Murder at The Actuary's House

K T BOWES

Dedication

For my beautiful son.
I love your road trips when we can talk unhindered on
the phone for hours.
You drive while I scan receipts, choose book covers, or
clean the house.
Because neither of us can bear to be still.
And somehow, we put the world to rights.

1

Club Chair

♥

"Look at this!" Freda flapped the flimsy newspaper in Emma's face. Her thin fingers shook in a Mexican wave, which began at her neck and ricocheted through her delicate left shoulder. Raw fury turned her irises milky behind the cataracts.

With a squeal of glee, baby Stephie snatched the paper and shredded the top sheet before Emma could rescue it. A tug of war ensued, Freda balancing her weight on her cane and rescuing all but the sheet she wished to complain about. It fluttered to the floor as Stephie released it. She grunted and peered at the ink stains on her palms. "Oh, no!" she wailed, presenting her pale pudgy fingers to her mother. "Oh, no!"

Emma reached for a packet of wipes on the kitchen table and wasted valuable time dabbing ink from between her daughter's fingers. Stephie's bottom lip poked out, a ledge signifying her dismay. Freda sank into a dining chair, her cane clattering on the tiles beneath the table. "Can you believe it?" she protested. "Bloody woman!"

"Children!" Emma hissed. She clapped her hands over her toddler's ears, spreading the black ink through the delicate blonde curls. "Oh, damn! Now look what I've done."

Stephie turned to her and beamed. Mischievous blue eyes glittered like diamonds from beneath enviable curled lashes. Rohan's eyes. Emma's heart ached. "Where's your daddy?" she whispered to the baby. She popped a kiss on the end of Stephie's button nose. The child balled her fists and shoved them into her eyes. Emma regretted her unfair question. She knew the score.

Rohan Andreyev took the train to London ten days earlier. He'd warned he might be radio silent for a few days. Emma hadn't appreciated his candidness until she called her friend Susan for a chat. Frederik answered the phone, his tone sulky. "I'm still in the dog-house," he growled. "But he took the other operatives with him."

It shocked Emma. He'd taken his ex-military squad on the job. Emma's nerves hiked. Angst set in with a vengeance.

"Steph's tired," Emma announced. She rose and hoisted the little girl onto her hip. "I'll take her over to Allaine's apartment now. What time did you agree the catering company could set up?"

Freda turned over her delicate left wrist. She peered at the ancient Timex, which dictated her routine. No matter that it ran ten minutes slow. "Five o'clock," she said, her tone gentler. "Thank you for recommending Luscious Lunches. Mavis messed up the dates with the original caterer." Her gaze softened as she tilted her head and regarded the young woman opposite her. "What would I do without you?"

Emma bit back her response. She'd recommended no particular caterer. A Google search netted a list of local companies who provided buffet style food for functions. She'd just shown the list to Freda. The elderly woman spent all her time living at Wingate Hall. She'd taken up residence with the ease of an adopted cat, never considering that perhaps she should seek permission for her overstaying.

The recent disaster with the Literary and Historical Society's awards night caused Emma a considerable headache. She didn't want them in her home. Not again. She sighed and rose. Stephie's temple bumped her cheek as the baby settled over her shoulder and dug her tiny hands into the warm space between them. "What time is everyone arriving?" Emma's tone held more tiredness than she'd intended.

"Seven," Freda declared. She slammed her palm onto the newspaper and a dull thud echoed from the wooden table beneath it. Stephie grunted but didn't take the tempting, rustling bait. "Look at this!" She jabbed a gnarled finger against the tiny print.

"You'll have to read it to me," Emma said, patting Stephie's back with a gentle palm.

Freda's querulous voice rang out in the kitchen, each syllable bouncing off the tiles in a distorted echo. *'The Market Harborough Literary and Historical Society wishes to congratulate a long-time member, Kathleen Dubois, for her recent Laureate award from the University of Leicester. Mrs Dubois commences her role as Poet in Residence after the Christmas holidays. A generous scholarship has provided accommodation and living costs for six months. During her time at the university, Mrs Dubois will give a series of monthly lectures on poetry of the twentieth and twenty-first centuries.'* Freda snorted, a throaty, congested sound which communicated disgust, and a looming chest infection. "If that woman's a poet, then I'm the queen of England," she declared.

Emma raised a dark eyebrow and pursed her lips. The debate about Freda's patronage ran deep and dank. Not a subject for a busy afternoon. As the bastard daughter of the former local lord, she might have ties to Buckingham Palace. Who would know?

"Right," Emma said, using her heel to send her chair skittering beneath the table. "I'll take Stephie across to Allaine's apartment and come back to help you set up for this evening. She should have made it back from school by now." Her eyes narrowed as she peered through the kitchen window at the angry sky beyond the mottled glass. "It looks like snow is coming," she mused. Within the privacy of her thoughts, she imagined a sudden blizzard cancelling the doomed evening. She could imagine no greater pleasure than reading her children a bedtime story, enjoying a hot bath, and then settling in the bed she shared with Rohan. A weight lodged in her chest at the thought of her husband. He'd tried to warn her, but what had she missed? He'd taken his squad with him, and that never boded well. Emma pressed a kiss against her daughter's downy head. If only she hadn't gotten so wrapped up in her children and in Freda's dramas, she might have understood the gravity of his latest mission.

"I bet her poem is shit!" Freda declared.

Emma whirled around to face her. "Well, that explains my son's latest swearword," she snapped. "Please think about your vocabulary around little ears."

Freda snorted. "You raised your son in a ghetto. He has his own mastery of inappropriate diction. I've learned all my dirty words from him."

Emma clamped her teeth onto her tongue to avoid the futile argument. Freda had lived for almost a century. Emma quit the fight long ago. "Ray is outside on the quad bike." She moderated her tone. "He'll open the gate for Luscious Lunches. I'm taking Stephie to Allaine's now. She's minding the children for tonight. So, I'm free to help you with your guests."

She stepped towards the door after snatching a blanket from the kitchen chair. It spread over Stephie's sleeping body. "Listen for the caterers. Ask them to set up in the morning room."

"The morning room?" Freda cocked her head. "Why not the ballroom? Doesn't the Market Harborough Literary and Historical Society deserve the ballroom?"

"It's an enormous room and far too cold. You gave me twenty-four hours' notice of the event and the ballroom takes three days to heat during the winter." Emma turned a determined glare on the elderly woman. Her chin flattened into a hard line. "There are thirty people, not a hundred and thirty. The morning room is adequate. Ray already lit the fire. He set up trestle tables along the back wall for the food and there are power points for the warmers. It's fine." She raised an eyebrow and waited for the bomb to go up. But Freda capitulated with surprising haste.

"Thank you for your kindness," she conceded. "It's all Mavis's fault. She goads me and I just can't resist. We've always held the last meeting of the year at the town hall, but she didn't bother to book it this time. She says I agreed to phone them, but it's not in the official minutes." Freda spread her hands with the palms upwards in a pretence of innocence. "I can't imagine what happened."

Emma growled low in her throat. She could imagine very well. But arguing with Freda held as much satisfaction as banging her head against a brick wall. She pressed her child closer and raised the blanket over Stephie's snoring head. "It's freezing outside," she advised. "And this big old house resists all attempts at warming it up. I've placed slippers in a line just inside the front door. There are enough pairs for the caterers, too." She raised a brown eyebrow and dropped her chin as she glared at Freda. "Make sure your guests use them this time!"

"I will, I will." Freda pursed her lips and bent to retrieve the crook of her cane. Worn smooth by age and the soft palms of her forebears, it creaked as she pressed its rubber foot against the red quarry tiles and rose. The fragile bones in her knees popped and chattered like dice in a tin. She shuffled towards Emma, her feet encased in fluffy boots with rubber soles. "I've apologised for the garden party fiasco. I didn't realise they'd poked around inside the house and left a mud trail throughout every room."

Emma swallowed the rebuke. The muddiest prints matched Freda's orthopedic soles. She couldn't resist showing off Wingate Hall to her contemporaries. It vindicated her after years of scorn at her pretentious genealogy. Rohan hadn't trusted her. He'd locked the family rooms and barricaded every known entrance to the secret tunnels. But it still took Emma and Allaine hours to clean the worst affected carpets afterwards.

Emma thought she'd made herself clear to Freda. Despite the elderly woman's Ayers family connections, the house belonged to the Andreyevs. Yet after the subsequent apologies and commiserations, they'd arrived back at the same place. Perhaps the Lit and His Society always planned to host their annual event at the Hall. But no one bothered to inform its owner.

"Back in twenty minutes," Emma said, tucking the ends of the blanket around Stephie's sleeping form. "Watch out for the caterers."

"Yes dear." The tone of contrition masked a lifetime of disobedience as Freda followed her from the kitchen. But instead of turning left and heading along the corridor to the lobby and the front door, she turned right and shuffled towards the servant's stairs.

"Bloody hell!" Emma hissed as Freda rattled her way up the first flight to the dog-leg. *Tap, tap, tap,* her stick replied as it carried her around the corner and onto the floor above. With her appropriated room at the back of the house, it became obvious to Emma that her house guest had no intention of watching the front gate for anyone's arrival. Not the caterers or her guests. The rightful lady of the manor would need to do it all. As usual.

2

Side Chair

♥

Emma hurried through the darkness. A bitter wind nipped at her ankles. Her boots pattered against the cobbles in the old stable yard. Allaine's friendship and her warm apartment urged Emma to stay. To sink into the sumptuous sofa cushions and accept a fortifying mug of tea. But she'd promised Freda.

So Emma kissed her son's upturned forehead and placed her daughter in Allaine's capable arms. Stephie roused as though tickled, beaming with delight at her changed surroundings. She'd burbled nonsense and reached for Allaine's earrings. Nicky focussed on the board game between him and Allaine's youngest child.

Emma hadn't prolonged the separation. Leaving her children caused her distress, but they remained unconcerned. "You should feel grateful," she chastised herself. Her breath puffed as white clouds into the frigid air. "You would have given anything for this five years ago."

And she would. Five years earlier, her life had looked so different. A single mother with an absentee husband, she'd battled through each day surviving on her wits. Nicky had run wild, and they'd owned nothing but the clothes on their backs. Emma drew her coat tighter around her stomach and considered the commodity she'd most taken for granted since inheriting Wingate Hall. "Safety," she whispered to herself.

An early winter darkness shrouded the rural mansion. It rolled across invisible lawns and outbuildings. Light pollution rose from the nearby town of Market Harborough in the north. But the fathomless black didn't hold the same threat anymore. Anton bequeathed more than a neglected manor house abandoned by the Ayers' family. He'd given her security and independence. From Rohan. From everyone.

Anton's death, painful and tragic, had restarted her life. She missed him. His loss created a continuous ache in the pit of her stomach. A tear slid from her left eye and halted halfway down her cheek. The freezing air seized it, struggling against the salty content as it turned it to ice on her skin. Emma brushed it aside with her mitten.

A spotlight flared to life as she rounded a corner and faced the main house. The solar bulb in the security light ticked as though woken from a deep sleep. It lit her way along the gravel drive, her shadow striking out sideways like an eerie companion. Her boots crunched in the gravel.

Twin headlights bobbed across the lawn as Ray's quad bike neared the front entrance. Emma had employed the ex-army sergeant as a groundsman. She'd needed help with basic maintenance. But Ray proved a capable foreman for the renovations and a wise and trustworthy confidante for her. The children adored him.

The quad bike buzzed across the grass, its motor loud in the silence. Another security light flashed above Emma's head. She raised her hand in acknowledgement as Ray's face turned towards her. She sensed him wave back, though she couldn't see his hand lift in the darkness. But someone else saw her through his myopic lens. Her wave acknowledged him as well.

The security light picked up a disturbing sight. Emma groaned. Snowflakes tumbled through the beam in fluttering, tumbling tufts like feathers burst from a pillow. "Great!" she exclaimed. She reached the wide steps leading to the front door, turning as another light gleamed yellow against the blackness of the evening. It spewed across the driveway near the road and picked up the opening of the automatic gates. The ornate bars cast perpendicular shadows across the driveway. They created the effect of a cattle grid guarding the entrance. It elongated and shape shifted until Ray locked the mechanism. The headlights of a transit van winked in the entrance.

A bark sounded, its pitch cutting over the low rumble of the van's engine and the higher buzz of the quad bike. An ebony shape bounced in the streams of light as the family dog made his interest known. Anton's dog, then Rohan's, and now Emma's. Farrell spent his days outside with Ray. Rohan's training long forgotten, the spaniel yapped and danced beside the transit, his paws lifting to touch its metallic sides before curling over. Even he sensed it would be a step too far.

The van moved into the driveway and began its slow, tentative journey towards the main house. Ray followed, the gates already closing behind him. The dog's ebony coat made him invisible in the wake of Ray's bike, but Emma knew he still followed in anticipation of unfamiliar smells and experiences. He missed Christopher. Emma's shoulders slumped. They all missed Christopher, though no one ever mentioned the treacherous man's name.

In the days when Wingate Hall formed the social hub of Market Harborough society, all tradesmen veered left beside the lodge. They clattered over the cobbles before passing under the wide arch beside the stable yard. A rear door gave access to the kitchen, and the transit followed the ancient protocol, though the driver would not have known of its written and enforced existence in times past.

Emma tutted as she wiped her damp boots on the doormat. She flicked the hood from her head, her ears already reddening in the chill. She'd asked Freda to watch for the caterers, but doubted the nonagenarian could make it downstairs in time. *If* she'd even intended to put in appearance before her guests arrived.

Emma whipped off her right mitten and her fingers closed over the front door handle. Her heavy ski jacket rustled as she reached out. Rohan insisted they keep all external doors locked since Christopher's departure, but carrying Stephie made it too difficult to battle the giant brass key. Besides, a locked door presented no barrier to the tricky Irishman.

A sense of foreboding crept along her spine, prickling the skin at her nape. The rounded handle twisted beneath her fingers, the metal worn by the gloved hands of generations of footmen and butlers. Its coolness bit into her skin, its speckled patina conducting the freezing air. But the ice which slid through her veins came from inside her soul.

Someone watched her.

She sensed their gaze from within the shadows. A prickling sensation moving along her spine. The tang of lavender and winter green reached her. Emma gulped. A void yawned behind her, sucking her into a world built on false premises. Christopher Dolan had both loved and deceived her from the same well of despair. She'd refused his affection, rejected him, and sent him into obscurity. A terrible end to their friendship.

"Christopher?" Emma whipped around. Her mitten fell to the floor. "Why would you come back here?" Her lips stumbled over the words. She patted her pockets for her phone. If she screamed, the man watching through the cameras would act. The terrible sense of foreboding would dissipate on the wind. He would send help, acting on Rohan's careful training. But it would set into a motion a plan she couldn't stop. Emma tugged her phone from her pocket, the flap catching against the smooth plastic case and delaying her salvation.

Scream or call? Scream or call?

Her rational mind soothed her. "He isn't here," she whispered. Panic released as condensation from her chattering lips. "He won't come back." The revelation sent a stab through her chest. Her shoulders hunched. Because she missed him. She ached to laugh about his Catholic upbringing and his overbearing mammy in the warm kitchen. But the urge faded. Christopher Dolan had used a child to hack a government site. And he'd double crossed her husband. Then he'd smashed her world apart with his two powerful fists.

"Goodnight," Emma called to the ghost who waited beyond the driveway's brick lintel and the flower border she'd planted herself. Her voice held a brave note, a trace of defiance and strength, as she bent to retrieve her fallen mitten. Acknowledging the hidden presence helped her to focus as she reached again for the door handle and turned the icy brass knob.

"Goodnight," he mouthed back, though the creak of the heavy door covered his voice.

3

Armchair

♥

Emma stepped over the threshold and closed the heavy door behind her. A bolt into the floor locked it against her fear. Her hand shook as she turned the brass key.

Lights flickered to life in the stone porch. Wall mounted and new, they appeared antique. The worn tiles revealed their history as indents. Fine dresses had brushed over the threshold, rubbing grooves over the centuries.

Emma kicked off her boots and tucked her cold toes into her slippers. She closed the inner door with her bottom, listening for the click before carrying her footwear to the renovated armoire. She opened the door, setting her boots on a shelf beside Ray's spare pair of work boots. Sleeves from the family's coats brushed her cheek as she bent. The Russian greatcoat

Rohan never wore rustled, its heavy sleeve protesting the closing of the door. Emma's heart ached, missing him like a wave yearning for the beach. The family at Wingate Hall orbited around Emma Andreyev, but Rohan provided the gravity and the stake to keep her anchored.

The cool breeze discouraged her from removing her coat. It whipped around her calves and bit through her jeans. Emma stuffed her mittens into a pocket. She stared at her phone's empty screen. The porch lights winked out, and she fumbled for the switch in the wide lobby. Wall sconces flared to life. She woke her phone screen with a swipe of her index finger. Pulling up Rohan's emergency contact number, she paused. "This is silly," she coaxed herself. "It's nothing. He hasn't returned." If she called Rohan at the wrong moment, he'd ignore her. He wouldn't risk his operation. Knowing he'd taken his squad of ex-military tacticians didn't help her mood. He expected trouble and guarded against it.

The clattering of something heavy and metallic echoed along the narrow corridor leading from the kitchen. It shocked Emma from her course of action, and she killed the call.

"I think it's the caterers, dear." Freda's voice warbled from the second floor. She leaned against the balustrade, backed by a soft light. The scent of fresh Dior wafted into Emma's nostrils, forcing a sneeze from her sinuses.

"You think so?" Sarcasm edged her voice as she stared up at her friend. "You promised to look out for them and tell them where to set up their gear."

Freda tossed her glossy curls. A wide band cut across her forehead and fluffy white crests. She'd abandoned the cane in favour of a cigarette holder. Her thin arms resembled chalk sticks in the muted light. "They dropped something. I hope it isn't the hors d'oeuvres." Her accent contained a plummy British edge as though she'd morphed into a 1930s flapper.

Emma exhaled. Freda had adopted the character lodged in her imagination. The delicate dress poked through the wooden spindles, revealing knobby knees above her fluffy slippers. Like soft rose petals fluttering in the updraught, the shadow muted its vibrant pinks.

"You'll freeze dressed like that." Emma shivered at the sight of Freda's bare shins. "It's below zero out there. It's about seven degrees inside."

"Beauty before comfort, dear," Freda replied. She turned away, showing no inclination to join the busyness in the kitchen. "I'll take tea in my room." She released a dramatic exhale. "Be a darling, won't you?"

Emma swallowed the groan in her chest. She couldn't blame Freda's behaviour on an undiagnosed medical condition. Or her longevity. Freda Ayers could run rings around them all on a bad day. "Nope," Emma grumbled. "And nope to your tea."

She glanced down at the phone in her hand. The noise levels increased along the corridor. The Ayers family had abandoned the original kitchen in the basement after the second world war. They moved it upstairs. When liberated servants left the big houses, it changed the face of the gentry. Four maids, a housekeeper, butler, and cook managed the Hall in the 1970s. The Ayers finally discarded their dilapidated pile to appease a bankruptcy court. Another metallic clatter galvanised Emma. She couldn't leave Ray coping alone on his night off.

Her fingers sped across the phone screen, sending a text to a contact named Lear.

'Check the cameras? I sensed someone outside. Front door.'

Dropping the phone into her jacket pocket, she crossed her arms and rubbed her biceps through the heavy fabric. Her jog towards the kitchen ended with her blasting into the kitchen. Frigid air met her, snatching away her breath. The rear door stood wide open, snowflakes pitching through the gap. Metal containers already filled the pine table and most of the counters. Emma crossed the room in five quick strides. She poked her head into the darkness.

"Here you go." Ray's words created a white condensation haze over the metal tray he pushed into her arms. "There's more." He waited until she'd got control over the tray before whirling aside and disappearing.

A happy wine at her feet indicated the dog's presence. He sneezed and wet droplets cascaded onto Emma's jeans and slippers.

"Out of the way, Faz!" Ray grumbled. He approached the doorway bearing two more trays.

Emma backed up, turning and setting her burden on a corner of the table. "I hope they don't expect me to fund all this?" she exclaimed as Ray stacked his trays on a growing pile. "Bloody hell!" she huffed, covering her mouth with her hand.

Ray's eyebrows rose and fell in a curious Mexican wave. The cocker spaniel entered the kitchen, tentative steps testing how far he could get before being shooed back outside. He edged towards the Aga, aware of Emma's scrutiny but pretending she couldn't see him. With a grunt of pleasure, he flopped into the squashy fabric bed snuggled against the warm stove. Having reached last base, he settled in for a ringside view of the activity.

"This is madness," Emma mused, widening her eyes at Farrell. He responded with a deep sigh and rested his long jaw on the rolled side of his bed.

"Two more." Ray carried in the last tray dumped it on the kitchen table. His wet footprints interspersed with Farrell's paw marks to create the tracks of a strange, clawed night creature. "I need to get home now. Paul's visiting."

"Okay. Thanks." Emma surveyed the feast. She ignored Ray's comment about his son's presence at Wingate Hall. The detective's sharp observation skill could pick away at Rohan's veneer of respectability. But they couldn't ban Ray from seeing his son. She raised an eyebrow, and Ray offered a shallow nod. He knew the score.

His retreat left Emma alone with a mountain of food. It resembled a banquet for hundreds, not the thirty people expected for the Lit and His Society's annual bash. Still sealed in foil wrappers, it signified an unlimited budget. An invoice fluttered to the floor, and she bent to retrieve it. Her eyes popped at the four-figure amount written in the blue ballpoint pen at the bottom.

A woman wearing a white chef's coat and black and white checked pants staggered through the door bearing a tray of fruit. "Hi, I'm Chloe from Luscious Lunches. You must be Mrs Ayers." She dumped it on the counter and turned to Emma, her right hand already outstretched.

Emma shook her head. "Emma Andreyev," she said, seizing the icy fingers. The woman's blue eyes sparkled with life as though feeding multitudes appealed to her and filled a well in her soul. Droplets clung to the hair, escaping her bun in glittery blonde tendrils.

Two men clattered through the door, stamping their feet on the coarse coconut mat. The younger one sported a footman's outfit, the jacket a little too large and the trouser cuffs turned up above his shiny patent shoes. Both men wore white gloves, the older one dressed in the full rig of an 1800s butler.

"I've roped in my boys to help," Chloe said, her lips parting in an amiable smile. She indicated the older man. "This is my husband Gareth, and Dyfed. I've added their time to the bill."

Emma stared, Freda's flapper outfit making sudden and horrible sense. "Is it fancy dress?" she stuttered. Her gaze flicked to Ray, who gave a smirk and a wave before banging the rear door closed behind him. The Aga clicked in the corner. Farrell's tongue made a wet slapping as he licked his toes, oblivious to the surrounding chaos. It only mattered that he got to dry beside the ancient stove and hide there until morning.

"Can you pay that before we leave?" Chloe jerked her chin towards the invoice in Emma's hand. "Cash please."

Emma cleared her throat to test her voice. She regarded the chef with her bleached hair, the roots already showing brown in the parting. The woman's sloped shoulders held a stiffness, as though she expected trouble over the payment. A scar to the left of her upper lip twitched.

"I own the house," Emma began, her tone faltering. "I've given the Lit and His Society use of the kitchen and morning room just for tonight." She laid the invoice on the only square of pine table not covered in trays of food. "I'm sure their chairperson will sort out your payment."

Gareth's brows furrowed into a long line and his lips parted as though he might challenge her. With dark hair cropped close to his scalp and a piercing in his left eyebrow, he glowered at her as though she'd robbed his granny. Only Dyfed smiled, his white-gloved hands resting across his stomach as though he'd already got into character.

A vibration rippled through Emma's coat and tickled her hip bone. She tugged the phone free and turned aside. "Excuse me," she said, though her heart pounded through her chest wall. Anger fizzled from Gareth's side of the kitchen, and it unnerved her. She absorbed his negative energy, the silent accusation making her feel irrationally guilty.

'*Roger that. Nothing spotted except occupants of white transit, Ray, and you. All clear.*'

Lear's response should have comforted her. It didn't. Christopher Dolan had installed Wingate Hall's security. Despite the added features deterring a skilled hacker, nothing could hold him back if he visited. Only Rohan's presence would keep him away. But Emma hadn't heard from him in over five days. Too long. Something had gone wrong. She sensed it in her bones.

"I'll leave you to it," she said, infusing brightness into her tone. She glanced at their shoes and swallowed the offer of slippers. A butler and a footman couldn't clop around wearing fluffy slides without appearing ridiculous. The invoice contained a charge for food, a chef, and three wait staff. Emma raised an eyebrow as the outside door opened to admit another blast of freezing air. An older man stepped over the threshold, stamping snowflakes from his shoes. He closed the door behind him and when he turned, Emma saw skin the colour of stained oak. Deep wrinkles furrowed his brows, and missing teeth marred a cautious smile.

"Where did you get to?" Gareth demanded, his tone acidic.

"Sorry," the man mumbled, cowed despite his seniority in age. His suit appeared rumpled, the fabric shiny and worn at the knees and elbows. An open jacket revealed a shirt untucked on one side and his zipper stood at half-mast. Farrell sat up in his bed and lifted his chin to taste the air. Emma winced, guessing where the man got to and hoping he'd urinated nowhere her children might walk.

"Stand with Dyfed," Gareth growled, and the man edged close enough for their elbows to touch. The situation appeared incongruous, the young, smiling man in his early twenties offering solidarity to one closer to sixty.

Emma cleared her throat. "You can use the soap by the sink to wash your hands," she suggested. Both men glanced at Gareth before acknowledging her words. He nodded as though giving waiting dogs a signal to eat their food. They rushed towards the sink, shoulders jostling but their lips still silent. Dyfed removed his white gloves and tucked them beneath his left armpit with care. The Black man splashed in the funnel of water like a child.

"Gareth is a builder," Chloe offered, as though in explanation. Her eyes sparkled, darting around as though afraid. The man's presence had charged the atmosphere. "The boys work for him."

"Okay," Emma responded. "The Aga is on if you wish to warm or cook anything. The dog will move out of your way, eventually. I'll introduce Mavis as soon as she arrives. You can sort out the invoice with her."

Cursing Freda, she slipped from the kitchen and pulled the door behind her to leave a tiny gap.

Something about the caterers bothered her, and she channelled her son's relentless curiosity. She stuck close, pulling out her phone as a ready excuse in case one of them yanked open the door and discovered her eavesdropping. Farrell grumbled as he pursued a more comfortable position, a noisy eater settling in with popcorn for a coming show. But Emma didn't need to wait for long before Gareth spoke. "You needed to make her pay that invoice," he snarled. "She's loaded. Must be in a place like this. You said she agreed to pay with cash!"

"That woman didn't book us. She told you that," Chloe responded.

Dyfed spoke with a clipped Welsh accent, but his tone held a note of caution. "What shall we do now?"

Emma tensed as Gareth turned his ire on the young man. She peeped through the narrow crack, seeing him spin to face the smiling footman. Farrell emitted a low growl, not liking the builder.

"Shut your face!" Gareth rebuked Dyfed. Emma watched his broad shoulders tense, and he lifted a pointy index finger and jabbed it towards the young man. "Just keep your eyes open for anything we can grab. Nothing obvious. I don't want her to miss stuff until long after we're gone."

Dyfed made no reply, but Emma reacted with anger. She shoved the door open with force. Its brass knob clattered with the pantry. Men like Gareth had made her former life a living hell with their entitlement. They'd taken everything and still demanded more. Their poor-me stories sickened her. Emma observed the gathered occupants. She dropped her chin to add emphasis, glaring at them through the tops of her eyes. "Every centimetre of this house is within view of a security camera. Leave the food and go. We'll manage it ourselves."

"No! Please!" Chloe rushed forward, a gushing river meeting a dam wall. Desperation oozed from the lines in her forehead. "He didn't mean it. Please, let us finish our job. Mrs Ayers promised us an excellent review. I need the work." She swallowed, a lump rising and falling behind her soft throat. "He won't do anything." Her body swivelled to face her companion, the crisp white coat sleeves swishing in the silence. "Will you?" she growled.

Emma exhaled. Her heart thudded in her chest. She'd left the violence of the council run estate in Lincoln behind her, but not the powerlessness it fostered in her soul. Conflict blurred the lines she needed to follow.

Chloe's desperation created a haze, which Emma could almost taste. But her gaze flicked to Gareth, and she detected no shame behind his hooded lids. Rohan would have thrown him off the property without a second thought.

And still Dyfed smiled at her, his lips drawn wide in a manic expression which didn't reach his almond-shaped eyes. Emma swallowed and crooked her finger towards Chloe. "Come with me," she said, her tone severe.

4

Wingback Chair

♥

"What's going on?" Emma demanded. She'd closed the kitchen door behind them and led Chloe along the corridor and into the lobby. She faced her, digging her freezing fingers into her jacket pocket. The fabric crinkled and her index finger brushed the smooth plastic cover of her phone.

Chloe fidgeted. She shivered against the icy air. The oak panels clung to the walls with indifference. They'd seen many tough conversations across the centuries. "I'm sorry," Chloe gushed. A strand loosened from her bun. It covered her left eye. "Dyfed has Moebius Syndrome." "He had facial animation surgery to create a smile. His muscles couldn't form one for him. It's left him with that inane grin."

Emma huffed out an exasperated breath. "Dyfed isn't the problem!" She raised her voice in frustration. "Your husband encouraged you to steal! I can't have him here."

A pink tongue swiped Chloe's lower lip. She gave a reluctant nod. "Gareth gambles," she said. "As fast as I make money, he loses it. He overheard my conversation with Mrs Ayers. She promised cash. That's all he needed to hear."

Emma swallowed. Her shoulders slumped until the fur fringing her jacket hood brushed her earlobes. "I don't know what to say," she admitted. "I'm not comfortable having your husband on the premises. And I'm even less keen to ask the Lit and His chairperson to pay you in cash." Reaching out, she rested her fingers over Chloe's cool wrist. "This can't continue, can it?"

A single tear slalomed down Chloe's cheek and she brushed it away in an angry, futile action. "I know," she agreed, her voice a whisper.

"Can you send him away in the van?" Emma asked. "I can get someone to run you home at the end of the evening, or drive you myself."

"Home." More tears glittered like crystals on Chloe's lashes. A glob of mascara pitched onto her cheek and formed a dark track across her skin. It met with a blue line peeking beneath her white collar, only visible when she turned her head. "Home is likely to be the van at the rate he's going." She sniffed. "Unless he sells that, too."

"I'm sorry." Emma exhaled. She'd watched the men on the estate gamble online, hooked by the glitzy, whirling, addictive colours on their battered phone screens. Lured by the promise of dreams-come-true but blinded by reality, they'd risked everything. Stuck in a cycle of loss. Their self-respect disappeared with their possessions. Morality followed. They whored out their women to fund the next lucky spin of the wheel.

Emma had struck lucky because of Anton. She'd still have traded it for one more hug from her effervescent, exuberant step brother.

A shudder ran through her. She'd left the estate, abandoning her former home and meagre possessions. She prayed no one would find her or Nicky. A two-hour car journey would bring them to her door, and they'd camp there until they'd wrung her out too. Pity flooded her heart for Chloe's predicament. Running. Always running from something.

She swallowed and fixed her gaze on the other woman's face, determined her message would hit home. "You can work here this evening," she stated, her tone harsher than she intended. "But Gareth leaves. Right now. He doesn't come back here for any reason. I'll speak to Mavis. She'll pay online into your business account." Emma rolled her eyes. "And just in case your husband gets any ideas, I doubt Freda has over a thousand pounds of cash tucked into her handbag. I imagine she said that to get you here at short notice." Emma yanked on the hem of her jacket and squared her shoulders. "Right," she said with a sigh. "Let's do the deed."

"You're coming with me?" Chloe's eyes widened as Emma turned towards the corridor. "He can get nasty." Her fingers fluttered to her neck, and she tugged her collar to cover the bruise.

Emma nodded. "So can I," she stated, her tone dull.

They entered the kitchen to discover the men hadn't moved. The most recent addition hid behind Dyfed as though using his grin as a shield. Emma glanced at the wet prints from Gareth's shiny shoes. He'd created no new ones. She'd half expected him to dig through drawers and cupboards, but he hadn't. The black dog in the squashy bed indicated the reason. Farrell's wise brown eyes studied Gareth, his ears pricked and his jaw open to reveal sharp teeth. The overhead lights turned the man's cropped hair into a shadowy crown and deepened the lines in his forehead. He appeared anxious.

Chloe narrowed her eyes at him. Emma's presence at her shoulder seemed to give her courage. "This lady wants you to leave," she said to her husband. She held out her hand, the palm bobbing with the force of her trembling. "Van and house keys, please?" Her jaw was set in a harsh line. Emma watched in her peripheral vision as Dyfed just smiled and smiled.

"How do I get home?" Gareth's brows drew into twin lines of disgust. An ugliness entered his expression, beginning at his down-turned lips and finishing with the sneer which ran bone deep.

From his bed in the corner, Farrell sat up and contributed a snarl from his chest as the atmosphere communicated Gareth's hiked antagonism.

"I don't know." Chloe stammered the denial. "Just go." She drew aside the collar of her chef's coat to reveal a long black line encircling her throat. The bruise Emma spied was only the tail end of the damage. "I needed the money for the rent. You ruin everything. Just go. I can't take what you do anymore. What you're doing to all of us." Her frantic gaze encompassed the two men lurking against the counter. Electricity sparked in the loaded air.

Gareth took a step towards his wife, his eyes widening as though his brain required more clarity from a greater field of vision. "You little bitch!" he snarled. He dropped a set of keys into her palm and glared at his shiny shoes. "It's snowing out there! I can't walk back to Market Harborough in this monkey suit."

Chloe blanched. Defeat roiled off Gareth in a nauseating wave of self-pity. Emma tasted victory, but daren't hope he'd leave without a fuss. Another step carried him closer, and Emma steeled herself for a fight. Her fists closed in a reflex action, middle fingers shifting higher to create spiteful spears. Her thumbs eased out of the way, and she slid her weight into her right foot. She readied herself to swing her body and lay Gareth out flat on the red quarry tiles. "Just leave," Emma growled, hoping to provide the definitive sentence which would strip away his power.

But her words acted as a catalyst. Gareth unleashed his fury on her instead. He swore, syllables and spittle leaving his open mouth in dual arcs of depravity and accusation. His morality had departed. It left when he put his knotty fingers around Chloe's throat and squeezed. And it didn't reappear as sanity left his hazel eyes. Their colour dulled to a muddy brown as vitality and decency slipped through each heaving breath. He reached out for Emma's throat, his fingers wiggling like a comic zombie. His rage reached her in a wave, its sonic boom almost knocking her off her feet.

Farrell barked, the deep sound echoing off the wooden cupboards and metal appliances. A snarl backed it, filled with threat.

Behind Gareth, his feet on the coir mat, poor Dyfed still smiled. And smiled. And the older man hid. He turned his face towards Dyfed's left ear. And he tried to pretend he didn't exist.

5

Recliner

♥

Chloe's panicked inhale seemed to last a lifetime as Emma reacted. Her mind filtered her responses into a series of choreographed movements, pushing her limbs through paces as familiar as her own reflection. In less than a second, she'd pressed her hands together as though clapping, forcing them between Gareth's advancing forearms, and splaying his elbows outwards.

His arms shot out to the sides, the maneuver unexpected enough to delay his recovery. With his throat unguarded, Emma reformed her right fist and landed a punch into his Adam's apple. Gareth reeled backwards, already bending at the waist. Uncertain of his defeat, Emma bent her right toes backwards inside her furry slippers, pivoted on her left foot and launched the hard ball of bone into the vulnerable space between his legs. Gareth collapsed onto the tiles; his fingers jammed between his legs. His body bowed so his forehead touched the cold floor.

As though waiting for Emma to finish, Farrell launched, clamping his teeth around Gareth's right forearm. Chloe stared from beside Emma, her lower jaw dropped far enough to reveal amalgam filled molars.

Emma grappled for the phone in her pocket as a low rumble reached her ears. The quad bike halted outside the kitchen window and the door flew open. Ray's gaze took in the room's occupants, Emma's defensive stance as she readied herself to go again, and Chloe's shock. He glanced at Dyfed and frowned at his ceaseless smile before his lips peeled back in disgust. Gareth bowed on the floor, the dog still gripping his right forearm. Farrell's body created a perfect triangle, his front legs bent and his backside higher. His nose and tail closed the hypotenuse, which pointed straight at Gareth.

Emma blinked as Paul Barker entered the kitchen behind his father. The detective's irises glittered with curiosity, although his brows drew into a concerned line.

"He assaulted me," Emma stammered, adding urgency and feigned emotion into her voice. "I heard him talking about stealing from the house and asked him to leave." She added a sob in her throat for good measure. Ray's left eyebrow quirked upward, and he cocked his head as though wondering how far Emma would take the ruse. He stepped aside to allow Paul to move past him. A sharp whistle through his teeth called off the dog. Farrell ran to Ray's side and dumped his backside on the tiles. His fluffy tail waved like a sail behind him, sending white flakes spinning around his head as though he belonged in a snow globe. The dog grinned at Emma, his tongue lolling from the side of his pink mouth as though he'd experienced the best and most unexpected fun of his life. "Good boy," Emma told him, and the wagging increased.

Snowflakes billowed through the door, increasing in strength. The outside freeze surged through the opening, filling the room with its icy tendrils. Ray used the side of his left foot to shoot the door closed, though it made no immediate difference.

"Is this your version of events?" Paul stared at Chloe, relaxing as she gave a shallow nod. Tears dripped off the end of Gareth's nose in a steady stream, an indication of the ongoing agony radiating from his groin and the inverted chode which hid behind his zip. "Up," Paul said to him, bending and clasping Gareth's left elbow.

"Hurts," the man groaned, his breath still leaving his chest in gasps.

"I need this to end." Chloe's fingers drew down the collar of her shirt to display the bruising for the newcomers. "He strangled me because I hid my purse from him this evening." She gulped and avoided Gareth's furious glare as Paul hauled him to his feet.

"Don't I know you?" Paul clasped the bent elbow and cocked his head at Gareth. "Yeah, I do." His nod bobbed his head with certainty. "You missed your court date," he said, his speech slow as he sifted through a mental library of names and images. "Demanding money with menace. I guess all those old people you robbed didn't like how you left their building work unfinished. You know you're meant to complete the job before demanding payment, don't you? One of your victims is still in hospital. Dude, your mugshot is on the wall of our office at the station."

Chloe released a sound which contained shock and a sob. "I didn't know," she breathed. She turned to Emma. "I promise, I didn't know."

Gareth gave a rough shrug, attempting to shake off Paul's grip. But his body still sagged at the waist and his nose had joined his leaking tear ducts in sympathy. He swore at Paul and the detective jerked his chin up at his father.

"Dad," he said, his tone unhurried. "Do you have your phone on you?"

Ray shook his head, his left nostril rising in disgust at himself.

"I have mine," Emma said. She leaned across Chloe, expecting Paul to take it. But he shook his head.

"Dad can dial," he said, reluctant to release Gareth.

Paul held onto Gareth while talking to his colleagues on speaker. Ray balanced Emma's phone on his wide palm.

The kitchen door flew open hard enough to hit the cupboard behind it. Freda clacked over the threshold in shoes dragged from a museum display. Covered with a cream silky fabric, they sported a giant bow over each instep. The clever decoration hid a strap which curved over Freda's narrow foot. They appeared at least three sizes too large for her and she walked as though struggling to keep them attached. "What's going on here?" she demanded, her accent exaggerated enough to give her status as a Windsor. She carried a cigarette holder in her left hand.

Ray groaned low in his throat and his lips parted in amusement. "Hey," he said to Freda in jest. "Is England missing a monarch?"

"Are you missing a brain cell?" she clapped back, too fast for conscious thought. Emma imagined her practicing the retort and her mind flicked to her son. It sounded more like something Nicky would say than a nonagenarian dressed as a 1930s relic. She sighed.

"Chloe, this is Mrs Ayers," she said. "You spoke to her on the phone." Emma lowered her chin and peered at Freda through her lashes. "Freda, I told Chloe the Lit and His Society would pay online into her business account."

"Oh, yes." Freda flapped her hand in dismissal. She fixed her gaze on Ray's son. "I'm surprised at you, officer. And anyway, I don't carry that much cash."

Chloe's jaw flapped open, and she took a step away from Freda. Emma rolled her eyes at her. "Inside joke," she whispered. "Don't worry about it."

"Oooh!" Freda's gnarled forefinger picked at a layer of aluminum foil on a nearby tray. She peeked inside, her string of over-long pearls trailing across the tinkling surface as she dipped to inspect the food. "Vol-au-vents!" she exclaimed and clapped her hands together. "My favourite." The cigarette shot from the end of her holder and landed at Farrell's feet. In two snaps, he'd eaten it.

Emma gasped. "Don't kill my dog!"

"It's sugar." Freda's fingers shook as she popped open the tiny bag at her hip and withdrew a packet of fake cigarettes. She fitted another one in the end of her holder. The dog's eyes widened, and he shifted on his bottom, as though expecting Freda to launch another one for him.

"How old are they?" Emma demanded. "Those sweets went out of production two decades ago."

"I know." Freda waggled her eyebrows, revealing twin wonky brown lines hand drawn using one of Nicky's permanent marker pens. They didn't match, giving her an expression of permanent surprise. She shrugged, completing her affected guise. "They're sugar sticks now. Nicky helped me colour the ends in red."

"A squad car is on the way," Paul advised, stepping back from the phone and cutting off Emma's reply. Nicky's imagination ran to enough crazy feats without the encouragement of a disenfranchised, deluded ninety-something year old. Ray ended the call with the stab of a sausage finger stained by hard work and handed it back to Emma. "They'll meet us at the gate," Paul concluded.

Freda's eyes widened. Her fingers stalled as she pushed the offending packet back into her cloth bag. Emma recognised her son's immature handwriting on the cardboard and noticed he'd spelled Marlboro wrong. He'd turned the end of the word into 'borough', perhaps confusing it with Market Harborough. "I can't have the police here!" Freda's voice rose to a shriek. "The Literary and Historical Society members are due to arrive." She jabbed her cigarette holder towards Paul Barker. Farrell bobbed and his jaws snapped in anticipation, though the sugar stick remained wedged into the stick. A frown crossed the dog's furry brows, and he sighed in disappointment. "You need to smuggle this man out another way," she declared. "Hide him, bury the body. I don't care which, but he can't stay here. Mavis already sniggers behind my back, and I refuse to give her more ammunition."

Gareth rose to his full height with a grunt. Paul produced a set of handcuffs from his back pocket and clipped them over the man's wrists. Gareth towered over the detective, and for a moment, Emma feared for him. But Ray, the ex-army drill sergeant, edged close enough to stare into Gareth's sweating face. Ray's blank expression invited the man to try it and suggested without words how much he'd enjoy retaliating.

Freda turned over her thin wrist, the skin rolling and sagging like curtain fabric as she peered at her watch. "One hour to showdown," she declared, her eyes lighting with an inner delight. She clapped her hands and Farrell lurched for the next flying sweet cigarette. He released a howl of disappointment as it bounced off the cupboard and snookered itself beneath the Aga. Farrell dived after it, sniffing and snuffling around the warm stove. He whined with anticipation and disappointment poking his paws beneath it.

"You there," Freda intoned, her eyes closed to convey her superiority. She directed her empty holder towards Dyfed and bobbed it in command. "You look like a lovely, sunny chap. Help me set up the morning room for supper." *Jab jab.* "And get that criminal out of here before my esteemed guests see him."

Ray smirked at Emma as she ground her teeth. "Have a nice evening," he offered, the laugh catching in his throat.

6

Lounge Chair

♥

Freda did little to assist the group as they carried the trays along the corridor and set them up in the wing at the southern end of the property. Dyfed followed the old lady like a lap dog, keen to fulfil every barked instruction. She thanked him profusely while ignoring Emma, the distraught Chloe, and the other unnamed footman.

"It'll be fine," Emma whispered to Chloe as they set out platters of delicate savouries beside the tiny cakes and pastries. "If Gareth already missed his court date, the police won't just let him out on bail. They'll keep him overnight."

Chloe made a dismissive grunt and set her tray of sausage rolls between the delicate sandwiches and thin slices of fresh pineapple. Emma pursed her lips and wondered if Chloe knew her audience. Most of them wore false teeth. Drippy, chewy pineapple presented a challenge they would avoid, like Marmite on toast.

"Ridley, put those here." Chloe spoke to the older man with the dark skin. He dumped the plates with shaking hands. His zipper still hung open. Chloe moved away. In Emma's peripheral vision, she noticed Ridley snag a sausage roll. He ate without chewing, as though sucking out the life and flavour. Only the crumbs betrayed his theft. Gnarled fingers edged another sausage roll over the gap.

Emma snapped a surreptitious photo of the banquet, as though thrilled with its enticing artfulness. She left Chloe to fuss over placing her wares. As fast as the chef moved around the table to display her creation at its best, Freda walked behind her shifting plates and sampling items.

Gareth's attack had unnerved Emma. She texted Allaine, warning her to lock her apartment and contain Nicky.

'I saw the cop car arrive,' Allaine responded. *'Is everything okay?'*

'It is now,' Emma replied. *'But just to be sure...'*

Her next message went to Rohan's technical support guru. The young man occupied Wingate Hall's folly, a mile away from the house. He changed his operational name to Lear, eager to leave his misspent online past behind him. The avatar betrayed his love of Shakespeare. Rohan disliked its path to his real name of Regan, King Lear's fictional daughter. Regan sat in his eerie and ran technical operations for the Actuary. And he monitored Wingate Hall's security.

'Has that asshole left the property yet?' she demanded.

Regan's curt reply reminded her a little too much of Christopher Dolan. *'Which one?'*

Emma ached to ask about Rohan. He wouldn't tell her. She turned the flashing cursor into a sentence. *'The cops and the guy in custody. Ray's son arrested him for threatening to steal from us.'* Her thumb hovered above the unfinished message. Should she mention the man's attack? Did she want Rohan to know?

Emma sent the message with no additional information. Regan's response warmed her. *'I sent Ray back,'* he commented. *'It didn't feel right.'*

Emma exhaled. Her breath released in white puffs. She'd lied to Gareth. The house boasted state-of-the-art security, but only outside. The kitchen camera had picked up the caterers as they arrived. Regan had acted on an unease which mirrored Emma's. The police couldn't learn of the footage. But Rohan would. It chalked up another black mark against Freda.

'*Thanks,*' Emma responded, her gratitude genuine. Though Regan could check the security monitors, she still forwarded the photograph of Dyfed and Ridley taken from her phone as they circled the feast. '*I know you're busy,*' she said, acknowledging Regan's proper task, '*but in between, please, can you find anything on these two?*'

Regan replied with a thumbs-up emoji, leaving Emma staring at the picture. Both men appeared malnourished. Their eyes contained a soul-deep darkness born of fear. Emma knew it because she'd lived through it herself. Crumbs dotted Ridley's left sleeve; the only evidence of the vol-au-vent he'd scarfed with no one else noticing. Dyfed smiled, rearranging the platters at Freda's direction. The camera caught him looking at Chloe, his gaze softening with veiled adoration. Emma frowned, sensing a mystery lurking between the odd trio. She gave herself a mental shake and jammed her phone back into her pocket. Asking Regan to check them out seemed like overkill as she sifted through the scant information. A glance at her watch showed the hour hand edging towards the seven. Three more hours and the white van would drive away, carrying Chloe and her companions into a different tomorrow. Emma admitted to herself she'd rather not get involved.

A master key locked the family rooms. Only the kitchen, morning room and the bathroom off the lobby remained open. Emma repeated the action on the first floor, but left Freda's bedroom unlocked. A maelstrom of moth-eaten clothing covered the bed and floor. Stockings clung to a vintage free-standing mirror as though sent there by an explosion. Emma sighed. The devastation imprinted itself on her retinas. The old lady had raided someone's dressing-up box.

Emma didn't lock the door to the original servants' quarters. Beyond the narrow staircase, the tiny attic rooms awaited renovation. A snapshot of history, each contained a bed, a dresser, an empty bowl, and a matching jug. One bathroom serviced that floor, a 1970s addition. The original high flush toilet and stained sink still worked, but air in the pipes made the taps wail like a trapped siren. A leaky bath plughole required a complete refit. But the council's infamous heritage officer resisted the cast iron bath's removal.

The last servant left Wingate Hall in the 1980s. In a coffin and following close on the heels of his wife. The butler's suitcase still sat on the floor of his old room, his monogram of FLD preserved in history.

Apart from Freda's, Emma's and her children's rooms, the renovation of the second floor had stalled. Anton had left Emma the money to continue but couldn't bequeath her the energy to deal with the heritage department. "I'll begin again after Christmas," she promised herself. She meant it, just like she had the previous year.

Emma's bedroom faced south. The Ayers family had bricked up the original window and added the ensuite. It created an architectural atrocity which gave the frontage the appearance of a lazy wink. Emma had shifted the ensuite and removed the eye patch.

She used the toilet in the new bathroom. Non-slip tiles and tasteful hand rails added to the practical design. She'd improved her husband's life without alluding to his missing leg or his laborious, daily struggles.

As she washed her hands and dabbed smudged eyeliner from her cheeks, Emma heard a faraway toot from outside. Running to the front window, she saw a bus parked in front of the gate. Exhaust fumes puffed into the haze as though released from a dragon's nostrils. Emma used her phone to log into the gate's intercom. The camera view revealed a bulbous nose filled with hair and the upper regions of a bushy moustache. Emma pressed a symbol on the screen and spoke into her phone. "Hi," she said, forcing brightness into her tone.

"It's the Market Harborough Literary and Historical Society," came the reply. The man shouted into the camera, giving Emma an altered view of chapped lips and yellowing dentures above a bow tie and a formal dinner jacket. "It's Major Mallory-Eaves here. We all came together." He enunciated each word in his exaggerated plummy accent. "It's snowing jolly hard out here."

Emma winced at the passive aggressive demand for entry. "I'll open the gates now." She pressed another icon and heard the motorized whirr of the mechanism engage. Unable to resist a laugh at his expense, she added, "You'll need to hurry. They'll only remain open for a few seconds." She smothered her snort with her hand as the major waddled back to the bus, slipping and sliding on the icy surface. Snowflakes added to his fluffy white crown. The lie gave Emma devilish satisfaction. She watched the pompous man slither past the headlight beam and huff up the steps. He'd treated her like a servant at the garden party in the summer and probably planned to repeat the exercise.

Emma watched the bus pass through the aperture. She registered the glow of indiscernible faces reflecting the glare from the security lighting overseeing the main entrance. A blur of feather boas tapped the interior windows as though the occupants had enjoyed a pillow fight. "Rather you than me," Emma whispered to herself as the tail end of the bus flew past the camera. The mechanism whirred again, closing the gates behind it.

She gazed with a sigh at her inviting bed. Did Freda intend to greet her own guests? "Probably not," she admitted.

Emma left the bedroom with leaden footsteps. She locked the door behind her.

7

Rocking Chair

♥

Once in the lobby, Emma discovered a crowd on the front steps. And no Freda.

She pulled the inner door open, groaning at the freezing air which assailed her cheeks. She'd just released the bolts and turned the key in the storm doors when it barged inward, almost knocking her off her feet. Mavis Dickinson waded past her, slamming the younger woman against the wall of the vestibule. The heady fumes of chilled Dior filled Emma's head, the bitter wind nipping at her nose and exposed cheeks. She swore with volume and aggression.

Mavis sneered. Her plump bleached curls coiffed into cumulus clouds. The hair stood like antennae on her bare arms. A pink feather boa wound around her ridged neck. Her costume mirrored Freda's, a fact guaranteed to irk both women once they met. The crowd behind

Mavis had halted in shock at the violence in her entry. They at least had the decency to pause at the threshold.

Emma stepped from the vestibule into the lobby and fixed her hands on her hips. "Excuse me!" she shouted, her voice echoing off the panelled walls. She jabbed a finger at Mavis's shoes and the trail of water she'd tracked along the polished floorboards. Emma's temper flared. At Mavis. At Freda. At Rohan. But mostly at herself. "No outdoor shoes!" she snapped. "There are slippers to choose from."

The reticent crowd filtered through the doors and into the lobby, bringing with them their icy, uninvited weather bomb. "We'll do this my way!" Emma asserted as Mavis's lips parted in protest. It was a fight she should have picked during the summer fete. She took a determined step towards Mavis. "This is the last time. Do you understand?"

Mavis's painted lips withered to a thin line like two pink worms bridging her wide mouth. She didn't apologise but eyed the slippers like a child regarding a candy filled piñata. Snatching up the fluffiest pair, she wedged her oversized rump on the nearby wooden pew and wrestled her feet from shocking pink shoes which appeared too big for her.

The rest of the crowd conducted themselves with more dignity. Sir Robert Holden KC nodded to Emma. The men sported rented black suits with white bow ties. Someone had stitched leather patches to the elbows of Sir Robert's jacket. He filed past Emma wearing fluffy moccasins. The barrister added KC to the end of any introductions. It indicated he'd acted as the king's counsel. He hadn't, but only because England's queen still reigned when he retired. Freda declared after three large glasses of Merlot that the KC stood for Kennel Club. Emma returned his lop-sided smile and turned to the next guest.

Montgomery Jones approached Emma with his usual affection. "Now then," Monty said. He wrapped an arm around her and pressed a cold kiss to her cheek. "Thank you for this. I hear Mavis cocked up the booking for this year's bash. She dumped it all on Freda to sort out." He leaned closer and lowered his voice, the scent of sweet coffee enticing. His Welsh accent reminded Emma of happy times spent in Aberystwyth. Her heart craved the pebble beach and the effortless, rolling surf. "Some of us think she did it on purpose," Monty continued, his greying eyebrows waggling in time with his accusation.

Monty's grin held a natural lightness. He'd retired from teaching but not from life. The school children had adored him, including Nicky. Damp speckles glinted in his luxurious brown hair. His dash through the snowfall had mussed it. Streaks of grey added to the salt and pepper effect. Flakes scattered across the shoulders of his mahogany smoking jacket. "What do you think?" He patted the wide, silky lapels. "All I could rustle up at short notice." He flicked the matching bow tie with an index finger. "Borrowed from the drama cupboard at the school."

Emma smiled. "Very Fred Astaire," she remarked. "Apart from the slippers." Ignoring the men's array, Monty had stuffed his feet into fluffy pink slip-ons from the Pound Shop. He waggled his toes and winked at her.

The outer door closed, and Monty's wife stepped into the lobby. She looked around her and saw Emma. "Am I locking this?" she asked, lifting her voice above the hubbub of slipper related disputes happening to her left.

"I'll do it," Emma said. She shivered against the breeze which had entered with the group, wishing she'd remembered to light the lobby fire. Ray had set it, banking up the sticks and coal at the same time as he lit the one in the morning room. Emma hadn't thought they'd need it. But as she locked and bolted the front doors to seal out the freezing air in the vestibule, she changed her mind.

Flora squeezed and kissed her from within a sumptuous fur coat. Tall and attractive, she served as the perfect pair to her handsome husband. Apart from the height difference. She towered over Emma, her stunning face giving her heavy boned frame an added lightness. She oozed beauty and grace. Emma jammed the door keys into her jacket pocket, where they tapped against her phone and the master for the internal locks. "I hope that's not real," she said with a smile, running her fingers over the soft black-and-white sleeve.

"It's rabbit," Flora replied in a hushed whisper. "I've had it for years and never wear it in public." She pressed an index finger over her red lips. "Thank you so much for hosting us," she said, lowering her chin to inspect Emma over the rim of her glasses. "Monty has a theory."

Emma rolled her eyes. "I agree with him. She wanted to come here but knew I'd say no."

"The signal black-spot out here is a nightmare." Flora peered at her phone screen. "I can just about get texts and calls, but I can't use my data. I wanted to take pictures of the awards ceremony and post it on the Society's Facebook page." Her painted lips turned down in a frown.

"You'll need the Wi-Fi code." Emma stared at the chandelier as she recited it. "Action_Man_Rules," she said with a wince.

"Thanks." Flora connected her phone to the signal. "Can I share it with the others?"

Emma nodded. She studied Mavis as the woman pushed to the front of the group in anticipation of making her grand entrance into the morning room. She chatted with a slender, emaciated looking woman beside her. Their heads bowed like old friends. Only the constant bobbing of Mavis's chin suggested more of a sycophantic relationship.

A tall man approached Flora. His cologne preceded him in a musky cloud. Straight-backed and handsome, he oozed confidence. His hazel irises glittered in the light from the chandelier. Emma recognised the same dangerous mischief which graced Christopher Dolan's. "And who's this?" His voice reverberated against the Tudor panels. His fingers closed around Emma's wrists, warm and strong. He kissed her right cheek and then her left. A tingle shot through her nerve endings as his skin lingered against hers. The faint hint of bristles scratched her cheek, intentional eroticism in the action. "Thank you for hosting us." His gaze gave the impression of the sun giving its glow. He clicked his heels together and bowed, the action ruined by the slap of rubber slippers instead of leather shoes.

"You're welcome," Emma lied, the words couched around a laugh which vied for freedom. He wore a long tailored coat over a matching waistcoat, his dress pants and shirt of an expensive cut. Younger than the other Lit and His Society members and confident enough that she knew his identity, he didn't introduce himself. He dipped his chin to Flora in a suggestive smile and stepped away with slow, precise movements. Emma ground her teeth together, sensing a man who enjoyed playing with fire. She'd met many of his type before and married the worst offender. The stranger showed enough restraint not to glance back over his shoulder, but Emma sensed him judging his effect on her. The stiffness of his spine and the way he angled his head to the side indicated he expected her to follow him. Many women would, she reasoned. Such males exuded excitement and sex appeal, risk, and adventure. Emma released a snort of mirth to herself, knowing this man couldn't match her absent husband.

Flora pursed her red lips together, but a flush crept up her throat. Emma steeled her heart against its murmured misgivings as she followed the babbling throng from the cool lobby and into the warm morning room. Three hours of her life and they would all leave. They'd return to Market Harborough until the next time they needed a last-minute bolt hole.

But then she watched Freda's face light up like a spotlight at this chance to play the fine lady. In that moment, she wasn't a bastard daughter of the Ayers family or a woman facing her final stage exit. She was Freda Ayers, wife of John and genealogically linked to the British royals.

Emma watched Freda lift her chin, extend her gnarled hands, and approach the waiting group. Perfect deportment masked her age. A genteel gliding action carried her across the vast room. She no longer looked like the woman who tapped around the Hall with a cane or taught Nicky swear words. Lady Freda presented her right hand to the stooped man beside Mavis, her fluttering lashes shutting out her nemesis. "Arnand

Dubois," she said in a simpering tone. "My, haven't you grown into a handsome young man?"

8

Chesterfield Chair

♥

Arnand Dubois was a decade past pensionable age. Wrinkles created a patchwork of his face and made a liar of Freda. A brown tweed jacket and matching trousers rebuffed the fancy dress memo. A chocolate shirt clung to his rounded stomach. The button holes stretched across his midriff. Belly hair peeked through the gaps. A lank fringe curtained his forehead, at first glance lush and full. But he'd parted it at the back, dragging the reluctant ash coloured tendrils forward to hide a balding pate.

The volume in the room rose as everyone greeted Freda. Eager eyes grazed the buffet tables. No one removed their jackets or shawls despite the fire sending out its best heat. Dyfed approached, wearing his customary smile. His dark fringe spread across one eye.

He bore a tray loaded with wine glasses and tumblers. It bounced with the removal of each glass.

Emma frowned as she surveyed the room. Chloe had catered for thirty, though ill health and indifference had shrunk the gathering from the expected sixty. "Eleven," Emma murmured, performing another head count. She glanced at Freda in confusion, though the host perhaps hadn't yet noticed.

Emma left the morning room. She closed the heavy door behind her. A woman sat on the pew alone, stuffing her feet into fluffy booties. She smiled at Emma through features drawn by a light hand. Her nose and lips formed a smudge in her thin face. She set her outdoor shoes at the end of the long line. Her low courts had the raggedness of something dug from a disused cupboard. "I love how you've provided slippers for everyone." Age had frayed the hem of her dress, the colour faded from russet to a washed out beige. It had the rumpled texture of fabric kept in a closet for decades and bruised by shifting against heavier items. A run in her stockings told more of her story. Either she didn't know or didn't care.

Emma's shoulders relaxed. She felt grateful for the chit chat after Mavis' blistering antagonism. "This house is freezing in the dead of winter. The heating system is gravity fed and, according to the plumber, it's working fine." She wrapped her arms around herself. "It just doesn't seem like it." A left turn took her to the mantelpiece. Emma stepped onto the hearth to reach the lighter. Ray stored it high enough to thwart small, mischievous hands. She located it by touch. He'd pushed it to the very back of the oak beam which straddled the fireplace. Emma bobbed down, flicked the lighter until the flame appeared, and held it to the newspaper stuffed between the kindling. The flame took, the orange stain spreading across the paper to leave a curling black fringe in its wake. Still squatting in the giant hearth, Emma jumped as the woman spoke from behind her.

"Is it difficult to light?" she asked, bending to watch the enticing colour spread like an infection. Short brown wiry hair escaped from beneath a fascinator the colour of diarrhoea.

"Sometimes." Emma edged back to sit on her haunches. Fire lighting summoned a latent pyromaniac's spirit in her soul. It gave her voice a faraway quality. The edges of the kindling blackened, fed by the gnarled sticks and the pine cones favoured by Ray. The bundle in the grate shifted as the flames chewed at its core. Sparks floated up the chimney. Satisfaction bloomed through Emma's chest as the shards of pine kindling caught, turning ebony as she sacrificed them to the fire's hunger. "That's good," she remarked to herself. Rising, she used both hands to heft a heavy log onto the top of the pile. "It might make a difference."

"I guess the heat rises upstairs." She turned to find the woman staring up at the balcony rail overhead and the bedrooms beyond. "Doesn't it make the bedrooms toasty?"

Emma debated adding another log but resisted, not wishing to risk dousing the fledgling flames. "It warms the hallway, but not the rooms." She stepped over the tiled edge of the hearth and inspected her fingers for traces of soot. "In the past, maids lit every fire in the house to push the heat around. It's inefficient." She sighed and flapped her left hand, spotting a smudge on her thumb. "It's all smoke and mirrors with the heritage department at the council. They want everything left in its original state and refused an application for better heating."

"It's beautiful." The woman stared again at the main staircase. Her blue irises twinkled as though imagining herself gliding down the steps in a wedding gown. "You're so lucky." Her observation caught Emma in the raw spot which Anton's death left in her soul.

"Fortunate," she agreed, avoiding eye contact. Rohan's suggested response to such statements. Anton's hard work and speculation raised the money to purchase the property. Not Emma's. His gift had wrapped around her shoulders like a warm hug on a frosty night. Right when she needed it. But his death brought devastation and loss, which reverberated through the bones of the old Hall. Like a knife wound in her heart. He hadn't trusted her with his terminal diagnosis.

"Oh, sorry. I haven't introduced myself." The woman held out a hand with the integrity of a sparrow's delicate foot. Emma stared at the protruding bones, almost afraid to accept the fragile offering. "I'm Bunny Cathcart, secretary to the Market Harborough Literary and Historical Society." She bobbed her head at the same time as administering a handshake hard enough to take Emma by surprise. Bunny's cool fingers clamped around Emma's freezing digits and pressed until her bones ached.

"Right," Emma replied, drawing out the word and extracting her hand. She pushed it into her pocket in case Bunny expected more painful physical contact. She cocked her head to observe the other woman. "Freda's mentioned you but I figured you were older."

Bunny snorted. "Everyone assumes that. I can't imagine why." She smoothed a hand over her spiky strands and made a motion of tucking them behind her left ear. But without the length, they rose back up. Emma frowned, wondering if the pixie cut represented a new image which Bunny now regretted. The woman's fingers fluttered down and abandoned their futile activity. Her hand rested in line with the tiny mound where her left breast might hide. The woman shrugged, a slight, spasmodic movement. "I guess it's the name," she tittered. "And the role. It fits the librarian stereotype."

Emma smiled in acknowledgement. "I'm an archivist. I understand the ironies of uninformed perception." She waved her other hand towards the closed door of the morning room. "At least you won't lose your teeth eating the buffet," she commented. "I'm not sure what

Freda told the caterers, but I don't think it included a warning about the average age."

Bunny tittered again, an insipid, irritating croak. "Oh, I contacted them," she said, dropping the statement into the conversation as a veiled rebuke. "Freda gave me two phone numbers, but only Luscious Lunches could cater at short notice."

"What happened to the other company?" Emma's brows drew into a line as she pondered the reason someone would ditch the lucrative event at the last minute. The Lit and His brigade might resemble a band of bigoted old folk enjoying their last hurrah, but they were each connected in the highest echelons of Market Harborough society. The wrong word in the right ear could damage a local business's reputation with ease.

Bunny shrugged again, her knotty fingers fixing the wonky bow across her chest. It sagged to one side; the outfit desperate for the attention of an iron. "Building work at their place," she replied, as though her answer sufficed as an explanation. When Emma continued to frown, she added, "Their chiller defrosted overnight and ruined all their food. It's the season for Christmas parties. Only Luscious Lunches seemed interested."

Her lips flattened into thin lines; her teeth dull behind them.

Something about the woman repelled Emma, though she couldn't say why. She pondered her reasons as the fire crackled and spluttered behind her. The log hissed as it released the damp hiding in its pores. The heat made little difference to the lobby, but it warmed Emma's bones. "You'll find everyone through that door," she remarked, pointing again towards the morning room.

"You're welcome to join us," Bunny replied. "It doesn't matter that you're not in costume." Her gaze took in Emma's ski jacket, and the worn jeans hugging her knees and shins. A strange sensation prickled Emma's skin, as though a hidden hand had frisked her without warning.

Emma's lips parted. She leaned towards a denial but that invited offence. Bunny had given permission for her to enter her own morning room. A room hijacked without proper discussion.

A heavy thud issued from the outer doors, followed by a distinct slithering and then a wail. *Bam, bam, bam!* A flat palm hammered against the original leaded glass and Emma tensed. Powerlessness whispered in her ear that she'd lost control of her home and surroundings. And that just wouldn't do.

9

Dining Chair

♥

The hammering ceased. It resumed as the security light picked up movement. A maw of nothingness ate the world beyond the light circle. Emma opened the inner door and stepped into the freezing vestibule. She held her breath. Snowflakes fluttered beyond the distorted antique glass. They danced on an invisible breeze as the temperature fell.

Emma gasped. She jerked back as a white face appeared against the glass. It popped upwards like a garish jack-in-the-box. There. Not there. Feathers brushed against the warped glass like craggy fingers. Emma grounded herself against the cold stone wall. A shiver rocketed through her. Fearing Christopher's return, she turned to Bunny. "Someone's at the door," she stammered. Bunny watched, but she didn't move away from the fire. The flames crackled and spat, enjoying the feast of pine logs and willow sticks. She stood too close, the heat wafting her flimsy skirt. She appeared frozen. The knocking resumed.

With shaking fingers, Emma unlocked the outer door. The face bobbed up before her as she tugged the heavy wood inward.

"You locked me out!" Indignation filled the shrill voice, adding an entitled quality. More annoyance than hysteria. The woman glared up at Emma from the top step.

"Who are you?" Emma demanded. "How did you get here?" She leaned forward enough to see the bus sitting at the bottom of the stairs. An icy fog already dulled the windows as though it had spent hours and not just minutes parked there. A dusting of white flakes obscured the windscreen and roof.

The newcomer bobbed upright again, waving a pointed shoe in Emma's face. The cerise heel dangled from a green-stick fracture with the sole. "My shoe broke!" she announced. Her warm breath oozed across Emma's cheek. "Let me in!" she demanded, her voice rising to an even shriller pitch. "Or do you want me to die out here?"

Emma considered the question with seriousness. But she stepped aside and allowed the colourful creature to stamp past her. She locked the outer doors, then followed her up the step into the lobby. An icy blast nipped at her calves and buttocks, seeping through her jeans.

Emma closed the inner door, a thousand curses rumbling through her mind. Rohan would have rumbled Freda's secret plan and nuked it days ago. He wouldn't put up with this charade.

"Sorry, who are you?" Emma fixed her hands on her hips and glared at the newcomer. Blonde curls cascaded from a glittering headband as the woman turned to face her. Her movements held grace, despite balancing on one leg with her broken shoe held out to Emma.

"Can you fix this?" she demanded.

Emma ignored the question and the slight. "Who are you?" she asked again, her tone acerbic.

"Perhaps I can clear this up." Bunny hopped forward in a jerky movement. Long ears and a fluffy tail would complete the rabbit image. Placing her body between the two women, she spun on the spot to regard them both. "Gwendoline Dubois," she said, bobbing her chin to the blonde. "This is Emma

Andreyev. She's allowed us to use Wingate Hall at short notice." Her statement held a veiled warning, as though she suspected Emma might expel Gwendoline for further rudeness. "Gwendoline's mother is Kathleen Dubois." Bunny jerked her chin down and raised an eyebrow. When Emma didn't respond, she blinked in rapid succession before speaking as though to a fool. "Kathleen Dubois is the celebrated poet who won the scholarship for Writer in Residence at Leicester University. She's our keynote speaker tonight."

Emma shrugged, shivering against the cool air encircling her shoulders. The name, the accolade and the daughter's presence in her home meant nothing more than an irritation.

"I got left on the bloody bus!" Gwendoline raged. Bunny's appraisal didn't touch her. "You just left me! My foot caught in a hole in the floor of that rust heap, and the idiot driver took off so fast, it snapped the heel!" She levelled her accusation at the tiny woman before her as though holding her personally responsible.

Bunny licked her lips. She stared, transfixed, at the newcomer. Emma relaxed. Amusement lifted her lips. The 1950s showgirl had insulted Major Mallory-Eaves' driving without reserve. This woman might shake up the boring Lit and His Society awards night.

Emma surveyed Gwendoline's ostentatious feather head dress. A tight black and red corset ballooned her breasts. Her lithe thighs appeared blue with cold. And her skirt only just covered her buttocks. The woman's ageless face, though beautiful, resembled melted plastic. She'd had cosmetic surgery.

"Nice to meet you, Gwendoline Dubois," Emma said, infusing her words with the opposite meaning. She jabbed her index finger towards the extensive line of slippers. Thirty pairs of cheap but passable warmth, purchased from the Pound Shop at late notice. And only nine gaps showing, nine pairs snuggled around cold feet. Nine guests excluding Freda. Not thirty. "Help yourself," Emma stated, her tone flat. She turned to Bunny and spread her hands. "Where is everyone else?" It occurred to her with a wave of discomfort that she might need to open the door countless more times to admit late guests. "Ray already closed the gate," she added, though she knew she could open it again via the app on her phone.

"Ah, about that." Bunny linked her fingers, the knuckles glinting in the fire's hungry glow. The joints moved beneath the skin as though she tried to squeeze a ball between her palms. "People dropped out as the event drew closer." She lowered her voice to a whisper. "In protest."

"At what?" Emma pursed her lips as Bunny remained silent. "Because it's at Wingate Hall? Or because of me?" The machinations of local snobbery stole the wind from her lungs. Her mysterious ownership of the manor house and acreage caused gossip about how she acquired it. They constructed stories about her past, her Russian surname, and her husband war injuries. Each element added fuel to their conspiracy theories.

Bunny offered only a flat smile of extreme sympathy.

"Okay." Rejection rose from Emma's soul like a blight. It contained the stink of poverty and the scorn of those who had once judged her from behind a desk. "Right. Have a lovely evening. I'm sure Freda can take care of everything." Emma checked her watch, though she knew the time. "I'll return at ten o'clock to say goodbye."

She made her escape. The rubber soles of her slippers scuffed the corridor's tiles. Her shaking legs carried her as far as the kitchen. She paused against the panelled wall. Her palms sought the smoothness of the painted wood and she grounded herself in the house's energy. She'd sanded each chocolate stained section in the months before Stephie's traumatic birth. The heritage officer had grumbled as she painted the wood with a delicate duck egg green. Ray mended the ceilings. He washed them, stripped the peeling wallpaper, plastered, and sanded them smooth. A gentle cream reflected the ornate ceiling lights. No more stains from water leaks, hanging swathes of dusty wallpaper, and nicotine.

Emma ran her fingers over the familiar knots in the wood and sighed. Why did it matter so much what the townsfolk thought of her?

She didn't know why. Just that it did.

10

Swivel Chair

♥

Light and heat bloomed from the kitchen as Emma pushed open the door. Ridley crouched by the Aga, his craggy fingers smoothing the soft hair on Farrell's head. The scent of garlic-infused chicken filled the air, explaining the dog's immovable stance beside the baking savories. The man didn't rise as Emma entered the room, but the air of pretence hung around his shoulders. It contained a silent prayer that she didn't notice him.

Emma wondered how he expected her to miss his bulk occupying the warmest corner of the room. He hunched there like a raven in his ill-fitting footman's uniform. His eyes squeezed closed as he stroked his fingers across Farrell's fur. Emma sidestepped the kitchen table and strode towards the coffee percolator. She'd need a caffeine hit to remain awake and expel the house invaders. Dumping in too much milk meant shoving the lukewarm brew into the microwave.

Farrell released a whine. He wriggled free of his bed. His claws tapped against the tiles. He nudged Emma's thigh with his wet nose. His feet had dried by the Aga, his toe beans leaving no tracks across the tiled floor.

"Good boy," she soothed. She buried her fingers in the soft ruff around his throat. The microwave pinged after fifty seconds. Emma tasted the result in her mug. Not great, but not terrible. A snapshot of Christopher's smiling face filled her imagination. His lithe fingers, capable of such greatness and such harm, scooped coffee into the machine. The sadness in his gaze added to the list of what she'd lost by banishing him. Friendship. And great coffee.

Farrell sat on her foot, not allowing her to leave without him again. Ridley remained like an ink stain in her peripheral vision, one knee of his worn black pants resting on the stuffed edge of the dog's bed. Fine hairs from Farrell's white blaze dotted the threadbare fabric. Emma glanced at the kitchen door, imagining the grown man slinking from the morning room and past her in order to escape. But escape what?

She took another sip of her coffee and winced. "This is horrible," she murmured. Turning with the dog's bottom still perched on her foot, she tipped the murky brown liquid down the sink. She ran water over the lurking stains in the mug and left it to soak. A sigh pushed through her lips at the awkwardness of Ridley's behaviour. "Are you okay?" she ventured, her tone light. "Did someone upset you?" Her lips drew back as her mind ran through the possibilities. The Lit and His Society comprised an offensive bunch of entitled fools.

Farrell bumped her knee with his ears as he turned his adoring gaze on her. His eyes narrowed to happy slits and his tongue poked from between lips which parted in a grin. Emma's mood lost its severe edge. "You're always okay," she said, running her fingers over the dog's glossy cheek. "But I asked Ridley, not you." His tail thudded against the tiles. He released a low whine of innocent appreciation.

The man in the corner rose, and he pressed his backside against the Aga. He offered a shallow nod but refused to meet her gaze.

"Can I get you something?" Emma asked. Crumbs dotted his lapels. She noticed an aluminum crest rising in the corner of a tray like a glittering tsunami ready to plunge over the side. Pointing to it, she said, "You might want to smooth that flat." Her gaze strayed to the kitchen door.

A shaking hand reached from the end of Ridley's frayed jacket cuff, drawing with it a dirty grey sleeve. He pressed the foil back into place with a deformed index finger before jamming his hands behind his back. Black lashes shuttered eyes the colour of charred mahogany, but emotion leaked through the cracks in his weathered skin. "Is Ridley your first name, or your second?" Emma asked. Her empathy soaked up his pain and confusion like an overfilled sponge. It lodged in her gut as though she'd eaten too much. He shrugged in answer to her question and stared at the red quarry tiles. "You don't know?" she pressed, her tone gentle. "Or you don't want to tell me?"

"I don't know," he whispered. The words tumbled over lips which contained a purplish hue against his dark skin. His lashes fluttered, stroking the craggy contours of his cheek. His reply left Emma floundering. She'd offered the suggestion as a loaded choice, expecting he just didn't want to engage with her. She hadn't foreseen him telling her he didn't know his own name.

"Do you need help?" she whispered. She imagined a man who attacked a woman would think nothing of meting out his ire on an older, feebler employee. "You work for Gareth, right?"

Ridley's eyes widened until the whites seemed to obscure his irises and pupils. His gaze turned towards the kitchen door as it opened in a rush. Emma inhaled, her reaction causing Farrell to stiffen. He administered a low growl in response.

Chloe jammed her hands on her hips. She stared at the empty tray on the kitchen table. As though weighing the silence, her gaze slid to Ridley and then to Emma. "Problem?" she demanded.

Emma clamped her lips closed. She didn't need to justify her presence in her own kitchen. She observed Ridley's exaggerated head shake with interest. A new checkered cravat hid the bruising on Chloe's neck. She'd also tidied her unruly blonde curls. The bun gave her face a severity. She edged Ridley aside with the backs of her fingers. He shifted away like a horse threatened with a whip. Oblivious, Chloe tugged on the Aga's handle. She examined the contents simmering in its cavernous stove. "These are ready," she announced. Snapping a cloth dangling from her smock, she reached one-handed into the oven. A tray of steaming savouries filled the kitchen with wonderful scents. Emma's mouth watered at the sight of flaky pastry and melted cheese.

"Lovely," she remarked, despite Rohan's warning in her head. It told her to go upstairs and not reappear until ten o'clock. She should have listened to her wise inner Rohan.

Chloe dumped the tray on the metal lid of the Aga's left burner. It appeared precarious because of the hinge. Tomato juice dribbled down the side of the container and pooled, hissing on the Aga's spotless cream surface. Emma studied it, having not factored a clean-up operation into Freda's promises of requiring nothing from her other than to host her arrogant friends. *'One tiny favour,'* she'd called it. Emma held on to the snort of derision building in her throat.

Chloe didn't offer Emma a sample, but her gaze rested on the owner of Wingate Hall. A hint of aggression projected from behind her blue irises. "I catered for thirty," she snapped, spittle flying from her lips and landing on the uppermost empty tray on the kitchen table. "Hardly anyone's come."

Emma pursed her lips. Guilt tapped a beat in time with her pulse. Bunny had intimated no one came because of her. Blame stained her safe place and left a blot on her sense of home. She missed Rohan's like a physical pain in her chest. The eternal umbilical cord connecting her to her children gave a twang of misery. She wanted them all around the fire in the comfy lounge with its squashy furniture and the toys littered across the floor. Her family.

Emma straightened her spine. The dog's weight numbed her left instep. She glared at Chloe. "I own the Hall." Her spiky tone oozed with the bad breeding of which she stood accused. "You need to speak to Mavis about tonight's event."

Chloe took a step towards Emma, the table blocking her passage. The hem of her white coat dangled over a tray of mini pizzas, their red sauce blotting the edges like blood. She dipped forward at the waist for emphasis. "I want my money," she stated, reiterating a moot point. "That old woman said I needed to speak to you."

Emma's jaw dropped with dismay. "What?" she hissed. Her head shook as though a mechanism had failed in her neck. "Which old woman?" she demanded. "Because I can assure you, she lied!"

11

Chippendale Armchair

♥

Emma stamped from the kitchen. White-hot fury surged through her veins. She'd expected Chloe to describe Freda, but she hadn't.

Emma's soles squeaked against the floorboards of the lobby. Farrell jogged beside her, his ebony tail wafting like a flag. It tapped a rhythm against her thighs. She welcomed his solidarity in confronting the correct *old woman*. Her fingers trembled on the brass knob of the morning room. She'd polished it until it shone. These people didn't deserve her efforts.

Taking a deep breath, she strode into the room. Her room. In her house.

"Oh! Not the dog!" Mavis cried, lifting a loaded tea plate above her head. "We don't want hair in the food and on our clothes! Get that mutt out of here."

Ignoring the protests which followed Emma across the room, she strode towards the roaring fire and pointed at the hearthrug. "Farrell, wait," she told the black dog. With a grin of appreciation, he dumped himself onto the rug with a sigh. His fluffy ears remained pricked for her next instruction, but his eyes narrowed with pleasure at the warmth on his fur.

"This will not do!" Mavis hissed. A cake crumb perched on her lower lip, a blot in the rose pink gloss. She rounded on Emma, smaller, dumpier but emphatic.

"No, it won't!" Emma replied. She stared at her with brown eyes flashing with fury. "The caterer informed me you sent her to me for payment." Emma raised her voice and flapped the tatty invoice between them. "Explain!"

Mavis swallowed a lump of cake. It turned to concrete in her throat, and she struggled to speak. "Let's go outside for a moment," she croaked. Turning to the guests edging nearer the dispute, she flapped the hand holding the tea plate. A scone plunged to earth. Farrell's jaws snapped. The perfect vacuum cleaner. Mavis stared at the floor in confusion.

"No." Emma folded her arms across her chest. "Let's do it right here. Why don't I inform your committee members about how your tale of financial woe led to me funding the summer fete? You claimed to have a little cash flow issue and promised to refund it within a few days." Emma dipped forward to make her point. She focused on a mole clinging to Mavis's chin. A single dark hair sprang from it to create a waving antenna. "I'm still owed for the last shindig you held on my property. I won't allow you to take advantage of me again." She jabbed her index finger at the door leading to the lobby. "Pay the lady. Tonight."

Mavis gulped. "Or what?" She threw her shoulders back and her breasts battled beneath the thin cream fabric of her lacy dress. Her body language oozed defiance, but the hissed question hinted of an inner fear.

"Is there a problem here?" Monty Jones gave Emma's elbow a light touch. The rouge dots on Mavis's cheeks remained the only colour in her flaccid complexion.

"No, no!" she insisted, a waxy smile tugging at her lips. She spun her body to form a barrier between Monty and Emma, shoving at his arms with her hands. "Have you tried the mini pizzas? They're to die for." Farrell's tail thumped against Emma's foot as though he agreed.

Emma exhaled as Mavis led Monty away, his elbow gripped between her white-knuckled fingers. He shot a concerned look over his shoulder. Emma gritted her teeth and watched him leave.

"Is that true?" A wavering voice from behind Emma broke through her angry thoughts. It explained the sudden wag of the dog's tail. Not for pizza, but at the sight of a friend. And one who fed him naughty things which dogs shouldn't have.

Emma turned to face Freda. The haughtiness of earlier had vanished beneath an expression of horror. "Is what true?" Emma replied, her tone flat.

"That she didn't pay for the food in the summer? Or tonight?" Freda pressed a shaking finger to her lips. "But the Lit and His Society sold tickets for the summer fete, and you charged us nothing to hold it here." Freda took a step forward, the worn toes of her antique shoes touching the soft fronts of Emma's slippers. "Is it true, Emma?" Her voice wavered. "Have I allowed them to take advantage of your generosity?" Her blue irises swam with saline, creating pools along her lower lids. She'd missed the mark with her eye liner, and it formed a black, crusty line just above her cheekbones. Dots of mascara covered her paper thin skin like dirty snow.

Emma exhaled. An impossible question. Had Freda allowed her elite group of social climbers to exploit her kindness? No doubt, she'd overstepped. Again.

Freda had visited the Hall for a few days two years earlier. She'd never left, taking the first of the renovated bedrooms as though entitled to it. Emma hadn't challenged her. She squared her jaw and tasted the words as though testing for poison. "You backed me into the corner," she replied. Her brown eyes lost their habitual gentleness. "And let them take whatever they wanted." Emma cocked her head. Her mind strayed to Rohan. He'd seen this coming. And he'd tried to warn her. Again, his radio silence stabbed at her. Was he lying injured and alone, as he once did in Afghanistan?

"But I didn't mean to," Freda whispered, dragging her back to the conversation. Her gnarled fingers closed over Emma's, and she shook them as though needing to force her meaning through the joints. "I didn't know!" Her voice rose higher, and Monty frowned from across the room.

Emma sighed and shook her hand free of Freda's grip. "I don't care anymore." Her tone held an uncharacteristic bite. "But I'm not paying for tonight's food, so make sure Mavis does." She swallowed, but the words spilled over her tongue and became airborne before she could stop them. Emma suspected nothing would have prevented her final retort. "Do not invite your insular friends to my home ever again!" She meant every word. Her gaze strayed to a flouncing Gwendoline in her showgirl outfit. Pickle plunged from beneath the triangle of sandwich clutched in her fingers and bounced on the expensive rug at her feet. She tilted her body to stare at it before grinding it into the wool with the toe of her slipper. Emma's teeth clenched until her jaw ached. Even the sad wobble of Freda's chin didn't quell her rage. She needed to leave before she lost her temper.

"Hey, Em?" Flora Jones slid a cool arm around her rigid shoulders. With lips pursed in sympathy, the older woman dipped her head towards Emma's, creating an air of confidentiality. "Monty said he'd sort it out," she whispered.

Emma raised her gaze. She concentrated on a huddle near the buffet tables. Dyfed and Chloe circled the nearest group. They handed out bubbling flute glasses filled with champagne and tiny snacks. Monty had bailed Mavis up against the tea urn. Her large buttocks threatened a line of white mugs as she squirmed. Bunny,

Major Mallory-Eaves and Sir Robert stood as though defending an invisible goal.

Emma sighed, releasing enough of her pent-up aggression to speak. "How can Monty sort anything? It happened months ago. Your chairperson shafted me for the cost of catering and the hire of crockery, marquees and furniture. I paid it like a fool. I'm not doing it again."

"We didn't know." Flora employed the same tone she used on the seven-year-olds in her class, coupling it with a pat to Emma's forearm. Strands of her fading red hair escaped from her complicated chignon and merged with her rabbit covered shoulder. "I just overheard what you said to Freda." Flora jerked her head towards the knot of rigid bodies near the buffet. "Monty just agreed to act as the treasurer until they find another sucker. He'll sort out tonight's payment and look at everything else." She frowned. "We knew nothing about the cash-flow issue."

"I'm so sorry, Emma." Freda pressed the back of her hand to her forehead and squinted around for somewhere to collapse while preserving her dignity. She edged towards a restored Victorian wing-back chair and sank into it. Her entire body seemed to disappear into the folds of the sumptuous fabric.

Guilt rampaged through Emma's chest as a condemnation. She now appeared petty and vengeful, choosing the society's big night to air her grievance. A chill entered her body through her feet and eased along her bones. Her shoulders sank. She ached to hug her children. A wet kiss from her baby daughter and a bear hug from her son always put the world back on its axis. Emma cleared her throat. "I'll leave you to it," she managed, her tone emotionless. "I'll come back down before ten to see you all out. Freda knows where the fire exits are and what to do in an emergency."

"Oh, no you don't!" Flora soothed. "I won't let you slink away by yourself. Stay here in the warm and eat some of this delicious food." Strong fingers closed around Emma's right wrist. "If I have to weather our esteemed guest doing a poetry recital, then it's only fair you should suffer, too." She pulled up another chair and shoved Emma into it.

And Freda's gaze bored into the side of her crestfallen face.

12

Hanging Chair

♥

"Just kill me now," Emma murmured to Farrell as he crawled along the rug on his belly. He reached her and butted her fingers with his head. Emma peered over the side of the chair to see him splayed out like a frog. His back legs unfurled behind him, in the epitome of laziness.

"I didn't know." Freda leaned sideways. Her right breast squashed against the chair-arm. "I'm so sorry."

Emma relented. She stared up at the ceiling rose. The heritage officer from the local council complimented the finished work. He'd have fainted with chagrin had he known they'd done it without expensive professional help. Ray moulded the delicate filigree with his fingers "We'll talk about it later." Emma distracted herself with the softness of Farrell's head. He crawled on his belly like a commando, removing stray crumbs and a blob of jam from between the tufts of the rug. Emma forced herself to play nice. "I know Flora and Monty from Nicky's school. Tell me about everyone else."

She listened as Freda detailed the names and occupations of the gathered guests. The old lady edged past her misery as she launched into a gossip festival fit for a lady's maid. "That's Christos Smaragdis," she whispered, pointing to the tall man wearing the expensive suit. "The divine one with the naughty eyes." She fluttered her lashes as though contemplating how long she could keep him busy in the bedroom. The wrinkling of her nose suggested she'd reached a conclusion and decided not to bother. "He's offered several times to act as our treasurer. I'm surprised Mavis won't allow it."

Emma stroked the dog's head and stared at Christos as he flirted with Gwendoline. As though aware of Freda's adoration, he glanced across and winked at her. She jumped as though he'd kissed her full on the lips. He appeared sophisticated in his bow tie. The gold chain of a fob watch snaked into a side pocket of his waistcoat.

"She thinks he's a bad boy," Freda hissed, her mood turning to acidic. Her bottom lip poked over the top one to spread lipstick over her philtrum and the underside of her nose. When she released it, the smudge created the impression of a giant mouth. She glared through slitted eyes at Gwendoline as the other woman orbited Christos like a moth to a flame.

"And is he?" Emma frowned and leaned closer, guessing Freda hadn't finished her sentence.

"Just a philanderer." Freda flapped her hands as though trying to fly. "God's gift to women." She sighed. "He's Greek!"

Emma shot her a sideways glance, wondering about the relevance of his nationality. Dark-haired and handsome, he could have held an Italian or a Ukrainian passport. Who would know?

Emma observed him, feigning interest. Anger still roiled on her gut. At Freda. At Mavis. At Rohan, but mostly at herself. "He looks young." She stiffened at Freda's pointed sniff. "Younger than I expected," she added. Freda appeared mollified. The wise inner voice in her mind sounded a lot like Rohan's as it absolved her of blame. The Lit and His Society, with Freda's help, had wronged her. Not the other way around.

"He's a banker," Freda sniffled, and Emma hid a smirk behind her hand.

"I'm sure he is," she managed. But the smile faded from her lips at the memory of Christopher's play on words. A banker on his tongue became something quite offensive. Without his immature snorts of mirth, the joke lost its humour. It tumbled to the rug where Gwendoline flattened it beneath a coquettish pirouette as she showed off her wares for Christos.

Flora approached the pair. Her height seemed diminished as though her confidence had abandoned her. She spoke to Gwendoline but turned her feet towards Christos. Emma studied the strained interaction. "I don't eat carbs." Gwendoline sneered at her plate. In a flash of movement, she dumped a scone onto Flora's. Crumbs scattered far and wide.

"Thanks." Flora glanced from her to Christos. She drifted away.

"I see you've met Bunny Cathcart." Freda had left Emma behind. She fought to catch up with her labelling. Freda rested her chin on her fragile wrist. A prelude to gossip. "She lived with her mother until she died in the summer. Monty took pity on her. He and Flora voted her in as our secretary. It doesn't pay much." Her wonky eyebrows waggled, creating a comedic image. Courtesy of Nicky and his felt tips.

Emma felt honour bound to instruct her son on the correct positioning of eyebrows if the ill-advised alliance continued. "Mind you," Freda continued. "She doesn't do much. Her computer keeps breaking." Her lips pursed into painted lines smudged as far as her left nostril. She drew her owlish spectacles along her sharp nose and peered at Emma over the tops of the thick lenses. "I could ask Monty to fire her." The eyebrows danced near her hairline. "He's rather partial to you."

Emma cleared her throat and squirmed against the inference. "No thanks," she bit, her tone acerbic. "I have a job, remember? I'm renovating Wingate Hall and raising two children."

Freda's head jerked back on her neck. "I see little renovation happening," she commented. "It all stopped after Stephie arrived. What about your archiving job at Nicky's school? Weren't you meant to go back to it?"

Emma blew out a ragged breath. Freda had exposed her failures. She'd spent the last two years coasting, not grasping anything. Healing, she'd called it in her guiltiest moments. Rohan had offered a gentle nudge towards solidity before he left. And they'd argued. She ached to see him, speak to him, convince him of his mistake. Her chin dipped as self-pity took root. Because he was right.

She studied Farrell's unusual commando crawl as he clawed his way as far as a coffee table and waited beneath it. He resembled a crocodile, biding its time beneath the lapping waves to snap up a victim. The crumbling section of cake which pitched from Gwendoline's plate didn't even hit the floor. *Snap*. Gone. She glanced down in confusion, but without caring about the damage her carelessness might cause to the vintage furnishings. With a shallow shake of her head, she continued wooing Christos Smaragdis with her fluttering lashes and smoky laugh. When he turned his head to meet Emma's gaze with a smile, Gwendoline stepped between them to block his view.

"What about her?" Emma demanded, pointing at Gwendoline's lithe thighs. "Who is she, and why is she here?"

"That's her mother." Freda jabbed a bent knuckle towards a rakish woman with a horsey laugh. She wore a mustard ball gown three sizes too big for her. Vomited up from the nine year Regency period in the 1800s. Her skin had a greenish tinge, enhanced by the awful dress colour. And she covered a barking cough with her thin fingers. Short grey hair rose from her scalp in spikes. Like Bunny's. Mavis had chatted to Kathleen Dubois in the lobby. "She's won the scholarship for Writer in Residence at Leicester University." Freda's voice held irritation. She disliked the woman and her success.

"What did she write?" Emma turned in the armchair and tucked her right leg beneath her. Farrell glanced back at her with a grin, as though assessing her need for his company against the important role of vacuuming the floor. He made his choice and edged closer to Gwendoline's foot, scooping up a fallen blob of mayonnaise. His lips drew back from his teeth at the taste of the hidden cucumber, and he bobbed his head as though revolted. It reappeared on the rug like a ball of green slime. Emma forced herself to look away from the minor devastation of her home and life's work.

"Well!" Freda settled in for the long haul. A proper nonagenarian prayer chain download then. "She wrote a poem about food. It's rather cute. Her daughter, Gwendoline, entered it into a competition and here we are." She clapped her frail hands together and grinned. "Kathleen, Arnand, and Gwendoline moved away from Market Harborough ten years ago. Mavis invited them back for our end-of-year celebration." She shrugged, her thin shoulders shifting through a series of gears from her earlobes and back again. "She doesn't have many good ideas, and we couldn't afford a big celebrity. I haven't seen the Dubois family since before the you-know-what."

Emma screwed up her features. "No, I don't know. How could I? They left before I arrived in town."

Freda leaned closer, and the action enlightened Emma on the reason behind her erratic behaviour. She'd found the ancient cooking sherry hidden in a locked cupboard inside the old butler's pantry in the cellar. Emma's lips twisted in consternation. She needed to check the safe in her bedroom, which housed the only key. Ray left it off the master for a reason. Because beyond the shelving of the innocuous cupboard lurked an ancient system of tunnels which spread across the grounds. And she didn't want her son in them again.

Emma glared at the old woman and shelved her misgivings. "Why did they move?" she asked, not sure why it mattered. But the query bought her time to sift through her inner demons while Freda droned on about an affair with a church warden. "The vicar of St Dionysius didn't want the scandal," she concluded. "They left rather fast after that."

"Sorry, I missed that. Who did the vicar have an affair with?"

But as Freda dipped forward again to redeliver her truth bomb as she knew it, the piercing tinkle of a metal spoon against a fragile crystal flute drew her attention.

"I'd like to call everyone to order." Mavis lifted her shrill voice above the hum of continued conversations. Her breasts clashed beneath the lace fringe of her inadequate dress, barely constrained by the greying bra straps leaving dents in her shoulders. Mavis dipped forward like a marionette with the strings cut. Bobbing back up again, she beamed at the gathered crowd. "We're privileged to have here tonight our esteemed Poet Laureate." She spread her hands with the palms facing upward in welcome.

"Couldn't afford anyone else," Freda muttered, loud enough for Emma to hear.

"Kathleen, er, Kathleen!" Mavis clapped her hand to get the woman's attention.

The esteemed Kathleen's husband had commandeered all her interest. They debated in hushed whispers, foreheads together and noses almost touching. Arnand pressed Kathleen's palm before slipping something into his pocket. She lifted her hand to her mouth as though suppressing a cough.

Mavis cleared her throat and started again. "Your family proved such a loss to our society." She cranked into second gear, this time with Kathleen turning to face her.

"Not really," Freda muttered.

"We're hoping you'll read your winning entry to us." Mavis swivelled from the waist, her breasts moving independently like Chinese Baoding balls.

"She needn't bother," Freda sighed. She jammed her cigarette holder between her lips and mimicked puffing on the sugar stick.

"First, let's eat some more of this wonderful food!" Mavis instructed, waving towards the laden buffet tables. "There's plenty."

Freda gasped and jabbed her holder at Mavis' broad back. "Well!" she exclaimed. "She could have thanked you for hosting the event in your home at late notice!" Her lips puckered like a frayed sock, and she turned to Emma with eyes widened by righteous indignation. "It was her cock up after all!" The fake cigarette sailed through the air, enjoying a quick but exhilarating flight before Farrell snagged and ate it with consummate ease.

13

Bistro Chair

♥

"I'm going upstairs," Emma said. She unwound her legs from the seat and gave herself a moment for the circulation to seep back into her left foot. "Rohan's dog is eating crap, and I can't bear how your friends are treating my home." She sighed as a pickled onion rolled across the expensive rug. Farrell sniffed it as though not quite believing the horror experienced by his taste buds before he spat it out. Another lick confirmed it and he squeezed his eyes closed and pretended it wasn't right there by his left paw. Major Mallory-Eaves sat on the renovated arm of a priceless Queen Ann wing-back chair. It released a woody creak of protest, and Emma forced herself to look away. Freda had wanted the bare ballroom, but Emma had granted her the warmer, furnished room if she promised to take responsibility. She regretted that decision. Among others.

Emma rose and clicked her fingers to the dog. But Freda's hand clamped around her wrist. "Don't go?" she begged, the plea more in her eyes than in her voice. "You're an extra body. If you leave, it will look as though no one came."

"Because they didn't!" Emma replied. "In protest!"

Freda dropped her chin and sighed. "Oh, you heard about that?"

"Yeah, I did." Emma straightened her ski coat and patted her pockets. "I have my phone. Call me when you're ready to leave." She added the pronoun as a futile salvo, wondering if Freda understood Emma had included her in the list of those exiting the building.

"Take a seat, take a seat!" Mavis urged. "Keep your food and drinks with you. Kathleen has agreed to read her poem to us. So, let's give her a rousing Market Harborough welcome."

Freda yanked hard enough on Emma's jacket sleeve to topple her back into the seat. Christos slumped into the chair beside her. He stretched out his long legs, making leaving difficult. Emma shook her head and rose again, a violent narrative in her head assuring her she didn't need to stay. But as Freda clung to her sleeve, she stood like a totem. Expectant eyes turned to her. Monty bounced upright. His bottom had barely kissed the seat of the antique Georgian dining chair pulled up beside Flora's. He held out his hand towards Emma. "On behalf of the Literary and Historical Society, I'd like to thank Mrs Andreyeva for hosting our gathering at short notice." A twitch tugged at his right cheek at the pathetic applause which dribbled from the hands of those gathered.

A sudden influx of noise sounded from beside Emma as Christos hammered his palms together. He grinned up at her, his perfect white teeth shining from lips pulled back in enthusiasm. "Bravo!" he cried, nodding around the group. Eager to please him, Gwendoline added a flutter of her fingers and gazed at his handsome profile.

Emma fought the urge to vomit as Freda gave a gargantuan tug on her sleeve. She relented, piling back into the squashy seat with a sigh. She'd allowed them to trap her in their circle of falsity and entitlement. The remaining few hours stretched before her. Resigned to her fate, she turned her gaze to the snowflakes as they tapped a gentle beat against the long windows facing the extensive gardens. The loaded clouds and gentle covering created an eerie greyness which matched Emma's mood. "Kill me now," she murmured to herself.

"Pardon?" Christos leaned towards her. The tang of cheap champagne laced his breath. "It really is most kind of you to host us," he reiterated. His expression oozed sincerity. But Emma detected a predatory spirit encircling him as he reached out in a feigned accidental movement and stroked her rigid fist. In her peripheral vision, she noticed Gwendoline tapping the exposed wrist of his right hand to regain his attention. Her blonde brows drew together in irritation as his interest in Emma trumped anything she could offer.

Emma returned a wan smile. If she lied to him, would he notice? "It's fine," she replied, testing her theory. The slightest frown drew his dark brows together in concern, as though he'd plugged into her soul. Emma withdrew, mentally and physically. She tucked her hands between her thighs, afraid he might try to seize one and enfold it. Poverty and riches attracted the same type of man. Both were hard wired to exploit those within their grasp. She turned her shoulder to cut Christos from her field of vision, recognising a player and keen not to join his proffered game. Gwendoline released a sigh aimed at grabbing his attention. It ended with a moan, sexual enough to draw a raised eyebrow from Sir Robert. Rapid blinking betrayed his surprise and then interest. Feeling betrayed by her fellow females, Emma winced and focussed on the dog.

Farrell continued to crawl and feast. His fluffy spaniel's tail flowed behind him like a snake. It joined with his trailing legs, disturbing the weave of the carpet until he left dark tracks. He diverted for interesting crumbs, his progress silent and effective. Emma imagined herself leaving the room the same way and smiled to herself. Glancing up, she met Monty's quizzical gaze. She hid her grin behind her hand and manufactured a genteel cough.

A glass of lurid orange liquid appeared near her right elbow. She forced her lips into a smile and waved away Christos's help. The man behaved like a wasp, circling her, and buzzing into her face. A shiver of foreboding ran through her torso, indiscernible from the cool air seeping through the wooden window frames. Farrell reached Mavis and recoiled at the glare she shot down at him. He sent his wet tongue up the side of her stockinged calf, and she kicked out at him. He moved fast enough for her to miss before retreating under the coffee table. Turning his back on her, he rested his head on his paws.

Emma gave him a sympathetic dip of her chin and studied Mavis's breasts as the woman warbled on about her precious but irrelevant society. Farrell bestowed the pleading white half-moons of his eyes on Emma and she ignored the emotional tug. Just like her, he'd walked into this disaster. Mavis's breasts possessed a language of their own, jiggling and bumping within her creamy lilac dress. Her waistband had increased to provide them with a suitable shelf, giving her the appearance of a football. A section of the underskirt had caught in her knickers, creating a bulge to match all the others. The swipe of Farrell's tongue had removed a section of the line drawn from the heel to the hem of her skirt. Emma pursed her lips, a giggle rising from her stomach like an air bubble. She struggled to hold on to it, whimpering with the force of the threatened explosion.

The battle continued throughout Mavis's introduction of Kathleen. The innocuous giggle turned to hysteria in Emma's head, as though she'd found herself trapped on a plane plunging to earth cockpit first. She ached to run from the room screaming, not stopping until she reached Allaine and her babies. But she foretold Nicky's first question even without him asking it. *'When's Papochka coming home?'* And she didn't know.

Emma dropped her hand into her lap, the smile lost between her head and her heart. She edged her phone from her pocket and peered at the screen. Nothing. Not from Rohan or Lear. She shoved it back with a sigh containing enough desperation to earn herself a feathered pat to her sleeve from Christos. A pointed glare from Gwendoline followed his caress. Rebuking herself, Emma concentrated on Kathleen Dubois.

"It's so wonderful to come back to Market Harborough," she said, her voice a low warble. She swayed on her feet, a sapling struggling against a gale force wind. Her physical appearance invoked pity, with her vomit hued dress clinging to her emaciated frame. But her words cut through the air like razor blades. "It's strange to return to a place and find nothing has changed," she stated, her weak voice throwing the barb without care. "You're all still here, right where my darling Arnand and I left you." She clapped her hands together, the fingers fragile enough to snap. Her husband studied her with rapt attention, perched on the edge of his tub chair with his feet pressed together.

He wavered as though expecting his wife to collapse. Their dynamic appeared odd, as though they'd tied themselves in an irreversible knot. She waited to fall while he poised himself to catch her.

Emma glanced at their daughter, sliding her gaze sideways and avoiding the instant smile which lit Christos's lips. Gwendoline played with a flake of pastry on her plate, her mood distracted. Or disinterested. With her long legs crossed at the ankles and her skirt barely covering her underwear, she resembled a petulant teenager. Emma frowned, certain she'd passed the two decade mark a while ago.

Major Mallory-Eaves released an extended throat-clearing as Kathleen twisted her body and snatched a notepad from her seat. The atmosphere in the room became charged. Farrell lifted his head and stared at Emma, picking up the hike in gathered anxiety. His brow furrowed into an ebony line, and he stared at her, ears pricked and limbs poised to lift his body from the rug. Sir Robert Holden rubbed a nervous hand across his bushy moustache, directing his attention to the leatherette slippers on his feet. Emma didn't recognise them. He'd brought his own with him.

Kathleen's voice strengthened, and she studied the paper trembling in her fingers. It rang out, clear and strong, as she released her poem's title into the silence. "It's called *Food for Thought,*" she said. She paused a moment, balancing the notebook on her left hand and placing a finger near the top of the page. Soft purple ankle boots peeked from beneath the hem of her lavender dress.

Emma blinked as Arnand erupted from his chair and whipped a pair of bifocals from his nose. He presented them to his wife, his body bent at the waist and his palms outstretched like a courtier afraid of losing his head. Kathleen plucked the glasses from his hands and offered him a smile of gratitude. "Thank you, my darling," she said, her tone soft. She jammed them onto her nose and smiled down at her winning entry.

"In the lofty realm of feelings, where our dreams reside,

Let's go on a journey, where passions collide.

For emotions, dear friend, are like flavours profound,

A gastronomic symphony, which makes our senses abound.

Love, the sweet nectar, like sap on our lips,

The taste that uplifts, with each honeyed sip."

The poem didn't interest Emma. But Kathleen's emaciated state perplexed her, especially considering her poem's juxtaposition between food and emotion. The three components jarred like badly fitting shoes.

"She's usually much more spiteful." Freda's informational dubbing sounded louder than intended. She fiddled with the device in her left ear and a high-pitched whistle cut through Emma's brain. Her hearing aid needed a new battery. Freda leaned closer to Emma, drawing the interest of both Christos and Gwendoline. "She wrote a limerick about me," Freda stated. Monty leaned sideways to peer between Flora and Kathleen as the poet kept reading. Emma cringed, picturing the former Year 6 teacher making her stand up as a punishment. She fixed her gaze on Kathleen and hoped he assumed Freda's indiscriminate rambling related to age and too much sherry. "She likened me to a faggot," Freda continued, her voice rising. "Do you know what a faggot is?"

Gwendoline snorted and Christos leaned forward to stare at Freda. She waved to him and nodded. Grateful for her fresh audience, she led her diatribe in a circle from offensive gay slurs and back to food with consummate ease. "You have it with peas," she said, guileless, oblivious and entirely without shame. "Faggot and peas. I just never worked out if she meant it as a compliment or an insult."

Despite the lingering cold in the enormous room, Emma sank into her ski jacket and sweated with embarrassment.

14

High Chair

♥

Emma escaped during an impromptu interlude. Mavis forced Kathleen to hand out irrelevant prizes for random, made-up roles exercised by the committee members throughout the year. The embossed certificates created a riot of colour and hinted at the desperation of a rainy afternoon at the mercy of grandchildren. Kathleen sank into her chair for extended bouts of coughing until a concerned Arnand handed her a glass of water.

"A slight break," Mavis called in her shrillest voice as Kathleen deteriorated. "Five minutes. Don't wander too far."

Gwendoline rose, lithe and elegant. She floated towards her parents as though on wheels. Bunny poked her face between Mavis and the bent Kathleen. "Would a hot drink help?" she asked, her tone infused with the desire to help.

Gwendoline gave a dramatic eye-roll. "She's already got water!" She added enough pique to her voice to send Bunny recoiling backwards. "Stop interfering!" she jibed, and Bunny skittered away. She headed to the other side of the room as though scorched.

Emma jerked her head at Farrell, and they bolted for the door. She closed it behind them, intending to disobey Mavis and wander as far as possible. She laid another log on the lobby fire and remained crouched in the wide hearth. The flames sneaked from beneath the round wooden feast, sensing its quality like snakes tasting the air. Sparks flared from the bark as the orange tendrils licked the craggy surface clean. Emma absorbed the wholesomeness of the scene before rising with a sigh. "Let's go up to my bedroom," she murmured, turning to speak to Farrell. The sentence trailed from her lips as a gasp.

"A little forward perhaps," Christos said with a smirk. "But I'm game if you are." His left hand contained a vape. The reflection of the fire sent yellow sparkles across the empty glass tube which shielded the atomiser.

Emma stepped over the tiled lip of the hearth and navigated the metal guard rail. Christos observed her with dark, glinting eyes, which bored beneath her winter layers. The experience left her feeling vulnerable. He didn't move aside to assist her progress, forcing her to brush against him as she passed. "You can't smoke in the house," she stated, her tone flat. "Where's my bloody dog? Farrell!"

Claws tapped from the corridor which led to the kitchen. They sped up as he trotted back to her, jaw open in a smile, and his ears pricked. The whine he emitted from between his lips indicated his need for a bathroom break. Christos lifted the vape to inspect it, his long fingers encasing the tank. "It's not smoking, it's vaping." He licked his lips and smiled at her, the wink of his left eye offering a challenge.

Emma used the moment to take a step backwards, buying herself an extra metre of space between them. "Smoke, vape, I don't care what you call it, but you can't do it indoors" Her jaw clenched. She turned her back on him.

The signal to escape this predatory male yammered in her ears. Her heart rate increased. Blood surged through her head until her temples ached. But the dog's needs committed her to the kitchen instead of her safe bedroom.

"But I can vape outside?" The reasonable question acted like nails on a blackboard in Emma's brain. Farrell whined and ran towards the corridor, staring back at her in hope. His furrowed brow cast a shadow over his eyes, his tail swaying without enthusiasm. "It's snowing. I'll get wet," Christos stated, his voice mirroring the dog's anxiety. Emma cringed as the soft swish of his slippers followed her towards the narrow passage.

Frigid air hit Emma in the face as she turned the knob and stepped into the kitchen. The rear door stood wide open. It edged back and forth in the gathering wind, prevented from slamming only by the stack of empty food trays in its path. Ridley appeared in the gap, his eyes widening as he spotted Emma. He spun on his scuffed shoes, the tail of his footman's jacket thwacking the backs of his thighs. "Mum!" he yelled, his voice echoing in the courtyard beyond the door. His single word bounced off the cobbles and buried itself in the dense cloud, bringing snowflakes cascading onto his tight black curls. "Mum!"

"What?" Chloe snapped, her tone aggressive and her accent less clipped. She clambered from the rear of the open van, landing with a heavy tread. Stamping and blinking into the light of the kitchen doorway, she spotted Emma. "Right." Her lips pursed, and she hauled on the rumpled hem of her chef's jacket.

Farrell dashed past her, his ribs clattering against the door frame when she didn't shift for him. Undeterred, he disappeared into the grey light outside to head for his usual toilet.

"Would you like some help?" Emma asked Chloe, keen to detach herself from Christos. He edged past her, his palm lingering over her shoulder as he shifted her aside. Chloe noticed the gesture and her eyes narrowed in condemnation. Guilt flamed Emma's cheeks, though she'd done nothing wrong. She hated the man for his misguided attempt to woo her. She set her jaw and renewed her determination to avoid the guests until forced to wave them off the property. Chloe stepped aside to allow Christos to pass. Her irises glinted with harsh judgement, which she directed at Emma.

"We're fine," she stated, her tone harsh. Lifting her left wrist, she examined the hands of an old Garmin. Its cracked pleather strap matched the colour of faded raspberries. "We're paid for another two hours yet," she concluded, but her brows furrowed together like a line drawn in straw. "The snow is falling fast. If it gets any worse, we'll transfer the food onto your crockery and leave early." Her blue irises became intense. "But not until we're paid."

The veiled rebuke reminded Emma of her earlier mission. "It's just a misunderstanding. The acting treasurer promised to sort it out. He's the man with brown hair and pink slippers." Her words ground to a halt as though powered by a fading battery. Her gaze switched to Ridley with his skin as black as coal and salt and pepper dotting his Afro hair. Snowflakes glistened on the tiny round coils as they dried. "Did he just call you Mum?" The question escaped, mistimed and ill-advised.

Chloe's expression hardened. "My family is none of your business!" Her voice rose and Christos's face appeared in the doorway amid a cloud of white smoke. The vapour swirled around him, creating a disembodied effect with his severed head. His brows rose into the artful swish of fringe crossing his forehead. He cocked his unattached face at Emma in question.

"You're right, I don't care." Emma straightened her spine, relief eking through her chest as Farrell pushed his way back into the house. A layer of snow covered his back. His tail twitched as he fought the urge to shake himself inside the kitchen. "No! Out and do that!" Emma cried, clapping her hands and shooing him back into the courtyard.

Chloe engaged Ridley in a hushed conversation. They moved towards the Aga as Emma walked outside. The icy air of the British winter stole her breath, infusing it with the cherry haze from Christos's vape. It chugged out white condensation as though powering an engine. Dolan had favoured the same place. He'd leaned his powerful shoulder against the door frame. He'd sucked down the nicotine with casual disinterest, unable to give up the smokes. Unable to give up Emma despite the consequences.

Emma's lower lip wobbled, and a hand landed on her right shoulder. "Beautiful night for it," Christos observed. He didn't elaborate on what it was beautiful for. The fruity scent shrouded him, mingling with his musky cologne to create a sickly atmosphere.

Emma shrugged off his grip. She didn't wish him to touch her, flirt with her, or speak to her. His familiar behaviour reminded her of Dolan. She knew how that had ended for the handsome Irishman. He'd become a fugitive, a traitor. He'd pushed their friendship until it snapped. Emma still sensed his influence, watching, waiting, lingering like the ghost of Wingate Hall.

Was he out there in the dark courtyard? Did he see Christos touch her shoulder and bristle with fury?

A snowflake touched her nose and then another. Emma brushed it away, studying its crispiness as it faded to water on her fingers. She looked up, noticing how the moon lit the underside of loaded, angry clouds. They bore their burden with growing strain, ready to dump the contents of their fluffy baskets with relief. The sky held an eerie potency like a woman readying herself to birth a child. Expectancy and fear filled Emma's heart. She wanted rid of her miserable guests and their problems. Then she would jog across to Allaine's apartment, snuggle on the sofa, and enjoy a well-deserved glass of Merlot.

But the weather had other plans. The clouds split, the sky turned a washed out grey, and the moon extinguished its silvery lamp.

15

Slipper Chair

♥

The dog ran into the kitchen, his claws sliding on the tiles. Snow still covered his back and ears, though he'd shaken himself until his teeth rattled. Emma consigned him to his bed beside the Aga. He busied himself with licking the crystals from his coat. His sigh contained extreme contentment. Emma wished others were so easily satisfied.

Mavis glowered at her as she entered the morning room. The banked fire emitted a decent heat, flushing cheeks and creating a slush pile of boas, scarves and shawls. The discarded clothing lounged like a colourful drunk in a tub chair. Someone had hauled the expensive drapes across the windows to obscure the disaster unfolding in the courtyard. "Let's call this meeting to order," Mavis cried, her voice like tinkling glass slicing across every other conversation. She turned her shoulder towards Emma and clapped her hands, the fat knuckles dripping with twinkling gems set in expensive metals. Emma released a huff of exasperation, but Christos proceeded into the room and reached Mavis first. He smoothed his expert palm along her shoulder, his touch radiating through the thin fabric of her dress. Emma blinked as the woman gave a shudder which ricocheted through every skin cell and nerve ending. Mavis's thighs clamped together as though she feared losing control of her bladder. Christos leaned over her, disturbing her soft curls with his warm breath.

"Wow," Emma murmured to herself. "He's good. He makes Dolan look like a sweaty teenager."

"What are you muttering?" Gwendoline's sharp tones caused Emma to wince. The showgirl edged past her without care. She bumped Emma's elbow and dipped her head at just the right angle to blind her with the feathered headdress. Emma redirected flecks of red and gold from her face with a hurried breath. Gwendoline rubbed her damp palms together, her manicured fingers sliding against one another in a sexy, suggestive motion. She lifted her index finger and sniffed it. "Do you have Chanel in every room?" she purred, referring to the expensive hand cream consigned to the downstairs bathroom. Gwendoline reeked of its cloying floral scent, enough to have coated her entire body. She smirked at Emma, determined to shame her extravagance.

But Emma shrugged. "A gift," she replied. "From an idiot. Everyone knows Coco Chanel worked for the Nazis."

Gwendoline's pink lips parted in shock to reveal chemically whitened incisors. Perhaps not everyone knew then. As an archivist, Emma fed her thirst for information on historical facts. It gave her a jaded but informed view of human nature.

"There's a blizzard starting," Emma said, her tone as icy as the outside temperature. "The snow is laying fast. I think it's best you all leave early. The council won't send the snow ploughs as far as the side roads around here. If you leave now, you can make it back to town before it's too deep."

Gwendoline lifted her nose on one side to create a line of neat wrinkles. Small and pointed, it appeared too small for her long face. The slant of her eyes reinforced the illusion of a reasonable canvas altered by an inexperienced scalpel. Emma frowned at her, trying to match the sharp features with the buttery complexion.

Gwendoline resembled a sculpture, an earlier attempt at greatness by an artist who might one day become famous. "We'll leave when we want to," she asserted. "My mother has more poems to recite." Her gaze slid to encompass Dyfed as he lurked behind the food tables. He lifted a tiny savoury, stacked it with another and stuffed it whole into his mouth. His lips barely closed around the food, but his jaw remained static like a Venus fly trap. Death by disintegration. "Yuk!" she snarled. "Those weirdoes are disgusting!" She flounced away, her swishing hips creating a ripple in her short skirt. She made a bee line for Christos. Her long legs acted like pincers as she navigated the furniture. Emma noticed Sir Robert studying Gwendoline's lithe body. He sensed Emma watching him and turned back to the droning monotone of Major Mallory-Eaves.

Undeterred, Emma followed Gwendoline's path, deviating towards Mavis instead of Christos. Hearing her soft soles on the floorboards, Gwendoline turned back to her with a glare which channelled murder. "I want Mavis," Emma snarled. "You can have him." She overtook Gwendoline at a fork between Flora and a coffee table. "There's a blizzard," Emma announced to Mavis without preamble. "You should leave. Now."

A movement to her left stole her attention as Mavis spluttered. Kathleen Dubois slumped in her seat, a handkerchief over her mouth. Arnand sat beside her, his knees touching the delicate silk of his wife's ball gown. He'd draped his jacket over her bare shoulders, and he whispered to her. His fingers stroked her knuckles in silent devotion. "Is your guest of honour okay?" Emma demanded, reaching into her pocket for her phone. "She looks like she might need an ambulance."

"She's fine!" Mavis barked, causing Arnand to glance up at her. Mavis lowered her voice. "She's recovering from a nasty virus. There's no need."

The major appeared in Emma's peripheral vision. He squatted in front of Kathleen, murmuring in hushed tones. "Can I assist?" he whispered. "I served as a medic in the army."

"No!" Kathleen shoved at him with more strength than she appeared to possess. She forced her body upright in the seat like a crane arm rising beneath a heavy weight. "I'm fine!" she declared, her voice husky.

"But my dear," he continued, laying a tentative hand over her wrist. The middle finger shifted until it covered Kathleen's pulse. As though to distract her, he engaged her in an idle chat about her poem. "What inspired it?" he asked, his tone light.

Kathleen relaxed and didn't swat away his surreptitious action. But her expression didn't reflect the glow of an artist expounding on her craft. Her brows knitted, causing her sagging lids to shroud her eyes. "I like food," she said, the words a low growl to invite the major's challenge. The skin hanging from her withered muscles said differently, but the defensive set of her square jaw defied a response.

"Your pulse is rather higher," the major stated, removing his hand from her wrist. Emma frowned as he wiped his fingers against the lower pocket of his jacket. The surreptitious movement suggested a clamminess on Kathleen's birdlike wrist. "You should see a doctor," he stated. His knees clicked as he rose, and Emma adjusted her opinion of him. The flattening of his lips and the pained expression in his narrowed eyes reflected empathy. He jerked his chin towards Arnand, seeking the other man's solidarity.

But Arnand gave a series of rapid blinks and stared at his wife's profile. Fear sparkled behind his muddy irises. His body stiffened as though he readied himself to duck from a blow.

"Okay," the major replied, but deep lines of concern scored his prominent forehead as he returned to his seat beside Sir Robert.

Emma turned her attention back to Mavis. She slid away her phone. "The blizzard is already here. Look through the window if you don't believe me."

"I don't need to," Mavis maintained. A hysterical edge entered her tone, and she leaned forward and hissed at Emma, "You're determined to ruin this evening. I know things about you, young lady! Be very careful how you proceed."

Emma blanched but held her nerve. She forced her mind away from the worrying track which led only to derailment. "Right," she replied, her tone bland. She added a shrug for good measure while another part of her brain formulated ways to torture Freda for her loose lips. Emma smiled, forcing a disarming openness into her expression. She widened her eyes and acted the part of the Actuary's wife. "Perhaps you could entertain us all with your marvellous insider knowledge of my personal circumstances." She took a risk, fuelled by irritation but also by curiosity.

Mavis bristled, realising the members of her group had assembled as instructed and awaited her direction with sudden rapt interest. She cast her gaze sideways, revealing thread veins lacing her white sclera like a bloody patchwork. And so, just like Gwendoline, Mavis returned to batting away Emma's prediction about the weather. "Christos says we're fine for another few hours," she simpered, rising onto her toes and fluttering her lashes at the treacherous Greek god still returning to his seat. Mavis called the meeting to order with another clap of her fat fingers. Turning her back on Emma, she dismissed her.

One woman decided the fate of the Market Harborough Literary and Historical Society in a moment. A mere moment of thought spared for fourteen unwitting individuals there because of her.

Chairperson Mavis would have hours to reflect on that ill-fated split second decision. And she would live to regret it.

16

Corner Chair

♥

Emma waited in the lobby for her watch hands to reach ten o'clock. She sat on a two-seater sofa by the fire, still wearing her ski jacket. Minutes later, the morning room door snapped open. Farrell snored from his favourite spot on the hearthrug, not even cracking one eye. He seemed disinterested in the opening door.

Mavis waddled out first, crossing her arms over her chest as a futile barrier against the chill. Her leather handbag trailed from her elbow. She used it as a battering ram against anyone following too close. "To the bus!" she called in her strident voice as the other group members surged around her.

Emma said nothing as they discarded their borrowed slippers and reclaimed their outdoor footwear. Though good sense told her the snow would deter them from leaving, a vestige of hope remained in a crevice in her heart. She studied Arnand's bent spine as he slipped Kathleen's tiny foot into a small, rubber soled grey shoe and fastened the buckle. Exhaustion shrouded the poet, and a glazed look blurred her irises. Arnand left his jacket around her thin shoulders, committing himself to bracing the below zero temperature in his shirt sleeves.

Emma had already unlocked both the front and vestibule doors, ready for the big reveal. Major Mallory-Eaves hauled open the heavy door first and poked his head into the freezing vestibule. A wall of snow met him through the obscured glass, flakes slithering down the windows on either side. "Oh!" he remarked, appearing bemused. His head bobbled on his thready neck as though it might snap. He turned to the gathered group. "Oh, dear!" he announced, his anxious tones rising above the clamour of voices. "Oh, dear!"

Mavis popped her head up from wrestling her wide feet into her shoes. Her cheeks flared pink from the effort. "Just get the bus started," she directed. "Warm it up for us."

"I can't get to it." The major's keys shook in his hand as he flapped his arms. "The snow is too deep." He lowered himself into the vestibule and pressed his nose to the glass. "We shouldn't open the door," he mused. "The drifts have covered the front steps."

"Let's use another door," Mavis blustered, rolling up behind him. She scattered the observers crowding the threshold, battering them aside with her handbag. "We'll leave a different way. Then we won't need to navigate that treacherous entrance and those icy steps." She nudged her left breast with her knuckles as though bolstering it. "Someone could fall and break their neck on those stairs. I might inform the council of the hazardous nature of this establishment."

"No, you won't!" Monty barked from behind her. He tapped her shoulder and ushered her and the major inside. His aggrieved tone smacked of a man tired of having his patience stretched to its limits. "The snow is far too deep. It's unsafe to drive the bus in such conditions. If we get stranded outside in the darkness, it could prove fatal." His gaze slid sideways to Kathleen Dubois, the woman's fragility perhaps uppermost in his thoughts. The other members of the Lit and His Society milled around, listening to Monty's monologue. Only Kathleen appeared disinterested. She remained on the wooden pew wearing her husband's jacket, her body tipping forward and back as though she searched for her inner equilibrium.

"I must get home," Sir Robert protested. "My heart pills are there. I can't manage without them."

Major Mallory-Eaves patted his jacket pocket. "I have spares if they're the same as mine." But his gaze remained on the white bubble encasing the rented bus. Only its shadow showed in the eerie darkness, the defining features obscured.

"This is ridiculous!" Mavis barked. She shoved past Monty, her fingers closing around the ornate door knob stroked by generations of butlers with their white-gloved fingers. It spun at her touch, the door sliding inward with the faintest creak. "Aargh!" she cried. "Aargh!"

Farrell jerked to his feet with a yap of concern. Emma rose from the sofa, standing on tiptoes to see through the crowd. As though fighting her way through a blanket, Mavis waddled back into the lobby, her hair plastered to her forehead and her saturated dress clinging to every hill and furrow of her torso. People dodged aside to avoid the fresh disaster. Monty smothered a laugh behind his hand, waggling his eyebrows at Emma. "Mavis is a little wet," he managed, his Welsh accent infusing the sentence with more comic relief.

The bodies parted, allowing Emma to see the mess on the vestibule tiles.

Snow covered every surface. Her heart sank, but she forced herself not to react to the mess. Freda stood at her shoulder, puffing on the fake cigarette. "Oops," she commented without sincerity. "Snow drifts are dangerous."

"Yes, thanks for that," Emma growled.

"Don't suppose you have a shovel handy?" Monty's eyes danced with humour until he noticed Emma's struggle. "I'll clear it up," he assured her, raising his right hand as though swearing an oath.

Emma tapped a panel beside the fireplace. It slid sideways to reveal a cavity.

"That's a good one," Freda commented. "Does it lead to the tunnels?"

Emma ground her teeth, wishing Freda would cease talking. "No," she growled with irritation. She reached in and her fingers closed around the handle of a shovel. The pitch fork behind it slid sideways, creating a grating sound against the brick interior. Emma reached lower, noticing a crowbar leaned against the far wall. Nicky's

Action Man clung to its rounded edge, his legs bent in a rock climbing position. Emma exhaled. She retrieved the shovel and slid the panel closed. Turning aside, she found everyone staring behind her at the invisible hiding place. Monty took the shovel from her.

"It's freezing in here!" Mavis stamped her wet feet and hugged herself. She glared at Emma through narrowed eyes, holding her responsible for the sudden drop in temperature.

Freda shrugged and spoke with the cigarette holder in her mouth. "Well, you wouldn't listen, would you? You never do. Jenny Philbin told you not to marry that waste-of-space from Lutterworth. You knew better. He chased every piece of skirt from here to Husband's Bosworth. Would you believe anyone? No." She turned her rheumy blue eyes to Emma and added an aside. "Impressive really. He only ever rode a bicycle. I suppose it's a testament to his stamina, all that pedalling followed by his favourite endurance sport. Bonking other men's wives." Her thin hands made a double clap after the punchline like a comic ending a sketch.

Sir Robert cleared his throat, a loud, invasive sound intended to halt Freda's flapping lips. Mavis had turned puce. Her eyes bulged and her lips thinned into faint lines. Emma exhaled as Monty went into battle against the snow drift covering the vestibule floor. The flat edge of the shovel grated against the antique tiles.

17

Bar Stool

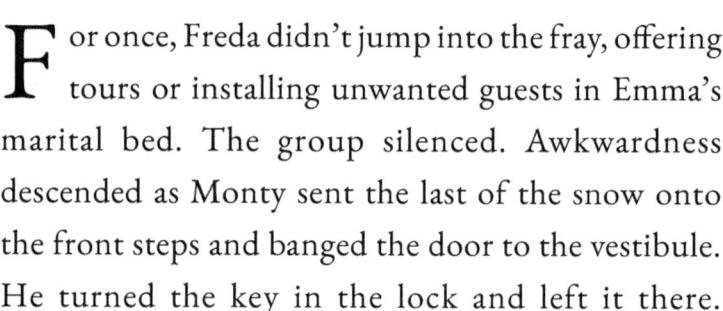

For once, Freda didn't jump into the fray, offering tours or installing unwanted guests in Emma's marital bed. The group silenced. Awkwardness descended as Monty sent the last of the snow onto the front steps and banged the door to the vestibule. He turned the key in the lock and left it there. "Right then." Monty closed the inner door and leaned against it. He handed the shovel to Emma.

"Thanks," she said, accepting it. She put the heavy spade back into its hiding space and slid the panel closed.

With the snow expelled and the chill trapped beyond the thick oak doors, the fire's heat spread out its orange fingers with more success. Emma considered the options ahead of her, wondering if she should just go upstairs to bed and leave them all staring at each other. Farrell sighed, seconding the motion.

Mavis brushed her wispy hair back from her forehead. "You'll have to host us for the night," she stated, directing her beady gaze to Emma. Her breasts conferred in a bouncy conversation, communicating her increased agitation.

"No." Monty crossed the floor to her side, his outdoor shoes clicking against the polished boards. "It doesn't work like that, Mavis. I think Emma's tolerated your rudeness quite enough for one evening." His lips tightened and Emma sensed discomfort radiating from him in waves. She might have enjoyed the fragile victory, if it didn't mean giving these horrid people house room for another twelve hours.

"Mum is stuck!" Dyfed screeched to a halt at the end of the hallway. His feet arrived before his head, creating the illusion of a stick man running against a strong wind. The smile still beamed from the nose down, mismatched with his distressed eyes. Emma contemplated the agony of his face, which betrayed his heart at every turn. "She's stuck!" he cried, pressing his palms against his cheeks.

Monty leapt into action, following the man as he retraced his steps. Mavis seized the opportunity to wriggle free of her dilemma. She directed the rest of the group into the morning room after switching her wet shoes for her slippers. Emma left Freda in charge, although she didn't consider what that might entail. She jogged to the kitchen with Farrell and surveyed the scene.

Half a metre of snow covered the kitchen floor where someone had opened the door and allowed the drift to collapse inside. A fresh snowfall speckled the sky, blowing through the gap to decorate every counter and appliance. Farrell disappeared into the drift with a happy whoosh. Flakes feathered upwards where he landed. Emma clambered over the mess, the toes of her slippers soaking through in seconds and wetting her socks. "What's happened?" she called, following the spiky-toed prints from Monty's dress shoes.

Emma gasped and cried out as the rear bumper of Chloe's van collided with her hip. The collision shoved her backwards the way she'd come. She tripped and slid over the drift before finding the door frame beneath her grasping fingers. Monty's voice rose over the revving of the engine. White vapour billowed from underneath the van, exhaled from an exhaust pipe buried in snow. "Just stop!" he cried. "You hit Emma!"

A door slammed and Chloe waded round the van. She frowned at Emma with fury in her narrowed eyes. "Why would you stand behind me?" she shouted. "It's obvious the wheels are stuck!"

Monty clambered over the melting snow and slithered into the kitchen. "Enough!" he demanded, holding up Chloe's keys. Orange indicator lights winked outside, casting an eerie yellow light over the snow covered surfaces as he locked the van with the remote. He tucked it into his jacket pocket. "No one is leaving here tonight!" he stated with authority. Ridley slunk around the corner. A dusting of icing sugar coated his black curls. He crept behind Chloe, hunching his shoulders and withdrawing his head into his collar like a tortoise.

"Where do we go then?" Chloe gnawed on her lower lip and brushed snow from her hair.

"We'll sort something out." Monty spread his hands and spoke to Emma. "Can I trouble you for that shovel again, please?" he asked.

While Monty bailed out the kitchen enough to close the rear door, Emma battled the disgruntled crowd that encircled the buffet in the morning room. Freda hurried towards her, the bows on her shoes flipping and flopping as she walked. "We don't have enough suitable rooms," she hissed through pursed lips. Lifting her left hand, she counted off bedrooms, including Nicky's and Stephie's.

"Nope." Emma dug in her heels, relieved she'd locked the private rooms earlier. "The servants' quarters have beds and sheets. I'll turn on the radiators and find more blankets. I'm sure your friends can cope for one night."

Freda's lips twisted into a grimace. She glanced sideways at Mavis and leaned close enough for Emma to feel her breath on her cheek. "Don't you think the stairs are a little steep, dear?" She moderated her tone to a wheedling, simpering whine. "They're all old people, don't forget."

Emma detached herself from Freda. Ignoring Mavis, she strode to the centre of the room and shouted, "Excuse me!" All eyes turned towards her, reluctant to acknowledge they needed her help after an entire evening of insulting her. "Monty has decided to keep everyone here for the night. I'll house you together on the third floor. There are beds and bedding, but the rooms aren't renovated. There's a bathroom on that floor and the one below. You can use the shower on the second floor, but the tub in your bathroom isn't usable. It leaks." Without delaying, Emma swung from the morning room, a line of grumbling pensioners and a yawning dog trailing behind her.

"Isn't there an elevator?" Mavis whined as they puffed along the second floor. Emma didn't rise to the bait. A glance behind her showed Gwendoline reaching out to turn the door knobs as she passed. She found each of them locked. Her pretty nose wrinkled in disgust. Smirking, Emma opened the door to the narrow stairs leading to the servants' level. She doled out rooms at speed, not wanting to hear the expected complaints.

"Mr and Mrs Dubois can have the first double room on the left beside the bathroom." Emma heard Flora calling for Kathleen but getting no reply. "Gwendoline takes the first on the right opposite them and Bunny beside her." Emma pushed open the doors to the sparse single rooms with their functional iron furniture. "Monty and Flora in the double to the left and Mavis and the major in the singles to the right." She paused for a second before continuing. "Ridley and Dyfed to the left and Sir Robert, Christos, and Chloe to the right." Emma reached the end of the corridor, where the space widened into the full width of the floor. Sofas created a cosy nook beside an empty grate. Emma jabbed her thumb over her shoulder. "The door behind me leads to the attic where my ageing husband's former mistress is a prisoner. She often screams at night, but we ignore her. There's also a store room and the spiders are as big as your hand." Emma smiled at her own sick humour, enjoying the only fun she'd had all evening. The archivist in her revelled in the impromptu history lesson. "Light a fire using the items on the hearth until the radiators get going. There's a box of matches at the back of the mantelpiece. The cupboards in each of the rooms contain blankets and extra bedding." Emma flapped her hand at the far wall. "This floor covers only half of the one below. The single rooms face the driveway at the front of the house. The windows in the double rooms are too high to look through. This is because the Ayers family didn't mind the lower classes watching their grand entrances, but they didn't want them spying through the reinforced skylights of the second-floor hallway. Married servants shared the double rooms, including the last butler and his wife. They left a few decades ago. Lower house servants slept in tiny rooms in the basement. Those have no windows and no heat source." Emma tried the knob behind her as she spoke. It turned, but the door didn't move. At least no one could fall off the roof and blame her. "Your bathroom is next to the stairs. It mirrors the family one on the second floor. Use either, but please remember not to touch the bath up here. It leaks."

"I'll take this room." Mavis's voice rose above the others. "Because of my arthritis." She jostled her way across the corridor and strode into the double bedroom nearest the stairs.

Emma sighed and shrugged at Flora. "So, she expects Kathleen and Arnand to share a single bed? She's an actual piece of work, isn't she?" Flora frowned in response. Emma stood on tiptoe to peer at the bobbing heads "Where are they? Didn't they follow us upstairs?"

Flora pursed her lips into a beak and herded Mavis back across the corridor. "Monty will flush them out of hiding and help them upstairs. I think he stayed down too," she called over her shoulder. "We really appreciate your hosting us."

Gwendoline squealed in the single room near the stairs. She ran from the bedroom and hurled herself at Christos. "A spider!" she squealed. "A massive one!"

Emma edged past the grumbling crowd and abandoned Flora to her shepherding. She could no longer keep a lid on her sarcasm. Flora might appreciate her hospitality, but no one else did. The only sentences reaching her ears contained complaints about the cold, the cramped rooms, the ancient metal bedsteads and the risk of fleas and bugs. She jogged downstairs and cranked up the heating using the dial in the airing cupboard near Freda's bedroom. The satisfying click signified the gravity fed pipes and radiators carrying more hot water to the uppermost reaches of the immense house. She jumped as Freda appeared at her elbow without warning.

"Why can't some of them stay in the coach house?" she demanded. "It sleeps four, and it's comfier than upstairs."

Emma exhaled. "I'm containing the hassle and the damage," she remarked, shutting the airing cupboard door with more force than necessary. "They'd rather go home, and nothing would make me happier. The coach house is off limits."

"But I don't want to share a bathroom with them," Freda whined. She still clutched the cigarette holder between her middle fingers. "I didn't know they could behave with such ingratitude."

"Well, you do now," Emma replied with a sigh. She whistled for the dog and a woof sounded from the far end of the hallway. Emma bit her lower lip, not surprised to discover Farrell had avoided the crush upstairs. He'd parked himself outside her bedroom door, already eager for bed. She left Freda to her grumbling, unlocked her bedroom for the dog and settled him on his blanket in front of the open fire. "Do you need the toilet?" she asked him as he snuggled beneath the top layer. "Right, well, don't complain in the night then."

She closed the door behind her and used the back stairs to get to the kitchen. Chloe glared at her from the sink, a metal tray in one hand and a cloth in the other. "Might as well wash these if we're staying," she snapped. Dyfed and Ridley dried and stacked them on the kitchen table. Emma snatched up a cloth and joined their chain gang in silence. Chloe frowned at her. "The boys ran all the leftovers back here," she said, her tone containing less bite. "They fitted most of it in the chiller." She turned to face Emma, her cheeks pink from exertion. "That's a fine chiller just for a family."

Emma dropped her chin and moved it from left to right. She glanced sideways at the stainless steel door. It housed such a tiny number of groceries in its vast bowels that it seemed indecent. She picked over her words, tasting them for their sting. They hurt less this time as she voiced them. "A friend lived here with us for a time. He loved cooking. I let him persuade me to add the chiller during the renovation."

"Where is he?" Dyfed's soft voice surprised Emma. The intensity of his question came from his piercing eyes. "Did he die?" He held the metal tray in his hands, the bones of his knuckles showing white through the skin.

"No!" Emma took a step towards him. "No, he lives somewhere else."

"Is he happy?" Dyfed asked, and Ridley halted to wait for the answer. Both studied her with frightening emotional depth seeping from their eyes. It hit her in a wave. Like grief.

"I don't know." Emma concentrated on drying the tray in her hands. MI5 caught Christopher crossing the border into Ireland four months after he'd run from Rohan's ire. He'd disappeared into a government facility on charges of treason after distributing the details of military personnel in a cache on the grey web. Emma hated what he'd done, but it didn't stop her from missing him. She forced her shoulders to relax. "He always made the best of an unpleasant situation, so yes, I imagine he's found happiness." Her smile held a listless, faraway look. Christopher Dolan was the chocolate pudding you gorged on and then vomited up. No half measures. All or nothing.

"Well, the food is all in there," Chloe repeated, setting the last tray on the draining board. "We'll leave first thing tomorrow."

Emma nodded. "Your rooms are on the third floor. I put you in the one beside Christos and the boys are opposite in a double room." She frowned and narrowed her eyes. "If you find Mavis has snatched the big room, get Flora or Monty to evict her."

Chloe nodded and ushered the two men ahead of her. She stopped at the door and peered at Emma through the tops of her eyes. "That man paid me like you said." She gave a gratified nod. "Not cash. Bank transfer."

"I'm glad." Emma touched the drying towel to her chest. "Monty is a man of his word."

Chloe left the room with Dyfed. He sprang ahead but Ridley hung close to her shoulder. Emma thought about the odd little group, and how a Black man in his sixties could call a woman in her late thirties, *'Mum.'*

She locked the back door and sat the key on the mantel above the Aga. The blizzard threw ice at the window panes to obliterate the darkness outside. Emma turned off the lights and closed the door behind her before using the main stairs to reach her bedroom. She found no stray guests on her way, but as she paused beside her door, raucous laughter issued from overhead in the servants' sitting room. Composed of male and female tones, it painted a picture of joviality rather than discord.

Exhausted, Emma let herself into her bedroom and locked the door behind her. She changed into warm sweatpants and a gym shirt belonging to Rohan. The clock recorded the time at just after midnight. Seconds after sending a goodnight text message to Allaine, she sank into an unsettled sleep.

18

Tête-à-Tête

♥

Emma woke with a start. The subdued light from the fire cast an orange glow over the room, creating long shadows from the furnishings. She stretched out her hand towards Rohan's pillow. Its cool emptiness condemned her.

Emma stretched her neck to look at Farrell. If something had woken her, she should find him pensive and alert. But the dog stretched over his blanket, paws twitching as he chased an imaginary quad bike across the lawn. "I'm thirsty." Emma spoke into the silence, expecting the dog to at least show an interest. He squeezed his eyes closed tighter, reluctant to leave the warmth of the fire on a futile mission downstairs. "Fine!" Emma grumbled. She used the bathroom, pushed her feet into her slippers, and padded to the door. The key ground in the lock and the hinges creaked.

The upstairs hallway had never appeared so pitch black. Apart from the nights with no moon, light usually shone through the glass skylight on the second floor. But the snow blanketing the house had covered the aperture and cast the hallway into a navy darkness. Emma returned to lift her phone from the nightstand. "Yuk!" she groaned. "It's half-past two in the morning!"

She searched the screen for her torch, hissing through her teeth at discovering Nicky's handiwork. He'd grouped her apps into categories and labelled them as the various spy agencies. "What the hell does 'torch' come under then?" Emma grumbled.

She called up her Google Assistant, irritated when the AI ignored her.

"Fantastic!" Emma spat. Farrell's tail bounced twice, and he rolled over like a lazy seal to warm his other shoulder.

Emma tugged on her ski jacket and pushed her feet into her furry slipper-boots. She padded into the hallway, leaving the door ajar in case Farrell changed his mind. The radiator outside her bedroom clicked but couldn't generate enough heat to banish the chill in the air. It wrapped around her like an unwelcome embrace.

She knew the house well enough to find the main staircase in the dark and count the steps to the lobby. The pathetic light from the digital time on her phone screen winked out as she reached the entrance to the tiled corridor. Emma's slippers released tiny squeaks as the surface changed beneath them.

A yellow sliver of light beamed from beneath the kitchen door, smearing its glow across the corridor. Emma frowned, fearful of running into one of her unwelcome guests scarfing buffet food in the early hours. She glided along the corridor towards the light, her mind presenting another, more thrilling proposition. Would she find Rohan sitting at the kitchen table, his blond head bowed over his laptop and a tumbler of vodka near his right hand?

Emma gasped as she pitched forward, all control gone. Her fingers paddled empty air and milliseconds of nothingness. The unforgiving tiles rose to meet her, and she heard the crunch of her knees. Her phone clattered to the floor ahead of her. Its case glinted in the light eking beneath the kitchen door. Her lungs struggled with the remnant of air caught in her chest as she lay splayed on the cold floor.

Emma remained there in the darkness, dropping her right cheek onto the cool tiles as her mind sifted through its most important checks. She couldn't tell if she'd broken anything until she moved. And she couldn't face that yet. The heritage officer had baulked at her idea of carpeting the busy thoroughfare. *'Oh no!'* he'd exclaimed. *'These tiles are original quarry, over three hundred years old and fired in Italy.'* He'd suggested a series of runners to mitigate the discomfort, and forbade the fixings required for a permanent carpet. But he'd overlooked Rohan's disability and his need for crutches when not wearing his prosthetic leg. Runners would create an unstable skating rink for him. So, the floor remained bare, as hard as concrete, and icy to the touch. Emma could testify to all three as she lay there, forcing air back into her lungs.

She spread the fingers of both hands and groaned. She'd crushed her left thumb. Pain blossomed across its fleshy heel and into her wrist. Rolling onto her side, she sensed the heat flaring in both knees. They ached when she tried to bend them, the left worse than the right. Darkness swaddled her in its heavy blanket, the accompanying silence containing an unusual eeriness. Emma knew the creaking old manor house by touch and scent, by the shifting air currents and the tilt of floorboards or tiles beneath her soles. Her fall made no sense.

Pushing herself onto her bottom, she let relief flood her mind. She focussed on her sore knees, ignoring the spreading numbness in her left hand. "Note to self," she mused under her breath. "Trip up the heritage officer in the downstairs hall and see how he still likes the quarry tiles afterwards."

A rhythmic ticking imprinted its odd sound on her brain. It increased like clock hands spinning out of control before ceasing with an abrupt slap against her cheek. It left a warm wetness behind, and Emma wiped it away with her sleeve. "Now you decide to get out of bed!" she exclaimed as Farrell wound his body around her. His tail banged her nose and dragged across her chin as he circled her with a concerned whine. He trod on both her painful knees, not careful where he placed the paws edged with sharp claws. Emma grabbed the ruff around his neck and held onto it, the dog's warmth transferring to her fingers. He turned to sniff her face and hair, another whine tugging free from his furry chest. "I'm fine," Emma grumbled. She edged her bottom backwards towards the wall, crablike and undignified. Her palms ached as she found the painted wainscot, meaning to use the wall to haul herself upright. But her left hand complained, sending out a series of agonising jabs.

Farrell whined again and released a low growl. His claws clicked away, and she heard his gentle puffs of air as he sniffed the floor. Emma groped for him in the darkness, his black coat giving him a cloak of invisibility. She found his hard crown on her left as he circled again and rested her aching palm there. "Shush," she soothed. "Please don't bark and wake the whole house. I'm not yet ready to face the masses."

Rohan Andreyev had the hearing of a pigeon, detecting even infinitesimal infrasounds. The kitchen door remained closed despite her loud tumble, meaning Emma's husband still hadn't arrived home. Disappointment enveloped her heart and squeezed. "Let's get some warmth," she told the dog, a shiver erupting through her torso. The shock of her fall enveloped her like an ice bath, even as her knees heated and swelled.

Her steps appeared wooden as she walked towards the narrow slit of light. She groaned as she bent to pick up her phone. An icy draught blasted across her ankles. Farrell stuck close, his shoulder rubbing her right thigh. Emma's fingers closed around the knob, and she turned it to the left.

The door swung open with the creak of old bones. Freezing air hit her as though she'd walked into a wall. Light flared from the overhead bulbs, revealing a room without human occupation. Through the window, Emma recognised the eerie greyness caused by moonlight reflecting off snow. Flakes had soused the windowsill to create a drift which half covered the glass. It sparkled with yellow dots from the kitchen light. Farrell gave a low growl, and Emma turned her feet to face the rear door. A bank of snow had drifted in through the opening, bringing with it icy temperatures which defeated the dull heat of the Aga.

Beyond the doorway, Emma picked out the edges of sheds and outhouses, already softened by banked snow and high drifts. Frigid air nipped at her bare fingers and attacked her nose and cheeks. It froze her in place, adding her as a statue to the picturesque landscape.

The dog whined and licked her hand, galvanising her into action. Her mind tipped her from inactivity to panic. She ran to the phone in the corner, lifted the receiver and listened to the silence. Nothing. She jammed her index finger over the buttons, to no effect. She examined her mobile phone, grateful to see no obvious damage from its fall. Her fingers scrolled across the screen as soon as it bloomed to life. "Ray!" she gushed as soon as he answered. "Ray, the kitchen door is wide open. But I locked it last night."

Her keen gaze picked up a set of dark footprints spaced a metre apart in the snow beyond the doorway. The blizzard had stopped, but the freezing temperatures continued. They had immortalised the footprints as evidence. Emma gulped as she edged towards the door. Squinting helped her to separate the rounded heel prints from the toes, the heavy tread belonging to a man's boot. "Someone's in the house," she hissed to Ray. The toes pointed towards the doorway, not someone leaving Wingate Hall, but entering.

"Can you close the door for now?" Ray demanded. "I can't get out of my apartment without clearing the balcony and stairs."

Emma stared at the icy drift blocking the doorway and sighed. She cast around for the shovel from last night. "I'll get rid of the snow. Then it'll close."

"Great." Ray's voice held relief. "I keep some tools behind the false panel in the hall, in case you need them."

"What else should I do?" Emma closed her eyes and swallowed her rising hysteria.

"Emma," Ray urged. "Tip the snow outside, then close and lock the door. Go to your room, barricade yourself in, and wait for me."

"Okay." Emma took a deep breath. "I think Monty took the shovel back to the cubby. I'll fetch it." She stepped into the corridor. The rubber soles of her slippers squeaked against the tiles. Farrell moved with her, a shadow sticking close. The glow from the kitchen light spilled out before them like a carpet of daffodils in the gloom. Emma stepped into it. She kept the phone pressed against her ear, needing Ray's comforting presence as she set off on her brief journey. Her slippers squeaked to a halt in the spot where she'd fallen just moments before, the explanation in front of her. "Oh no," she said, her voice a croak.

"What's wrong?" Ray demanded. "Emma, what's happened?"

"I fell." Her voice rose and pitched as she fought her terror. "I thought I just tripped in the dark, but now I can see it." She blew out a wavering breath through her icy lips.

"See what?" Ray's voice rose to a shout. "See what, Emma?"

She swallowed, a moan escaping with her words. "A body," she whispered, turning away from the shadowy figure lying prone across the corridor.

"Oh, shit!" Ray cursed. "That changes everything."

19

Bubble Chair

♥

"You can't leave me to deal with this alone!" Emma protested. She flicked off the corridor light, retreated inside the freezing kitchen, and stared at the drift. A panicked glance at her watch showed the time at just before three in the morning. Snowflakes dribbled from the sky in threat as the voice in her ear changed.

"Hey, Emma, it's Paul Barker here." His tone held a note of apology. Ray never let his son stay long in his apartment, aware of the risks a detective posed to Rohan's clandestine activities. But Paul lived twenty minutes away, which meant he also got caught out by the blizzard. It explained the tightness in Ray's voice.

"Hi." Emma slumped into a kitchen chair. The dog rested his chin on her thigh. Her hand shook. She put the phone on speaker and set it on the table. "I did everything you asked. I checked her pulse, and she's dead. Please, you need to come and get her. Take her away." Her chest hitched at the memory of the staring, unfocussed eyes. The woman's cool skin possessed a waxy quality. Emma's stomach roiled again. Her mind likened the texture to raw chicken pulled from a refrigerator. The detachment seemed to help her, removing her a tiny step from the dead body in her hallway.

"Can you see any external injuries?" Paul demanded.

Emma swallowed and considered her response. She blew out a shallow breath. "I didn't look," she admitted. "Her left eye is open, and her skin is like raw chicken." Her stomach churned in protest. "There's a puddle spreading out from beneath her. She's wearing a long grey coat, and the hood is over her head." Emma's heart rate hiked, forcing her breaths into staccato pants. Nausea rose into her throat from an empty stomach, leaving behind a bitter, acidic taste. "It's Rohan's greatcoat," she whispered. "He brought it back from Russia years ago, but I've never seen him wear it." Her voice rose in a wail. "His DNA will contaminate the evidence! But he's not even here! She's taken it from the armoire in the lobby."

"Is she wearing shoes or boots?" Paul continued, dismissing Emma's growing hysteria. "Could she have made the footprints outside the back door?"

"Please, don't make me look again!" Emma groaned. "It feels wrong. She needs someone to come and take care of her."

"We'll get there as soon as we can," Paul promised. "The snow ploughs are working on the main roads, but they won't reach this district for hours. That means the police can't come yet either."

"Fly them in!" Emma pleaded. Her mind flicked to her husband's impressive resources, calculating if this latest calamity might bring him home. He'd mentioned the Bank of England, which meant a decent payout and a limitless operational budget. But thoughts of her husband progressed to her children and her nosy, indefatigable son. "You need to come now!" Emma gasped. "Stephie and Nicky can't arrive home to a dead woman on the hall floor! You must take her away."

"If I can't get out, then Allaine can't either." Ray's voice crackled as though speaking from a distance. "I'll text her to explain. She'll keep the little ones longer, I'm sure."

"What about Regan?" Emma grasped at flailing tendrils of hope. "Can't he help me?"

"Who's Regan?" Paul directed the question at his father, and Ray's silence stretched to painful limits at Emma's blunder. Lear's presence on the estate relied on secrecy. The nerdy introvert had faded from society's memory, the gawky teenager lost in the system. He no longer appeared on official records. He'd become a ghost, overseeing Rohan's activities through screens and data and interacting with a chosen few. It suited him, and Emma had almost blown it.

"A friend of Emma's. He lives at a neighbouring property." Ray shoved his inquisitive son off course with a half lie. "No." Exasperation leaked through his voice. "It's down to us for a while, at least."

"And you need to preserve evidence."

"What?" Emma blinked at Paul's statement. The snow fell heavier, intruding through the open doorway as though invited. "I need to do what?"

The light flickered, and the microwave released a sad beep. Ray groaned through the phone. "The power might fail, Em," he said, communicating his concern as he shortened her name. "Make sure you have enough phone charge to last. If the Wi-Fi goes down because of a power failure, we'll only have mobile calls or text. The land-line is already dead."

"I dunno," Paul added. "This snow is unprecedented. It's minus twelve degrees centigrade outside. If it affects the cellphone towers, we're screwed."

Emma released a ragged breath. A heavy shroud of doom engulfed her. She struggled to shake herself free of it. "I know how cold it is!" she snapped. "The bloody door is wide open, so it's the same in here! I'm getting the shovel and clearing it away. Then I'm closing the door."

"No!" Paul cried. "Now I know there's a body, I need you to preserve the footprints. And take photos of the victim."

"But I'm not a cop!" Emma growled. And killed the call.

Outrage warmed her. These people had invaded her home and treated her like unpaid help. After availing themselves of her hospitality, one of them had the audacity to die outside the kitchen wearing her husband's coat. Paul couldn't put all the responsibility on her. Could he?

Reluctant to face the thin woman's body on the way to fetch the shovel, Emma dragged a tub of flour from the pantry and set it on the table. Activity dragged her mind away from the calamity. It stopped her from sinking into despair. The woman in the corridor had left behind friends and family members who would grieve for her loss. Her ending seemed undignified and tragic. A sob wracked Emma's chest, and she pressed her lips together. She ached to pass the problem onto someone more qualified, a paramedic, an undertaker, a detective. "Preserve the bloody footsteps," she raged, fetching a bowl and upending the container into it. A puff of white powder rose into the air before sinking to speckle the table.

Digging in the cupboard under the sink netted a tub of Nicky's craft PVA glue, and Emma yanked off the lid. She added it to the flour before filling the empty container with tap water. The liquid swam with blobs of flour as Emma used a spoon to stir it. "This is as good as it gets, Mr Detective," she muttered. Her fingers became clumsy with the cold as the temperature plummeted even lower. The mixture slopped onto the table, but she made more mess by trying to scoop it back into the bowl one-handed. Adding flour made it too thick and more water too runny.

Without warning, it formed into a paste as though tapped by a magic wand. With a flash of inspiration, Emma added red food colouring, turning the makeshift plaster a garish pink. Farrell watched, his black brow furrowed in confusion. The scent of the flour and water attracted him, but the chemical tang of the glue caused his nose to shift from side to side in repulsion.

At last satisfied with her stringy goop, Emma stepped towards the open doorway. The soaked tiles proved slippery underfoot. She gripped the door frame to prevent herself from falling, leaning out over the nearest defined print. Her left wrist smarted before settling into a numbing ache.

The footprints seemed close enough to the house to avoid the latest falling barrage, but not the coming drifts. The wind turned towards the doorway and sent the dancing flakes into a frenzy.

Emma poured the crazy, lurid blend from the bowl into the footprint. It filled just the bottom centimetres of the heel and toe. A narrow pink bridge linked them together. "That's as good as it gets," she grumbled, casting the bowl into the sink. "It might not even set in the cold."

Still reluctant to pass the body in the hallway, Emma hunted a dustpan from beneath the sink. She scooped up the drifting snow, casting it beyond the doorway and onto the hidden cobbled surface. Farrell edged past her, slipping into the darkness. It swallowed his black coat until he became a shadowy blot in the grey light.

Emma used towels to mop up the remaining water. The dog shot back inside as she closed the door. The snowfall had turned him into a dalmatian, and he licked water from the end of his nose. Emma pointed towards his bed in front of the warm Aga, and he ran there as though afraid she might change her mind. He grunted with pleasure as he sank down beside it, his haunches against the warm iron surface.

Emma snatched her phone from the table and glared at the screen. She'd missed two calls from Ray. Ignoring the accompanying frantic texts, she turned up the radiant heat on the Aga, braced herself and stared at the door knob. She narrowed her eyes and pondered it. "I closed the door when I went to bed," she mused. "So, the only fingerprints on the inside of the knob belong to the intruder." She stared at it, searching her memory for her own actions. "I just pushed it closed with my hand on the wood," she said. "So, unless they wore gloves, Paul can lift their prints off the inside."

Stepping back, Emma walked to the pantry and sifted through the container of sandwich bags and wrappers. She needed to protect the handle. Even though her fingerprints had blurred those on the outside, she coated both knobs with plastic wrap and added a sandwich bag for good measure. It produced a gaudy, comical effect as she secured them with elastic bands. She knew in her heart it wouldn't work. One careless touch would smudge any fingerprints, including hers. In desperation, she used parcel tape to secure the handles from turning and deter anyone from touching them. Another length of tape placed horizontally across the door frame prevented the lock from engaging. If the door wouldn't close, no one needed to use the handle to open it.

Satisfied, she faced the long corridor and the body lying across its width. She'd thought at first that Bunny had just collapsed. She'd told Paul the woman's name without a doubt. But as she flicked on the overhead light again, she frowned in confusion at the woman's short grey hair and high cheekbones. Easing the hood away from her hair with the fork she'd grabbed from the cutlery drawer, she saw it wasn't Bunny Cathcart at all. Farrell scrabbled at the door. He wanted to follow her, but Emma sent him back inside. "I'm fine," she whispered, her tone infused with fake lightness. "Get back into your bed."

But she didn't feel fine as she used her phone to photograph the woman's position on the tiled floor. She'd fallen sideways, her neck at an odd angle like a dead bird's. Her right shoulder rested on the floor, her cheek against the wide skirting board. Emma took as many photos as she dared, turning her gaze aside as she snapped an image of the one visible staring eye and the lips tinged with blue. She wondered how she'd mistaken her for Bunny. She sent furtive glances along the corridor, fearful that a member of the Lit and His Society might arrive to witness her ghoulish actions.

Rising, she sent the photos to both Ray and Regan using a social media message app. The icon spun but nothing happened. The photos didn't send. In frustration, she opened a text box and sent them that way instead. The process took far longer. Minutes later, her phone vibrated in her hand, and she dashed back to the kitchen to answer the call.

"Well done," Paul said.

"We got worried." Anxiety caused a wobble in Ray's voice. "You took ages."

"I sent the photos via direct message in bulk, but the app isn't working. That's why I texted them. I had to send them one at a time. I also made some plaster and filled the biggest footprint outside the back door," Emma continued. "It's bright pink. I hope it sets but I'm not sure it will. The snow is falling fast and covering them. I needed to get some warmth into the room."

"You did great." Paul's admiration travelled the distance between them in his soft, lyrical Leicestershire accent. Emma heard his smile through the thickening of his words. "That's quick thinking."

"What should I do with her body?" Panic raised Emma's heart rate again. She experienced the irrational desire to hide the fallen woman, as though making her disappear might also expunge her death from reality. The Aga worked fast, radiating heat to chase the icy air into the furthest corners of the room. "I can't just leave her lying in the corridor and pretend she isn't there."

"Sorry, but you can't move her." Regret laced Paul's tone. "A forensics team needs to see her in situ."

"No!" Emma wailed. "She's stone cold and in the middle of my hallway. I have a house full of people wanting breakfast in less than three hours. She's blocking access to the kitchen. What do you want me to do?"

"You need to cordon off the corridor." Regret turned to determination as the detective-spirit won through. "It's against the law to do anything different." His tone contained steel.

"This is a disaster," Emma breathed. "Can I at least cover her in a blanket? For decency."

"Only if you want your DNA on the victim. It'll raise some provocative questions about your involvement in her death."

"I'm not involved!" Emma protested. "And my DNA is already on her. I tripped over her in the corridor! She's wearing my husband's coat! How much more contamination do you need?"

"A woman is dead. Remember that." Paul's words acted like a slap to her cheek. "This Bunny Cathcart might have passed from natural causes, but we owe it to her to discover the truth. I'm sorry for your ruined weekend, but a woman died."

Emma gulped, the sound loud in the silent room as she digested his rebuke and owned her selfishness. "About that," she began, guilt creating a prickling in her chest at the thought of alerting the woman's family to their loss. It landed like a brick in her gut. "I got it wrong. It's not Bunny Cathcart. It's Kathleen Dubois, the honorary guest from last night's event. And any minute now, her husband or daughter will come looking for her."

20

Folding Chair

♥

Emma raided the armoire and added more clothing beneath her ski jacket, also finding a pair of waterproof pants. The next hour involved her running from the kitchen to the French doors in the morning room, via the courtyard at the rear of the main house. Each trip involved navigating the footprints and the growing drifts. Chloe's van didn't help matters, parked with the rear bumper jutting across her path. Emma set out some of the remaining buffet on the tables at the back of the morning room. Her left wrist throbbed, but circumstance forced her to use it, anyway.

The electricity held, enabling her to heat an urn and provide a bottle of milk, a tub of instant coffee, and a bowl of tea bags. She used a wheelbarrow abandoned outside the kitchen door to transport the crockery and enough mugs to suffice, wishing she'd thought of it earlier when she'd tripped and dropped a tray of tiny quiches into the snow.

Despite her mittens, the frigid air nipped at Emma's bare fingers until her nails turned blue. She steamed beneath her many layers. Sweat trickled down her spine and into her underwear. The journey back and forth across the courtyard proved treacherous. The temperature rose enough near dawn to melt the new layers of snow, but then turned them to ice as a weak sun painted the laden sky a mottled pink.

Emma began by removing her boots at the threshold of each door. But as the laborious journeys continued, she abandoned propriety. Slimy water trailed across the kitchen tiles and the morning room's gleaming floorboards. An ice skating rink spread outward from her steps.

Light flicked on from the third floor. It cast a glow across the roof. Panicking, Emma abandoned a tray of cold sausage rolls in the morning room and locked the French doors behind her. Emerging into the lobby, she dragged aside a two-seater sofa from beside the extinct fire. The wooden legs squealed against the floorboards, loud and high pitched. She jammed it across the entrance to the corridor. A heavy 1950s curtain swished across the gap in a haze of dust motes. It blocked the view of the corridor beyond it. And the body.

Then she switched from boots to slippers and dialled Ray's number again. "I've done what I can," she said, her breath emerging in staccato gasps. "But everyone is waking up now. Paul must get here before her family comes downstairs. He can't expect me to break the news about what's happened!"

"Is there something I should know?" The voice came from behind her, and Emma jumped. Her thumb slid across the screen. She killed the call before Ray could reply. Turning, she met Monty Jones's quizzical gaze. He cocked his regal head onto one side and peered at Emma. "You look terrible. Haven't you slept?"

"Not much." Emma ran a hand through her tangled hair. Her fingers snagged against the damp knots from the blizzard, which had hampered her work. She stuffed her phone into her pocket, ignoring its incessant buzzing. "I've set up the buffet in the morning room again. Most of it's still cold." She narrowed her eyes at Monty. He still wore last night's clothes, but his slicked hair had a damp sheen. He smelled of soap. "Did you take a shower?" she asked, her words released with slow precision.

"A bath. Freda said you wouldn't mind."

Emma gaped, rendered speechless at the extent of Freda's liberties. She glanced towards the main staircase and blew out a ragged breath. "You didn't use the third floor bath, did you?"

"Yes. We're taking it in turns."

Emma released a curse and pushed past him. She took the steps two at a time, almost breaking her neck in her haste. "Go into the morning room!" she shouted behind her, aware of his expression of bemusement as she reached the third floor.

Running water met her ears as Gwendoline pushed the bathroom door closed in Emma's face. Wrapped in a fluffy towel, she screamed in shock as Emma barged the door open with her shoulder and wrenched on the tap. "Get out!" Gwendoline shrieked. "It's my turn!"

"It leaks, you bloody idiot!" Emma retorted. "That's why we haven't renovated this floor yet! I told you that last night!"

"But Freda said we could use it!" Gwendoline protested. "Monty already had a bath!"

"Just get out." Emma seized a screwdriver from the worn cupboard beneath the stained sink. She dug it underneath the hardboard between the 1970s avocado toned plastic bath and the frame. It came away with a tearing sound to reveal the flood spreading outward from beneath the plug hole. Emma snatched the second towel clasped in Gwendoline's arms, yanking it with enough force to set her off balance. She swore to herself as she mopped at the flood. Rising, she jabbed an index finger in Gwendoline's face. "I don't care if you lot pay a tractor driver to take you home. This is not a free hotel. Get dressed. You're leaving!"

Emma hauled the metal plug from the hole, releasing the foamy water with a gurgle. Steady dripping added a plop to the already soaked towel. She fumed. Another yank on the plug snapped the fragile chain. The metal came off in her hand. She jammed it into her pocket, where it clanked against her phone. "Get out!" she reiterated.

Gwendoline scurried backwards. Her lips drew into thin, vengeful lines. "I know all about you!" she snarled, clutching her remaining towel to her bouncing breasts. "You're just a nobody who struck lucky, so don't think you're any better than the rest of us!" As Emma floundered before her, Gwendoline snaked her elegant neck towards Emma and spat, "My mother made up a great poem about you last night, Miss Snooty." A cackle, loud and long, issued from her throat. The sound held an eerie, grotesque note. "She read it to us, and we all laughed." She dipped her chin and her eyes narrowed. "You're a piece of shit and everyone knows it."

Emma backed from the bathroom, her chest tight. She gripped the plug in her pocket with fingers which burned from the pressure.

"Is there a problem?" Freda stood in the doorway. Her knotty fingers twisted a string of expensive pearls around her throat. She'd dressed in another vintage frock, which seemed familiar.

Emma halted. The tirade on her lips died. "Did you raid the box from the attic?" Her brown eyes widened. Freda took a faltering step out of range. She clattered with Flora. "It is!" Emma spoke through gritted teeth. "I just fetched it from the dry cleaners. The Market Harborough Museum wants to display it!" She pictured the clothing cascaded like an exploded bomb over Freda's bedroom. The treasured pieces she'd set aside as a legacy of the Ayers family would require cleaning again. At Emma's expense. "I can't do this anymore." The statement held a strange, releasing finality. She adored Freda, but the gravy train had drawn into the station with a metallic squeal of brakes. Freda had sunk into her fantasy as the rightful Lady Ayers. It needed to stop.

"Is everything okay?" Flora's voice held a waver, as though anxiety pressed close to the surface.

Emma turned to the knot of people crowding the doorway. "There's a cold breakfast in the morning room." She ignored the ugly sneer on Gwendoline's face. "Eat and plan to leave."

Major Mallory-Eaves and Sir Robert rose from the sofas clustered around the fireplace.

"But what about baths and showers?" Mavis complained. She clutched a pink fluffy towel to her chest as though it might strengthen her claim. "It's bad enough having to wear the same clothes from last night."

"Use the sink. Roll in the snow. I don't care!" Emma snarled. She jabbed a finger in Mavis's direction. The other woman flinched. "And you can pay me back for the summer garden party, Mavis. I'm giving your personal address and phone number to a solicitor. Don't think you can slither away again!"

She pushed through the hushed crowd and clattered down the narrow stairs. Her footsteps pounded along the lower hallway until she reached her bedroom. Water slapped against the tiles of her ensuite. Her last nerve frayed. Someone had also appropriated her unlocked bathroom for a shower.

Her chest ached with the effort of holding in the looming explosion as she battled with her emotions. She'd learned to swallow her hopes and fears over countless disappointments, but this nasty collection just wouldn't get in the box. Emma pressed her palms against her sternum, sensing she needed to leave the room before the interloper emerged from her shower. And she killed them. With her bare hands. And enjoyed it.

But it reminded her of the body in the hallway. The dead Kathleen Dubois laid there like a discarded rag. Emma's knees ached as she shook. The joints threatened to drop her onto the carpet. She covered her face with her right hand, frozen in the nightmare her life had become.

"Emmaline." The soft male voice stole into her mind. Gentle fingers pulled her hand from her face. Emma looked up into the twinkling blue eyes of her father-in-law, unable to form a suitable response. This man invaded her home and her marriage without invitation, stealing in and out at will. He seemed to her no better than the ungrateful, complaining crowd upstairs in the servants' quarters. "Emmaline, come," he urged, tugging on her wrists.

At that moment, a screech of fury and dismay echoed from the family bathroom at the other end of the hallway. Winston's lopsided grin graced his handsome, angular face. He focussed his efforts on her left hand, enfolding her fingers into his strong, craggy palm and leading her towards the door. The blackening bruise from her fall earlier sent an ache of protest, and Emma hissed. She drew her hand from his grasp. And frowned at Winston's mischievous expression. "You turned off the hot water," she stated, her tone bland and devoid of emotion.

His grin widened to reveal white teeth which, despite his age, were still his own. Creases appeared in the corners of his eyes as though he spent more time in laughter than Emma realised. "A simple solution dorogaya," he soothed, dropping the Slavic endearment into his sentence with ease.

He led her into the hall. The space appeared darker than usual. Snow obscured the long glass skylight. "We should talk before these morons filter downstairs." He jerked his head towards the third floor. Maids and footmen had once gazed through their tiny windows at the front. They'd watched the bedecked guests who'd graced the gentry of Wingate Hall. But they'd never crunched the lime grit beneath their shoes or listened to the whispers of the tree-lined avenue. They looked but were forbidden to touch. The guests occupying their beds now knew no such boundaries.

Emma sighed out a ragged breath and nodded at Winston's expectant frown. "I'll come," she whispered, defeat slumping her shoulders.

"Good," Winston replied, bending his regal head to speak into her ear. "We must discuss what to do with the corpse on your hallway floor."

21

Adirondack Chair

♥

"The cop said I need to leave her there," Emma said with a sniff. "I'm breaking the law if I move her. If I cover her with a blanket, I'll contaminate the crime scene with my DNA." She glanced towards the far end of the hallway and the stairs leading to the servants' quarters. "But her family is here. Won't they notice she's missing?"

"Families only miss the ones they love," he replied, lifting a neat grey eyebrow and dipping his chin. "As you crave Alexei in his absence."

Emma nodded. It seemed futile to correct his son's legal name to Winston. Rohan would always be Alexei to the man who'd overseen his child's life and education like a colonel rather than a father. "We argued," she admitted, knowing as the words slipped free that sharing anything with Winston would anger her husband.

"Corpse first," he replied with a stroke of her cheek. His fingers held a surprising softness. "Save your anguish." His dismissal cauterised the well of despair brewing in Emma's chest. It occurred to her that perhaps he didn't want to know or understand the finer details of her relationship with Rohan. He hadn't approved and perhaps still didn't.

Chloe met them at the bottom of the stairs, Ridley close on her heels. "I need to get to the kitchen," she stated, pointing towards the corridor. Her chef's coat appeared rumpled and creased, as though she'd slept in it.

"No!" Emma cried as Dyfed's fingers closed around the arm of the sofa. His spine bent and his limbs tensed as he readied his muscles to pull the heavy piece of furniture aside. A cloying scent reached her nostrils and provided her with a ready excuse. Though her stomach roiled at the obvious cause. "A drain leaked in the hall," she lied. "It's spread everywhere. You don't want to go down there."

Winston set a course for the sofa. His expression became stony, a threat projecting from his blue irises. "Leave it!" he commanded.

"But Mum said," Dyfed began. He waved his right hand towards Chloe. "We need to load our stuff into the van." His wispy hair stuck upright as though he'd slept hanging from the ceiling. It occurred to Emma too late that she knew little about her unwanted house guests. If Kathleen Dubois hadn't died from natural causes, she'd assumed the unknown intruder had killed her. But what if someone from the Literary and Historical Society put a premature end to Kathleen's life?

Emma stared at Winston, and he waggled his eyebrows at her. "In there," he snarled, jabbing his finger towards the morning room. "Now go!" Dyfed skittered across the lobby towards Chloe, his eyes wide with fright. He carried the tangy scent of dried sweat with him.

Emma spoke to Chloe. She noticed Ridley fondling the hem of her chef's coat between finger and thumb. He didn't look at Emma, perhaps wishing himself somewhere more welcoming. "You can use the French doors in the morning room to access your vehicle. That corridor is out of bounds for now." Chloe jerked her chin upward in understanding and released a tired sigh. Emma gnawed on the inside of her cheek, considering what might face the woman once she returned home. "Have you heard from the cops about Gareth?" she asked, her tone softening.

Chloe snorted, a harsh, animalistic sound. White condensation puffed from her lips as warm air met the cold of the lobby. "They let him go last night," she stated, her tone harsh. She turned her shoulder towards Emma. "No thanks to you, lady."

Emma released a gasp. "He attacked me!" she argued to Chloe's retreating spine. "What did you want me to do?"

"Not make things worse," she snarled, walking away with Dyfed and Ridley hovering like stray flies.

Emma sighed and let her hands slap her thighs as they fell. Voices drifted from the morning room as the group complained about the cold breakfast. Farrell gave a mournful howl from the kitchen to complete Emma's misery. Now even he hated her.

"Er, slight problem." Monty stuck his head into the lobby, holding the edge of the door like a shield.

"What now?" Emma demanded, her tone heavy and filled with defeat.

"I don't think anyone is going anywhere," Monty replied. "Have you looked outside?"

Emma left Winston guarding the corridor and entered the morning room. A chill air met her. In her haste to retrieve the food from the kitchen, she hadn't resurrected the fire. And her constant passage through the French doors had infused the room with the icy temperatures from outside. She shivered, noticing her guests rubbing their arms and stamping their slippered feet. "Let's make a fire," she suggested, forcing lightness into her tone. She raised her hands for their attention. "Look, none of us imagined you'd spend the night stranded here. I found myself unprepared for fourteen unexpected guests." Including Freda in their number despite her absence, Emma took a deep breath and studied the individual faces turned towards her. Some scowled. Others just observed her discomfort.

Sir Robert Holden leaned over to examine a stray thread on his left slipper. He appeared not to listen, but the major studied her with narrowed eyes. "I realise very few of you like me. I've heard the rumours of how I gained ownership of Wingate Hall." She shrugged. "I actually don't care." Confidence caused her chest to rise and her spine to straighten. Her beloved Anton had given the Hall to her. Not to Rohan, his mother, or his half-brother. To her. "Your opinions don't matter, so please show some respect and keep them to yourselves. I love this house. I'm raising my children here. This is our home, not a hotel." She tossed her tangled curls behind her shoulder in defiance and narrowed her eyes. "I have the phone number for a local farmer. He might prove amenable to giving you a ride to the nearest ploughed road." Emma glared at Mavis. "For a small fee."

"Good, because I'm not spending another night in that freezing cage!" Gwendoline bit. A general shushing sound drowned out her words.

"Enough!" Monty growled. He stepped towards Emma and offered his raised hands in a truce. "I can light a fire," he said with a placatory smile. "Just show me where to find the things I need."

Gwendoline continued her whining complaints. Emma turned her back on her, concentrating on Monty. "The matches are on the mantel," she said, her voice sounding less confident in the face of continued opposition. "Ray brought in extra logs. There's also a bucket of coal." She lifted the lid of a wooden box situated to the right of the fireplace. "We keep the sticks for kindling in here."

"Don't worry about those ingrates," Monty urged. He squatted in the hearth and used the poker to rake through the coals. Tiny orange sparks flared to life. "Pass me some of those sticks, please?" He held out his left hand. "I think I can get this going again." Ash piled through the grate as he raked. Emma dug her fingers into the kindling box. Something white and crunchy brushed against her thumb. She pulled the sheet of lined paper free from beneath a pine cone and spread it out against her thigh.

"A poem," she said, recognising the four-line stanzas written in cursive handwriting.

Monty's eyes widened, and he ceased his raking. He held out his left hand. "I'll chuck it in here," he said, his tone firm. "It'll help the flames to spread to the sticks."

"But I want to read it." Emma stood up straight and held the paper closer. Her lips moved as she read, the colour flaming through her cheeks. "Who wrote this?" she demanded, her tone acerbic.

Monty held out his hand again. His gentle eyes held sadness. "Just give it here," he said with forced calm. "It's not worth reading. She didn't even finish it."

Emma's hand shook as she folded the page along its original creases. She pushed it into her pocket. "I'll call the farmer," she said, drawing her phone from the other pocket. "Enjoy your fire starting."

Emma stepped into the lobby and closed the door behind her. Monty's words suggested a woman had written the poem. That put seven of her guests into the suspect's circle. No, six. She dismissed Chloe without challenge. The woman had taken a cooking gig, not launched her career as the next Poet Laureate. Emma hung her head as she peered at her phone screen. Nothing from Regan, which seemed odd.

"What did he want?" Winston's question made her jump, and Emma breathed out and cocked her head. She shoved her phone back into her pocket.

"Who?"

He'd remained on guard by the sofa, his hands behind his back like a professional bodyguard. Emma softened at the seriousness with which he'd taken his task, protecting the body while she cried over a spiteful poem. "The man called you into that room." He jerked his head towards the door behind her. "He wanted to show you something."

Emma turned to face the panelled wooden door. "You're right," she mused. "He wanted me to look outside." But unable to face the uncharitable crowd, she strode towards the inner front door instead. Hauling the heavy wood by the knob, she stepped into the freezing vestibule.

A wonderland scene greeted her. Snow shrouded the bus from above and below, creating a narrow aperture of glinting glass. Emma covered her mouth with her hand, at first dismayed and then amused. "Oh, wow!" she breathed. "Gwendoline went back for something last night. I think she forgot to close the bus door behind her." In the time since Emma had ferried food from the kitchen to the morning room, snow had covered her tracks. At least a metre had fallen in the last hour.

Winston joined her at the inner door. His ramrod straight spine and smooth hands showed not even slight discomfort at the cold. The immaculate three-piece charcoal suit hung from his shoulders, tailored to his lithe frame by an expert hand. Emma wondered if it contained hidden heating elements as he gazed at the landscape without a discernible reaction. The sight of a snow bank covering the bus steps and edging towards the driver's seat tugged at the left side of his upper lip. "Imbeciles," he mused. He turned his regal head towards Emma, his hooked nose and sharp features weighing her reaction as he said, "We should make them all disappear. The world would miss none of them."

Emma shot back into the house, elbowing him aside as she closed the front door. "Oh, my goodness!" she hissed. "Did you kill that woman?"

22

Egg Chair

♥

Winston Wright's laughter echoed off the wooden panelling and drifted up the main stairs. Her question had entertained rather than shocked him. "Why would I?" he chuckled. "I have no vested interest in these morons. They're stranded here like rats on a ship." The Russian accent he'd covered with plummy English inflections leaked through his words. He pressed a manicured hand to his chest and his blond lashes fluttered. "I seek only to provide comfort and reassurance to my daughter-in-law. You have nothing to prove to that dubious crowd, Emmaline. You are enough."

The statement took her breath away. It sheared through the wall of protection she spent her life sheltering behind. *'You are enough.'* Winston had validated her, giving his fatherly approval. She'd never asked for or expected it. Emma floundered, unable to thank him or process the revelation. But it rang in her ears. "Please, will you help me?" she begged, brushing over her murder accusation seconds earlier. She jerked her head towards the morning room. "Monty is right. Even a tractor can't drive through such deep snow." Her shoulders drooped. "I'm stuck with these ingrates."

"Da." His affirmation seemed to hollow out her chest.

"You'll help me?" she repeated, falling on his mercy. She took a risk, knowing one day he'd demand a payment, which she may not want to deliver. Rohan rarely spoke of his relationship with his father, choosing to focus on not replicating Winston's mistakes with his own son. But she'd gleaned enough to understand that her father-in-law could play both antagonist and saviour within the same conversation. She promised herself she'd show caution. Right then, though, she needed him, a state she hadn't anticipated when she awoke that morning.

"The corpse stinks." He stated the fact in hushed tones. "It has lost its bodily functions. We should move it and clean up the mess."

Emma squirmed before his observation. "Detective Inspector Paul Barker threatened me with obstruction if I touch anything," she replied. He'd intimated it, but she'd understood his point.

"He is not here." Winston spread his hands and shrugged, as though expecting Paul to pop up from nowhere and prove him wrong. "Give me his number. I will contact him and explain."

The notion of abdicating responsibility filled Emma with hope. But Winston couldn't interact with Paul Barker. "He might go digging," she replied. She gathered Winston's cool hands into hers. Her left wrist twanged along the tendon. He didn't resist. His brow furrowed as though finding the contact alien. "It's not worth the risk." Emma sniffed the air and blew out her breath. "I'll make the call."

She stepped away to dial Ray's number. Winston returned to guard the corridor. Emma added another fact to her mental file on Rohan's elusive father. He'd accessed the house yet again triggering no security. And amazingly, he also possessed enough control over his sense of smell to endure prolonged sentry duty alongside Kathleen Dubois' corpse.

"Yup!" Ray answered the call with a breathless grunt.

"The poor woman stinks," Emma replied without preamble. "We can't leave her there." Her bottom lip poked out as she considered Gwendoline's reference to the nasty poem about her. Of course, Kathleen Dubois wrote it, the spiteful Poet Laureate. "I want her moved," Emma demanded. "Everyone is stuck here because of the snow. I can't cope with a dead woman in my hallway. She wrote mean poems about people and in the hour since everyone woke up, not one person has missed her." Farrell gave another howl of distress from the kitchen and Emma walked towards Winston. "I'm moving her onto a tarpaulin and dragging her downstairs," she stated, finalising her decision. "It's freezing in the wine cellar."

"Emma, no!" She registered Paul's distant wail of fury as she ended the call.

"They're not coming," she said to Winston. "It's down to us."

Winston helped her to move the sofa aside so they could squeeze past it. They tugged it into place just as Freda drifted down the main staircase. She still carried the cigarette holder. She halted to observe Emma's fingers clinging to the open curtain. "What's he doing here?" she demanded, her tone curt. She jabbed the pointy prop in Winston's direction. "I've told him he's not welcome in this house!" A determined edge caused her to sound every syllable, as though Emma didn't understand English.

Emma turned her back on her. "Then you lied to him, didn't you? And overstepped again."

"What are you doing?" Freda peered down the dark corridor through her rheumy eyes. Emma swished the curtain across the aperture to block her view of the body. She left the overhead lights off. Freda could just about see her own feet without her glasses.

"Look after your guests," Emma called as she walked away. "They're your responsibility."

Freda's slippers swished against the floorboards as she shuffled across the lobby towards the morning room. "I corrected an accident with the hot water." Her voice held an unfamiliar waver. "Someone turned the switch in the airing cupboard."

Emma heaved a sigh of exasperation, though she sensed the woman had immunised herself against guilt. Winston stepped over Kathleen first, pausing to study her face. He made a sound like a harrumph and kept walking. Emma navigated the woman's long, splayed legs, keeping her gaze on Winston's retreating jacket. She reached him as he stopped to stare at the kitchen door knob. "What is this?" His grey eyebrows disappeared into his hair.

"I'm protecting the fingerprints." She pursed her lips at the inadequacy of her DIY detective effort. Winston allowed Emma to push open the door. The tape had curled away from the frame to create a sticky, obstructive ball. His nose wrinkled once in the kitchen.

Farrell barked before noticing Emma. He threw himself at her legs, spinning and whining with joy. She pulled open the rear door and stood aside as he took a flying leap from the threshold.

The happy woof died in his throat as he hit an unexpected blockade. Farrell yelped, disappearing face first into the drift. He left a dog shaped dent in the soft snow. The blizzard had buried the pink footprint. In response to the opening door, the wall cascaded inside. It spread across the kitchen tiles and covered Emma's feet. She sighed. "Can the day get any worse?".

She turned away from the calamity as flakes puffed upwards from Farrell's eager burrowing. Winston's expensive shiny shoes remained dry. Winston Wright could fall into sewage and walk away without a stain. She sighed. "I'll get the dustpan again," she said.

But as she bent to retrieve it and her fingers closed around the plastic handle, the spiteful poem crinkled in her pocket. The words burned in her mind, imprinted on the insides of her eyelids.

'Her Ladyship.
Her voice, like onions, such a pungent assault,
Harsh and crunchy, our ears to halt.
Her laughter, like the bitterest citrus zest,
Leaves tongues twisted and hearts unimpressed.'

23

Womb Chair

♥

"You detested the dead woman?" Winston asked without guile.

Emma shrugged and shovelled another layer of snow outside. She gasped as the dog tunnelled himself from the drift and hit her in the stomach in his haste to escape. Her butt gave a twinge of protest as she rolled backwards. The dustpan flew from her fingers and skittered across the tiles. "Ouch!" she groaned, rubbing her stomach through the waterproof pants. "Bloody dog."

Farrell retreated to his warm bed and hurled himself into the soft fabric. He released a prolonged grumble in a doggy apology. Emma flipped onto her sore knees and resumed her work. She uncovered the dripping towel she'd placed there earlier and dragged it free of the doorway.

"Do you not have a shovel?" Winston watched her from a seat at the kitchen table. He'd crossed his legs and his arms, making a defensive statement which Emma couldn't fathom.

She slammed the door closed again with a sigh and dragged the soaked towel to the sink. Freezing, dirty water dripped from the fabric as she twisted it over and over. She struggled to perform the action one-handed. "Monty used it last night," she replied. "I meant to check the lobby for it, but then Freda appeared."

Winston made a low growling sound in his throat. "Doesn't she always?" he asked.

Emma turned to face him. Her body twisted as her fingers squeezed water from the towel. "You wish to make an observation?" Her exaggerated politeness raised a smile from his lips.

"Alexei has concerns." Winston lifted the foil edge of a tray in front of him and peeked inside. His nose wrinkled, and he pressed the wrapper back into place.

"That's news to me." Emma's cheeks flared, and she busied herself with the towel to hide her fear. But she'd fibbed. Freda's presence had also featured in their argument, another matter which remained unresolved.

Winston snuffed out a laugh. "You lie." The simple statement acted as a knife in Emma's chest.

She spread the towel in front of the door and leaned against the sink. Folding her arms across her stomach to support her left wrist, Emma scowled at him. "Enlighten me," she invited him.

An iron grey brow shot into his fringe as he studied her. She waited for his verdict, her chest tight with condemnation. "She gossips," Winston stated. "Can't help herself. You've allowed her too much liberty within your family. She has become your weak point."

"But she knows nothing important," Emma countered. She glossed over his assertion that Freda's presence affected only her. He hadn't included Rohan in the division of weakness. Confusion drew vertical lines through her forehead. Doubt entered her voice. "Does she?" Gwendoline's comment returned as a faint echo. *'I know all about you!'* And Mavis had said something similar. *'I know things about you, young lady!'*

Winston studied her, giving nothing away in his bland expression. He'd perfected the art of warfare and espionage. He would reveal only those details which suited his immediate purpose. "Your heart is too soft," he stated. Emma listened for the rebuke and found it there, waiting for her. "It took you too long to expel the Irishman. He threatened Alexei's credibility from under his nose. Freda Ayers poses the same risk, but through ignorance rather than misplaced affection." He lowered his chin and regarded her through the tops of his eyes. It created the effect of a displeased teacher seeking an apology. Emma's gut twisted. He knew about Christopher Dolan's bleeding heart.

"What should I do?" She lowered her voice to an agonised whisper. "She's an old lady with nowhere else to go."

Winston snorted, the sound causing Farrell to lift his head from his paws. "She owns an apartment in town and a cottage in Great Arden, yet she lives here."

"She doesn't seem happy anywhere else," Emma countered. The words sounded pathetic even to herself. Her shoulders slumped. "Does she know what she's doing?" she asked, her tone filled with dread. Her chest caved in on itself and she hunched her shoulders.

"No." And with that declaration, Winston let Freda off a nasty hook, which would have permanently terminated her friendship with Emma.

She sighed and acceded with a shallow nod. "Just another problem," she mused. After all, in the grand scheme of things, she had a missing husband, a house filled with strangers, and a leaking body on the floor of her hallway.

Emma jumped as a scream pealed from beyond the closed door. The sound rolled through the house, pitching and tossing. She froze in place. Farrell shot to his feet, barking and growling. He scrabbled at the kitchen door, assisted by the sticky tape which prevented it from closing. Emma reacted too late as the door opened inward and the dog pushed through the gap. She reached the cold corridor and glanced back at Winston. His gaze rested on his jacket sleeve, his index finger picking at a tuft of lint. He showed no sign of accompanying her into the disaster.

"Get that dog away from my mother!" Gwendoline's voice rose to a deafening pitch, joined by Farrell's exciting yap. "Help! Someone help!"

Emma steeled herself, forcing confidence into her steps as she met the mixed reactions of the Literary and Historical Society's overstayers. Gwendoline had collapsed to her knees in the corridor, her fingers fluttering over her mother's ashen face. She knelt in the puddle beside Kathleen Dubois, unaware of its origins. A man bowed over her, rubbing her shoulders and whispering words intended to soothe. Emma had expected to discover Christos in the role of gallant hero. She frowned when Monty tilted his face to look at her. "What the hell happened?" he growled. "Did you know about this?"

"She killed her!" Gwendoline lashed out sideways, catching her bunched knuckles against Emma's painful left knee. "She tried to cover it up!" Despite her obvious agony, she still took time to load her bow and fire the spiteful arrows in Emma's direction. Monty hauled Gwendoline upright with his forearms supporting her weight from beneath her armpits. Emma took a calculated step back, uncertain of what she'd just seen in the dim light.

Monty's eyes flashed a dangerous blue, and he shouted at her, "Do something! Don't just stand there!"

Emma halted just out of range of them, a sense of misgiving fixing her in place. She whistled to the dog, and he obeyed, abandoning his excited dance beside the body. His bony bottom dug into her foot as he sat. Tongue lolling and his chest heaving. The hall light flicked on, revealing a trail of wet paw prints tracking urine in every direction.

"What's happening?" Sir Robert Holden demanded. "Who's screaming?"

"She's dead!" Gwendoline roared, her voice throaty and slick with tears. "That bitch killed her!"

The wooden legs of the sofa squeaked against the floorboards and the retired lawyer advanced on faltering steps. A knot of other sightseers followed at a safe distance as though wishing to observe the scene without engaging in the drama.

"Oh." Sir Robert arrived on the other side of Kathleen, peering over her as though assessing a steak for rarity. "Police," he stammered. "We need the police. And an ambulance."

His last suggestion quieted Gwendoline with instant effect. She pushed herself away from Monty, latching onto the tendril of false hope. "Yes," she cried. "Call an ambulance." She wrung her hands before her, eclipsing the dual mounds peeking over her red bodice. Reaching across her mother's prone body, she clung to Sir Robert's sleeve hard enough to skew his bow tie. "Call for help?" she pleaded.

Sir Robert blanched, grunts and growls of embarrassment leaking from his throat. "Sorry, old girl," he grumbled. "I don't carry a phone. Not since the incident with that tabloid journalist. Bloody idiot. Terrible case of mistaken identity." His words trailed to a murmur as Gwendoline transferred her distress back to Monty.

"We already called them." Emma included Winston in her flapping hand, but he hadn't followed her into the fray. "A detective is coming, but the snow means he'll take a while." Her voice trailed away at Gwendoline's obvious and genuine grief.

"What about an ambulance?" she wailed. "Mum!" She knelt by the body and shook Kathleen's shoulder. "Mum, wake up!" Her mother's cheek thudded against the skirting board, but her body tilted. The angle held for a moment before she rolled onto her back. Her neck remained bent, driving her chin to touch her chest. Her head followed her body's awkward movement.

Emma gasped and covered her mouth with her hand. Mottled purple skin showed on Kathleen's right cheek. Gravity had pooled her blood at the lowest part of her body. But a long gash bisected her face, deep and bloodless. It began beneath her right eye, creating a diagonal line which stretched as far as her chin. Gwendoline's shocked inhale seemed to last for minutes, long enough to fill her lungs. Ready for the bloodcurdling scream which followed it.

24

Tube Chair

♥

Emma slammed the kitchen door behind her and leaned against it. Farrell muttered as he skittered ahead of her. He almost lost the end of his tail in the door jamb. Winston still occupied the chair and hadn't moved a muscle. Emma jabbed her bottom into the seat beside him. Her breath caught in her chest and a tremor rippled through her torso. She leaned forward, placing her hand over Winston's bent knee and squeezing it. A life raft on a rolling sea. "Kathleen looked sick last night," she gushed, her lips uncoordinated and her mind in free fall. "Terminally sick. So, I assumed she just dropped dead in the hall, but she didn't." An agonised gulp truncated her next sentence. Her eyes widened, and the words stuttered freely. "There's a killer in this house!" Her voice rose to a squeak. "Another one apart from you." She qualified the statement, but the lifting of Winston's iron grey brow made her regret it. He didn't appear amused, his expression deadpan and his lips unmoving. "Please tell me you brought some goons with you?" she pleaded. An image rose into her mind, painting an SUV filled by dark-suited men with muscular torsos and expressions of steel composure. Slavic men who worked for the former spy without question.

"Goons?" The word spat from his lips. They sealed after its expulsion, creating harsh lines infused with white from the pressure. His nostrils flared, and he tilted his gaze to observe Emma's hand gripping his knee. "Goons." He repeated the descriptor and then barked out a laugh. "I like that," he said with a long blink. "Golovorezy. I'll tell them."

"No!" Emma bowed her head until her fringe tapped the knees of her sweatpants. She withdrew her shaking fingers from his leg. "Please, don't. But did you bring them?"

Winston exhaled and his shoulders lost their tension. "To visit Alexei? No. They aren't welcome."

Emma wondered again in that instant how the elderly man gained access to the Hall. Lear believed he'd sewn up all the entrances and exits. Winston's presence suggested he'd missed something crucial. It seemed less relevant in that moment than it would have the previous day. "I wish Rohan was here," she breathed, her chest still tight. "He'd know what to do."

Winston made a sound low in his throat. It suggested neither agreement nor dismissal. "You saw the injury?" he asked, his tone even.

Emma's head moved upwards by slow increments. Nausea threatened her with every distant scream released from Gwendoline's chest. "You knew?" she gasped.

Winston shrugged. "I assumed you checked the body. The angle of her head indicated fractures from a blunt force trauma." He tilted his own head to the side. "It's not possible, see?"

Emma blew out a ragged breath, interspersed with the first hints of a retch. "I thought she just died," she hissed. "Came downstairs in the night for a drink and tripped."

"Wearing your husband's greatcoat and her own flimsy outdoor shoes?" He blinked with rapid flutters of his long lashes, as though aghast at Emma's naivety.

"Okay, fine!" Emma ran her left hand through her fringe before hissing at the pain in her wrist. She examined the bruise spreading across the heel of her hand. "Will they think I did it?" Devastation robbed the question of logic.

"I don't know." Winston's unhelpful reply offered no reprieve. "She didn't die from contact with a hand, Emmaline. The killer hit her with something long and sharp. Hard and from the side. Perhaps she saw and felt nothing."

Emma doubted that. But the kitchen door creaked open to cut off her reply.

Monty glared at Winston from the doorway. His keen blue eyes flitted over the elderly man seated at the kitchen table. Winston's muscles remained relaxed. His legs stayed crossed at the knees. The raised cuff of his trouser leg revealed the blood-red hue of his sock before it plunged into the smart, shiny ankle boot.

"Who's this?" Monty stepped through the door and pressed it closed behind him. The tape caused resistance. He stared at it in confusion. Monty turned his interest to Winston. "Are you with the police?" His hand shook as he ran it through his fringe. "Did you bring an ambulance? Gwendoline fainted." He licked his lips, focussing on Winston's expressionless face.

Emma's tongue poked free with disbelief as Winston patted the pockets of his expensive jacket. He repeated the action with his pants. "No," he concluded. "No ambulance in there."

"You ludicrous man!" Monty yelled. His voice echoed around the kitchen, reverberating off the stainless steel white ware and leaving a shock wave of residue. "A woman is dead! Do you find this funny?"

Winston cleared his throat and returned to his examination of the threads in his sleeve. Emma recognised Rohan's fastidiousness in the deliberate movements of his father's long fingers. She rose. Her knees shook in their effort to support her. Kathleen's bisected face haunted her inner vision, the diagonal gash revealing the yellow fatty layers beneath her cadaverous skin. "Monty," she whispered. Her voice box produced only a hushed half measure of what she'd ordered. "This is my father-in-law, Winston Wright." She opened her left arm in an arc of acknowledgement to encompass his presence. "Winston, this is Monty. He taught Nicky in school last year and he's married to Flora. She teaches the baby class."

Winston sniffed, a haughty, disinterested snuff which halted Emma's diatribe. "I do not care," he replied, not even trying to hide his boredom. He fixed his intimidating azure stare on Monty. The other man quailed and appeared to shrink. "The woman was murdered. Emmaline called a detective. He's on his way." Winston made a flapping motion with his left hand, the fingers sharp and clean. It created the effect of a complete dismissal of an inferior. "Return to your friends and await instruction. You have already destroyed the crime scene." His Slavic accent infused his speech, oozing from his tongue as though refusing further imprisonment. "And do not burst into Emmaline's private quarters with your demands again." Monty blinked with a rapid frenzy of lashes. His cheek twitched, adding to the palsy effect as Winston leaned forward in his chair. The older man's gaze never left Monty's face. "Or I will cut out your tongue, durak!" Spit from the Slavic insult landed on Winston's hand. He winced before flipping his wrist and wiping it against his trouser leg.

Monty got the message. He fled. The sticky thump of the door against the wadded tape provided his exit anthem. Winston raised an eyebrow and observed Emma with a sigh of disdain. "He was not meant to be a murderer."

"What?" Emma screwed her features into a knot and stared at her father-in-law. "That's ridiculous. Monty couldn't hurt a fly."

"Cadfael," Winston mused, examining the section of knuckle he'd wiped on his trouser leg. "By Ellis Peters. Brother Cadfael always said those words before he sought a way to absolve the sinner of their crime."

Emma blew out a stressed breath. Her arms ached to squeeze her squirming daughter. She longed to hear Nicky's shrill voice demanding something outrageous. "Edith Mary Pargeter," she corrected Winston. He raised the condemning eyebrow again and stared at her. "Ellis Peters was a woman." Emma's smile broke wider, though she sensed it would do her no favours. "She spoke fluent Czech, did you know?"

The Slav frowned. He dropped his gaze to the scarred pine surface of the table. And Emma wondered, not for the first time, who exactly her father-in-law was.

25

Ball Chair

♥

Emma left Winston in the kitchen. The dog eyed the elderly man with furrowed brows, never sure of the vibes which radiated from him.

She trooped along the deserted corridor. Was Winston a friend or a foe? She couldn't tell. To Rohan, his father proved an irritant. A fickle dictator with the violent potential. Emma experienced a shiver of gratitude that he couldn't see Winston Wright making himself at home.

Kathleen Dubois had shifted beneath Gwendoline's justified hysteria. She laid on the cold tiles like a snow angel. Her fingers curled inward towards her palms, the nails ragged and bitten. The overhead light picked up the grey flecks in Rohan's greatcoat. It cast the dark patch of postmortem urine into shadow.

Monty's russet jacket covered Kathleen's battered face. He'd tried to preserve her dignity. It created the illusion of a ruddy apple replacing her head. And they'd contaminated her body with fibres and DNA.

A sensible voice in Emma's head urged her to step over Kathleen's splayed legs. Not linger. As though to amplify its wisdom, Gwendoline's shrieks of grief reverberated through the solid walls.

"I'm sorry, Mrs Dubois," Emma whispered. She glanced at the curtain hanging askew at the end of the corridor. With exaggerated care, she lifted the edge of Monty's jacket. The sleeves collapsed on either side of Kathleen's head like an elephant's folded ears. Her grey complexion was a ghastly hue, her lips and eyelids blue. Her eyeballs showed through her pale lashes. Postmortem rigidity stiffened the lids.

The diagonal cut across her right cheek had just missed her eye. Bone showed through the parted layers where the weapon slashed as far as her cheekbone. "Who did this to you?" Emma whispered. She stroked the curved knuckle of the woman's index finger. Not the palm or finger pads. Rigorous forensic testing might later reveal her touch. The knuckle resisted Emma's gentle push, the rigidity lacking the completeness of rigor. Kathleen had seemed fluid and relaxed at first. But hours later, she appeared cast from cement and in the latter stages of curing. Emma released her held breath and tugged the jacket to cover Kathleen's empty stare. She avoided the sticky stain. It dried at the tiled edges of the pool like a lake cut off from its source.

Emma gazed down at Kathleen, nauseated by the indignity of death. The freezing temperatures would confuse her time of death.

Emma had checked the time before she ventured downstairs in the night. Half-past two. Her guests laughed raucously around midnight. Gwendoline said Kathleen entertained them with a poem about her. She needed to find out what time they retired to bed. And if anyone remembered Kathleen going back downstairs.

Emma stared at Kathleen's unsuitable shoes. Constructed of man-made rubber and a cloth upper, they resembled the genuine antiques adorning Freda's feet. But the plastic bows shone in the light. Emma frowned at the glint of a staple clasping the left one to the thin bridge over Kathleen's instep. She pursed her lips. The footprints now filled with her hasty and garish plaster work were larger. A man's print with the grip pattern of a heavy boot.

A shiver ran through Emma. It started at her spine and radiated outward. Her phone bounced in her hand. She'd found the footprints five hours earlier. Yet their owner still roamed unchecked in her house.

Emma stepped over Kathleen. She hurried to the lobby. The light held an eerie by-product of the weak sun. It reflected off the snow drifts beyond the narrow front windows. The chandelier offered a twinkly dimension to the scene. Bunny knelt in the hearth, a poker in her outstretched hand. She jabbed at the embers of last night's fire as though willing the flames to materialise from her futile strokes.

"Leave it!" Emma snapped as she headed for the armoire. "I'll revive it after I check something." She hauled open the oak doors and sifted through the contents. Coat hangers tinkled against each other as she examined their wares. An empty wooden hanger dangled beside Nicky's winter Parka. It rocked as Emma swiped it aside, no longer bearing Rohan's forgotten greatcoat. Poking into the darkness, Emma unearthed Ray's lost overalls. They'd disappeared the previous summer. She tugged them aside, realising they'd become home to three Action Men deserters, and a crumbled packet of biscuits.

Emma opened both doors of the cupboard. She stepped back to survey the cavernous interior. Shelving occupied the right side, lined with shoes and boots of varying size. Her index finger stabbed into the air as she counted them off in search of an absent pair. An ominous patch of mud and dried grass surrounded a section of bare shelf on the lowest rung. Emma lifted her phone. She cursed as the digital assistant again failed to rouse to her command. "Bloody kids!" she raged.

"Let me help." Bunny appeared at her elbow, her phone screen already aglow with yellow light. "But my data isn't working. It's weird because it was fine last night."

"Thanks." Emma took her phone and shone it into the cupboard.

"What are we looking for?" Bunny asked, leaning closer.

Loneliness and responsibility gnawed at Emma's stomach. She'd spent so long managing by herself it seemed alien to return to such isolation. No Rohan, no Christopher and no Ray yet. She turned to face Bunny, needing a friend but aware that a killer walked undetected through her home. "Someone entered the house in the night," she said, lowering her voice to avoid causing further hysteria. "They left the back door open and came inside. They didn't leave the same way. It's possible they killed Mrs Dubois."

"And they're still here?" Bunny's head reeled back on her neck. Emma instantly regretted her candidness. The other woman's lips pinched together as though she'd sucked on a lemon and couldn't rid her mouth of the taste.

Emma exhaled. Tiredness seized her muscles. "I don't know. Perhaps." She turned her back on Bunny but retained the phone. She examined the cupboard's interior while admitting another unintentional error. Her recent sifting hadn't helped the police investigation. She stepped backwards, clattering with Bunny. The woman squeaked like a mouse as Emma stepped on her left foot.

"Kathleen didn't wear a coat last night," Bunny observed. Her nose wrinkled in pain, but she didn't complain about her squashed toes. She shifted her weight into her right foot to provide silent relief to its twin. "Do you think she borrowed the grey one from in there?" She pointed a slender finger at the armoire.

Emma nodded. "I know she did. It belongs to my husband." She tilted her head, eager to stamp on any suspicion. "Rohan left on business almost two weeks ago." She jerked her chin at the cupboard. "I saw it last night when I grabbed my ski jacket." She shrugged, and the fabric rustled against her arm. The vacant space emphasised Rohan's enduring absence. And his unusual and prolonged silence. He'd accused her of emotional paralysis and offered to help. Her wounded pride had resisted.

Emma pushed back her sadness. "Ray's spare boots are missing." She pointed to the gap. "His new boots hurt his heels, so he left his old ones there in case." Emma's lips flattened as she turned to Bunny. "The footprints belonged to a man. Someone took Ray's boots. The killer didn't come from outside. They're in here. They stayed the night in my home." Her voice cracked, and she blew out a breath to cover her fear.

Bunny drew closer, her shoulder touching Emma's. She'd wrapped a shawl around her thin dress. Her forearms glowed like bone where they poked through the flimsy wool. "So, if we find the boots, you think we'll find Kathleen's killer?" Her white sclerae glowed in the light from her torch, resembling two golf balls in her dainty face. Pinpricks represented both irises and pupils. The eerie glow threw her features into sharp relief, a forlorn landscape of ridges and crevices. "But that means it's one of us."

Emma nodded, at once alarmed by the flash of excitement which flitted across Bunny's face. "We can't tell anyone!" she demanded, her voice a throaty hiss filled with threat. "Help is coming, but we aren't safe here." She glanced down at her phone as it vibrated in her hand. A tut escaped from between her lips.

'*Signal lost*,' said the message on the screen.

26

Wassily Lounge Chair

♥

Emma cursed her missed opportunity. She'd avoided waking Allaine too early. Now, she couldn't phone her at all. "What's happening?" she murmured. "This is a nightmare."

The gentle hum of voices rose and fell like surf from the morning room. Emma glanced at the closed door. "They're all in there." Bunny raised an eyebrow. It performed a Mexican wave with its mate across the bridge of her hooked nose. "Even the caterers. That woman says she's on strike. Monty paid her for last night, but I heard her saying she's not working today for free." She frowned and paused in thought. "Do you think they're a little strange?" She cocked her head to one side like a hawk surveying a mouse. "Those men slept on the cold floor last night, instead of in the bed. I saw all the bedding in a heap as I used the bathroom early this morning. The quiet one joined the queue behind me, but I saw the smiley man's feet sticking out from under the quilt as he closed the door. And they speak to that woman as though she's their mother. Have you noticed that?"

Emma nodded. Ridley couldn't be Chloe's son. But it presented a mind bending problem which Emma lacked the energy to contemplate. She blinked. Her gaze returned to her phone screen to plead with the icon depicting an aerial. The red line slashed through it intensified her dismay. Bunny continued speaking. Emma scrambled to make sense of the last flourishes of her question. "Pardon?" Her fingers brushed over the screen as she opened a social media icon. The Wi-Fi would allow her to send a private message on social media, surely?

"I asked if you had any other form of communication?" Bunny repeated. She'd moved on from gossip about the caterers. "It's an extensive property. How do you reach your estate manager if he's out of range of a phone signal? We've all had to use your Wi-Fi. Is that usual?"

Emma's shoulders slumped. "The men use radios. But I never learned how to use them. Christopher was here, and I just ran to him with problems whenever Rohan worked away." She pursed her lips to stem the flow of regret. She clamped her teeth over a ridge on the inside of her cheek, finding she couldn't do both actions at the same time. "The phone signal isn't reliable out here. It's a black spot. We can usually get a mobile signal, but the internet became hit and miss a year ago."

Her mind flicked to Lear. Unlike Christopher, Regan spent little time in the house. Neurodivergent and introverted, he preferred his own company. The folly in the depths of Wingate Hall's extensive grounds provided him with a geek's fantasy. The tiny, two-storey building had enough tech to rival NASA. From his throne room, Regan lived a life he'd only ever dreamed of. He'd replaced Christopher's technical knowledge and hacking ability, but in choosing to maintain an emotional distance from the family had left a gaping hole in Emma's world. Rohan had bridged the gap in the time since Christopher fled the authorities. And the Andreyev's marriage had strengthened without the meddlesome Irishman. Until now. Rohan's absence slashed Emma's soul.

"Oh," she breathed. Her eyes widened as she turned to Bunny. "I think I can get help," she whispered. She jerked her head towards the morning room. "Can you think of a way to occupy them while I slip out?"

"Slip out how?" Bunny's fluffy brows joined again to create a single line. Vertical creases bisected her forehead and vanished into her fringe. She pointed at the wonderland revealed through the panes of glass on either side of the front door. The latest fall of snow had obliterated all but the bus roof. A snarly, twisting wind had wrapped a white blanket around the vehicle. It temporarily hid Gwendoline's error in not closing the bus door behind her. "We can't open any of the external doors. The snow has banked against them." She blinked, her mismatched blue eyes accentuated by faux horror. "Christos stopped Mabel from opening the French door in the morning room. He thought an avalanche falling from the roof might crush her."

Emma bit harder on the inside of her cheek to suppress the barbed comment. It seemed a fitting end for the awful woman. And then she thought of Kathleen Dubois, lying spread eagled on her hallway floor. She sobered. Something about the wound to Kathleen's face snagged at Emma's subconscious. She reached for it, only to find it snatched away by the urgency of her current crisis. "Play charades," she suggested to Bunny. "It's a parlour game from the early 1900s and it'll kill some time. You'll find pens and paper in the bureau to the left of the fire. Just keep them busy and buy me a precious few hours."

"Righto." Bunny saluted, the action giving the impression of a spring working her elbow. It was the left arm and the wrong salute for a British service person, but Emma accepted her obedience with a nod. An involuntary shiver reminded her the journey wouldn't take her outside the Hall. But it would involve colder temperatures than anything offered by the lobby or morning room. She switched her gloves for ski mittens from the armoire.

"An hour if everything goes well," Emma hissed. "Longer if it doesn't."

Bunny gulped and nodded.

Both women jumped at the clatter of heels on polished wood. Emma widened her eyes at Bunny as the newcomers made a liar of her. Not everyone was in the morning room. Freda's gnarled fingers gripped the banister rail as she navigated the main staircase. She wore a winter coat which stroked the stairs behind her as she descended. A floral headscarf wrapped around her hair. The ensemble jarred with the fluffy slippers on her narrow feet. Dyfed followed with Ridley hot on his heels. Only the men's faces showed above towering piles of clothing in their arms. "Are you moving out?" Emma delivered the question with a fraction of the barb she'd intended. A pure act of will maintained enough passable levity to avoid offence.

"Just sharing some warmer things, dear," Freda replied. She offered a regal wave before adjusting her headgear. It seemed impossible to believe she'd spent the previous day wandering around in a light cardigan despite the threat of snow. The Hall's radiators grunted and clanged as they did their best. They worked without fanfare to take the spiteful edge from the air. Freda's extremism served as an affront to the house's weak efforts to please.

"Right," Emma remarked, unable to trust herself further. She fixed a smile on her face and watched the procession edge towards the door of the morning room. The expression didn't reach her almond-shaped eyes. As Dyfed fumbled with the door knob, a woman's coat slithered to the floor. Emma took a threatening step forward. She recognised the antique fabric rescued from the attic.

Freda blinked and sought a distraction. "Mabel thought Rohan's things might fit some of the men," she stated. Her eyes widened with practiced innocence. She dipped at the waist, her tone confidential. "I didn't believe you'd like that."

Emma maintained her silence at the ridiculousness of the suggestion. Except for Christos and the major, most of the men would fit into Rohan's top pocket. Her mind ran riot with all the reasons Freda might have turned on their friendship. But the old woman redeemed herself with a single act of charity. "Someone used your ensuite," she said, her voice reeking of scandal and her brows furrowed. In the absence of Nicky, the permanent marker scribbled above the rim of her glasses pointed to her self-sabotage. "I locked your bedroom door," she said with finality. As though bestowing a gift of great importance on Emma, Freda shuffled across the distance between them. The weighty master key wobbled in her outstretched fingers.

Emma took it with a grateful nod. "Thank you," she conceded. "I left it upstairs by accident."

"Well dear." Freda ventured into the kind of territory containing sarcasm by the ton. "I know how much your privacy means to you." She patted Emma's cool hand and swirled towards the morning room. She resumed supervising the two borrowed builders whom she'd buried beneath ancient rags. Emma searched for a suitable retort and found nothing.

Freda left behind her familiar Tweed scent to fill Emma's gaping mouth.

27

Wiggle Chair

♥

E mma waited for the motley band to enter the morning room before waving her thanks to Bunny. The elfin woman closed the door behind her. An echoed report reached Emma's ears as she clapped her hands and announced the game.

Taking the main stairs two at a time, Emma reached her bedroom in record time. She moved aside a stunning landscape of rolling Northamptonshire hills. A roller swished on a hidden rail behind it. She didn't pause to admire the stunning autumn colours of the paint daubed orange leaves, though she loved it. Her index finger stabbed a code into the digital pad behind it. The mechanism pinged, and she entered a second set of numbers. With a gentle sigh, the heavy door swung open.

Emma snatched up a brass key hanging from a metal hook inside the safe. She pushed it into the inner pocket of her jacket. After closing the heavy door and dragging the picture to cover its secret, she glanced at her cavernous walk-in wardrobe.

Hanging dresses concealed the entrance to Rohan's armoury. Beyond it, a crisscross pattern of narrow passages wound their way through Wingate Hall. Once, they'd served as escape routes. The Hall's chequered history included civil wars, religious uprisings, and political turbulence. Nicky adored the tunnels. Too much. But his fascination with Rohan's weapons led to the erection of a breeze block wall. It cut the main bedroom and armoury off from the tunnels. Permanently.

Emma entered the downstairs corridor after yanking the sofa back into place. She tugged the curtain closed against Kathleen's potential morbid spectators. Her steps pattered over the tiles, and she apologised as she stepped across the stricken Kathleen again. She kept her outdoor boots wedged beneath her left arm as she jogged to the kitchen. Her rushed entry into the room caused Winston to jump in shock.

Rohan's features stared up at her from his handsome face. A noble heritage shone from a guileless expression and twinkling irises. Winston in repose had lost his customary mask. If Emma had ever doubted Rohan's spurious parentage, any musing ceased. Her husband's blue eyes and high cheekbones glowed from beneath a momentary contentment. Winston's hand caressed the dog's soft ruff. He blinked, and the portcullis crashed back into place. His expression returned to its usual rigid severity, without compassion or interest.

Farrell offered Emma his doggy grin. His tail thudded against the tiles. His allegiance hadn't altered for the price of a few strokes. He licked his lips with enthusiasm, sausage roll crumbs collected around his mouth.

"Did you feed the dog?" Emma frowned at Winston. She used her bottom to push the door closed against the tape. Her boots thudded onto the floor. Farrell rose, his ears pricked in expectation.

"No."

"I need to tell you some things," Emma puffed. She sank into the chair beside Winston. She tugged off her slippers and stuffed her feet into the cold boots with a grimace. "The land-line isn't working.

Something has happened to the cell tower. I also can't seem to get internet apps working either. We have no communication. I've left Bunny Cathcart supervising a game of charades in the morning room. That will buy me an hour before they get bored or rebel." Her brows waggled. "Or both."

"Where are you going?" Winston studied her flailing laces before his gaze flicked to the back door. "I checked. Snow blocks every exit." As Emma looked up, a grey shape blasted past the window, fast moving and heading to earth.

She nodded, surprised to find herself agreeing with Christos. "It's coming off the roof," she observed. "It's not safe near any of the buildings."

"So, why are you dressing to go outside?"

"I'm not." Emma fastened her left boot and patted the pocket containing her useless phone. She pulled the master key free and held it out to him. Winston peered at it, raising his head to peer through the half-moon spectacles he'd perched on his hooked nose.

"Oh," he remarked. "I have one of those."

"Of course, you do," Emma bit. She shoved it back into her pocket. "I bet Ro didn't give it to you."

A steel grey eyebrow rose and fell. Winston whipped his glasses from his face and inserted them into his jacket pocket. The summit of a perfectly folded scalene handkerchief bent a little to admit their bulk. "Ways and means," he murmured under his breath.

Much as Emma wished to uncover the traitor in her small household, time slipped away from her. She shelved the issue of the rogue key for another moment. It explained Winston's ability to float around Wingate Hall like a resident ghost. It didn't solve the mystery of how he gained access through locked external doors.

"Look." Emma leaned forward. "One of the guests murdered Kathleen. She came downstairs in the night and borrowed Rohan's heavy coat from the armoire. It must have drowned her."

"She intended to go outside?" Winston leaned back in the chair and folded his arms. It creaked, the groaning of the wood a paradox with his slight build.

Emma shook her head. "I told them where to find extra blankets. Why not wander around draped in one of those?" Her gaze tracked to the sash window as a falling icicle slid past like an arrow. She blew out a breath filled with exasperation. "Kathleen and her husband didn't come upstairs when I showed the others to their rooms. Perhaps no one told her about the blankets." She gazed at Winston. "I'm not convinced she intended to go outside at all."

He cleared his throat and the eyebrow of condemnation rose again. "But she wore shoes," he stated, his tone flat. "You gave slippers to everyone. Why switch into outdoor footwear?"

"True," Emma conceded. "But those little shoes wouldn't cope with snow drifts. And I found the kitchen door wide open in the night. There are footprints under the drift. A man's size. Walking towards the house and not away from it. The killer borrowed Ray's spare boots from the armoire. That means it's one of us. They went out and then returned."

Winston shrugged. "Don't include me in your amateur murder mystery," he grumbled. "I would have disposed of a fragile old woman with more flair. But yes, it's possible the killer exited the house through the kitchen and the snow covered their tracks. They returned later, leaving only one set of footprints."

Emma gave a slow nod. "I don't believe Kathleen went outside. Her shoes appear dry. Do you think she intended to meet someone?" Her mind whirred with possibilities. "There's a past issue of misconduct with either her or her husband. Freda mentioned an affair. The whole family moved away afterwards. Do you think she planned to remake her lover's acquaintance?"

Winston gave a visible shudder, not from the cold but rattled by unsavoury mental images. "You saw her!" His upper lip pulled back from perfect white teeth. "A pile of bones and sinew. The woman suffered from a terminal illness. Someone ended her suffering early. Perhaps an act of love."

Emma gaped at him. "She'd had a virus." Her thoughts rampaged through lost snippets of information as she sought the identity of her unwitting informant. "Freda," she murmured, though sensed herself reaching. "Or Mavis."!

Winston snuffed through his nose. "Think what you will," he replied. A long sigh deflated his chest. "I do not care."

Emma dipped towards him. "I need you to do something for me," she said, her tone serious. "Bunny is occupying the guests, but I'd like you to search the third floor. Find the missing boots." She exhaled and rose. "The rooms aren't on the master key yet, but they're unlocked. Search wherever you need to. Find those boots and we'll have the killer."

"Where are you going?" Winston demanded. His voice remained level and unaffected by the drama.

Emma feigned deafness. The wooden door thudded against the tape in answer. Farrell slipped out beside her and glued himself to her right leg. Emma fondled his ears, grateful for his company as she faced the secret depths of Wingate Hall.

28

Accent Chair

♥

The key taken from the hidden safe unlocked a door beside the entrance to the coach house. A set of narrow, twisting steps took Emma to the basement of the Hall. Farrell's claws clicked on the stone, matching her turns. The dim blue light of her phone's digital clock guided her feet. It timed out as she reached the bottom, plunging her into darkness. Unconcerned, Farrell nudged her knee with his nose.

"There's a torch in the butler's pantry," Emma whispered. Her voice echoed as though a hushed crowd waited to surprise her. She shivered. The temperature seemed closer to that of the world outside with its quilted blanket of snow.

Emma found the architrave surrounding the butler's pantry through blind groping. Her toe kicked against the step leading up to it. The dim light from her digital display helped her slip the same key into the lock. The heavy brass rod grated against the mechanism.

Emma jammed her phone between her teeth to free up her left hand. The knob turned, the Bakelite still solid despite its age. While the knobs and handles above the stairs shone and glistened from their brass construction, Bakelite ruled below stairs at Wingate Hall. Emma had digitised the dusty inventories discovered in the butler's office. The neat, cursive script of successive men complained how the brass knobs worked loose under constant use. The mechanisms rusted from the damp. A footnote recorded how a maid became trapped in the servants' hall. She required sedation after her experience. Bakelite appeared in the 1900s. The hard moldable material didn't slip under wet fingers like brass. Constructed from temperature and pressure stressed phenol and formaldehyde, it still worked.

Dust assailed Emma's nostrils as she pushed open the door to the disused room. She'd had such good intentions for the house. Anton had entrusted Wingate Hall into her care, knowing she'd love it back to health. But she'd stalled after Stephie's birth and subsequent hysterectomy. And Christopher's betrayal had rocked her world. She both hated and missed him.

She fancied she caught his scent in the air as she stepped into the butler's former pantry. Her phone screen lit her way to the light switch, and she placed her index finger over the porcelain. The rotary mechanism clicked. A single overhead bulb flared to life, appearing naked and unloved as it dangled from its cord. Farrell's tail brushed an empty shelf and Emma sneezed at the cloud of dust which rose from its surface. He blinked up at her as though concerned before expelling his own whoosh of damp air.

"Yeah, maybe don't do that again," Emma told him. Turning with a sigh, she dragged the key from the lock and closed the heavy door. The brass turned with a clack, sealing them inside the room. Emma withdrew it and pushed it back into her pocket. "No point taking risks by leaving it here," she murmured to the dog. "I have no idea who is coming and going in this house." The remark encompassed Christopher, Winston, her unwanted guests, and a killer.

A crumpled wrapper caught Emma's eye, and she bent to inspect it. Christopher Dolan's sweet tooth dictated he always carried some treat in his pocket.

Emma's fingers shook from cold and emotion as she retrieved the yellow cellophane from beneath the shelving unit. It whispered in her fingers, reminding her of Christopher's tinkling laugh and his permanent scent of mint, coffee and expensive cologne. "Feckin eejit!" she breathed, borrowing the Irishman's favourite expletive. She rose, dropping the wrapper onto a shelf.

Christopher favoured the butler's pantry for access to the main house. The folly hadn't contained his world as it did Regan's. Christopher Dolan's influence stretched far beyond the technical wonders housed there. He'd built it, but it couldn't hold his interest. Only the possession of Emma would satisfy him. And he couldn't have her.

"Here goes nothing." Emma's fingers closed around the knob. She pulled the heavy door towards her. The mustiness of disuse filled her nostrils. She pursed her lips. A nearby switch engaged a bulb which fizzed and complained. The light flickered. But it held, releasing a painful whine. Tap, tap, tap, tap. Farrell's claws followed Emma past empty shelves where expensive glassware once rested. Anton's solicitor auctioned the limitless antique crockery, candlesticks, crystal, and appliances before Emma learned of the generous bequest. The profits funded the renovations. At least, they were meant to.

Emma banished memories which pricked at her soul. She lifted an ancient wax candle from a shelf. Dust coated one side. Emma blew at it, shoved it into her pocket, and added a box of matches. The dog sneezed, and her nose wrinkled. Condensation billowed from her lips as she spoke. "Sorry." Her words sounded overloud in the empty cupboard. She stowed away her phone and patted her bulging pockets.

Farrell released a snort of excitement as Emma lifted a heavy torch from the shelf. She brushed off the dust and tested the bulb. It disturbed a long-legged inhabitant busy with a sizable web. The spider froze as Emma gazed at it in horror. "Rohan's right," she breathed. "I need to continue with the renovations and expel all unwanted guests."

She braced herself and faced the shelving unit occupying the end wall. The dog's shoulder bumped against her knee as she prepared herself for what lay ahead. Forcing a moment's delay, she retrieved the ski mittens from her pocket and tugged her hood over her head one handed. The torch light picked up more resident spiders in its white glow. A glance to her right found Farrell shivering, not with cold, but with anticipation.

Emma pulled one mitten over her hand but kept the other secured beneath her right arm. She edged her free index finger along the side of the shelf at eye level. The catch resembled a raised knot in the wood. She pushed it, exerting pressure until she heard the familiar click.

The entire unit seemed to fall towards her, the effect creating a terrifying visual disturbance. Farrell jerked backwards with a whine, but Emma didn't move fast enough. The circle of light from the torch bounced as though loosed from captivity. A line of shelves bumped her, each smacking against a different body part. The one at eye level jabbed her in the cheek at the same time as the lower shelves attacked her knee and ankle. She took an overlarge step backwards, clattering with the fleeing dog and dropping the torch.

The door swung in a wide arc until halted by the unit behind it. It clattered once and rebounded, coming to rest against the adjacent shelves. Frigid air crawled from the cavity, attacking Emma's nose and fingers. She rubbed at the painful ache to her cheek, irritated at having forgotten the violence of the door's opening. Once loaded with the weight of clean linen bound for the Hall's residents, it would have yawned with less enthusiasm.

Emma blew a ragged breath into the darkness and retrieved the torch. It proved as shatter and waterproof as the manufacturer claimed in the embossed font scrolled along its handle. She waggled it from side to side in her hand. It remained alight. Trailing webs hung overhead, thwarted by their reliance on a false wall. The weight of the torch reminded her of her fall over Kathleen's prone body as an ache bloomed from the heel of her hand to her elbow. She switched it into the other hand. "Enough messing around," she told Farrell in a stern voice. He wagged his tail to show he knew who'd caused the delay.

Emma stepped over the threshold and into the tunnel. The light from the pantry spread before her like a glowing boundary marker. Beyond it, darkness loomed. Rough bricks blinked back at her from the bobbing, shifting spotlight of the torch. "There's a murderer in my house," Emma whispered to herself.

Farrell trotted past, and the tunnel swallowed his ebony coat.

She didn't want to follow, but necessity dictated she must. Emma's fingers closed over the freezing bar. It stretched the width of the tunnel side of the door. She gave it a valiant tug. The structure swung back towards her. It clanged shut, a dull boom which reverberated along unseen walls.

The darkness overwhelmed her, icy fingers stroking her exposed skin. Farrell's eager sniffing echoed like the snorts of imagined monsters. Emma's teeth chattered in a symphony of icy percussion.

No one could follow her now. They'd need keys and an intimate knowledge of Wingate Hall. She was alone in the bowels of the house.

Emma used the torch to guide her steps along the earthy floor. Shadows bobbed and danced off the walls in response to the light. The glow caught the dog's waving tail and padding feet. Emma shoved her other hand into its mitten and resumed her journey. But snippets of information intruded into her thoughts and her fear caught hold of them.

Who knew she'd stowed the key to the kitchen door on the mantel above the Aga?

Who'd roamed her house in the middle of the night, confident enough to raid the armoire for outdoor clothing?

Emma stumbled along the tunnel, sensing the subtle gradient changes. It passed from beneath the main house and progressed into the open at a sharper angle. The torch light bobbed against the arched ceiling. An ancient, unknown architect designed it that way. It offset the weight of the earth overhead as the tunnel angled downward and threaded deeper. Emma navigated spiteful, jutting rocks protruding through the dusty floor. Her mind remained busy as she pondered a new, unwelcome notion.

Rohan owned a pair of work boots, just like Ray's. Emma wondered if he'd taken them with him or left them inside the armoury.

Rohan's greatcoat and boots just like his.

She puffed out white clouds. They fogged her vision as she wondered who would kill a poet and frame Rohan Andreyev for her murder.

The answer brought her no pleasure.

Lots of people.

And some of them were far nastier and more dangerous than others.

29

Office Chair

♥

The tunnel leaked. Green slime collected in puddles. Moss occupied cracks between the bricks as life thrived without light or air flow.

Emma kept her arms at her sides. If she stretched them out, she could touch both walls. She jumped the puddles, but Farrell strolled through them. His earlier fugue left him with depleted energy. He swept the darkness ahead without his usual enthusiasm. The torch picked up his waving tail. With his nose a few centimetres from the earth, he halted at subsequent forks. He tolerated Emma's guidance, though his body demonstrated a preference. He adored Christopher Dolan. The loyal dog still tracked the fading scent of his final, frenzied journey.

A partial collapse blocked the route to the derelict chapel. The arch had given way to the left of the keystone, raining down bricks, earth, and water. Sadness filled chest. Such destruction forced her to make tough choices. She'd avoided them for too long already. Repairing the damage meant allowing tradesmen onto the property. They would gossip in the nearby town. The Andreyevs valued their privacy. The tunnels didn't appear on the estate plans. Emma rued the day the heritage officer discovered their existence.

Anton entrusted the Hall into her care because of her skill as an archivist. He knew she'd preserve the Hall's history. She'd failed. Perhaps Ray could help. He'd stopped offering assistance as she'd squirmed beneath her overwhelm.

Emma waved the torch towards the right-hand tunnel. It rose in a gentle gradient beyond the reach of the beam. Farrell jerked into action, his steady, rhythmic four beat trot extending as he sensed victory.

The frigid air bit through Emma's padded mittens. Farrell halted to wait for her. The incline grew more taxing. White breath clouds obscured the view beyond the torch beam. Emma followed the dog as he sloshed through narrow streams of water. It saddened her. Her neglect had allowed rainwater to damage the tunnel's integrity. She would put it right.

The torch beam picked out Farrell. His tail swept the earthen floor beside a heavy wooden panel. He stared at it and whined for Christopher. The wood still contained the scent of newness, its varnish glossy in the torch light of her torch. Ray and Christopher had designed it to withstand a sledgehammer blow. Yet the mechanisms would bend beneath a gentle touch.

"He's not here anymore," Emma told the dog. She knew he didn't understand. Christopher had worked for Anton when her step brother acquired the cocker spaniel puppy. He'd served as a constant in Farrell's life until the day the government came for him. Emma pushed away her morbid regrets. She removed her right mitten and knocked on the panel with her knuckles.

The sound reverberated through the tunnel, forking and echoing back as far as the house. Emma feared someone might hear it. She covered her ears with her hands. The carabiner from the loose mitten slapped against her eye. She cursed, adding her bile to the echo. "Fine!" she snapped at the bewildered dog. "I'm sick of playing Mrs Nice. I'm going in. Hold these!"

She paused for long enough for Farrell to accept the mittens in his soft mouth. He carried them like a limp pheasant. His eyes winked with concern from above them.

Emma pressed her boot against the bottom edge of the panel, pushing but not kicking. A click reached her ears. She repeated the action, using her palms against the top edge of the door. She struggled to maintain contact, forced to rise onto tiptoes and balance on the incline. But the click resounded along the tunnel and faded at the first fork.

The panel slid inward, turning on a pivot at its centre. Farrell dodged sideways as the far edge encroached on his seat. A mitten fell to the floor. He scuffed through the earth in his efforts to retrieve it without dropping its mate. Emma relieved him of his burden and bent to fetch the other one. "Good lad," she told him, running her palm over his soft head. His dangling ears held an aching chill as she fondled them. "Let's get in the warmth," she whispered to him. His tail wagged in response.

The panel closed behind them with a push of Emma's palm. She stood in a deep but narrow cupboard. The light of her torch confirmed her bearings. A magnetic catch offered an easy exit, but Emma faltered as she pushed against the wood. On her last visit to

Christopher, she noticed a padlock. He'd cut the folly off from the main house. Panic lit a fire in her chest. She'd come this far.

Emma shouldered the door, prepared to break the hasp if she needed to. The dog rose onto his back legs to help.

The door flew open and catapulted the pair into the spacious lower floor of Rohan's hidden tech hub. Farrell recovered faster. He regained his balance with consummate expertise and landed on all four feet. Emma proved less fortunate. She hit Regan's skinny chest and slid to the floor, taking his raggedy jeans with her. "What the hell?" he shouted, kicking his feet to shake off her grip. Fluffy, knitted socks bounced before Emma's face as the denim puddled around his ankles. A pair of stripy boxer shorts maintained his remaining dignity.

Emma glanced up from the restored floorboards. "Sorry," she managed, though the word stuck in her throat. A laugh bubbled out, covering any genuineness in the apology. Regan battled with his jeans, hauling them over his narrow hips and holding them against his thin belly. Farrell alternated between them both, bumping Regan's legs before running back to sniff Emma's hair.

Regan proved unmollified as Emma pushed herself to a sitting position. Farrell retrieved her fallen mittens. He placed them into her lap, one at a time, like an offering. Her second fall of the day reminded her of earlier. She'd hit the ground in almost the same way. Her left wrist protested with more violence. "That's torn it. Do you have any anti-inflammatory pills?" Emma sighed. "I'm going to need some."

30

Chaise Lounge

♥

Emma sat on a plush sofa beside a roaring fire. Regan clattered down the stairs, settling an oversize tee shirt across his narrow torso. His arms protruded from the sleeves like twin strands of spaghetti.

Loose and stringy, his nondescript brown hair hung across his shoulders. It defied the ragged band at his nape. A long fringe obliterated one eye. He'd attended Nicky's last birthday party under duress. Staying only long enough to scrounge food in a faded Tupperware container, bolted. No one noticed him leave. He'd drifted back to the folly using the overground route and disappeared into oblivion. Emma sighed at his dishevelled appearance. His step mother would blame her for any ill health.

"Are you well?" She cleared her throat and saw confusion pass across his customary mask.

"What?" He seemed thrown by her question, tilting his head to peer through his left eye. His Adam's apple bobbed in his throat. His fingers threaded like churning water. The knuckles appeared too large for his hands. "Oh, no!" he breathed. "Am I fired? Do I need to leave? Did the Actuary send you? I messed something up, didn't I? Is this because of what happened?"

Emma blew out her ragged breath and lifted the mug of tea to her lips. She assumed he knew about the body in her hallway. The fact gave her hope. Brown bits floated on the surface and the milk smelled sour. She changed her mind and set it on the coffee table. "Why would Rohan fire you?" His alarm infected her. Her chest tightened.

Farrell stared at her through wide brown eyes. He balanced his chin on his paws and warmed himself on the rug beside the hearth. But his ears pricked high, hard angles rising from the silken folds. Emma shifted forward on the sofa and indicated the armchair opposite her. "Sit down," she commanded. "Tell me everything."

Rohan's mission went well, according to Regan. At first. He'd taken four of his ex-soldiers, including the one who drugged Emma on their first meeting. The Bank of England's chief officers had engaged the Actuary to hunt for forged twenty-pound notes. He followed the trail to the Debden Printing Works in Essex. He'd focussed on finding a leak at the single true source of English bank note manufacture. Posing as a company accountant, he'd expected to find a crooked delivery driver in league with a high-ranking employee. Only a few executives controlled the audit trail of the unique polymer paper. Regan cleared his throat. He still possessed the treble voice of a teenager. "The Actuary found something else." His eyes bulged.

Emma tilted forward in her seat as he continued. "An entrepreneurial former executive from a polymer manufacturing operation set himself up on the same industrial estate as Debden. Here's the clever part. His building adjoined the printing works. And his output required more accuracy than volume. His equipment only needed the capability for producing biaxially oriented polypropylene. That's a complicated and exacting process. If he got the paper right, the printing could happen anywhere. And did."

Emma frowned. "Explain the relevance of the location."

Excitement lit Regan's face. Baby fluff dotted his top lip and chin. "Well," he began. "The back-to-back proximity of the warehouse to the Debden site gave it the same street and postcode number. The exec added a tiny letter *b* to the Langston Road number." Regan wrinkled his sharp nose. "Legitimacy by location. Very clever. And he knew the exact recipe for the paper. He ordered the ingredients from black market suppliers. No one noticed the adjacent operation. Debden functions as a printing works and this warehouse produces paper. It seemed a natural fit. Despite the location of the genuine polymer manufacturer being a state secret."

Regan relaxed, his slender hands falling into his lap. "The truck drivers delivered supplies to the address on the docket. They believed the lie about a warehouse fire and the need for extra storage. The exec took great pains to ensure everything appeared the same. The uniform of the guard at the gate matched the header on payments and invoices. Even the fencing copied Debden's. It gave the impression of a site extension. He carried out his operation in plain sight. Leaving the signage of the previous warehouse occupant extended the ruse. Only one truck driver remembered a conversation with the gate guard. The man told him a new sign was on order."

"What did Rohan find?" Emma asked.

"He turned the legitimate company's books inside out searching for a leak. Someone must have stolen the polymer sheets and shipped them elsewhere. But only an accountant with Slavic ancestry would notice the Cyrillic б, the letter b appearing as an off kilter б in the header of a payment sent to the local power company. It replaced the third letter of Debden in all correspondence, including the email address." He clapped his hands together with glee. Pride rippled through his body like a current. "It was so subtle. Just that tiny inaccuracy facilitated the dual manufacture of the special polymer paper. It then travelled to a decent counterfeiting operation for printing overseas. Not one person in Debden gave the mirror operation a second thought. And yet they'd paid its power bill for over a year."

"Wow," Emma said with a sigh. She reached for the cooling tea with fingers which shook less. "So, Rohan spotted the anomaly and solved it. I know he took his hench mob. Guess he didn't need them. Is he on his way home?"

Regan's lips twisted in his narrow face. He cleared his throat before licking his lips. "My hacking accidentally set something in motion." Emma tensed at the flash of fear in his one visible eye. "Don't get cross," he began, his iris huge with earnest concern. Emma swallowed and set the mug on the low table.

"What?" she growled, her heart rate increasing fast enough to cause a visual disturbance. She edged forward on the deep cushion, wrestling to extract herself. "What happened?" she demanded, her voice rising.

Regan pinged from his chair with youthful ease. He watched Emma fight the cushion without helping. His lips opened and closed with an irritating click, and he clasped his hands before him. But his feet pointed towards the stairs as though he readied himself to run. "I ran over a bug at the power company. It set off an alert. So, the fake company knew they'd been discovered. It sounds worse than it is," he stated, releasing the preamble in a sing song voice. "A flesh wound. The boys promised. They got him out in time."

"What kind of flesh wound?" Emma spoke through gritted teeth. "The man has very little flesh left uninjured. What happened and how bad is it?"

"We all feel terrible. Especially the Home Office agents. And me. I didn't prepare them for opposition." Regan folded at the waist. He seemed nothing like the formidable persona of Lear which he projected online. He backed away, continuing his bow. "Just a rogue bullet from a semi-automatic when they raided the warehouse. It's gone straight through."

"Went through what? And where is my husband?" Emma shouted. "Is this why he's late?"

Regan blinked as he ordered the questions, replying in a staccato beat. "Left shoulder, missed everything important. He's at a private hospital in London. Sniper stayed with him, but the others left. His crew saved him and got him out, thank goodness. The Bank of England execs are murderous, and the Home Office is beyond embarrassed." Regan continued to back towards the stairs, clapping his palms before him in a futile act of placation. "They thought they'd arrive back here before the snow came, but the hospital wouldn't let the Actuary leave." He fixed his palm over his quavering mouth. "Infection," he mumbled.

Emma took a giant stride forward. She made it long enough to unsettle her balance, wavering as she hit the floor with her front foot. "He's sick? You're saying my husband is sick from a gunshot wound?"

"No, no! Yes! Just a precaution." Regan's spine touched the curve of the ornate wrought iron banister rail, and he bounced forward. "He wanted to tell you himself, after he got home."

"I bet he did!" Emma snarled. She jabbed a sharp index finger into Regan's concave chest muscles. "Have you forgotten where your loyalties lie?" She jabbed again. Regan's lower lip folded over on itself to reveal sparkling clean front mandibular teeth. His Adam's apple bobbed twice before she released him.

She sank into his vacated armchair and put her face in her hands.

Regan inhaled as the sob rocked Emma's body. Her emotion froze his unique brain. He owned no blueprint for extreme female emotion. Susan, his step mother was blind and stoic. It split his loyalties between Emma and the Actuary. He couldn't answer her question. Instead, he squirmed in discomfort.

Emma reached the end of her last nerve. Rohan was missing in action again. People who hated her had invaded her home. And a dead woman leaked on her hall floor.

Emma wept, comforted by Farrell's wet nose pressed against her knee.

Regan watched like a statue by the stairs. Emma sensed his misanthropic introvert's mind exploding. He couldn't help her.

31

Papasan Chair

♥

"Mrs Andreyeva?"

Emma had dried her eyes on her jacket sleeve and sat with her forearms resting along her thighs. She missed her children with a palpable ache in her soul. They were less than a mile away, but without communication it felt like the other side of the earth.

She sniffed, a disgusting, guttural sound. Not yet ready to face Regan with her puffy eyes, she picked at a strand of moss clinging to Farrell's fluffy neck. "Do the tunnels go beneath the old stables?" she asked, her tone flat. If Regan answered yes, it meant she'd walked right under her children without knowing it. She could have touched the damp brick roof and perhaps felt their combined energy coursing through the earth.

"I don't know." Regan's knotty fingers appeared in her peripheral vision. They held a glass of water. It sloshed with his nervousness. The other palm opened like a bud to reveal a blister pack containing ibuprofen. "For your injuries." The hand bobbed and Emma took the offerings.

"Thanks." She blew out a steadying breath before popping the tablets into her mouth. The gulp of water made her cough. She catapulted the empty plastic wrap onto the sparking logs. It melted, sighing blue flames. "And sorry." She bowed her head, ashamed of her meltdown. Especially in front of Regan. She'd known he couldn't cope with it, but the emotion had burst from her like shards of glass exploding from a smashed window.

Emma set the glass on the table beside the cooling tea. She forced herself into a mental state of acceptance. "I have a problem," she began, lifting her gaze to Regan. "More than one. I need your help." He shifted before her, every muscle in perpetual motion. It created a blur around his edges. Her eyes tried and failed to pinpoint a landmark. As though sensing her difficulty, he backed towards the curved banister and pressed his spine against its constancy.

Emma told him about her unwanted visitors. She described her fall in the downstairs hallway and the discovery of Kathleen Dubois' dead body. "I sent you some photos," she told him. "Didn't you see them?" Her fingers closed over the phone in her pocket, but she paused.

"Perhaps you didn't get them. I lost my data and now my phone signal. The land-line isn't working either. The snow must have affected the cables."

Regan's nose twitched on one side, like a cute mouse scenting cheese. To her surprise, he reached out his hand for the phone. He crossed the distance between them before retreating with the device. Glancing at the screen, he scrolled through the morbid gallery.

Emma edged forward on the cushion and sighed. It sucked her bottom into its stuffing. She stroked the hard fabric with her right palm, sensing Christopher favoured this seat during his long, lonely evenings. Probably making mischief on his phone and luring a young man into peril. Emma gulped, the sound high and squeaky. "Ray received them, so they must be on your server."

Regan blinked up at her. "I haven't seen them." He bowed his head in a solemn, jerky nod. "The Actuary told me to grab some sleep for a few hours. Perhaps they arrived then. You woke me with your hammering on the cupboard door."

Emma pursed her lips but didn't apologise.

Regan turned the screen from side to side. "What makes you think someone killed her?" His fingers performed a pinching action as he enlarged the image. "She looks sick. Maybe she wanted fresh air and fell in the dark."

"I thought so too," Emma admitted. "Until her daughter turned her onto her back. There's a cut which runs in a diagonal across her right side." Her eyelids fluttered closed as nausea rose into her chest. "There's no blood. It looks like someone tried to chop off her head with a straight object. It hit her cheek bone hard."

"Ah yes." Regan seemed intrigued. His shoulders hunched around his concave chest. He scrolled until the gory images ended. The twitch of his lips suggested he'd found the images Nicky took of Stephie's tonsils. He didn't hand the phone back to her. His deft fingers scrolled through something Emma couldn't see. "You need to reset the main router," he mused. The mousey lashes fringing his eyes fluttered. "I'll do it from upstairs. That should restore data. There's no reason for that failing." His lower jaw twisted as though sliding itself free of his skull. "Unless someone sabotaged it."

"The router is in my bedroom with the Wi-Fi unit," Emma said. "Rohan installed boosters around the house to improve connectivity. Someone could turn off the boosters and it would become glitchy. But not near my bedroom. Then I'd pick up a direct signal."

"So, what happened when you tried that?" Regan nailed her with the glare of a strategist. His quick mind gathered data for a theory.

Emma coughed with embarrassment. "I didn't try my phone up there. Too much happened at the same time." Her brows drew together in concentration, thinking of the damaging flood beneath the bath and Gwendoline's ire. "I didn't lock my door when I went downstairs in the early hours. Someone used my ensuite shower but I'm not sure who. Freda didn't lock the door until much later. It's possible anyone could have unplugged the router or Wi-Fi unit. But why?" She shook her head, struggling to order her thoughts. "It makes no sense."

"Winston Wright appeared in the main house this morning. Did you know that?" Regan's lashes fluttered like butterfly wings.

Emma tutted. "Who made that decision? Rohan?" Her jaw clenched at the twitch of Regan's left shoulder. "Nice! He tells me to stay away from his father and then invites him home!"

"Only for the weekend. He had his reasons. The team expected to arrive back on Thursday night, but the bullet wound scuppered that plan. He made a split decision. Ray fetched Mr Andreyev's father from town on Friday morning while you took the children to school. He's staying in the coach house."

Emma exhaled. "That explains why he appeared suited and booted so early in the morning. The coach house is close to the downstairs hallway. I wonder if he heard me fall over the body in the night."

Regan shrugged. "He can't contact me and he's off limits from me calling him. I have no visibility inside the house."

"Unlike your predecessor," Emma muttered. She wondered if she regretted forcing Rohan to strip out Christopher's nanny cameras in the main house. He'd seen and heard everything. The notion still induced a sense of bone weary sickness. Everything.

She gave herself another mental shake. "I felt someone's presence last night when I visited Allaine.

Why didn't you put my mind at rest? I could have settled, knowing Winston went on the prowl."

Regan blinked through his visible eye. His fringe clattered the lashes of the other. "I checked the cameras, Mrs Andreyeva. Even the recording. I traced your walk from the stable yard to the front door. You were alone."

Emma dropped her chin. Disbelief beat a tattoo in her chest. "I'm losing it," she murmured. But the surety didn't leave her. "Where's Christopher Dolan?" she asked, her tone tight.

Regan tutted. "Mr Andreyev asked that same question before he left." He lifted his free hand and scratched his scalp. More fine tendrils floated from the band's weak captivity to frame his slender face. He sniffed, a portend of doom he'd rather not share. "I can't find him. The government kept him in a maximum security jail after the trial. He's disappeared." When Regan shook his head, his hair tapped his jawline. "He's still in custody. We just don't know where."

A groan broke free of Emma's pursed lips. "I don't suggest you bet on him still being in prison." Her tone held an unexpected spikiness. Regan frowned as she added. "The odds are not in your favour."

32

Eames Lounge Chair

♥

"Do you have camera footage from outside the kitchen? Rohan told me he'd covered the weak points. Can we look at what happened during the night?" Emma gnawed on the inside of her cheek as she focussed on her more pressing matter. The body in her hallway. She headed towards the stairs leading to the second floor and Regan's technology centre. "Do you still have data in here?" she demanded. "Or a phone line?"

"We use satellite phones for jobs." Regan sprang up the stairs behind her. "And yes, I have internet. I told you, someone's disconnected the router for the main house."

Emma halted on the landing, grunting as he catapulted against her spine. "Why don't I have a cell phone signal? And no land-line? Did someone deliberately remove our communication so we couldn't get help?"

Regan shook his head. "No, there's a problem with the nearest tower. The overhead wires for the land-line failed under the weight of the snow." He navigated around her and entered his throne room. Once, massive cables hung from the ceiling, ferrying information and power to the vast servers. Black and cornflower blue, the heavy wires resembled mismatched washing lines. None remained.

Emma gaped at the clinical space. It resembled a NASA mission centre. Not the chaos Christopher favoured. Tiny steps carried her over the threshold and into a space which had once seemed familiar and safe. She no longer knew this place.

Regan slumped into an expensive swivel chair and frowned at her confusion. "I couldn't cope with the disorder he left." He flapped his thin fingers towards the wall to his left after following her gaze. "I'm affected by visual disturbance. It plays hell with my brain. Ray helped me to hide the mess behind trunking."

Emma studied the odd shadow beneath the coving. She blinked, recognising the thin, boxy plastic structure running along each junction with the ceiling. It extended in perpendicular lines down the corners, creating gentle angles which created a rotund illusion. An immaculate spirit governed the fastidious cleanliness of the hub of the Actuary's business. Rohan couldn't function without this hidden data centre. She sensed the new order would gain his approval. Though still young, Regan oozed capability within his sphere of existence. His fingers coursed across the nearest keyboard like bubbling water over rounded stones. Windows popped open on his monitor. They vanished before Emma saw their contents. Pop, pop, pop. They appeared at the speed of a blink, boxes overlapping like Tetris. When their colours darkened to navy and the fonts winked white on the screen, Emma knew he'd delved into code.

"Unplugged." He smacked his lips as he spoke. "Whoever knocked off your Wi-Fi just unplugged the router."

"But it's in my bedroom." Emma's voice wavered. With no other chair on offer, she dug her shaking fingers into her pockets. She stared at the glass wall which bisected the room. Red lights blinked from the racks of black servers staged within the transparent vault. As Regan scrolled through another set of windows on his monitor, a white light flickered like a dying star. His fingers blurred across the keyboard.

"Yeah, I can't ping the router at all," he declared. His lips twisted into a grimace. "You need to plug it in."

"You realise the killer went into my bedroom?" Emma enunciated each word.

Regan shrugged. "They killed a woman in your hallway. What difference does it make?" He grinned. A chipped front tooth hindered an infectious smile. His expression faded as he remembered his manners. She'd saved him. He hadn't forgotten. His body jolted as though electrified, and his eyes widened. "Sorry, Mrs Andreyeva," he breathed. He employed the female intonation of her Slavic name.

She sighed. "Regan, it's fine. You're right. They're in my house and apparently have access to my bedroom." She turned her head to see the blinking light had slowed its frantic strobing. "Please, can we see the camera footage?"

Regan attacked his keyboard with fervour. Emma sensed his growing discomfort as his head jerked back on his neck. "Can't. I need the Wi-Fi to access the footage stored on the server," he declared. His fingers slowed their frantic stroking. "They might have recorded the images, but I can't link to them." His neck clicked as his head bobbed from side to side. "It's a significant weak point to the system. I'm pleased we've found it."

Emma's feet tapped the floor. She didn't share his enthusiasm. It meant she couldn't catch the murderer with the ease she'd hoped. Glancing down, she realised she hadn't removed her damp boots and grimaced with shame. A cursive peek behind her showed a drying trail of footprints. "So, nobody foresaw this security weakness?" Her tone held a bite to cover her guilt.

Regan shrugged. "It's never happened before."

"So, the internet has never just gone down before today?" The last five words of her sentence rung in the airwaves, filled with sarcasm and frustration.

"Not in the hub." Regan's lips flapped like a fish, desperate for its final breath. "But it's a vulnerability. We'll rig up a fix. Soon."

"But not now?" Emma's voice sounded brittle. "Right now, I have to go back to a house full of murderers and plug in the router?"

Regan cleared his throat. "Sorry, but yes. Do you want me to come with you?" His body gave an involuntary shudder as he contemplated the awful scenario of communing with other humans. He also hated tight spaces. The tunnels would cause him to freak out way beyond her ability to soothe or cajole him through them.

Emma exhaled. Her shoulders slumped. Every one of Regan's shortcomings made him perfect for Rohan's operation. Better than the wandering Christopher, always out for a smoke or a one-night stand when Rohan needed him at his keyboard. Emma squeezed Regan's bony shoulder, regretting the intimacy when he squirmed away from her. His lips widened in a horrified grimace.

"You're good," she said with a shallow nod. "Stay here and monitor things." The words hung in the air. The downed router rendered him blind to her peril. He couldn't assist her in any forthcoming disaster.

Emma shook herself, an action like Farrell's. As if on cue, the dog whined from the bottom of the stairs. Emma popped her head over the banister rail. He wagged his ebony tail. Hope blossomed in his sparkling brown eyes. He'd placed his front paws on the lowest step but hadn't dared to venture further. Emma imagined Regan breaking out the vacuum cleaner as soon as they left. Would he expunge their existence from his clinical eyrie immediately? Or would he tease himself with the traces of dog hair woven into the rug and Emma's damp footprints on the floorboards? Until he could stand it no longer.

Emma clattered down the stairs and met the dog's happy whines. He twisted and turned around her legs, bumping her knees and bounding towards the cupboard. "Let's go then." She forced enthusiasm into the words. Yet she dreaded the dampness, the fetid scent and the echo of her lonely footsteps. Farrell snatched up the torch she'd left beside the door. The weight of its batteries hauled his head into a lopsided angle. But his eyes still smiled as dribble coated the handle. Regan spotted the speckled saliva and tears filled his eyes as he held in the burgeoning vomit.

The cupboard door opened with a click. Emma pressed her palm and heel against the requisite catches to deactivate the lock on the hidden panel. The dog bounded into the darkness. Damp air circled Emma's face and licked at her cheeks. Farrell took the torch with him, bashing it against the wall and almost knocking out his teeth. "Fetch it here!" Emma called. Her voice echoed beyond the panel as a plea.

Regan gave a sharp inhale of breath. He perhaps expected the dog to drop the torch on the hard floor and smash the bulb. But he didn't. Farrell poked his head back through the gap, bashing his teeth for a second time. Emma took the long torch, and he released it with extreme care. He paused to shake his body as though throwing off the accident. A shudder ran from nose to tail. He bounded away in the darkness as though he hadn't just brained himself twice. His claws clicked away into the tunnel, leaving Emma behind.

"Is he okay?" Regan wrung his hands before him, the knuckles white. "Will he wait for you?"

Emma forced a smile onto her lips. "He's fine." She brushed off the dog's foolhardiness. "Spaniels never stray far. He'll sweep ahead and come back for me."

"Right." Regan blinked as though disbelieving her. But Farrell's clicking claws echoed louder as he returned, proving Emma right.

She stepped into the tunnel and halted, her hand on the panel. "Did you check out the caterers?" she asked.

Regan's brows drew into an unkempt, mousey line. "Oh, yes!" Panic flitted across his sharp features as the cold air seeped into his warm existence. He swallowed, caught in indecision.

"The quick version," Emma suggested.

"Something isn't right," he gushed, taking a step closer to the cupboard. "I searched the police database and found a complaint about the husband. Gareth. He uses several names and runs a cowboy building firm. I found an outstanding warrant for him. They arrested him last night, but then released him on police bail. There's nothing about the woman. It's as if the two guys with her just don't exist. Not with facial recognition software or those first names."

"Yeah." Emma gulped. "Chloe said they let Gareth out. What if he travelled here and killed Kathleen Dubois?"

Regan's lips spread in discomfort to reveal his teeth. "The weather turned nasty. He'd struggle to get a ride this far. And even though the cameras at the main house stopped working, I still had oversight of the gate and the boundaries. I'd get an alert if he came back onto the property."

Emma raised her eyebrows. "A text alert?"

"No. It's an app. I got an alert for the main house cameras but didn't see it." His features creased with failure and regret. "It came in after midnight. I'm sorry."

"Then it's incorrect," Emma replied. "I only left my room unlocked once last night. I returned to the kitchen after doling out bedrooms. Farrell would have barked up a storm if a stranger walked in and poked around." She shook her head, unable to solve the mystery. "What's the complaint about the husband? Gareth." Her features screwed into a grimace at his name.

Regan tutted. "That's the weird part. I can't see all the information. Someone redacted things like the complainant's name."

"What does that mean?" Emma frowned, her fingers gripping the edge of the panel. She flicked on the torch with her other hand. Its beam played over the fine tendrils of a dangling cobweb. She glanced at Regan and shifted the angle so as not to send him into an extended cleaning frenzy.

He shrugged, bemusement creasing his brow. "I don't know," he mused. "Something big."

"Like terrorism?" Emma's eyes widened. Had she left the companions of a terrorist running amok in her home? "I felt sympathy for his wife last night." She gnawed on her lower lip. "But she's prickly. Her relationship with Dyfed and Ridley is odd."

"The Actuary will know," Regan concluded. He anointed Rohan with the crown of omniscience like a star struck teenager.

Emma nodded and stared into the tunnel. She'd put it off long enough. A pair of sparkly eyes winked at her from the darkness. Farrell waited with forced patience for her to join his adventure. "Do you have a spare satellite phone?" she asked, her voice little more than a squeak.

Regan pursed his lips. "Sorry. I need the one I have. Sort out your router. I'll message you as soon as I hear from the Actuary."

"Thank you," Emma replied. Her voice reverberated as though a crowd of grateful onlookers lined her way. "I'm guessing Ray has a satellite phone?" She raised an eyebrow, but Regan neither confirmed nor denied the question. His features remained symmetrical and rigidified, as though he'd hauled a mask over his proper face. He didn't even blink. Emma stepped into the tunnel. She tugged her mittens from her pocket and hauled them over her already frozen fingers. "Well, if Ray has a sat phone, call him and tell him to get a move on." She pressed the panel closed behind her without waiting for a reply.

33

Ghost Chair

♥

Emma hadn't used the tunnels much during her time at Wingate Hall. It took her a while to catch on to their existence. Only her son's mysterious appearance in places she least expected him, made her question his wizardry. She'd used the underground route to the folly once. Christopher spent most of his time in the family's kitchen. Her thoughts turned to him again. She hated the thread of betrayal which wormed its way through her mind. "Till death do us part." She murmured the words of her marriage ceremony, aged sixteen. She'd stood opposite a pink cheeked Rohan, nineteen, fresh from army maneuvers, and king of the world. And she'd married him, because she loved him. She still did.

A warm flush worked its way into her chest as she hurried through the tunnel. Regan said the bullet went straight through. He'd survived. Rohan would return soon. Emma's lips curved upward as she imagined his polite disdain for the fussing of medics. Stoic and brave, he'd meet their concern with a stone wall constructed of past disappointment. Emma hugged her arms around herself, the torch light bouncing off the ceiling. "Sorry I behaved like an idiot, Ro," she whispered. Her words returned as an echo, caressing her soul as her boots settled on level ground. A change in the temperature warned her to slow, not wanting the echo of her steps to boom below the house.

Farrell waited at the panel leading to the butler's pantry. His eyes glinted in the torch beam. His tail engaged in its constant swishing.

"Faz, sit," Emma commanded. His bottom hovered over the cold ground. He didn't want to. With a grimace of disgust, he planted it on the earthen floor. The tail ceased its motion in protest. "Listen," she told him. His head tilted from side to side, his ears spiked and angular. Emma remained still. She allowed him to filter out her breathing from noise on the other side of the door. He turned to her with his lower teeth showing. A smile, not a snarl. He blew out a sneeze. Emma's shoulders lost their tension. He'd sensed the way clear beyond the panel. "Okay," she said, pushing on the metal bar. It opened with such unexpected ease, she lost her balance and tipped forward.

Strong fingers closed around her flailing forearms. A scream bubbled into her throat. One hand released her, and she crashed face first into a hard, muscular chest. The same hand shifted over her mouth, gripping her cheeks and trapping the breath in her nostrils. Her brain relayed its terror of suffocation. She forgot every lesson in self-defense training. The heavy torch gave a metallic clang as it hit the floor and rolled out of reach. Emma slid the length of the man's body until her sore knee smashed against the unforgiving tiles. A grunt burst through her gritted teeth.

The dog's tail whacked her in the face. A rough voice said, "Emma, it's me." He supported her elbow as her other knee sank to the floor with less force. She knelt there as though in prayer. His familiar scent filled the narrow space, overlaid with a hint of sweat.

"That dog is useless!" Emma wiped her shaking hand across her mouth. The mitten tasted of dust. "He didn't warn me." She knelt between the shelves and pulled both gloves from her hands. Then she scrubbed her fists over her face. The overhead glare from the bulb made her eyes water. It distorted her vision. The torch beam shone on a spider's web beneath the furthest shelf.

Ray spoke. "The command to *listen* tells him to stay alert for a threat." He ruffled the dog's ears as Farrell stood on his back legs. His front paws rested against the man's flat stomach. "I'm not a threat, am I Faz?" His voice drawled a syrup-laden tone as though he spoke to a baby.

"I didn't know that." Emma blew out her ragged breath and pushed herself upright. Farrell dropped to all fours. He rammed his nose against her thigh, as though apologising. When she resisted his beseeching gaze, he retrieved both her mittens and dropped them at Ray's feet. The big man bent, collected them in one hand, and stuffed them into the pocket of his camouflage jacket.

Emma pressed her hand over her heart. The painful thudding dulled to a steady throb. "I'm glad you're here." She avoided Ray's gaze. "Did Regan contact you?"

"Lear." He corrected her without rebuke, his voice retaining the gentle instruction of a loving parent. "Yes, he told me to hurry. So, I did."

Emma nodded. "On your satellite phone." Tiredness nagged at her skull, forming an ache which rose from neck to temples. It clamped with the gentle vice of a knitted hat. A greater pressure threatened. "Is Paul with you?" Her voice sounded small and distant. "Did you know Rohan got shot?"

"Yes, and yes," he replied. "I left Paul upstairs staring at the body. He thinks I'm using the bathroom. He can't know about the tunnels. And the captain was unlucky. It sucks."

"It all sucks," Emma murmured. Ray's presence seemed to lighten her load. But it left behind a crushing emptiness. "Did you see the children?" Her arms hugged her torso as though she clasped them tight against her chest.

"They're fine," he promised. His gaze softened. "The snow blocked the stairs, but I scraped away as much as I could manage off the balcony. I'll need to reinforce the supports before next winter. That drift must weigh a ton. We tipped all the salt I could find onto the balcony. The kids can at least come outside once it melts. But we left the stairs impassable. Otherwise Allaine won't manage to keep your son out of danger." He patted his top pocket. "The sat phone is useless, Em. We've called the cops and they can't get here. The snow is too deep, and the blizzard prevents helicopters from flying or landing. We're trapped here."

Emma nodded. "Did you tell Allaine what happened?" Tears prickled her eyes. "She can't let Nicky come home while there's a murderer on the property."

"She knows." Ray's heavy hand landed on Emma's shoulder as though holding down a helium balloon. "She'll keep them safe."

Emma sighed, her chest tightening. "Perhaps Allaine should just tell Nicky the truth," she said. "He's more likely to cooperate."

"Are we good now?" Ray tilted his head to observe her.

Emma nodded. "Did you see Winston?"

Ray growled low in his throat. "I sent him back to the coach house. We don't need Paul asking questions about him." He frowned and the pressure on Emma's shoulder grew as he kept her in place with his giant hand. "But why did he find my old work boots on the hearth in your bedroom? Is there something I should know?"

34

Bean-bag

♥

"My bedroom? My hearth?" Emma stared down at the newer tan boots encasing Ray's enormous feet. Her lips flapped, but no more sound emerged.

"Yes." Ray squinted at her. "The old man said you told him to search for some missing boots. He found mine in your bedroom by the fire."

"My room?" The puzzle pieces slid around in her mind. They ground together in protest as she fitted them into the wrong spaces. "The murderer wore them outside." Her voice rose. "How did they put them in my bedroom afterwards? I was asleep. I locked the door." Hysteria bubbled beneath the surface, seconds from an eruption.

Ray slipped his arm around her shoulders after dipping to recover the torch. "We'll sort it out," he promised.

"And how did Winston get a master key?" Emma halted and turned to face Ray. "Do you think he did this? He wanders around my house at night like an uninvited ghoul. Could he have killed Kathleen and draped her in Rohan's greatcoat? What if he got your boots and made stamping marks outside the door before hiding them in my room? Is this his revenge on Rohan?"

To her surprise, Ray snorted. Laughter rumbled deep in his chest. "That old man is too leery to do his own dirty work. If he wanted revenge on his son, he wouldn't play games with him first. He owns guys who don't ask questions. His justice is fast and clean. No one sees it coming."

Emma swallowed, the sound a loud gulp in the narrow room. She didn't ask Ray how he'd learned such information. She didn't doubt its truth. Winston Wright had a fluid edginess to his movements and a keen eye. It withered any beauty it encountered. She'd sensed his intensity many times. His tolerance for her stretched only as far as his toxic relationship with her husband allowed. She shivered, knowing he hankered after Nicky. He wanted another protégé to twist into a killing machine. As he had his own son.

"Regan. Sorry, Lear," she corrected herself. "Lear said Rohan invited Winston to stay in the coach house. Why would he do that? He doesn't want him near Nicky."

Ray shrugged, the movement ricocheting through Emma's shoulders. "Take it up with your husband," he replied.

"Is Paul here?" Her voice wavered.

"Yeah. He's seen the body. I left him speaking with the victim's husband and nipped down here to intercept you."

Paul Barker greeted Emma with an amiable smile, despite Kathleen's body still splayed at his feet. He wrapped his arms around her and kissed the top of her head. Ray's eyes bugged wide behind him at the over familiarity. "Sorry you had to go through this," Paul crooned. "You did great with the photos before the cell tower lost signal." He released her but held her at arm's length. His fingers gripped her shoulders. His doleful eyes peered at her with concern. "You're freezing," he noted, his keen gaze picking up her pink nose and cheeks. "How did you get outside? Snow drifts have blocked all the external doors."

"I didn't," Emma replied. She couldn't look at Ray. "I went into the basement to check the old freezer in the servants' hall. I thought we could store Kathleen in it for now." Nausea bubbled into her chest in a rising tide of fear and acid. But a giggle burst from her lips instead. "Put the poet in the freezer." The hand over her mouth couldn't stem the flow. She swore, but it wouldn't stop. The giggles just kept coming.

Alarmed, Paul glanced at his father. His expertise didn't extend to hysterical women.

"She dropped the torch," Ray said, waving it in his right hand. But another sight distracted him, and he also swore. "The bloody dog's licking the corpse!" he announced. "Farrell, get here! Bad dog. Leave the lady alone."

Emma barked out another laugh as Paul hauled the dog away by his collar. His fun spoiled, Farrell slunk to Ray's side. His tail curved between his rear legs like a hook. "She wrote a horrible poem about me." The words escaped before she could stop them. Paul's alertness pushed the hysteria down and nausea replaced it again.

"She what?" His eyes narrowed and his shoulders squared. Emma just handed him a motive for killing Kathleen. She landed in the frame with the deft footing of a ballerina. "Where is it?" Paul demanded, his tone hardening. His handsome features became hawk-like and predatory.

Emma glanced at Ray too late, seeing the tail end of his emphatic head shake. And she wondered in that moment of doom what she'd ever found to laugh about. Or if she'd ever laugh again.

Crinkles and dents had added themselves to the sheet of lined paper during its sojourn in Emma's pocket. The tunnel's dampness had blurred the ink. She tugged it free, the folds already furring and torn. "Sorry," she murmured, her tone loaded with contrition. "I forgot about it until now." As she spoke, the wax candle plunged to the tiles and snapped in half. It appeared sausage-like by the wick which trailed through both parts. The matches followed and Emma pursed her lips.

Paul reached into his own pocket and disgorged a translucent bag. It bore the words *freezer size* across a white label. She recognised the brand from her pantry. He parted the bag like a zippy mouth and flapped it at her. "Open it out and put it in here," he ordered.

Emma's hand shook as she obeyed. The corners snagged against the opening.

Ray watched, paralysed at the spectacle of his son besting his employer's stupid wife. Emma saw him shake himself in her peripheral vision. He stepped forward, dislodging Farrell from his seat on Ray's left boot. A heavy hand clamped over Emma's shoulder. "For goodness' sake!" he blurted, fixing narrowed eyes on his son. Paul ignored him, his fingers pinching along the seal of the bag. "Emma didn't kill her!" Ray's voice rose and Paul blinked up in surprise.

"Then she' has nothing to worry about," he replied.

"That's no kind of answer!" A warning vein pulsed beneath Ray's jaw. "I didn't strap tennis racquets to my feet and tramp across a bloody snow drift so you could arrest Emma." His nerves frayed. Ray placed his body between his son and Emma. He spread his arms out wide, his fingers tickling the air before he found her frozen body. Then he pressed her against his spine as though readying himself to defend her. Even against his own son.

"I'm not arresting her, Dad!" A gasp accompanied the sentence. "I don't believe she did it. But I'm a cop! It's my job to follow the evidence." He waggled the bag in his left hand. Air had created a dome around Kathleen's spiteful poem. "This is evidence."

"Of what?" Ray demanded. His voice boomed along the corridor, bouncing off the walls like a dinner gong. "Of a set-up?"

Emma blew out a tired breath. Her forehead touched Ray's jacket. She closed her eyes as his shoulder blades bunched beneath the contact. "Rohan can't arrive home to this mess," she whispered, keeping her voice low. His arms tightened around her in a backward embrace. He'd come to the same conclusion. "I need to sleep," she announced, releasing herself from his grasp. "Use your own key to the basement. Check the freezer before you plug it into the mains. It's ancient but empty." She knew this from memory, but the information covered her journey into the bowels of Wingate Hall.

Ray turned to face her. His expression paled as she walked towards the back staircase on heavy steps. Farrell set off with her, the clicking of his claws ceasing as his paws transferred from tile to carpet. Emma paused half way up to lever off her boots. She dropped them over the banister at the first dogleg, enjoying the satisfying twin clunks of them hitting the tiles. She padded up the rest of the way in her socks, pressing her feet into the plush, plum coloured carpet on the second floor. The dog's head bobbed level with her right knee.

Finding her bedroom door still locked, Emma withdrew the master key from her jacket pocket. "Did Winston plant those boots?" she asked. Farrell waited with intense patience. The door slid open, and he dashed through the gap, almost catching himself on the door frame. Satiated by his breakfast and exhausted by his stressful dash through the tunnels, he pounced on his bed beside the fire. The force of his arrival skidded the squashy cushion so one side peeked over the edge of the tiled hearth. Emma locked the door behind her.

Crouching beside the fire, she reached over the prostrate dog and threw another log into the smouldering ash. Though tiredness tugged at her eyelids, she resisted clambering into the wide bed without Rohan. She settled onto the sheepskin hearthrug, still wearing her outdoor jacket. Through narrowed eyes, she studied the tongues of orange flame as they tasted the new fuel. Farrell snored on his comfy bed, his paws twitching as he relived his explorations through the tunnels. Emma reached out and touched the smooth, tiled edge of the hearth, wondering where Winston found Ray's work boots.

Sleep snatched her, sucking away the stress, the fear, and the ache in her bones. It plunged her into a different darkness to the tunnel's. This blackness included the warmth of the fire as it crackled to life. And it sheltered her in a safe nest with her babies and her husband.

Until it expelled her with a cruel rush of blood and the sense that something was very wrong.

35

Hammock

♥

Emma loomed from the rug like a leviathan seeking the surface. Her scratchy eyes refused to open, and her fingers found a stickiness on her cheek. The dog towered over her, whining low in his chest. With his gaze fixed and staring, he regarded the bedroom door and then Emma, as though unable to choose between them. Emma braced her palms against the rug. She struggled to raise herself from the deepest part of her sleep cycle.

The frantic knocking on the bedroom door caused Farrell to whine again. He dropped his nose to Emma's head and ruffled her hair. She crawled across the bedroom floor with him flanking her. Lifting her left arm to unlock the door, her wrist tweaked. The blossoming ache took her breath away. "Just wait!" she urged, crawling sideways as the door edged open.

Farrell greeted the newcomer with enthusiasm. The swishing strokes of his tail blinded Emma. She recognised the brief flashes of Freda's slippers as they padded past her before arriving at her knees. After having his welcome ignored, Farrell blinked against the draught which poured in behind the guest. He stood on his back paws and pushed at the door. It slammed, and he dropped to all fours and padded back to his bed. He slumped onto the warm cushion with an extended groan which matched his irritation at the rude awakening.

"Why are you wearing waterproof pants? Do you have the vapours?" Freda crouched in front of Emma, oblivious to the fart which escaped her compressed intestines. It exited her buttocks with a loud pop.

Emma grunted. "Nice to note that despite a catastrophe and a tragedy, you're maintaining your 1950s persona."

"It's not a persona! This is who I am." Freda rose and released another fart. She swished her fallen scarf around her head. It looked more mummified than 1950s duchess. Farrell raised his head and shot a glare of indignation at Emma. It served as a silent denial of culpability. Nicky would have cackled like a parrot. She missed her son's antics and her daughter's kisses. She twisted her wrist as though the physical pain might banish her maudlin thoughts.

"So, did you faint, or what?" Freda demanded.

"I'm tired," Emma grumbled. "You woke me. I hope it's not to ask what's for lunch. Let them eat cake." She wriggled free of the crinkly waterproof trousers without standing up. Folding them into a neat square, she threw them onto the armchair.

Freda lowered her spectacles onto the end of her nose and stared down at Emma. Vertical lines scored her pale forehead. She ignored the cake reference to Marie Antoinette. "I'm sorry," she whispered. "I know you're cross with me. You look terrible."

Emma exhaled, too tired to discuss the disastrous weekend with a woman wearing her slippers on the wrong feet. Freda stood with her toes rounded like an ocean wake embracing the bow of a ship. "I've moved beyond irritation, through the river of mortification, and washed up on the banks of despair," Emma replied. She rubbed her eyes with the knuckles of her hands. Again, her wrist protested. She tugged back the sleeve of her heavy jacket to see a blue bruise snaking from the heel of her left hand. It headed along the underside of her radius. "Great! I think I've broken my wrist," she announced. "I fell over Kathleen, but my fingers were so cold I didn't notice the extent of the damage. Repeating the experience again didn't help." She avoided mentioning her trip to Regan's lair.

"Can Ray fix it?" Freda sank into the armchair beside the dressing table. Air from the plastic pants sighed beneath her weight. "He's messing around downstairs with his son." Her eyebrows waggled above her glasses. One had smudged almost into oblivion, leaving her with a startled expression.

"What are they doing now?" Emma smothered a yawn with her good hand and sent a longing glance at her bed. She could change her mind and clamber onto the comfy mattress, with or without Rohan.

"That's what I came to tell you." Freda shifted in the armchair. She fiddled with the floral headscarf but had discarded the heavy overcoat. "Gwendoline can't stop crying. I'm surprised her screaming didn't wake you earlier. She soaked Christos' lapels with her tears. I'm not sure why. Her mother behaved like an absolute bitch to her. Kathleen robbed every ounce of confidence that girl ever possessed. But it all started when the major wanted more tea. That Chloe woman refused to fetch it. She's commandeered the seats by the fire with her weird companions. Claims she's not lifting another finger unless we pay her an hourly rate. So, the major ventured into the kitchen to find you. Instead, he discovered Ray mopping up a lake of urine on the hall floor." She bugged her eyes as though waiting for Emma's full attention. "Kathleen is in the basement freezer." She delivered the sentence by bobbing forward in the seat. "Like a joint of lamb." She snapped her fingers. "Take that! Who's the old faggot now?"

Emma grunted. "Paul needed to preserve the scene, but he couldn't. So, he's done the next best thing." She yawned again. "I'm glad they've moved her, though. It felt wrong with her splayed across the hallway with that hole in her face."

Freda reeled back in shock. "What hole?" she demanded. "She died from a virus. Didn't she?" Her eyes lit with a surreal sparkle. She pressed her hands together at her chest until the knuckles whitened. "Did someone take the bitch out?" She clapped with glee.

Emma exhaled, blaming exhaustion for her error of judgement. She raised her hands in a placatory gesture. "Freda, you can't tell anyone," she begged. "Not even to get one up on Mavis."

Freda's lashes fluttered closed. One appeared wonky, a creature with fake bristles making a hasty exit. "Did they shoot her in the face?"

"No!"

"Chopped her with a machete?"

"No!"

"A cleaver? A mallet?" She dipped forward and back, rocking in a haze of dramatic ecstasy.

"Freda! Stop!" Emma begged.

"A rake? A bread board? A shovel?"

Emma's lungs stuck on an inhale. She stared at the old woman in shock. "Damn and double damn!" She pushed herself to a standing position with the help of the door knob. It turned beneath her fingers as she rose. "The shovel!" she hissed to Freda. "I think the killer used my shovel to kill Kathleen!"

36

Director's Chair

"Amystery!" Freda clapped her thin fingers together. They looked brittle enough to snap at the knuckles. She followed Emma down the main staircase at a geriatric trot. The headscarf swept across her right eye, the fringe bumping her nose. Still, she glided down with the blind grace of Mata Hari. "Won't you lock your bedroom door?" she called after Emma. "What if someone goes in there again and uses your stuff? What if they unplug the fangle-dangle thing again?"

"I told Farrell to guard the room." Emma glanced back at her. She gasped as Freda tripped. Emma swung her arm out wide to catch the old woman's hasty descent. "Be careful!" she warned. Freda ignored her. "Someone has a key. They unplugged the router and placed Ray's boots on the hearth to cause confusion."

"But even I don't have a master key," Freda mused. "Perhaps they picked the lock?" She grasped Emma's forearm without warning. Perhaps momentarily aware of her own frailty, she didn't wish to discuss it. She paused on the third stair from the bottom and forced Emma to halt beside her. "What would Rohan think if he arrived home and discovered another man's boots by the fire in his bedroom?"

Emma exhaled. "Terrible, murderous thoughts. You think this is more about my marriage than Kathleen's death?"

Freda closed her lips like a clamp. She wouldn't pursue the matter further. But the question set Emma moving along a path filled with dark surmising and zero facts. The boots belonged to Ray. Had ex-army sergeant Raymond Barker made it onto someone's nasty list?

Emma sent Freda into the morning room to mollify her guests. Then she ducked around the lobby sofa and the curtain. The faint scent of urine remained in the corridor, overlaid by a nauseating floral freshness. The mingling of pine and decay reminded her of a public bathroom. Emma strode along the tiles, a darker patch of grout highlighting the poet's ultimate resting place. She found Paul and Ray in the kitchen.

Paul nursed a steaming mug of coffee. Ray huffed like a dragon, expelling a cubic metre of snow from the open doorway.

"Hey Emma!" Paul rose to his feet. He set his mug on the scarred pine table and reached for her. Ray's late wife had nurtured a gentle son. He wished to coddle and soothe away Emma's trauma. He remembered his status at the last second. A police officer attending the scene of a vicious murder.

Emma had noticed the warning spark in Ray's eyes. She sensed Paul catch his father's horrified glance, too. He grappled for his mug after hastily re-routing his fingers. Emma wouldn't break after finding Kathleen. Ray knew that. She'd seen far worse and survived.

She sent Paul a smile of consolation, grateful for his compassion but not wanting his chloroform-like smothering. Again, she experienced a longing for Rohan's tough but fair responses to her woes. She ached for his logical mind and steadfast determination. He'd sort this mess out in minutes and restore her equilibrium. Emma gave herself a mental shake. It resolved itself as a physical shrug. She would think like Rohan and solve Kathleen's death for herself. He couldn't return home to this farce. Not with a gunshot wound which would raise questions from their unwanted house guests and resident cop.

Emma slouched into the chair opposite Paul. A new tower of clean baking trays provided a wall between them. The Lit and His Society had already scoffed most of the leftovers. She sighed and directed her attention to Ray. "Where did you get that shovel?" She watched his deft movements as he scraped up the white fluff and lobbed it into the courtyard. Clods hit the rear doors of Chloe's stricken van.

"We brought it with us," Paul answered. His expression softened as his gaze caressed her features. "We had to dig our way through the drift outside the back door. Loved the pink footprints."

Scrape, scrape, scrape. Ray continued working, but the set of his shoulders told Emma he waited for more. She considered her words. "I think the killer whacked Kathleen across the face with a shovel." She winced as Paul sat forward, alertness stiffening the hand cradling his mug. "Everyone watched me fetch mine from the panel in the lobby. We used it to clear the snow from the porch. Monty used again later. I haven't checked if he put it back. This morning, I used a dustpan to scrape up the drift in here, so I didn't grab the shovel."

"Right." Paul rose to his feet. His breath left condensation trails in the frigid air caused by the open door. "Show me," he demanded, his tone clipped. "Whose fingerprints will we find on it?" He used the plural pronoun as though an invisible forensics team dogged his words.

Emma closed her eyes and tilted her head back to stare at the ceiling. In the blank white space, she created a vision of last night's fiasco. "Mine. I lifted it from the cavity. Monty cleared the snow. Twice. He touched the handle and perhaps the shaft. Nicky left Action Men in the cubby. He can't resist fiddling with whatever he sees. So, his paw prints will cover just about every object in there."

"And mine." Ray ceased scraping the tiles. The teeth jarring sound caused Emma to tense. He'd made fast work of the drift. The door closed on the frozen scene beyond it. "I put it there in the first place. I dotted tools around the house for emergencies." He didn't state what kind of crisis might require a shovel. The downstairs toilet had once overflowed into the hallway. That started by needing a shovel. It graduated to a transit van with an on-board suction pump. A smelly investigation revealed an Action Man Bungee Jumper wearing bathing trunks. It followed a dramatic career change from bungee jumping to deep toilet diving. Nobody believed Nicky's excuse that he just fell in.

"Right."

Emma glanced up to find Paul scribing in a small notebook. Taking names, including his father's. "I can't think of anyone else," she added. "But that's not all." Her gaze switched to the sealed outer door and the worry lines etched on Ray's forehead. "Someone unplugged the router in my bedroom to cut off access to the internet. They might not have needed a key to do it, but the same person, or another, planted Ray's old work boots on my hearth. I believe they'll match the footprints under the ice outside the door."

Ray blanched. Paul swore. Emma guessed too late Ray hadn't told his son about the boots. But she wanted the truth more than anything. Because then Rohan and her children would come home. And she could breathe again.

37

Wicker Chair

♥

"Where are the boots now?" A stress pulse ticked in Paul Barker's neck, something he'd inherited from Ray.

Emma turned to stare at her property manager, regret snaking through her chest. "Ray hasn't touched them for months. He got new ones in the summer and left those here for occasional use. They haven't moved until today. There's still a ring of mud and dried grass on the shelf."

"You think the killer wore them? Where are they now?" Paul stared at his own feet as though Ray's tan boots might materialise on them.

Ray flattened his bottom lip. Emma winced. He'd told her Winston found them. But she hadn't seen them on the hearth earlier. She cast her mind back to the moment she discovered the stranger using her shower.

Winston Wright, destroyer of evidence throughout his lifetime. He could have put them there. But why would he? Her shoulders slumped. She needed to lie, to state she'd seen them, but they'd disappeared. Her lips parted, but Ray saved her the trouble.

"They're back in the armoire in the lobby." He gave an awkward bout of throat clearing. "Emma asked me to make sure she'd locked her bedroom door. I went upstairs to check. Sometimes she leaves the dog by the fire. I unlocked the door and walked around the bed. Didn't find the dog, but I saw my boots." His brow furrowed as he protected Rohan's father with a lie. It seemed a travesty. Winston didn't like Ray or his presence at Wingate Hall. He'd rather insert one of his own lackeys instead as a permanent spy. The thought blossomed in Emma's mind. All roads led back to Rohan's father.

"Why'd you put them back in the cupboard?" Paul cocked his head and looked from Ray to Emma and back again. The question seemed to choke him. "Are you two a thing?"

It broke the spell, the notion so incongruous it drew a bark of laughter from them both. Ray caved first. "She's like a daughter!" The colour faded from his ruddy cheeks. "Geez! What do you take me for? I work for the Andreyevs, Paul! That's all."

The police officer's gaze slid to Emma. He studied her discomfort as he waited for her denial. She sighed and shook her head. "I love Ray," she admitted. She heard the older man's inhalation of shock and watched Paul's irises harden to the density of coals. "Your father is one of the best things about this place." She lowered her voice as though attempting to spare Ray's embarrassment. "I couldn't run this property or renovate a single room without his help. But if you knew him as you should, you'd understand his high regard for my husband. Ray would give his life for Rohan. In a heartbeat. And I love my husband and my children. Neither of us would do anything to spoil what we have here. He spoke the truth. I'm like his daughter. And he's the closest thing I've had to a father for many years." She stared at Paul Barker, noticing the green haze of envy circling his head. Funny how she'd never seen it before. She stared at him. Through him. "You don't know how lucky you are," she stated, her tone flat.

Paul swallowed, creating an audible gulp which ricocheted around the room. It bounced off the stainless steel appliances and dispersed in the continued silence.

"Okay," he conceded. Bitterness laced his reluctant croak. "Who else touched the boots?"

"Me," Ray stated. "I assumed Nicky put them in Emma and the captain's room. He moves things around sometimes when he's playing. I put them back in the armoire. How could I realise they weren't just in the wrong place?"

"Who else touched them apart from you?"

Emma snorted. "The killer. Plus, anyone who opened that armoire within the last few months." She regretted sending Winston to search for the boots. He'd removed them from her room and she doubted Paul would find any prints. The old man hadn't made it this far without learning the subtle art of subterfuge and espionage. He'd have wiped both boots. Winston epitomised everything about deviousness and deviance. Emma didn't even know his real name.

She focussed on Ray. "You liked my pink footprints?"

He wrinkled his nose and nodded. "They're safe under the snow for now. It started to melt, but the temperature dropped again." He offered a rueful smile as though he'd inadvertently stamped on a child's triumph. Despite the agony of Paul's questioning,

Emma realised she'd found a new level with Ray. Father and daughter. She discovered she liked it very much.

"I'll fetch the boots in a moment and also the shovel, if it's there." Paul's manner switched back to businesslike. He'd exposed his jealousy and his minor crush on Emma on a single morning of doom. He worked to elevate himself back into the ranks of officialdom. Ray's lips twisted at the right of his mouth, allowing his son to reclaim his dignity.

"Did you really wear tennis racquets on your feet to walk over the snow?" Emma tilted her head and saw four scuffed bats leaning against the Aga's warm frontage. One had fallen sideways as though in a faint. "Very inventive. I'm impressed." Then her heart sank. "Please tell me Nicky didn't see you?"

Ray grinned, the expression genuine. "Yep." He chuckled. He jerked his damp head towards Paul. "Laughed like a drain when I tripped over that low wall before the kitchen garden. Paul had to help me upright."

Emma smiled as she pictured the scene. It became tinged with sadness. She wanted to hold her babies and pretend this awful weekend had never happened. She'd even tolerate Nicky clomping through the house wearing tennis bats on his feet. Her mood flipped. Nicky and Stephie couldn't come home with a killer in their midst. "These people can't stay here." Panic laced her tone. "I don't have enough food for them. They aren't happy, and I don't want them here."

"And one of them is a killer." Paul stated the obvious, and Emma repeated his words.

"Yes. One of them killed Kathleen."

Paul sighed. His expression softened at the sight of her misery. "Mrs Dubois is in the freezer for now. It's already cold downstairs, but Dad turned on the power for the refrigeration unit."

"As an alternative to propping her in the chiller," Ray added. He waggled his brows as Emma contemplated the horror of finding Kathleen on a shelf with the coleslaw. "It'll take the freezer a while to function at an optimum temperature. Longer because she's in there. But it's the best we could do under the circumstances."

Emma nodded. "Okay." She released a held breath. "Let's hope help arrives soon." Her phone vibrated in her pocket and her mood improved. The messages came from Lear.

'I can now ping router on system. Well done.'

'*Cell station and land-line still out. Roads impassable until just before Market Harborough.*'

'*Actuary recovering well. Home once the weather improves.*'

'*Send a list of guests. I'll do more digging.*'

Emma sent back a smiley face. She looked up to find Paul watching her through narrowed eyes. She floundered for long enough to make him suspicious. With impressive deftness, she tilted the phone so he couldn't see the screen and deleted three of the messages. She silently praised Lear's foresight in sending individual statements. Then she left the phone on the table. "My husband is stuck in London." She qualified the impromptu flurry of communication. "My friend just said the snowfall damaged the local cell tower. The overhead cables for the land-lines came down in the snow."

"So, how did you get that message?" Paul regarded her with his features sharpened like an owl's. He hadn't heard the vibrations and assumed she'd received only one. But he'd turned his unflattering crush into something hostile, as though he blamed her for attracting him.

"I told you." She cocked her head and regarded his new directness as though it pained her. "Someone unplugged the router in my bedroom. I connected it just before I came downstairs. My friend contacted me via a social media app. The Wi-Fi is now working." Emma pushed her phone towards him in an offering of truce. "Would you like to see?"

Paul recoiled, blinking and snapping his notebook closed. "No need." He squirmed with discomfort.

Emma's heart thudded in her chest, but she poked at the wall of mistrust between them. "I'll read it to you then," she said. Calling up the remaining message, she spoke out loud. She added a mention of Rohan without referring to the Actuary. "So, no one can leave Market Harborough," she stated. "I guess Northampton is the same."

"Yeah." Ray replied when Paul didn't. "The snow ploughs will make the towns safe first. But if it keeps laying after they've cleared it, they'll spend all day going back over the same roads."

"These are the questions we need answering," Emma continued, replacing her phone in her pocket and ticking items off her fingers. "Who used my shower this morning? Is it the same person who unplugged the router and planted the boots? Or do we have three different culprits?"

"And is the shovel the murder weapon?" Paul dug his hands in his pockets. Emma pressed her index finger against her opposite pinky to include his question in her list.

"Who left their room in the night too?" Ray added. "Apart from Emma."

"And did Kathleen Dubois go to bed? What clothes did she die in?" Emma frowned as Paul winced.

"A silky mustard dress thing underneath a heavy grey coat."

Emma snapped her remaining fingers. "Yes, my husband's coat. Did she take the coat from the armoire at the same time as the killer borrowed Ray's boots?" She gazed at Ray. "While you're searching in the lobby for the boots and the shovel, check for spare slippers. Kathleen died wearing her shoes. If she put them on in the lobby, she must have left her slippers there." She closed her eyes and stared at the inside of her lids. "Purple ankle boots. I bought them from the Pound Shop in the precinct in Market Harborough. I saw her wearing them last night at the awards ceremony."

"Okay." Paul nodded, happy to have a task list. He stepped from the kitchen.

Emma rose and caught Ray's sleeve before he could follow. "Problem!" she hissed. "My bedroom is on the master key, isn't it?"

Ray nodded, a frown drawing his brows into a line. "Yeah."

"But the external doors have individual keys?"

Again, Ray nodded. "Some have only one key. We leave those in the rooms they relate to. I have spares of others which I keep on my bunch. Changing all the external locks is next on my list."

"What about the morning room and the kitchen?" Emma hissed. Paul's steps halted in the hallway before becoming louder as he returned.

Ray nodded and his eyes widened. "They still have individual keys with no copies. We don't keep them in obvious places, though, do we?"

She shook her head and jumped as Paul popped his head back through the doorway. "Aren't you coming?" He directed his question to Ray.

"Yeah," his father replied. But his steps carried him across the kitchen to the high mantel above the Aga. He stretched across the warming plate and grappled on the shelf. His fingers withdrew the key from the place where Emma hid it the previous night. Her heart sank.

"So, whoever opened that door in the night removed that key and replaced it afterwards…"

Ray finished the theory for her. "Or they have copies of external keys and a master key to every room inside this house."

Emma groaned. "I don't know which is worse," she whispered. "Because both scenarios are terrifying."

38

Slipcover Chair

♥

Emma sat in the kitchen and pondered the questions. They behaved like loose sheep, evading an experienced dog in its efforts to round them up. The men returned with the boots and the shovel. Paul had covered the shovel's handle with another freezer bag. Ray carried it by the shaft. His old boots nestled in individual bags, separated by their disgrace.

"Do I have any freezer bags left?" Emma asked, a note of sarcasm leaking into the question.

"You won't soon," Paul stated without a shred of guilt. He jerked his head towards the counter. Butted up to the microwave, he'd piled the two remaining boxes. Sandwich size and large enough to encase a decent turkey. "I'll get through all of those before we're done."

Emma turned her upper lip until it almost reached her nose. "I think I broke my wrist when I tripped over

Kathleen," she stated. It ached as she used the fingers of her other hand to tug up her sleeve.

"Geez!" Ray exclaimed at the bruise. "That's a mess. Why didn't you say something earlier?"

Emma sighed. "You were busy. Can you fix it?"

Ray dipped as though to lean the shovel against the pantry door and Paul yelped. "No, don't contaminate the evidence. Just hold on to it until I've bagged it!"

A huff of irritation burst from Ray's lips. He held the shaft while Paul slipped the turkey bag over its blade. "I see blood on the right edge," he stated, peering through the transparent plastic.

Ray grumbled and spoke from between gritted teeth. "It's just clay from the front garden. I dug out a seedling gorse bush last week. The soil dries brown."

"It's blood." Paul took the shovel from his father and held it by the shaft. With great fascination, he mimicked swiping downwards with the tool. It shuddered as though making contact with an invisible person. "Look," he said, indicating the shovel's upturned face with a jerk of his chin, "that would do it."

Ray wrinkled his nose and pointed at Paul's fingers. "So, if they swung it like that, haven't you just covered their prints with yours?"

Paul frowned down at his gripping hands and sighed. "Yes and no. We'll get something from the handle because that's how people always grip it first. And we'll get the victim's blood from the shovel's blade."

Emma gave a visible shiver. Released from shovel duty, Ray pulled a first aid box from the cupboard above the microwave. The colour of a fire engine, it held his second best medical kit. He disgorged its contents onto the table, his large fingers sifting sticking plasters and antiseptic cream. The blue kit on the shelf above it held reminders of the time he'd stitched Emma back together. "Less blood this time," she murmured. He frowned at her. His slight head shake warned her not to bait Paul.

Five minutes later, Emma examined her bandaged wrist. A metal splint beneath the wadding immobilised the painful joint. As the heat from the Aga again banished the freezing air from the kitchen, Emma's bones and muscles warmed. But her pain increased. Her knee and hip added their complaints. Ray popped out two heavy duty tablets into her upturned palm. He placed a glass of water on the table beside her.

"What's that cream?" Paul studied his father's deft movements as he replaced the items in their box. "That one there." He pointed to a nondescript tube. Ray scooped it into his giant hand and deposited it beside a line of rolled bandages.

"Anesthetic gel." His low voice rumbled, comforting and safe.

"What's it called?" Paul persisted. He reached out to take it and Ray slammed the box lid closed.

"Just anesthetic gel!" His irritation rose, unable to admit the cream didn't belong in that first aid kit. Field grade and army issue, it had already reduced the throbbing in Emma's wrist.

Paul placed the encased work boots and the shovel on the kitchen counter. Ray scowled at the sight. "Is this appropriate?" he barked at his son. "Don't forget it's a family home."

Paul inhaled and Emma ground her teeth. He hadn't said it was *his* family home, but that's what his son heard. A home and a family which didn't include him. Emma regretted the pressure on Ray to keep his son at arm's length. She'd speak to Rohan. The segregation threatened to detonate their fragile relationship.

"It's fine." Her soothing tone cut through the male aggression like a balm. "But we need to do better with all this evidence. Chloe or her boys might come in here and move things just because they're in the way. It'll ruin the continuity of the evidence and it's bad enough already."

Paul raised an appreciative eyebrow. He didn't ask how she knew about continuity of evidence, sparing her the agony of another lie. Many of Rohan's investigations culminated in a prosecution of his mark by an irate client. She'd learned a wealth of information just by watching him prepare evidence for court. Or destroy it, depending on who paid the piper. Rohan didn't always walk on the right side of the law.

"What do you suggest?" Paul asked.

Emma glanced at Ray. "Well, we have a problem with access," she continued. "Someone with a master key unplugged the router and left those boots in my room. The other issue is keys. They knew where we kept the kitchen door key, or they had their own copy."

"And?" Paul looked from Emma to his father.

"So, that person might have complete access to every room in this house," Ray stated. He jerked his head towards the bagged shovel and the boots. "It doesn't matter where you hide your evidence, son. They can just let themselves into the room and do whatever they want with it."

Paul's gaze strayed to the kitchen window. He swore in disgust. Emma turned her body and tensed at the sight of the Paynes grey sky releasing another flurry of snowflakes. More than a flurry. A blizzard. Within seconds, it became a complete white-out. "What can we do?" Paul's voice held a strangled note as though he struggled to contain his despair. "I need somewhere safe to keep everything or it becomes inadmissible in court. I'll find the killer but won't secure a conviction." He whirled to face his father. "There must be somewhere in this giant bloody house which no one else knows about."

Emma considered Rohan's armoury. Would she dare to unlock it and hide Paul's evidence inside with the racks of heavy fire power and the shelves of ammunition? She glanced at Ray and sensed him thinking the same thing. But then Paul nixed that solution without ever knowing how close he'd come to the centre of Wingate Hall's best kept secret. "Only I can have access to it," he said. And that was that.

39

Bergère chair

♥

"I know one place." Ray cocked his head and surveyed Emma. "There are only two keys to the basement. I have one and you have the other. The victim is already down there in the freezer. Why don't we keep the evidence with her?"

Emma's lips twitched. She couldn't voice the objection in her head. It meant admitting she believed Christopher Dolan still roamed Wingate Hall. He could access every part of her life except for Rohan's armoury. She swallowed, knowing she'd sound paranoid if she didn't just agree. "Okay," she said, her throat constricted and her voice hoarse.

"Fine." Paul became businesslike again. "Then I'll need possession of all the keys to that area."

Ray studied his son. Emma's temper flared. "You can't do that. You can't just requisition my house. This isn't a mystery novel. You're not Inspector Poirot!"

"Someone committed a crime!" Paul snapped. "I can and I will exercise my rights under the Police and Criminal Evidence Act of 1984. Would you like the relevant subsection and its amendments? I can quote them for you."

"No!" Emma grumbled. "But as soon as this is over, you're banned from the property."

Ray's Adam's apple bobbed. She regretted her hasty fugue. But her bitchy, terrified side had risen to the surface, and she fed off its temporary surge of power. Paul pointed to his father. "Get the other key and bring it to me."

"I don't know the code to the safe!" Ray spluttered. "Contrary to what you believe, I spend very little time in Emma's bedroom!"

Paul released a hiss of victory before Ray realised his error. "And yet you retrieved your old work boots from there earlier without a problem?"

The lies piled up between them like forestry slash. They criss-crossed and tangled into a monster that could wash away houses. Neither Ray nor Emma spoke, unable to unfurl the sizeable mess. Where was Rohan when she needed him? She pushed away the natty reply before it took root. In a hospital. Injured.

Emma tugged the key from her jacket pocket. It thudded onto the scarred table. The brass had worn in places, the stem thinner from handling. She stroked her index finger over it and conjured up the faces of successive butlers. They smiled from faded black and white photographs, the family defenders loyal and austere. She wished they were here now. "Take it," she snarled. "Do what you must."

She rose then, keen to escape the jealous police officer. The door bumped against the tape behind her as she left the kitchen.

Freda met her in the lobby, her knotty fingers twisting in a dance of discomfort. "I don't wish to trouble you, dear," she began, her lashes fluttering. The rogue falsie had fallen off somewhere. Sweat dotted her brow. The delicate scarf had slipped behind her neck like a hood of rose petals.

"I need a shower." Emma strode towards the lobby fireplace and dumped two weighty logs into the dying flames. "Can you walk and talk?" Her phone vibrated in her pocket. The wrong pocket. She couldn't reach it with her strapped hand.

"They're hungry. And tired of parlour games." Freda winced, her lips pulling into dual tight lines. They'd nominated her as the sacrifice, sending the weakest into the fray to demand sustenance.

"What nice people," Emma murmured beneath her breath. But she smiled at the elderly woman shuffling up the main staircase alongside her. "Let me freshen up and we'll sort something out," she promised. "We could move the furniture to create a theatre. Perhaps dig out a movie to watch." She dipped her head to invite a sense of confidentiality. Freda's wilting smile betrayed the strain of the weekend's drama. "I have snacks," Emma whispered. "That's something we have plenty of here. Naughty food and a movie. Nicky's idea of heaven."

"Will I tell them?" Freda paused on the landing.

Emma brushed the fingers of her good hand across her daughter's bedroom door. She repeated the action across Nicky's. They should be at home with her, enjoying the sight of the blizzard through the windows. Dreaming up snowball fights and sled rides. But the Lit and His Society had separated them in a single act of pure selfishness.

Emma halted and forced a smile back onto her lips. She turned to speak to Freda. "I have DVDs in the family lounge. I'll fetch them when I come downstairs." She pushed open her bedroom door, hearing Farrell's faint woof of warning. "Just me, boy," she soothed.

Rohan owned a plastic bag. He used it to cover his leg in the shower when the stump became ulcerated or sore. Emma dug it from his bottom drawer. She covered the wrist bandage once she'd shed her clothing. The manufacturer designed the cover for a leg. Not a wrist. She kept the excess bunched in her fingers. But she shampooed her hair one handed, adding conditioner and struggling with the comb. The water didn't seem as hot as usual. Filling the upstairs radiators and depleted by potentially fourteen showers and a bath, it wasn't surprising. Emma washed just as the warmth cooled to an unpleasant tepidness. She shut off the spray, remembering Winston's earlier stunt with the boiler. He'd switched it off, just as it tried to reheat the temperature.

Emma emerged from the bathroom. She clutched one end of a fluffy towel beneath her armpit and the other in her mouth. The scream left her lungs at the same time as the towel fell. A woof echoed from somewhere else in the house. Claws scrabbled on a tiled floor.

"Sorry! Sorry!" Bunny covered her eyes with her slender fingers. She turned so her shoulder clattered with the door frame. "I came to find you." Her voice held a plaintive whine. "I kept them playing games for as long as possible. But it's been hours since you left to get help."

Emma dropped the plastic sleeve in favour of her towel. She wrapped it around herself with difficulty. Farrell's head poked between the door and Bunny's thigh. His alert expression and pricked ears invited praise for answering her distress call. Emma sighed. "Better late than never," she said in a soothing tone. Her words didn't match her delivery. Farrell smiled and wagged his tail.

"I saw him on the way down," Bunny said from behind her hands. "Freda said you'd come upstairs."

"Just come in and close the door." Emma pressed her splinted wrist over the corners of the towel. She dug in drawers with the other hand. "I might need help." She tugged out clean underwear and socks. The drawer below it stuck, requiring a levering action to get it open one-handed. Emma pulled out a fresh pair of sweatpants and a tee shirt before pairing them with a hoodie belonging to Rohan. He used it in the gym. The constant washing had faded the army emblem into a dirty grey patch. Much of the word had flaked away, though his body retained the injuries with more definition. She lifted it from the couch where she'd placed it in his absence, her fingers gentle as she sought comfort from the contact.

"The others held a vote." Bunny had dropped her hands from her eyes and gazed around the palatial bedroom. "They made Freda ask about food. Nobody else wanted to. I think they're a little scared of you."

Emma snorted. She forwent the hooks and eyes of her bra. Instead, she tugged the tee shirt over her head. "They didn't seem afraid of me last night when they tried to force me to pay their catering bill. And I noticed little fear when they turned their noses up at the accommodation and the breakfast."

Bunny stared at her knees. Bare and slightly blue, they poked from beneath her original gown. Freda's jumble-sale grab of the antiques had netted Bunny a delicate shawl in gold and red. It didn't match her pale dress, but at least offered some warmth. "That was before." The words slid from her mouth like silk, the meaning ominous.

"Before what?"

Bunny gulped. She flapped her blue veined right hand. "I'm not saying this," she stammered. "I don't agree. But you asked me."

Emma froze in the process of hauling the sweatpants over the waistband of her knickers. She wished the dog had stayed with her, though he wouldn't have understood the context of the coming bombshell. "Before what?" she whispered, already knowing the answer. She left the ties of the pants dangling. The frayed ends brushed against her thighs.

"Before Kathleen died," Bunny said, her voice a spasm of jerky syllables.

Emma reached for Rohan's hoodie, clutching the grey fabric to her breast. The knuckles of her good hand turned white. "They think I killed her, don't they?" she concluded.

Bunny pursed her lips. And nodded.

40

Bubble Chair

♥

Emma restricted Bunny's assistance to bundling her hair into a ponytail. The slender woman's hands shook as she performed the simple action.

"Do you think I killed her?" Emma asked. She detected the faintest whoosh of air leave Bunny's lips.

"No," the other woman replied. Then with more positivity, "No." She finished wrestling Emma's curls into the elasticated band and stepped back to admire her work. "Kathleen Dubois required time to get under someone's skin and wreak her damage. You only met her last night."

"Yes, but Gwendoline said she wrote a mean poem about me. Perhaps that made me want to commit murder."

Bunny sank into the nearby armchair and crinkled her sharp features into a quizzical expression. She folded her legs beneath her like a swan. The fringe of the shawl covered her knees. "Did she?" she mused. "I didn't know that."

"I heard you all laughing." Emma's chest tightened with an old ache. She'd been that bullied child in school. Her elfin build and gentle nature made her a soft target. In primary school she'd cried silent tears. In high school she'd fought back and often won. Her step mother's cruelty behind their neat front door had changed her. A scarlet rage hovered near the surface.

Would she have killed Kathleen if she'd heard the cruel ditty? Emma cleared her throat and shook her head. No, she wouldn't. The idea seemed more ridiculous the longer she dwelt on it. Her shoulders relaxed. She sank onto the bed. Rohan's scent rose from the bedspread. Citrus with the faintest hint of musk. It filled her with courage. "So, what did you all find so funny last night?"

Bunny pursed her lips. She stared at the ceiling. "Those men. The caterers. They slept on the floor of the single room with Chloe. It seemed so ridiculous. The younger one tripped over his own feet in the hallway. Not that funny, to be honest. The poor kid hurt himself."

"Did they move their bedding?" Emma imagined the chill of a night on the floor.

Bunny's brow furrowed. Her gaze became unfocussed and dreamy. "Christos smuggled a bottle of whiskey and a glass upstairs. Everyone got a little drunk and silly."

"Including Kathleen?" Emma's eyes narrowed as she imagined the emaciated woman inebriated and entertaining a crowd. She'd struggled to read her own poetry and hand out fake awards.

"No." Bunny shook her head, her short hair waving in protest at the sharp jerks of her neck. "I didn't see her at all. Arnand appeared not long after you went downstairs. Gwendoline showed him to his room. I went to bed about half-past twelve. Most people filtered away once the fire died down. The major rather enjoyed lighting it. His moment of glory, I think. He did a good job, and he saved some logs for this morning. But the radiators kicked in during the night, so it wasn't as cold when we woke." She gulped and stared at Emma as though fearing reprisals. "Sorry, that sounded terrible. You didn't factor in thirteen extra guests for the night. You've done your best and I appreciate it."

"No." Emma sighed. "I didn't factor in any of it. I didn't even want the Lit and His Society to come here again." She shook off the black hood of depression as it settled on her shoulders. The snow couldn't last forever. It never did. This was not her life. Just a temporary blip. "Can you remember who stayed up after you went to bed?"

Bunny gnawed her lower lip with tortured incisors which crossed over one another. The delicate skin turned pink. "Monty used the bathroom just after me. He said he'd had enough. Flora went to bed much earlier. She had a headache. Mavis turned in very early. Arnand went straight to his room." Her slender fingers tapped the arm of the chair in a frenzied beat only she heard. Her features hardened. "Christos said goodnight just before me. He'd chatted to Gwendoline. She seemed a little worse for wear." A dramatic sigh punctuated her sentence, but it drew Emma's attention.

"You like Christos?" She swallowed her surprise. "Really?"

An audible gulp escaped Bunny's thin chest. "He doesn't know." She flapped her hand in front of her flushed face. "Please, don't tell anyone. I know it's ridiculous. He wouldn't look twice at someone like me." Her eyes sparkled with unshed tears, which tugged at Emma's heart strings.

Her expression softened. "I thought that about Rohan," she admitted. "All the girls at school fancied him. But he never spoke, so the illusion grew because he didn't sully their adoration. His elusiveness gave him even more strength. Girls allied themselves with me hoping to get closer to him. Until they realised Alanya didn't allow friends in our house."

"How did you snag him?" Bunny dipped forward in her chair. The cushions creaked. She set her gaze on Emma, a latent hunger in her eyes. "Mavis thinks it's some weird incestuous thing."

Emma shrugged. The revelation held pain but not surprise. "Mavis would." She focused on her bitter-sweet memories of childhood. "I beat up a boy at school. He bullied Anton for months, and I couldn't stand it anymore. Rohan strode into the middle of the crowd and dragged me out just before the teachers arrived. On the way home, he kissed me."

Bunny's expression froze as her mind whirred behind her thick-rimmed glasses. "You hit someone, and your husband fell in love with you?" She cocked her head like a bird. Her thin fingers bunched around the glitzy shawl in a weak fist.

"No." Emma regretted the revelation as soon as Bunny spoke. She'd unwittingly displayed a prior penchant for violence. If Bunny spread the tale around the guests, it would reinforce their view of her as a killer. "There's more to a relationship than that." She reached out to Rohan with her mind, sending healing vibes and waves of love. Wingate Hall wasn't the same without him. He'd have sorted out Kathleen's killer by now and expelled the ungrateful Lit and His Society members.

"Why didn't he speak?" Bunny asked. "To the girls. Why did he remain silent?"

Emma smiled. Her inner vision filled with memories of living with Rohan and Anton Andreyev. The theatrical younger brother adopted a plummy English accent worthy of royalty. Rohan didn't. And so, he kept silent until he'd beaten down his Slavic intonations. "He struggled to pronounce certain words. Still does sometimes." Plus, other things. The horror of living with Alanya. Of knowing deep down that she'd poisoned his siblings. Emma believed he survived because Alanya loved him best. And because Anton pulled her attention towards himself. He feigned sickness, drawing her awful healing in his own direction.

Time and adulthood had revealed the truth. Winston Wright controlled Rohan's life like a puppeteer. His oversight would have betrayed Alana's activities in a heartbeat. She hadn't treasured her eldest son. She hadn't even cared enough about him to risk it. He belonged to a man who'd abandoned her on the wrong side of the Iron Curtain. Unmarried and pregnant.

Emma forced the questions straight in her head. "Did you see the major and Sir Robert go to their rooms?"

Bunny shook her head. Her gaze had lost its intensity away from the subject of Christos. "I left them by the fire, but they'd gone when I came out of the bathroom." She shrugged. "I assume they went to bed."

"But not Kathleen?" Emma mused. "You didn't see her upstairs at all?" She tapped her fingernails against her top teeth as she thought. Nicky hated the sound. She wished he would appear and drag away her hand. "Something woke me at half-past two. I know that because I checked my watch. So, that's two hours with no one able to verify Kathleen's whereabouts. We don't know what time she died." Emma exhaled. "Where do we begin?"

She rose and wrestled herself into the hoodie. A cursory check of her ski jacket's pockets revealed the plug from the third floor bathroom, her phone, a master key, and a frayed tissue. She discarded the plug, replaced the other items and forced her splinted wrist into the tight sleeve. Bunny helped her to straighten the hoodie underneath, giving it a gentle pat into place. "I've tucked it into the jacket hood," she advised. "It looks quite trendy." The wasted sentiment fell to the rug unclaimed. Emma no longer cared how she looked. She fought the temptation to call Farrell and hide in her bedroom until the unwanted visitors left. But hunger gnawed at her insides. She couldn't remember the last thing she ate.

"Let's go downstairs and find some food." She infused her voice with a gentleness she didn't feel. The master key plunged to the floor as she fumbled it from her pocket. Bending, she retrieved it. But her gaze fell on Bunny's feet.

Purple ankle boots clad her slender tootsies. They appeared too big for her, the necks gaping against her slim shins. It caused her to shuffle rather than take proper steps. "What?" she demanded, staring back at Emma's frozen expression. "What's the matter?"

Emma jabbed her index finger at Bunny's slippers. "Where did you get those?" she whispered.

41

Swan Chair

♥

Bunny grunted as though Emma had raised a non-issue. She stared at the slippers without concern. "I found them in the lobby with the other spares this morning. My feet are tiny. I buy children's shoes. The ones from last night fitted to perfection." Her button nose wrinkled with disappointment. "These were the next smallest."

"So, what happened to your others?" Emma's feet remained glued to the floor. The socks she wrestled on one-handed shushed against the smooth boards.

"I used the bathroom outside Freda's room for a shower this morning. But I left my slippers and stockings inside by accident. Mavis nipped in after me. She wouldn't open the door. When I went back afterwards, she'd soaked them. I came downstairs and chose a fresh pair while my stuff dried on the radiator in my room."

"Where were those?" Emma stared at the purple ankle boots. She remembered seeing them on Kathleen's spiky feet at the ridiculous awards ceremony. She flapped her good hand. "Like, were they lined up against the wall beside the armoire or somewhere else?"

Bunny shook her head. "I found them beside the wooden bench in the lobby. I assumed these were spare. They're quite pretty, aren't they?" She lifted her toes from the floor and twinkled the furry purple fabric. She appeared oblivious to having stolen a dead woman's slippers.

Emma nodded. But it answered the mystery of Kathleen's missing slippers. She'd sat on the pew and swapped them for her flimsy shoes before leaving. But the group didn't go anywhere. But why go to the kitchen after everyone went to bed? Emma frowned. Did she even make it there?

"Shall we go downstairs, then?" Bunny tugged on the brass knob and admitted a blast of cooler air. "Sir Robert is a diabetic. He needs to eat at regular intervals."

Emma stuffed her feet into her own slippers. She pulled the door closed behind Bunny and fumbled with the lock. A grey haze settled over the occasional furniture in the darkened hallway. Restoration of the second storey had required a structural survey of the skylight. The heritage officer condemned Wingate Hall's residents to two months of flapping tarpaulins while the glass went away for reconditioning. Then it leaked for another month because the millimetre tolerance of the steel fabrication failed in one innocuous place.

Bunny followed Emma's gaze, studying the intricate glass panels which rose to a graceful apex. With a grunt of satisfaction, she turned and headed for the main staircase.

"No." Emma didn't follow her. "I'll use the back steps. Mavis will have stationed herself in the lobby, ready for an ambush. I'm not ready for that yet. Let me visit the kitchen and grab whatever food I have left in the chiller. I'll make Sir Robert a priority. If you see Chloe in the morning room, ask if she'd mind helping me." Emma raised her injured left hand. "Monty can sort out an overtime payment for her."

Bunny placed her delicate foot on the first step. Her fingers gripped the sweeping banister rail, but she turned an agonised expression on Emma. "You don't know, do you?" she asked.

Emma tilted her head and braced herself for another delivery of unwanted drama. "Know what?" she demanded.

"Monty's boiling." Bunny lowered her voice. She turned her body so far that she almost lost her footing. "All the money's gone. The Lit and His Society is broke."

Emma gaped at her. "But Monty paid Chloe last night. She told me."

Bunny rolled her eyes. "No. The major loaned the money to the society. Sir Robert found some lined paper in the bureau and drew up a contract between him and Monty. They argued after the awards ceremony. Monty didn't want to sign it and end up liable. The Wi-Fi still worked, so the major made an online bank transfer before the internet went down. He showed Chloe the receipt, but the money wouldn't reach her account until Monday. Nobody else knows. Just those three people and Mavis. Freda is unaware of the situation." Her index finger fluttered over her lips as though to silence Emma. "People just forget about me. I sat in the chair by the fire. Nobody noticed. That's why

I know about the missing fifteen thousand pounds, and the argument." Her lips puckered. "I'm the secretary. They should have included me in the discussion. What if they can't afford to pay my salary?"

"But where did all the funds go?" The puzzle pieces dropped into place. Emma knew the answer even before Bunny's lips parted with the latest nugget.

"Mavis!" They said her name together. Bunny relayed the argument between the chair person and Monty after the awards ceremony.

"Mavis claimed to have borrowed twelve thousand pounds. She couldn't account for the other three, but Monty didn't believe her. They argued again on the steps leading to the servants' quarters."

Bunny had eavesdropped from the bathroom, her clamshell ear pressed against the keyhole. "Mavis took out a loan to pay off her husband's debts. The magistrates released him on police bail pending his court date." Bunny's eyes bugged behind the magnified lenses. "But he skipped out on her after promising he'd help with the repayments. He's wanted on fraud charges. Her pension doesn't cover the loan. Not once she realised, he'd re-mortgaged the house. She's borrowed from the Lit and His Society's account since just before the summer. The last treasurer left in the spring. I remember everything being in order back then. Mavis hoped to pay it all back before anyone noticed. Or before we got a new treasurer who asked awkward questions."

"But you take minutes at every meeting!" Emma supported her painful wrist with her other hand. She'd put on too many clothes. Her arms didn't move with the ease she wanted. The hoodie had bunched beneath her armpits, too big to fit beneath the snug ski jacket.

Bunny shrugged. Gossip seized her mouth and body. The compulsion threatened to pitch her down the stairs like a child on a water slide. Emma's chest tightened. Nothing she'd confessed about her marriage would remain sacred. The miscalculation irked her.

"Mavis lied at the committee meetings." The statement involved even Bunny's eyebrows. "Without a treasurer, she could say whatever she liked. We believed she kept forgetting the bank statements because that's what she said. You know what she's like."

Emma swore. She imagined the dumpy woman blustering through financial enquiries as though affronted at the implied doubt. Mavis had managed a quiet civility with her until Freda suggested Emma become their treasurer. It made sense. Mavis needed to scare her off. Emma guessed she'd never get back the money for their summer fete. "Bloody Freda," she murmured to herself. "Why do I listen to her?"

"I'll go down and tell them you're rustling up some food, then?" Bunny seemed to have grown another half a metre with the catharsis of information sharing. The faded dress still hung from her narrow frame, but she pressed her shoulders back and carried her head high. Gossip became her. Or she became it.

Emma walked down the back stairs with care. Her wrist ached, but the banging in her head surpassed even that inconvenience. She pushed the kitchen door open with her hip and closed it behind her with her bottom, reluctant to smudge the fingerprints beneath the film coated door knob. She found Ray alone. He stood by the Belfast sink, legs splayed and his hands behind his back. The at-ease pose suited him and reminded her of a younger Rohan. Captain Andreyev, fresh faced and blond. That Rohan, not the one smashed in a war zone. He found the stance too difficult to maintain nowadays. Locking his knees played havoc with his prosthetic leg.

"Ray?"

He jumped as Emma slunk into a kitchen chair. "Hey." A new rigidity entered his burly frame. In Rohan's absence, he'd become her protector, her overseer. It pitted him against his own son. The weight of responsibility cowed Emma in her chair.

"Where's Paul?" She glanced around the empty room. Farrell smiled at her from his bed, his tongue lolling from the side of his mouth. Ray had stoked the Aga until warm air hung like a shroud. The stupid dog would stay for as long as possible before slinking away, panting.

"Interviewing people in the morning room," he replied. He pulled out the chair opposite, the wooden legs screeching against the tiles.

"I've discovered some things." Emma rested her wrist on the table. The ski jacket made her overheat, but the thought of removing it tired her. She'd need to wrestle back into it before leaving the warm kitchen, anyway. Ray dipped forward with interest, his hooded eyes sharp. "Mavis has cleaned out the Literary and Historical Society's bank account."

"Wow." Lines appeared and then vanished in his forehead as he digested the information.

"I don't think Kathleen went upstairs to bed last night at all." Emma closed her eyes and pictured the scene. "Everyone put their shoes on before we discovered the snow laid too deep for the bus to navigate. I last saw Kathleen sitting on the bench in the lobby. Arnand tied her buckles. Bunny Cathcart picked up fresh slippers this morning, unaware they belonged to Kathleen. She's wearing them."

"Who came here with the victim?" Ray brushed his fingers over Emma's left arm, smudging away a dark mark on her sleeve. His gentleness over the splinted wrist softened her mental anguish.

"A daughter, Gwendoline. Her husband, Arnand Dubois. Bunny says they both went to bed before Kathleen. I allocated Arnand and his wife the double bedroom beside the bathroom because she looked so sick. Someone told me she'd recently suffered from a virus. She looked like death warmed up." Her lips pursed at the unfortunate simile. "Sorry," she whispered.

Ray's eyebrows danced on his forehead. He'd seen more mortality in his lifetime than she could imagine. His capable fingers had assisted countless wounded soldiers but failed his dying wife. "Mrs Dubois is death warmed down now." His black humour cut through Emma's guilt. "Seven degrees centigrade if you're looking for facts."

She winced and gave a shudder. "What do we need?" she asked. "Can your son solve this before everyone disperses?"

"Yeah, he's good." Ray winked at her. "But we could give him a little help."

Emma turned to him, her hazel irises sparkling in the light from the overhead bulb. "Okay," she agreed, her mood lightening. "How?"

Ray dipped forward until their heads almost touched. "You say someone saw the husband go upstairs to bed on the third floor, but not the wife?" Emma nodded with enthusiasm. "So, let's work out where they spent their time until then. Did you see him or the victim before you went to bed?"

Emma frowned and studied the knots on the pine table. "No. I locked up the kitchen and turned out the lights. I saw no one on my way upstairs and presumed they'd all gone to bed."

"But if we assume the victim didn't go to the third floor at all, then where did she go until she died? No one killed her in the downstairs hallway before you went to bed, or you'd have seen her."

"I didn't check the morning room." Emma wrinkled her nose. "I should have." She leaned back in her chair, defeat shrouding her.

Ray shook his head, dismissing her assumption of blame. "They're grown adults," he stated. "And not your responsibility. Paul will find out where everyone went and cross reference it with others in the group."

"What can we do to help, then?" Emma demanded.

Ray waggled his brows again and offered a mischievous grin. "We can look at shoes."

42

Pod Chair

♥

"My boots are a size ten." Ray observed the line of shoes in the lobby, his hands on his hips. "Whoever borrowed them needed to walk without tripping. They'd make too much noise clumping along the hallway and risk the dog hearing them."

Emma stood beside him, her elbow bumping against his waist. "That's what I don't understand," she mused. "Multiple people moving around at night and yet Farrell didn't make a sound. He's usually so alert."

Ray towered over her. A force of nature. Emma studied the footwear the group had worn to the house. None of the women owned genuine 1950s flapper shoes, but a couple had stuck bows to the front of buckled courts to create the same effect. Emma closed her eyes and focussed on the moment of the group's arrival. They'd chosen slippers and lined their own shoes up against the wall in haphazard friendship groups. Emma named the owners one by one. "Only Kathleen's outdoor shoes are missing because she's wearing them." She shivered. Ray frowned and turned his head to stare at her with concern. Ignoring him, Emma squatted beside the footwear. "The women have tiny feet," she concluded. "How would they manage in heavy boots with steel toecaps?" She let her gaze drift across the men's shoes. Sir Robert favoured slip-ons with tassels. The major wore sensible ankle boots shined to army grade. Emma lifted the left of each pair to examine the size.

"Verdict?" Ray demanded as she squinted at the tiny letters.

"I'm converting from US sizes in my head for these." She bobbed the major's boot in her palm. "Major Mallory-Eaves is a ten, so he's a suspect. But Sir Robert has tiny feet for a man. He's a seven." She rose after replacing the footwear. "What if they carried them to the rear door before wearing them?" she asked.

Ray released a long sigh as he considered the suggestion. "Did the footsteps appear long and scuffed? Like someone dragged their feet or didn't put down proper prints?"

"No." Emma moved her head from side to side. "They looked clear. Placed in the snow by someone with a confident walk." She squinted at the ceiling. "The wearer didn't even run, otherwise I'd only have found toe prints, wouldn't I?"

"Yeah." Ray exhaled and squatted before the remaining shoes. "These look promising. In addition to the major's." He pulled his upper lip away from his teeth, perhaps reluctant to incriminate another military brother. Emma sensed he'd rather find an alternative culprit as he pointed to Monty's shiny patents. "Size eleven." Satisfaction bloomed as a smile. "He could wear my boots, but it would hurt. Not beyond impossible, though. They're old and stretched, so we can't discount anyone with bigger feet." He jerked his head sideways towards Christos' shiny black shoes. "Except him. No way a size thirteen foot can fit in a size ten boot." He used his toe to tip over a sensible brown shoe. Made from mottled synthetic material, it sported a grey rubber sole. "Eight," he announced. "So, probably not him either."

"Those belong to Arnand Dubois." Emma opened the armoire and observed the circle of dried grass and flaked mud left behind by Ray's old boots. The ones in Paul's makeshift evidence bags bore no sign of dirt. Tramping in the snow would clean the grips and wash away any trace of mud. She sighed and closed the cupboard door. "Chloe and her boys wore their original shoes," she said. "I need to get a look at them."

Ray straightened his jacket, his irises glistening with a faraway sheen. "So, we've discounted three of the men for definite, and maybe one more. But two could have done it."

"Done what, though?" Emma's brow furrowed into lines of exhaustion. She rubbed her right eye with her knuckles. "Even if we find the culprit, we only know they used your boots to walk outside during the night. Kathleen died in the corridor. The two incidents might be coincidence."

"Which puts them all back in the frame." Ray's head hung low enough for his chin to touch his collar. "Perhaps the boots are a red herring."

Emma tilted her neck from side to side, aiming to work the crick from her tendons. "They're a puzzle piece. Even if the boot thief didn't kill Kathleen, they had a reason for going outside. And they returned through the kitchen door. But why did they put the boots in my bedroom?"

"And how did they get in there?" Ray growled. "That's what I'd like to know."

Emma nodded, also keen to solve that mystery. "Do we clear all the women? Bunny has smaller feet than Kathleen." She lifted the women's shoes again, one at a time. Her fingers paused over a pair with a bow glued onto the patent toe. "These belong to Mavis. A woman's size nine. What do you think?" She squinted up at Ray, who nodded. "Oh, and this pair is interesting." Her nose wrinkled as she considered the possibility. "No." She set them down again. "Flora is a ten, but I can't imagine her killing anyone. She's too sweet."

"Right." Ray's tone held a veiled rebuke, which Emma ignored. The gentle school teacher taught Nicky during the Andreyevs' most tumultuous year. Her kindness had stretched beyond the classroom. She'd mothered him through Stephie's birth, Emma's hysterectomy, and the disappearance of the mysterious Harley Man. Nicky knew nothing of Christopher's arrest or incarceration, because an embarrassed British government held his trial for treason and espionage in secret. Emma hated lying to her son, but she'd done it, anyway. She'd allowed him to believe Christopher had returned home to Ireland to care for a sick mother. Flora knew none of the details, only that the child had suffered the loss of an idol, a companion, and an unsuitable mentor. She'd soothed him when Emma couldn't.

"Flora wouldn't do it." Emma rose, her manner staunch and her body stiff. "I don't care how big her feet are." She jabbed her index finger towards the pointy red shoes jammed against the skirting board. "What about those?"

Ray lifted the broken shoe and peered at the embossed number in the centre of the sole. He shifted it around in the light until he could read it, the heel flapping like a lid. "Six," he concluded. "She might have killed the woman, but she didn't wear my boots."

Emma blew out a breath and regarded the waning fire. "So, perhaps two of the men and one of the women."

"Two of the women," Ray growled.

"Do we have more logs in the basement? Seeing as we can't get outside to the wood shed?" Emma licked her lips and focussed on the flames to avoid Ray's subtle head shake.

"Yeah, I'll get the key from Paul and fetch some. If he'll let me have it." His boots ground against the floorboards as he turned to leave. Halting level with the entrance to the corridor, his coarse fingers brushed across the heavy curtain fabric. "Emma?" he said, waiting until she faced him. In response to her raised eyebrows, he continued, "This isn't the time for naivety, sweetheart."

His words stung. Emma registered each squeak of his grips against the red quarry tiles. He usually wore his woollen socks indoors, but the threat of a murderer had moved the boundaries. "Flora didn't kill her!" she hissed, her tone defiant. "She didn't, and I'll prove it."

43

Task chair

♥

The sky betrayed Emma not long afterwards. Intent on her misery, the weather bomb dumped yet more snow onto Wingate Hall. It buried it beneath a solid white blanket. All hope of digging the bus free faded. No one from the Literary and Historical Society volunteered to do the work.

Drifts reached as high as a man's chest. They collected against external doors as the wind hurled its fury at every side of the house. The windowpanes rattled in their antique frames like a death knoll. Occasional gusts tore down the chimney of the morning room. They caused the flames to roar and stretch towards the hearth. And the unintentional residents of Wingate Hall grew subdued as their extended stay appeared more certain.

Emma helped Chloe raid the chiller and pantry. Dyfed and Ridley hung nearby. They worked in silence, assessing the ingredients to feed their growing number. Paul and Ray swelled their company to eighteen, including Winston. Monty hadn't mentioned their awkward interaction. But it didn't mean he hadn't complained to the others.

"I can make soup with this." Chloe appeared from the chiller, carrying a joint of meat. "Is it beef?"

"Venison," Emma replied. "I hadn't worked out how to cook it. My husband helped a local farmer out of a bind with the tax office and he paid in meat." She curled her lips back in guilt at the potential waste. "Is it still okay?"

Chloe used a sharp knife to release the hunk of red veined meat from its packaging. "It's fine," she announced after making a series of cuts. "Let's roast it in the Aga and then I'll make soup from it."

Emma exhaled as she imagined the complaints they might get from her ungrateful guests. "I have a loaf of bread," she offered. "We can restrict them to one slice each." Her voice trailed off as she pictured issuing the dictat.

"No need. I found a sack of flour at the back of the pantry. We can make some bread rolls. That should keep everyone going for a while if you can locate some yeast and other basic ingredients."

Emma gathered the items Chloe requested. Standing on tiptoes, she found three limp looking muesli bars on a high shelf. She stepped into the kitchen and peered at the ingredients. With a low sugar content and high protein, they might suit Sir Robert's needs as a temporary hold. Emma pushed them into her pocket alongside her phone.

Chloe appeared more cheerful. She smiled as Emma set down a packet of yeast and a carton of sugar. The atmosphere between them lost its tension. "How many eggs do you need?" Emma asked. "I have a tray of two dozen in the chiller."

"I'll get them!" Dyfed bounced forward and slid into the metal room's interior.

Chloe raided the kitchen cupboards and found utensils. Emma watched her deft movements as Chloe washed her fingers under the hot water. She'd dressed in her chef's attire without another alternative, but Emma caught the scent of Freda's grapefruit shower gel emanating from her. It mingled with the sweaty, masculine aroma from Dyfed and Ridley. A casual glance at the intense creases in their clothing showed they'd slept in them. The stench betrayed their reluctance to shower. Not just in a strange house, but perhaps ever.

Dyfed's white gloves poked from the righthand pocket of his footman's jacket. His filthy fingers had dirt ingrained beneath his nails. Emma turned to Chloe, pressing forward with her amateur sleuthing. "I'm sorry this happened to you," she said, her tone soft. She angled her body to remove any sense of threat, pointing her feet towards the door and trailing her left shoulder. It created a triangle devoid of a confrontational element.

"Ah well," Chloe replied. She added a helping of yeast to the flour and stirred it with a metal fork. "Milk," she said aloud. Dyfed galvanised himself. His shoes squeaked across the tiles as he rushed to comply. The chiller door clanked behind him. Emma noticed the frisson of alarm which ran across Ridley's smooth features as Dyfed disappeared.

"Did you find everything you needed for a shower?" Emma asked.

"Yes, thanks. The older lady gave me a towel. I used the bathroom on the second floor."

"Freda." Emma nodded with satisfaction. She ticked names off the list in her mind. Monty used the bath and flooded the floor. She'd found Gwendoline following in his stead. But she couldn't have got downstairs to Emma's ensuite before her. Not wearing only a towel. Chloe used Freda's bathroom. So did Mavis. Bunny had told her that in explaining away her missing stockings and slippers. Dyfed and Ridley hadn't showered. Freda would have used her own bathroom. That left Flora, Sir Robert and Major Mallory-Eaves to account for. And Christos.

Emma released a gargantuan sigh. Why did it matter? Using her shower without an invitation didn't make them a poet killer. Her shoulders slouched in the heavy jacket as she faced the window. Snow had piled onto the sill. It pressed against the panes to create stunning ice patterns.

Chloe kneaded the flaccid dough into a ball. It slapped against the metal bowl as she punched its centre. Dyfed had returned to sentry duty.

"Did you sleep well?" Emma made her question casual. Her laugh sounded fake even to herself. "The servants' quarters aren't salubrious, I'm afraid. Best I could do at short notice."

A miniscule frown flitted across Chloe's brow. She gave a jarring shake of her head. Her blonde bun wobbled against her nape. "We slept fine, thanks," she replied, answering for all of them.

Ignoring the blanket statement, Emma fixed her gaze on the two men. She grinned, sensing the moment it became forced and inane. "How about you two?" She infused her tone with false brightness.

Ridley shrank back against the cupboards. He edged his body behind Dyfed. The younger man smiled, but the expression didn't reach his eyes. "We slept on Mum's floor." His words held no guile. Chloe's fingers stiffened in the mixing bowl, ceasing their steady beating of the dough.

Emma left a rigid smile on her face. "Wasn't that uncomfortable?" she asked, her concern containing equal percentages of feigned and genuine.

"No, we can do it," Dyfed began, but Chloe turned her narrowed eyes towards him.

"Find a pan to cook the venison in," she demanded, her tone severe.

A stab of electrical energy ran up Emma's spine. These hungry, dirty men had formed an unnatural attachment to Chloe. Why did the police release Gareth from jail? It made no sense.

Emma slipped her phone from her pocket. Dyfed clanked around in the cupboards. He searched for a pan. She watched his bowed head and curved spine as he peeked into the cavernous spaces. Christopher organised the kitchen storage to his preference. She couldn't help Dyfed. But found she didn't want to.

Her fingers worked fast as she opened a message panel and sent a request to Lear via the Wi-Fi. *'Any luck on the complaint against Gareth?'* she asked.

He replied within seconds. *'Yeah. It's linked to something much bigger and screened off. I can't get to it. The Actuary will know a way to hack in further. The Home Office is involved.'*

Emma frowned. Why would the Home Office care about a cowboy builder? She glanced up as Dyfed's head emerged from the cupboard. He smiled as he set a roasting tray on the table. Her heart sped up despite her mental efforts to calm herself. The mystery grew bigger by the minute. It sucked in her guests one at a time like a hungry vortex.

Emma cleared her throat and fixed her attention on Chloe. The men lurked near the Aga's warmth.

She sensed they'd share nothing with her. Lowering her voice to exclude them from the conversation, she focussed on Chloe. The woman's capable hands kneaded the dough on a floury wooden board. "Do you think Gareth came here last night?" she whispered. Her gaze slid to Dyfed and Ridley, but still noticed Chloe's fingers cease their abuse of the dough.

"Doubt it." Chloe spat the words into the air like bullets. "His truck is off the road. It needs repairs. The van is here." Her eyes narrowed. She glared at Emma, all good humour gone. "You think he'd walk out here in a blizzard? To kill a woman, he'd never met?"

Emma's mouth dried. Rohan always answered her distress calls. Only the weather had delayed him this time. Courage infused her. "Rohan would crawl across broken glass to reach me." She threw the words into the room, sensing the men's attention pique. Fear flickered like a strobe in Dyfed's eyes.

"Congratulations." The single word held a bite. Sarcasm and jealousy roiled beneath the surface.

"I'll leave you to it," Emma said. "Shout if you need any help."

Chloe's upper lip drew back from her teeth in a snarl. She turned to wash her fingers under the hot tap. "Tell that old bitch I'm charging by the hour," she warned.

Emma left the room. Her heart beat a tattoo in her chest. The thudding resonated like a drum. It signified a retreat from a war zone.

44

Wheelchair

Emma found Ray on his knees in the lobby. He jabbed an ornate poker into the flames as he worked to revive the fire. With his broad back towards her, his head bobbed in time with the action. The tap tapping of claws pursued Emma along the hallway as Farrell burst from the kitchen behind her.

"Ray!" she hissed as she picked up speed. Her bandaged wrist rested against the lip of her pocket for support. He turned on his knees as she rushed up behind him, a quizzical expression on his face.

"There you are," he said, as though he'd searched for her but quit in favour of fixing the fire.

Emma squatted to sit on the metal rail surrounding the hearth. Constructed from beaten metal, it warmed through her sweatpants. "I know who unlocked the kitchen door," she whispered. He leaned back to hear her, his irises glittering with eagerness.

"Who?" he demanded before she could reply.

"Chloe." Emma waggled her eyebrows. Her expression folded like a sheet tugged from a washing line. Doubt prickled her spine. "Well, I believe she did it. She's terrified of Gareth, and so are those two men. But I sensed a longing for approval there too when I asked her about him. She spent more time in the kitchen than anyone. I know he'd already primed them to snoop. I think she unlocked the door and put the key back on the mantel. She already knew the police released him before everyone went to bed."

Ray frowned. "He'd just go home, wouldn't he? Don't they live in town?"

Emma wrinkled her nose and batted away the obvious counterpoint to her discovery. "Chloe demanded the keys from him. She specifically asked for the van and house keys. I saw him give them to her. She used them later when she got the van stuck in the snow. Unless they had a spare set, he'd spend the night outside."

Ray exhaled and stopped short of blowing out Emma's candle of victory. "So, you think he walked miles in a blizzard, scaled the perimeter fence, got into the kitchen, left the door wide open behind him, and hid in the house somewhere?"

"No." The negation fell from her lips as though drawn from a sulky child. "You're thinking of the boots, aren't you?"

"Yep." Ray turned to his raking. Soot coated the back of one hairy knuckle. "He wore scuffed dress shoes and an old-fashioned outfit. Paul held him upright outside because his soles had no grip in the ice. The guy had massive feet and holes in the toes of his right shoe. There's no way he walked back here, especially not in time to kill that woman."

Emma groaned. "So, back to square one."

She drew her phone from her right pocket and a muesli bar plummeted free. It clanged against the metal surface of the rail before hitting the tiled hearth. Ray retrieved it in sooty fingers and flapped it across a break in its centre. "Getting desperate?" he asked.

"It's for Sir Robert. He's a diabetic." Emma's fingers worked over her screen. She sent a message to Lear. "This boy is so slack!" she complained. "He has the footage from the security cameras now I've plugged in the router. Why can't he fast forward through the hours from midnight to two-thirty and tell me who went outside in your boots?" She huffed out a breath of exasperation.

Her phone vibrated in her hand. She almost dropped it. Her lips turned down in disgust as she read the social media message. "Great! Regan has discovered the cameras don't record if the Wi-Fi isn't working." She tutted. "He wants to install memory cards in them all now."

"Bit late," Ray grumbled.

Farrell leaned against Emma's knees, his head drooping from his bent neck. At intervals, his front paws slid on the floorboards, and he jerked himself upright. Emma stared at his closed lids and sagging ears. Ray peered from the sleepy dog to her. "Are you thinking what I'm thinking?" he asked, his voice low.

Emma stroked the dog's head, and he shuddered. Sitting upright, he smiled at her, his tongue lolling from the side of his mouth. "It's possible," Emma mused. "He didn't wake at all during the night. I went downstairs without him. He only joined me after I fell over Kathleen. He flakes out at every opportunity, and he doesn't seem like himself, does he?" She wrapped the fingers of her good hand around a trailing ear. With the texture of silk, it slipped through her palm. Farrell yawned, a wide action which threatened to disconnect his jaw.

Ray's eyebrows rose to meet the creases in his forehead. His lips pursed. "Someone drugged the dog," he concluded. "Then that's a whole different story. It means the killer intended to murder Kathleen."

"And they didn't want the dog to raise the alarm." Panic nipped at Emma's feigned calm. She glanced at the closed door of the morning room. "Is Paul in there now?" she demanded.

Ray pressed his hand over her knee. "He gave strict instructions for you to leave the investigation to him."

"But I want to know what's happening!" Her voice rose in protest. "I have a dead woman in my downstairs freezer!"

Ray exhaled through his nose. "Paul is isolating people one at a time in the family lounge. I lit a fire, and he has everything he needs. Your interference won't help matters."

"Paul thinks I killed the poet, doesn't he?" Emma released an angry snort, and the dog jumped again.

"No." Ray rolled his eyes and turned back to the fire. "Stay out of it, Emma."

Her lips tightened and she bit back the snarl in her throat. She pitied the detective, thrown into a murder with only the resources to hand. No pathologist, no forensics team, no one else to question the other suspects. Just himself. She glanced at Ray's bowed head and a smile stretched across her lips. And her.

"I'll give these bars to Sir Robert," she said, pushing as much innocence into her voice as she could muster. "See you later."

Ray grunted, but Emma sensed his gaze boring into her spine as she walked towards the morning room.

The group turned towards her as one, a sea of eight expectant faces. Lips parted and eyes widened. But the hopeful chests deflated in an audible whoosh as Emma closed the door behind her. They'd drawn up every available couch and chair to form a mini-theatre around the fireplace. The wheeled cupboard housing the TV sat at an angle, cables trailing behind it. A black and white comedy played on the screen, a favourite of Nicky's. The plummy British accents sounded high and false as a post war cast of characters acted. Emma cleared her throat and focussed on Freda's wonky brow.

Despite the general disappointment, Freda edged forward in her armchair and smiled at Emma. "Hello dear," she said. "Is everything okay? Monty is with the detective in your lounge. I hope you don't mind." She clapped her fragile hands together, the sound more of a slap. "I hope it's my turn next. He's very handsome."

"Mine!" Mavis thumped the back of Freda's chair with a knotty fist. "He wants to see me more urgently."

They squabbled as Major Mallory-Eaves lifted the TV remote and stalled the movie.

"Chloe is making soup and rolls," Emma announced. She surveyed her guests, trying to see the disastrous weekend from their viewpoint. Most of them knew nothing of Mavis' fraud, the empty bank account belonging to the Lit and His Society, or of the woman's manipulation of Emma. They'd rather have found themselves stranded at home than in a freezing manor house. Emma smiled at Sir Robert and tugged the muesli bars from her pocket. Their rustle attracted the attention of the room's other occupants. They perked up on rigid spines like a family of meerkats, Flora and Christos tallest in the mob. Emma squatted beside the retired barrister's chair. She held up the bars in her right palm as an offering. "Will this tide you over until lunchtime?" she whispered.

"Thank you dear." He took them from her in fingers which bent away from his knuckles. The arthritis in his hands explained his slip-on shoes still parked in the hallway. Fluffy white eyebrows wavered as he smiled down at her. Like tangled wire, they crawled towards his creamy hairline. "Most thoughtful," he murmured. "I appreciate your hospitality." His lips turned downward as though joining her in consolation. Emma discovered at close quarters she liked the aging lawyer, responding to the twinkle in his blue irises.

"You're welcome." She rose, performing a rudimentary headcount as she surveyed the guests. Flora shared a two-seater couch with Christos, a blanket spread across their knees. Tall and angular, she realised how comfortable they appeared. Emma glanced at the seat which Monty must have vacated. A high-backed chair sat empty, the dent from a bottom still evident in the padded cushion. It sat at ninety degrees to Gwendoline's easy chair, the tips of the wooden arms touching in a gentle caress. The younger woman had lost her arrogant air. Slumped and deflated, she'd expelled the showgirl demeanor and bowed beneath her grief. Her hair hung in a matted blonde curtain, a feather clinging to a trailing tendril. Grey streaks of faded mascara lined her cheeks. She leant forward, cradling her stomach as though in physical pain. A shawl covered her lithe thighs, pale and insignificant against the vibrancy of her black and red outfit.

Emma ached for her loss. The dead poet had both horrified and inconvenienced her. But she'd shed no tears for Kathleen Dubois. They'd shared no direct interaction. Only an alleged spiteful poem about the owner of Wingate Hall linked them.

Emma's lips twisted as she contemplated speaking to Gwendoline. She wanted to commiserate on the woman's loss, knowing the ache of losing a parent. But an air of blame circled the room, as though all but Freda held her responsible. Emma smiled at Flora and backed towards the door. But in the split second before her friend glanced up, Emma saw something. A game of footsie continued beneath the blanket. She paused with her hand on the door knob. The game halted. Flora raised her hand from beneath the tartan fabric and waved. "Need any help with the food?" she called.

Emma flattened her lips into a reluctant smile. "Chloe and the boys have it all under control," she replied. "But thanks." She thought for a moment, sensing all eyes boring into her bowed head. "I don't suppose any of you brought sleeping tablets with you?" She rubbed her eyes, exaggerating her distress.

Sir Robert shook his fluffy head with regret. "Sorry, my dear. Only insulin." He flapped his hand towards the major. "Bill shared his heart medication with me last night." He turned to smile at the man beside him. Their relationship had moved from casual acquaintances to friends.

Emma looked at the other occupants. She studied each. Bunny shook her head, as did Christos. Flora offered paracetamol from the depths of a tan leather handbag. Freda smoothed her tongue across her false teeth. Her eyes narrowed as she considered Emma's odd request. She knew Ray kept a pharmaceutical grade medical kit in the kitchen. The major fiddled with the remote control, eager to resume their movie watching. Mavis had ignored everything Emma said once the subject switched from food.

"Thanks," Emma said. She closed the door behind her, frustration budding in her chest.

Ray finished laying a fresh log on the fire and rose, brushing his hands together. Emma jogged across the lobby to his side. She frowned at the dog collapsed on the hearth rug and irritation mixed with her anger.

"Come upstairs," she hissed to Ray. "We need to search through their belongings. Someone just lied to me."

45

Throne chair

♥

Ray didn't argue. He followed Emma up the main staircase and along the hallway. She saw him steal nervous glances at the glass roof with its hazardous white blanket. An eerie greyness replaced the usual daylight.

"Do you think the skylight might leak when the snow melts?" She matched his long stride with a trot.

"Don't know," he replied, his answer clipped and without emotion. She assumed he wanted to deal with each problem as it arose and not fill his plate with possibilities. At the steps leading to the servants' quarters, Ray paused. He licked his lips and studied Emma's upturned face. "Let me do this alone," he said. "I know what I'm doing. Why don't you go back into the tunnels for a while?"

"What?" Emma's head jerked back on her neck. The fluff around her hood rustled. "I don't want to." She pictured the dank subterranean passages with their icy temperatures and endless darkness. Her lips turned down as her muscles recoiled.

"Not those tunnels." Ray's brows waggled in a comical action. "Paul won't tell us anything about his investigation. But if you overheard the interviews by accident." He licked his lips and left Emma to finish the thought.

But her lips drew back from her teeth in revulsion. "Not the house tunnels, please? What if I sneeze? He'll arrest me."

Ray shrugged and stepped onto the first rise. "You either want to know, or you don't. Go into the coach house and use the panel at the back of the airing cupboard. It'll take you behind the south wall of the lounge. The cavity is wider close to the fireplace but don't touch the brick. I lit a fire for Paul." The door swung shut behind him.

Emma ran down the back stairs and bypassed the kitchen. Chloe's voice sounded from inside the room and though she listened, Emma heard no reply from Dyfed or Ridley. A pan clattered against the Aga. Food scents drifted into the corridor, and she clamped a hand over her growling stomach. The lounge door remained closed on the opposite side of the hallway. Emma pictured her pretty sitting room beyond it. The long sash windows caught the afternoon sun and bathed the long room with warmth, even in the depths of winter. But not today. The wind lashed Wingate Hall as though exacting a punishment and the sky groaned beneath the weight of laden clouds.

Emma knocked on the door to the coach house and let herself in. "It's me, Winston," she called. At the northern end of the main house, the apartment boasted more glass per metre than anywhere else on the property. The former owners of the Hall had retreated there when the costs of heating and maintaining the manor outgrew their budget or inclination. They'd refurbished it and then hidden there, avoiding the decaying monolith beyond the adjoining wall.

Winston appeared at the end of the narrow hallway. Yellow light flickered across his sharp features as he smoothed gentle fingers over his neat waistcoat. His tie hung at an angle. He'd discarded his shiny shoes. Antique slippers encased his feet. Relics of the 1900s. Moving towards her, he placed a palm against the wall.

He seemed unbalanced. Emma frowned, an unexpected beat thudding in her chest. She met him beside the doorway of the master bedroom. "What's wrong?" she asked, her tone tight.

He waved away her concern with a flap of his free hand and a feckless shake of his head. "You caught me napping," he stated. For once Emma saw through the lie. She placed her hand beneath his elbow and led him towards the lounge. Enormous panes of glass reached from floor to ceiling, a gaudy 1970s abomination according to the heritage officer. Lots of things upset the council's historical enforcer about Wingate Hall, but the coach house irked him the most. He declared the renovation a disaster of epic proportions.

Emma helped Winston into the armchair closest to the fireplace. The dead grate did nothing to enhance the room's warmth. "It's freezing in here!" she exclaimed, rubbing her right palm over her left shoulder. "Why didn't you light a fire?"

"I'm fine," he murmured with a sigh. "I spent my childhood in Siberia. This is nothing."

Emma stepped to the nearest radiator and laid a hand over it. Cold. She faced Winston, noticing the uncharacteristic weakness in his movements as he covered his knees with a ratty blanket. Frayed edges dotted the threadbare tartan. "Ray brought you here on Friday?" She continued, already knowing the answer. "He wouldn't just leave you here with no heat. Did you send him away before he could light a fire or sort out the radiators?"

Winston shook his head. "The pipes whine. I turned them off. And he lit a fire, but I didn't maintain it."

Emma's shoulders slumped. "You're sick, aren't you?" Her words emerged as a frightened whisper. She'd watched her gentle father die a prolonged and painful death. The memories filled her with horror.

Winston shrugged. He cast off her sympathy. "I do not need your charity, girl!" But his easy intimidation faded. Rohan's odd invitation made a painful sense. He didn't put Emma beneath his father's watchful eye. He'd placed Winston beneath hers. Only she'd failed. Tangled herself in the Lit and His Society's drama and missed her real task.

Emma set her jaw into a hard line. "Ray can bleed the radiators," she stated. "It will take ten minutes at the most. Until then, I'll fetch the heater stored at the bottom of the wardrobe and warm the room."

Winston didn't object. She wheeled the portable heater from the second of the bedrooms. Closing the internal doors contained the heat as she set the device running beside Winston's chair. Its burning smell faded after a few minutes. "Can I get you anything else?" she asked. "A drink, perhaps?"

Winston shook his head. He laid his crown against the cushions of his armchair. His skin had paled to the hue of a calla lily. He blended seamlessly into the greyness of the storm. Emma cleared her throat, desperate to ask questions he wouldn't answer. Instead, she promised to return soon. His eyes remained closed. He didn't respond.

Emma opened the airing cupboard door. A fortifying breath escaped her. She tugged aside an ancient vacuum cleaner. Behind her, snow spattered the uncurtained windows, pelting the glass as though begging for entrance. Visibility had lowered to just a few metres. The white deluge obscured the stable block opposite.

After steeling herself, Emma crawled into the narrow space between the hot water cylinder and the wall. "I can do this," she whispered. "I can do this."

The back wall of the cupboard gave way to her second shove. It shifted into the cavity, allowing just enough room for her to squeeze through sideways. A cloying dust met her nostrils. It stuck to the back of her throat like a skin. Emma slipped into the space with two major regrets. She neglected to bring a face mask, and she'd forgotten the torch.

The house tunnels differed from the others. Emma immediately regretted not removing her restrictive ski jacket. She moved with caution, desperate to make no sound in the narrow space. But her jacket sleeves still brushed the dusty walls in a gap no wider than fifty centimetres. She stopped often, using a mental map to take her bearings. Her feet scraped against brick dust and her jacket created faint susurrations against the walls. Emma retrieved her phone again. This time, she dug into the apps icon and selected the first three letters of *torch*. A relieved sigh escaped her as the welcome glow activated.

Emma tried not to focus on her limited surroundings as she edged along the dusty floorboards. The light picked out her footing, helping her to avoid hazards. But not all of them. Cables hung along the walls like streamers from a lazy rewire job. They cast ominous shadows over the floor and distorted her view. It created the effect of battling through lace and increased Emma's growing claustrophobia. She'd looped her injured arm through a power cable and pulled it tight before noticing. It meant retracing her steps to release herself.

Forced to walk sideways to make any progress, Emma persevered. She imagined Rohan limping behind her, his warm hand on her shoulder. Comforting. Safe.

The passage turned a corner. Emma followed. Increasing warmth and the low hum of voices drifted through the silence. The soft soles of her slippers made less sound than her heavier boots as she edged forward. A half-eaten mouse block evidenced Ray's quiet battle with the other residents of the property. It had crumbled across her path. An unnatural, vivid blue in her torch light. A few steps further along, a shiny jelly bean showed the root of the problem. Nicky. Despite their best efforts, he'd found another way into the tunnels.

Emma jumped at the sudden clearing of a throat. Her heart seemed to lurch into her mouth. She held her breath, gagging against the myriad dust motes. She braced herself against a jutting wall and hissed in shock at the unexpected heat. Withdrawing her fingers, she placed them against her lips. She'd reached the fireplace of the room in which Paul conducted his interviews.

Without realising it, she'd covered half of the room already.

The throat clearing came again, the questioner perhaps uncomfortable with his task. But when he spoke, Paul's voice resonated through the wall. "I understand this is difficult for you," he said. "But your mother deserves justice." His soft tones held a persuasive determination.

A disgusting sniff reached Emma. She'd missed Monty's interrogation. It didn't worry her. She'd already dismissed Flora and Monty from her list of suspects. But not Mavis. Emma imagined a handcuffed Mavis wailing her protestations on the front steps. Fraud and murder. It couldn't happen to a nicer woman.

"I know who killed her." Gwendoline's voice rose three octaves, cutting through the brick like a pneumatic drill. "That bitch Emma did it," she sobbed. "I know she did. Why don't you arrest her?"

46

Ergonomic chair

♥

"Emma Andreyeva." Paul's words held no hint of a question. Emma held her breath, afraid he might take the accusation seriously.

"I don't know her last name." Gwendoline sniffed again, dredging enough phlegm from the back of her throat to impress an emphysema sufferer. "But she did it."

For a moment, Emma heard only silence. Her mind ticked over the reasons Gwendoline wanted her in the spotlight for her mother's murder. It seemed illogical, her accusation lacking any of the evidential triggers required to satisfy the detective. But her lips pursed at the realisation she possessed both the means and the opportunity. She owned both the spade and the house. So, if Gwendoline could provide a motive, it would put Emma in a precarious position.

Paul cleared his throat before answering. "There's nothing to suggest Mrs Andreyeva knew your mother prior to the weekend. Why would she want to harm her?"

Gwendoline floundered. She bought time by blowing into a tissue and mopping up her tears. "She's just hateful." It sounded weak, even to Emma. "There are rumours about her. I believe she's done it before."

Emma held her breath, dragged again back to the rumour mill of the small market town. Could Freda have betrayed her more than she'd realised?

"What rumours?" Paul sounded interested. Emma gave a silent snarl, drawing her lips away from her teeth. She'd thought better of Ray's son.

Gwendoline spent five minutes making things up. Her diatribe comprised speculation and insult with no modicum of fact. Emma relaxed as much as she could in the narrow space. She released her rigid muscles despite not wanting to touch the walls. Splaying her feet helped, but her knees complained. Emma knew she couldn't stand there for the entirety of Paul's investigation. But she wanted to.

Paul turned the conversation to the previous evening, distracting Gwendoline from her overt hatred of

Emma. "I understand that you all settled on the third floor for the night," he stated. "Talk me through the next couple of hours, please."

Gwendoline warbled on about Christos, betraying an entitled crush which stretched almost as far as obsession. "He's just marvellous," she gushed. "He's been so supportive. I don't know what I'd have done without him." Emma frowned, irritated that Gwendoline had conveniently forgotten how Monty comforted her beside her mother's body. He'd used his jacket to cover Kathleen's ruined face.

Another dramatic sniff gave Paul a segue into the conversation. "Can you remember who sat with you upstairs?" he asked. "And for how long before each person went to bed?"

A cushion creaked. Emma pictured the detective sitting in Rohan's favourite armchair. The deep leather seat let him remove his prosthetic leg and rest his stump. The chair curved at just the right point to meet the back of his knee. As though its careful maker had foretold its extraordinary requirement.

Emma preferred the sofa. She couldn't imagine Paul lounging there, his pocketbook and stubby pen poised.

Gwendoline stumbled over her reply. "Monty came upstairs as that old man lit the fire. Everyone cheered when the flames took hold. Monty said he'd left my mother sitting in the morning room with Dad. We told him Flora had already gone to bed. Mavis didn't sit with us. Dad came upstairs by himself later. I showed him to the room by the stairs." A sneer entered her voice. "The caterers arrived. Those two weird men caused a fuss. They moved their bedding into the single room opposite theirs." Her tone held no sympathy for a family who'd already suffered violence and an arrest. Perhaps Freda hadn't imparted that piece of gossip yet. But Dyfed and Ridley had intended to protect Chloe from Gareth's return. But Gareth hadn't come back. Yet.

Gwendoline's voice piped through the walls like nails on a blackboard. "I sat with Christos until he went to bed."

"At what time?"

A pause. "Twenty past midnight, I think. I didn't check my phone until I got into bed. The screen said half past. Horrible little room. You'd think in a house this size she'd host us somewhere that didn't smell of old people. And the beds! We'll all need a chiropractor after this weekend. We should sue for mistreatment."

"Did you wake at all during the night, Miss Dubois? Do you recall any unusual sounds which caused you to leave your room and investigate? Any kind of disturbance, however minor?"

Gwendoline snorted. "I hardly slept! My bed sounded like a xylophone every time I turned over. I tried to watch a movie, but I couldn't get any internet signal. Monty gave me the Wi-Fi password last evening, but my phone couldn't connect. Now my mother is dead!" Her voice rose to an irritating wail, punctuated by a sob.

Paul paused for a moment of decency before pushing forward with his quest for information. "Do you remember what time you tried the Wi-Fi?" he asked.

Gwendoline sniffed. Emma imagined the nonchalant shrug of her shoulders. "How should I know?" she demanded. "What does it matter? My mother is dead. What are you doing about it?"

Paul lowered his voice. "Someone unplugged the router in the main house during the night," he said. "It seems the storm took out the land-line first. The nearest cell tower failed this morning. But the house has underground fibre cables. There's no reason to lose access to the internet."

Gwendoline huffed out a protest and stated the obvious. "You can't expect a group of geriatric visitors to understand something like that!" she spat. "It's her, I'm telling you! Why won't you listen to me?"

"Approximate time," Paul persisted.

Emma sensed Gwendoline's teeth grinding in her pretty jaw as Paul rebuffed her attempts to implicate Emma. "I slept for an hour," she conceded. "I logged onto the Wi-Fi at one-thirty. It didn't work. I knocked on Christos' door around two o'clock, but he didn't wake. He's in banking. I figured he might fix my phone."

Emma suppressed a snort. She guessed Gwendoline's real motive. She hadn't stopped pawing at Christos since she arrived.

Paul pressed on with his questioning. "Then what?" Emma sensed a latent excitement in his voice.

"Nothing," Gwendoline grumbled. "I returned to bed and dozed until I heard someone running a bath. That funny little man with the white hair got the fire going again. We huddled around it to keep warm. I'd just bagged the next bath after Monty finished, when that bitch assaulted me and banned me from the bathroom!"

Paul moved on without comment. If Gwendoline had fantasised about Emma's arrest, the detective disappointed her. "You told Mrs Andreyeva about a poem your mother wrote." Rustling cut across his words. "Do you recognise this?"

Silence. Emma waited for Gwendoline's response. For seconds, she heard nothing.

"Would you like me to rephrase the question?" Paul's tone remained polite.

"No!" Sulkiness entered Gwendoline's voice. "Mum didn't write that. And anyway, it's not about that stupid woman!"

"Who wrote it?"

A loud huff. "Not Mum!" But Emma sensed Gwendoline's lie. If it wasn't about Emma, then who?

"See, this is where there's confusion," Paul continued. "You placed your mother upstairs last night. You told Mrs Andreyeva that Mrs Dubois composed and recited a poem about her. Mrs Andreyeva heard laughing just after midnight. That coincides with everyone laughing at her expense. Is that not the truth?"

Cold seeped into Emma's muscles. She fought the urge to stamp her feet. The moment held a latent potency.

"No," Gwendoline murmured. Emma's fingers brushed the dusty walls as she leaned closer to listen. A cobweb attached itself to her fringe. She ignored it. She forced herself not to worry about the possibility of an inhabitant abseiling down on her head.

"No, your mother didn't write a poem about Mrs Andreyeva. Or no, she didn't read it to you all last night?"

"None of that!" Gwendoline shouted. "Mum didn't write it! So, she didn't read it! I just said that to upset her. Christos won't even look at me when she's around."

"Did you see your mother at all on the third floor last night?"

"No!" Gwendoline sighed.

Paul battled on. "So, when did you miss your mother this morning?"

Gwendoline's voice hitched. "Not for ages!" she wailed. "Mum and Dad have separate rooms at home because she gets restless. Dad slept later than usual. He figured Mum used the empty room vacated by those catering idiots. But I assumed she'd stayed with Dad. We didn't search for her until we got downstairs. Then we compared notes and realised neither of us saw her after we went to bed." Her tears held genuine misery. Emma couldn't doubt the pain in the heartrending sobs escaping the woman's slender body. But Gwendoline had lied about the poem.

Regan timed the router's unplugging around midnight. Monty used the Wi-Fi at the awards ceremony to transfer money to Chloe. It made no sense to disable the internet connection. Because they still had a mobile phone signal as an alternative way to summon help.

Gwendoline had revealed Arnand brought sleeping tablets with him. An odd thing to take to an evening event. He might have drugged the dog.

"Had you met the other members of the Literary and Historical Society before last night?" Paul's gentle enquiry slowed Gwendoline's tears. She gave a disgusting sniff.

"I'd seen most of them. We moved away years ago. I'm not interested in poems and old books. Or old people."

"You seem familiar with Mr Smaragdis."

"Well, I met Christos on a dating app last year. I liked his profile. We chatted on and off for a while." She cleared her throat. "I sent him photos. Of myself." She rushed on with her story, not elaborating on what sort of images she'd shared. "We lost touch. I wanted to meet. He's my kind of man. Handsome. Successful." She didn't add *rich*, but Emma imagined her biting back the word.

"He ghosted you online?"

Gwendoline glossed over Paul's question. "My father expected me to support Mum at the awards night. He forwarded the invitation to me. That stupid Mavis included everyone's name in the subject line. I didn't realise Christos belonged to the Society. It's the only reason I came to this horrible house."

"To meet Christos in person?"

Gwendoline sighed. Emma detected an edge of exasperation. "So? There's no law against consenting adults meeting up for... relationship building." Her tone held a sparkly giddiness, like a teenager intoxicated by a fresh love.

"And how did that work out for you?" Paul asked.

"He's the one," Gwendoline stated. No doubt in her mind. "He's the man I'll marry."

"Right." Silence. "Tell me about the other members of the Society."

"I don't know them. Apart from Monty and Flora. They visit my dad sometimes. They both taught me at school when we lived in Market Harborough. Mum doesn't like them." She cleared her throat. "Didn't like them."

"Why is that?"

Gwendoline stalled. A fake coughing fit, intended to buy her thinking time, dragged into valuable minutes. Her response appeared strained when she spoke, as though she'd mentally redacted important facts. "Monty writes poetry. He got a book publishing deal. Mum didn't think he deserved it."

"But your mother won a writing scholarship with Leicester University, didn't she?" In Emma's mind, she saw Paul cocking his head.

"Yes." Her snippy reply raised the hairs on Emma's scalp.

"So, they're both successful?"

A pregnant pause. "Yes. I suppose so." The brittle words cut through the air. "Can I go now?"

Emma chewed on her lip. She fought the tickle building in her throat. The layers of dust aggravated her airways. Gwendoline had no alibi for the relevant two-hour period. She'd also tried to rouse Christos and failed. Had he roamed Wingate Hall during the night?

Emma pressed a hand over her lips as the cough built. A movement sounded from next door. Footsteps accompanied the soft voices, Paul commiserating.

"What do you do for a living, Gwendoline?" he asked.

"I'm a model." A haughtiness infused the declaration.

"Oh." Paul's tone held interest. "Catwalks and clothing lines?"

"No." The conversation ended on that final note.

Turning in the tiny space, Emma retraced her careful steps to the airing cupboard. She squeezed past the boiler and pushed the panel closed. But she didn't replace the vacuum cleaner.

Winston still sat in the armchair. His motionless posture set Emma's heart racing. "Winston!" She touched his shoulder with trembling fingers. The blanket lay in hills and valleys of tartan fabric across his neat waistcoat.

He jumped as though she'd used a defibrillator. His eyes widened with shock at the sight of her. Relief flooded Emma. Her knees knocked in a palsy of confusion. She pressed her good hand over her chest. "You scared me," she admitted. Then she silenced.

"Two stiffs in one day." His voice held a creaky quality as he finished her unspoken thought.

Emma swallowed. "I'm coming back," she promised. "I've found the perfect place to eavesdrop on the detective. But I can't disappear indefinitely without causing suspicion. I'll see if the food is ready and bring some for you." She glanced around the darkened room with a frown.

The swathes of glass brought the continuing blizzard inside, as though no barrier existed. The furious grey sky showed no sign of releasing Wingate Hall from its grip. "Can I put the TV on for you?" Emma walked towards the cupboard housing the device, only stopped by a wave of Winston's thin hand.

"No," he rasped. "I don't want it." He blinked, his long lashes deepening the shadows beneath his eye sockets. "Perhaps some lunch," he conceded with a half-hearted smile.

Emma nodded. She left the coach house. The knot in her stomach increased with every passing minute. This blasted storm had filled her home with a slew of potential medical emergencies. The average age of the

Lit and His Society dictated at least one more calamity. Their number contained a diabetic, and two candidates for a heart attack. And now Winston. She didn't need a medical degree to discern his ill health.

She wished the snow would melt, her living and deceased guests would leave, and that life at Wingate Hall could return to normal. Whatever normal looked like.

47

Saddle chair

♥

E mma feared the group's growing hunger. And their tendency to roam. The entrance to the basement remained locked to her left. She stalled before making the turn into the corridor.

One stride would take Emma back into the fray. Six strides would put her in the kitchen. The heady scent of fresh bread wafted from the part open doorway. The earthy tang of venison accompanied it. Emma listened for company.

The light thud of a spine hitting a wall prevented her first step. She peeked around the corner.

"You don't understand!" Bunny stood before Arnand Dubois. Her tiny hands splayed against his chest in a mute appeal. Her shawl hung diagonally from her right shoulder and caught beneath her left elbow.

Arnand gulped. He pressed himself against the wall. His muddy irises darted at the kitchen door beside him.

Emma remained frozen in place.

"My wife is dead!" Arnand hissed. Those four short words contained more passion than he'd shown so far. His voice hitched. "Stay away from us!"

Emma heard a sudden gasp. She sped around the corner in time to see the tail end of his nasty shove to Bunny's slight frame. His curled fingers remained aloft, zombie-like. Bunny hit the opposite wall, banging her elbows on the wooden architrave of the lounge door. Her head hung low as she rubbed them, her expression unreadable.

"Stop this!" Emma demanded. She squatted beside Bunny.

"You started it." Bunny whimpered the sentence through a guttural sob.

"No!" Arnand's voice rose to a shout. "You did this! You made my life unbearable. We left town, our home, our jobs. Poor Gwen changed schools! Just to get away from your interference." He clasped his hands together as though praying. His knuckles balled on his writhing fingers. "You engineered this invitation." His head shot up and he took a threatening step towards Bunny. She cowered beneath his fury, lifting her arms to shield her head. "You're the reason Kathleen died." Arnand's usual bland expression lit with a hidden fire. Cheeks flaming and raw, he glared at Bunny's bowed head. "Did you kill my wife?"

"No!" Her chin shot up. She clapped one hand over her mouth. The shawl lost its purchase, and its fringe brushed the tiled floor. "Or I would have done it years ago!"

Arnand grunted. He stared down at her as though inspecting something distasteful. "Stay away from us," he commanded. His tone offered no compromise. Turning on his heels, he strode towards the lobby. Strands of loose hair rode his head, streaming behind him like bunting. He passed over the place where his wife died without slowing.

Bunny sank to her bottom on the cold tiles. Her arms hooked around her knees. She sobbed without shame, head bowed and chest heaving. She fought the demon which just stomped on her heart. The toes of the borrowed purple slippers peeked from beneath the hem of her ratty skirt.

Emma glanced up as the kitchen door flew open. Dyfed stood in the gap. His affable smile belied the terror in his blue eyes. Wide and staring, they glittered with unshed tears. Naked panic increased his grip on the meat cleaver in his hand. He kept it raised. White knuckles shone in eight visible mounds. He flicked his gaze to Bunny and then to Emma. He reversed back into the kitchen. "The shouty man isn't Dad." He pushed the door closed as though he hadn't just threatened two defenseless women with a knife.

Emma edged closer to Bunny. Her heart blocked her throat with its forceful pounding. She daren't turn her back on the kitchen and its dangerous occupants. Squatting beside Bunny, she lifted her beneath the armpits. "Let's go to the lounge," she begged. She shot a glance at the closed kitchen door with its blob of tape sticking to the frame. She doubted the door knobs contained any fingerprints or DNA now. Had Paul not already identified traces of blood on the spade, she'd have put money on the cleaver.

Dyfed. In the kitchen. With the cleaver. Like a game of Clue.

Emma dragged Bunny upright, shocked by the woman's fragility. "Come on!" she urged.

Paul hadn't locked the lounge behind him. Emma turned the knob and shoved the door open, gratified by the wall of heat which hit her. She dragged Bunny over the threshold and closed the door.

"You know Arnand Dubois!" she blurted. "But you said nothing!"

Bunny's shoulders shook as she sank onto the nearest sofa. "You heard." She ran a trembling hand over her eyes. Needing Rohan's guidance more than ever, Emma claimed his leather chair. She ran her palm across the rounded arm and pressed an index finger over an upholstery button. The cushion dug into her bottom.

"Tell me everything!" she demanded through gritted teeth. "You have less than two minutes before Detective Inspector Barker arrives back. So, get talking!"

Bunny wiped her mouth with the back of her thin wrist. "After secretarial college, I worked at the district council offices on the outskirts of London. I was seventeen. Arnand ran the museum next door. I did the typing for all the departments. We got close." Her lashes fluttered, loaded with saline speckles. "We had an affair. I got pregnant." Her throat constricted, producing a strangled tone to her words. "Arnand promised I could see the baby whenever I liked. It seemed the best solution. To let them raise her. My parents couldn't know I'd behaved like such a slut. My father would have killed me." Her chest hitched. Emma swallowed at the genuine grief swirling around the tiny woman.

"Oh, my goodness!" she breathed. "Gwendoline is your daughter."

An agonised groan escaped Bunny's chest. The effort bent her double. Emma squatted beside her, resting her palm on Bunny's heaving shoulder. "I'm so sorry," she whispered. She imagined someone whisking Nicky or Stephie away from her. Forever. Her heart gave a shudder. It robbed her of her next breath. Gwendoline Dubois? She'd behaved with such rudeness to her own mother. "You don't fancy Christos, do you? You're keeping him away from Gwendoline." Chunky Arnand and the waiflike Bunny had produced a glamourous, entitled child. The fact made Emma's head reel.

Bunny nodded, the action jerky on her thin neck. "It's no good," she stammered. "He's not interested in me. I'm too old. I don't have what it takes." She jerked her head upright, her sparkling eyes boring into Emma's face. "But you do," she pleaded. "He's attracted to you. Keep him away from my little girl. He only wants money."

"Money?" Emma knitted her brows.

"He's a conman," Bunny began.

The lounge door had always squeaked. Ray had oiled the hinges and reseated the heavy wood. He'd tried everything to stop it. But it provided Emma with a valuable warning. She threw herself across the room and landed beside Bunny. The sofa creaked. She pressed Bunny's damp face against her shoulder. Under her breath, she issued a whispered command. "Shut up!" she hissed.

"Oh." Paul put enough indignation into the single word to suggest he'd been non-violently robbed.

Emma rested her cheek against the top of Bunny's downy crown. She smiled across the room at him. The expression of benevolence put him back in his place as she retook ownership of her home. "Leave us for a moment, please." Her eyes held no softness as the stalemate ensued.

Paul remained in the doorway, his next interviewee at his shoulder. Emma noticed Sir Robert's fluffy white fringe as he peered around the detective. "What's the delay?" the barrister enquired.

Emma released her hold around Bunny's neck. She allowed her to sit up again. "Feeling better?" she asked, her tone bright.

Nodding, Bunny dabbed at her swollen eyes with a corner of the shawl. "Thank you," she murmured.

Hurried footsteps caused Paul to spin on his heels. Sir Robert clapped his hands together. Chloe's rasping voice echoed in the corridor. "Does no one want this bloody food, then?" she snapped. "That bloke said he'd pay me for making a meal. I'll charge extra for chasing everyone around the bloody house to eat it!"

Detective Inspector Paul Barker didn't lose interest in the murder of Kathleen Dubois. But everyone else momentarily did. Like geese flocking to sunnier climes for winter, the occupants of Wingate Hall flooded into the morning room with their very late lunch. Bowls of wholesome soup and crusty buttered rolls left a magical scent throughout the downstairs.

Like geese they ate. Squawking, clucking, and flapping.

48

Ottoman

"I'm not hungry." Bunny used a rumpled tissue from her sleeve to dab at her eyes.

Emma savoured the scent of fresh, warm rolls as her guests spirited them along the corridor. Her stomach growled, but she needed to pump Bunny for more information.

Paul unnerved her. He seemed fickle, shifting from comforting hugs one minute to barking commands the next. She couldn't trust him.

Emma settled on her bottom in front of Bunny. She rested her right forearm across the woman's knees as contact, but also ensuring she didn't bolt. The action seemed predatory, but Bunny patted her wrist as though grateful. "I'll stay with you." Emma raised her eyebrows at Paul, wanting him to leave her to interrogate Bunny.

"Grab some food," she said, jerking her chin at him. "Please ask Ray to salvage some lunch for me?"

Paul's jaw shifted from side to side. Rapid blinking accompanied his realisation she'd stymied him. Glancing behind him, he sighed. Sir Robert had escaped to chase his late lunch. "Fine!" Paul growled and closed the door behind him.

"I'm so sorry." Saline created damp trails along Bunny's thin cheeks as Emma's stomach released a sad moan. Her tears crested her chin and dived into the neckline of her dress. "You're hungry, and I'm keeping you from your lunch."

"I'm fine," Emma soothed. "Ray will set some aside for me." She pursed her lips at the lie. Anything Ray wrestled from the hungry mob would end up before Winston. Her brows furrowed at the thought of her father-in-law's obvious physical distress. Another mystery she couldn't solve. She sighed and Bunny glanced up at her, tears collecting on the end of her nose.

"Sorry," she whispered again.

Emma used the ensuing pause to collect her thoughts. She bypassed the pain radiating from her wrist with difficulty and filtered the overheard argument between

Bunny and Arnand. "Why did Arnand accuse you of stalking?" she asked.

Bunny groaned and winced. "That's his word for it, but it's not true. I just wanted to see my daughter, as per our original agreement." Her shoulders lost their tension. She drew the shawl around her like a kitten burrowing into its mother's fur. "He moved away from London without warning. I arrived at his house to discover he'd gone and taken Gwendoline with him. I lost her for fifteen years." Her chest hitched. Grief spilled over into her story. "I employed two private detectives. The first just wasted my money, but the second discovered Arnand's location and his change of name. It explained why I couldn't find him listed anywhere. He'd married Kathleen and taken Dubois as his surname. I guess it sounded more sophisticated than Jones."

"Jones?" Emma's eyes widened. "Like Monty and Flora Jones?" The innocuous fact tied in with Monty's visit to Arnand in Leicester.

Bunny's lips tightened into a sardonic smile. "And hence the reason he relocated to Market Harborough when he left London. They're cousins."

"What happened to Arnand's first wife?" Emma tilted her head back and stared unseeing at the ceiling. "And why would she accept a baby conceived in a workplace affair?"

Bunny swallowed. "She couldn't have children. Despite everything, I knew she'd love Gwendoline with all her heart. I had little to offer, but she adored that child. And she believed I should maintain contact."

"So, what changed her mind? Why move away without telling you?"

Bunny made a squeak of regret in her throat. "Sandra Jones died just before Gwendoline's second birthday. Arnand failed to return to work after a two-week break. A colleague mentioned his wife died. Bereavement leave. I visited his house when I heard he'd resigned." She pursed her lips. Her shuddered sigh contained misery at the blank windows and the hollow knock of her slender fingers on the door to a deserted house.

"I tried to forget Arnand and my baby girl. But as the years passed, the ache in my chest grew. I saved up to pay the private detectives. The second one's information renewed my search. I persuaded my parents to visit Market Harborough on a weekend jaunt. We stayed at The Swan Hotel and explored the town. They fell in love with the place. Months later, they retired here, and I came with them. By then, I'd tracked Arnand down in the local museum. He'd changed his name, but not his profession. Museum curator." Her irises became glassy. "I fell in love with a mild-mannered man," she mused with a sigh. "He possessed a certain charisma beneath the boring, beige cardigans." She blinked. Her expression hardened. "He'd changed." Knotty fingers pressed against her lips. "She destroyed him. He behaved like a whipped dog when he saw me at the museum."

"Kathleen?" Emma leaned forward as the tension hiked. "Kathleen destroyed him?" Bunny's thin bones pressed against Emma's forearm.

"Yes," she breathed. "Manipulative, controlling and cruel. She worked as a verger at the old church in the town square. Not a single member of the clergy or the congregation liked her."

"So, where does the stalking accusation come from? He sounded furious."

Bunny's lips pressed into white lines. "I just wanted access to my daughter. But Arnand refused to broach it with his wife. Said she wouldn't permit it. Gwendoline believes Kathleen gave birth to her. It's not what we agreed." A flap of delicate skin wobbled under her chin as she heaved in a giant breath. "I went to see Kathleen."

"Oh." Emma imagined the spiky woman greeting her husband's former mistress with disdain. "What happened?"

"Screaming, shouting. The police came. She lied more in five minutes than I'd heard in a lifetime. They arrested me for stalking. Without evidence. Eventually, they dropped the charges." Another tear coursed down her cheek. It plunged from her jaw and left a dark spot on the shawl. "My father fetched me from the police station." She exhaled, funnelling the breath through a tiny vent in her lips. "The event exposed my awful secret. Anand disappeared overnight yet again. Then my father had a stroke. I blamed myself. The next ten years were my punishment. I cared for Dad and then my mother. They never forgave me. For the shame. And because I robbed them of their only grandchild. It left little opportunity to hunt for a girl in her teens who didn't know I existed."

Emma pitied her. The tale made her heart ache. But she couldn't live with herself if she didn't issue the whispered warning. "If the detective finds out any of this, he'll think you killed Kathleen," she said under her breath.

"But I didn't." Bunny sniffed. "What's the point? Gwendoline is a grown woman. What would it achieve now to upend her world?"

"To get Arnand back?" Emma raised a speculative eyebrow.

Bunny's chin jerked downward, and her lips peeled back from her teeth in a grimace. "I don't think so. He ruined my life, Emma. Any pity I had for his disastrous marriage died when he let the police arrest me. Kathleen told them I was deluded. He said nothing in my defence. Not one word."

"But did Arnand tell the truth about the invitation?" Emma asked. "Did you ask Mavis to contact Kathleen Dubois without involving you?"

Bunny nodded. "Yes, I noticed an article about her poetry success in a literary magazine. I told Mavis my laptop broke, and I couldn't send emails. I urged her to call Kathleen on the telephone and beg her to attend. Mavis practically salivated. I only had to email the invitations later."

"Did you realise the Dubois would bring Gwendoline?"

Again, Bunny nodded. "Mavis sent three invitations. I hoped if I could see them together as a family, it might justify everything that happened." She dabbed her left eye with her knuckles. "You know what I mean?"

Emma nodded. Her thoughts turned to her brother. The brother she would never now meet. "I do," she replied. "You fill your mind with pictures of the wonderful life they had without you. And hope with all your heart someone loved them." She winced, avoiding Bunny's perceptive stare as she revealed her own painful secret. Hidden adoption wrought terrible consequences.

"You do," Bunny agreed. "The woman seemed as odious as I remembered, but Gwendoline worshipped the ground beneath her." She shrugged. "Kathleen Dubois' death achieves nothing for me. I've still lost my daughter."

Emma twisted her lips into a grimace. "Detective Inspector Barker won't see it that way."

49

Executive chair

♥

"Is it possible Kathleen recognised you?" Emma kept her fingers over the door knob and turned to face Bunny. "Did you have any interaction with her?"

"No!" She snarled the word, her body jerking backwards in revulsion. "I spent the evening hiding from her. That's why I hung around in the lobby." A hand lifted to brush back an imaginary fringe. She'd cut her hair and altered her appearance. "I tested it later when I offered Kathleen a drink. She didn't acknowledge me. Nor did Arnand." She pursed her lips. "Until just before. But I pushed the issue. He left the morning room, so I followed him to the kitchen. I intended to tell him I wouldn't pursue things with Gwendoline, but he went crazy. He brought up the stalking accusation and wouldn't let me explain." She gave a visible shudder. "This weekend has given me a chance to reevaluate my life. I've made some dreadful mistakes and wasted too much of it." Her lips flattened into even thinner lines than Emma believed possible. "I'll sell my parents' house and use the money to travel. I'll watch Gwendoline from afar. Make sure she doesn't end up with a loser like Christos." The decision gave her irises a sparkle.

She placed a hand over her flat stomach and raised a smile. "I feel much better now. Do you think there's any food left?"

Emma cocked her head. "How do you know he's a conman?"

"Instinct," Bunny snapped. "He wants to be the Society's treasurer far too much. It's a role people get pushed into. Nobody chooses the responsibility, not in my experience. He's asked each month since the summer. Mavis has blocked everyone, but now we know why."

Emma shrugged. "That's a thin reason."

Bunny snorted. "Monty asked him to take over last night. He looked like he'd won the lottery."

"Until he realised, he'd inherit an empty account?" Emma surmised.

Bunny nodded.

A miserable sight met them in the kitchen. Ray's back faced the entrance, his body bent in a deep arch. Plates clanked as he filled the dishwasher with almost all the crockery Emma owned. Yellow rubber gloves flashed into view as he rose. "Really?" Emma exclaimed. "This is just too much!"

Ray flapped a glove at the kitchen table. Jets of soapy water tracked through the air. "Yeah. These people think they're at a hotel. One of them asked for dessert and coffee." He snorted through his nose.

"Mavis?" Emma asked.

"No, the tall, willowy one who thinks she's a supermodel." Ray hefted a heavy saucepan into the sink and activated the hot water tap. "Soup tasted great, but the cook used every pot and spoon in the kitchen."

Emma turned as Bunny tapped her elbow. "I'll leave you to it," she said. "They've eaten everything by the looks of it." She leaned sideways to observe Ray's cleaning up operation. Emotional exhaustion created dark shadows beneath her eye sockets. Her thin chest periodically hitched from crying. "Forgive me for not helping. I'll take a nap in my room." She forced a smile. "Thank you for everything."

She left before Emma could dissuade her. The link to Kathleen Dubois made her nervous.

The door emitted a tired thud against the tape as Emma let it close behind her. Bunny's spongy soles padded along the corridor. Possession of Kathleen's slippers held a hollow irony.

"Where's the dog?" Emma frowned at the realisation she hadn't seen him for a while. His empty bed stood beside the Aga.

Ray glanced back at her and waggled his eyebrows. "Comatose by the lobby fire. I built it up again about half an hour ago and he didn't crack an eyelid."

Emma lifted a floury board and carried it to the sink. "Thanks for doing this," she said, raising her injured arm in a stiff wave. She retrieved as much of the dumped crockery as she could manage, loading it into the dishwasher one-handed. Ray splashed in the deep sink, brushing baked flour from a metal tray.

Emma jumped as a swathe of white flew past the window. It hit the roof of Chloe's van and shattered into fragments.

Ray grinned sideways at her. "Bit jumpy, Em," he mused. "Anyone would think there's a killer in your house."

"Not funny!" she jibed back. She lifted a dish towel and patted at the bubbles on a plate. "What did you discover upstairs?" She eyed him sideways.

Ray sighed. "I couldn't get access. The bossy woman shouted up the stairs that the food was ready, and people appeared from everywhere. That friend of yours didn't seem to want me upstairs by myself and encouraged me to follow them down."

"Friend?" Emma cocked her head. "Male or female?"

Ray mopped his brow against his shoulder. He plunged his hands deep into the sink. "Tall lady with a fur coat."

"Flora?" Emma frowned. "I thought everyone went to the morning room."

Ray snorted. "They're everywhere, Em. It's like herding ants."

She winced as her phone vibrated in her pocket. The groan started in her chest as she unlocked the screen. "Nicky again," she said with a sigh. "He's got into Allaine's Facebook account and keeps sending me photographs. It's probably a good thing we don't have a cell phone signal. He'd drown me in texts."

"Message Allaine on the app," Ray suggested. He wrinkled his nose and vetoed his own suggestion.

"Pointless exercise. He's already in her account. He'd see it before her."

Emma turned the screen so Ray could admire the close-up photograph of Kayleigh's nostrils. "This kid knows too much about life," she said with regret.

Ray shrugged, his broad shoulders blocking Emma's view of another falling chunk of snow. "Perhaps he's strategic like his daddy. At least if she gets blown up someday, he'll have the blueprint to stick her back together again."

Emma reeled back in shock. "Soldier humour, not appropriate."

"True." Ray laughed. "But you know your son is going straight into espionage as soon as he's of age. He has all the makings of a very fine spy."

The comment reminded Emma of Winston. "Did you take him some soup?" she asked. "Is he okay?"

Ray shrugged. "I left it with him. Chemotherapy knocks some people around worse than others. Awake all night and sick all day."

"Chemotherapy?" Emma gaped at him. "Is that why Rohan invited him here?"

"That, and other reasons. I told you, talk to your husband."

Emma shuddered and changed the subject. "I sent Winston upstairs to search the rooms earlier. Did he find anything apart from your boots?"

"Says not," Ray replied. A soap bubble clung to his left eyebrow. He stopped with his hands in the sink and stared at the ceiling. "But when he got downstairs to the second floor, he found the tall dude trying the door to your bedroom. Winston hid in the alcove and the guy gave up, but it bothered the old man." He quirked an eyebrow at her. "Asked some questions about your marriage and whether you might stray from his son."

Emma dropped her chin and peered through the tops of her eyes. "He thinks I'm having an affair with Christos Smaragdis?"

Ray squirmed, his muscles seething beneath his jacket sleeves. "You let him use your shower. Mr Wright's antenna is up and receiving."

"I did not!" Emma barked. She thought back to the moment in her bedroom after Winston shut off the hot water. "Christos?" she mused. "So, he might have left the boots there at the same time?"

"Maybe," Ray agreed.

"So Christos is our boot stealer." She ruminated on the thought for a moment. "Paul is releasing pieces of evidence as he goes. I wonder if Christos has realised the importance of the footprints."

"But he has massive feet, remember?" Ray countered.

"Yeah. Size thirteen." Emma exhaled and shook her head. "What if he drugged Farrell last night? Perhaps he always planned to go outside, and he didn't want the dog to wake the entire house." She tapped a fingernail against her teeth. "But why is Farrell still groggy? He slept like a brick until I found Kathleen. He seemed fine on the way to see Regan."

"Lear," Ray corrected. "Yeah, that has crossed my mind. I'm wondering if he scrounged food meant for someone else at the awards thing. He always eats crap off the floor and your guests are a messy bunch." He clattered the tray onto the draining board and reached for the mixing bowl Chloe used to knead the dough.

Emma frowned and loaded stained soup bowls into the dishwasher. Most of them appeared licked clean, a testament to Chloe's cooking skills. "You think someone brought drugs to an evening event with the express purpose of making their victim docile? For what purpose?"

Ray waggled his eyebrows, but didn't detail the horrible possibilities. Emma's brows knitted in horror.

"You think Mavis planned to seduce a comatose Christos?" She shuddered. "Or Major Mallory-Eaves fancied a bunk up with Gwendoline?"

"The major is gay." Ray blinked as sudsy water flicked into his face. He dunked a roasting pan into the sink. He wiped his eyes on his shoulder.

"How would you know a thing like that?" Emma demanded. "He strikes me as a very private man. I doubt it's public knowledge."

"I still have mates in the service. He served overseas and became embroiled in a scandal with a male attaché to the American ambassador. His wife divorced him, and he took an honourable discharge over a court marshal. I remember when it blew up, but it's old news now."

"Medical corp?" Emma asked. Ray nodded. "That's how I know him. He won't remember me, though. He'd already earned his stripes, and I was a lowly private."

"I kinda like him," Emma admitted. "He grew on me a little last night when he checked Kathleen's pulse. His concern seemed genuine." She gnawed on her lip and placed spoons in the cutlery rack of the dishwasher. "Perhaps his bluster is defensive."

Ray shrugged. "That bus out front is from the high school at Kibworth. He's driven it for the last ten years. I'm guessing he borrows it sometimes. It's the same one he used for the summer fete."

Emma leaned back against the counter and folded her left arm across her right for support. "What do you know about Sir Robert Holden?"

"You're asking me because you think Paul has shared information?" Ray plunged a hand into the deep water and hauled out the plug.

Emma smiled at him, a coy, knowing grin. "No. But you're nosey and you have ways of finding out things. And if Rohan wheeled in Winston for the weekend in his absence, I'm guessing my father-in-law took the responsibility seriously. I bet he's checked out the members of the Market Harborough Literary and Historical Society. So, come on. Winston can't help himself. What do you know about our local barrister to the king?"

Ray leaned back next to her. He peeled the rubber gloves from his hands as though performing a striptease. Emma's curiosity built until she ached to punch his arm. "Sir Robert Holden KC indeed served as a lawyer. You can check any London news article over twenty years old and see his face on the front cover. He prosecuted some big value cases in his time." He dumped the gloves on the draining board beside the clean saucepan. Water dribbled from its interior.

"And?" Emma demanded. "Something in your tone tells me his career came to a traumatic and abrupt end."

"Drank too much at a soiree and drove his Mercedes into the rear of a police car."

Emma winced. "Ouch. But judges have done worse and survived."

"Not in the middle of a high-profile case involving Alison Gerhardt. The media crawled all over it. He believes they hacked his phone. You can imagine. It didn't help that he fled the scene, leaving an officer injured."

"Alison the baby killer?" Emma scrubbed her eyes with the heel of her right hand. "I remember that case. Awful. Munchausen Syndrome by Proxy. She worked as a nurse on the neonatal ward at Addenbrookes, didn't she?"

"Yeah. Also known as Factitious Disorder Imposed on Another. Make them sick to look like a hero when you nurse them back to health again."

Emma blew out a breath, which ruffled her dark fringe. "Rohan's mother did that to us," she said, her voice tight.

"So, the question we need to answer is why Farrell is still zonked out." Ray pulled at a thread on his sweater cuff. "It's possible he's had a second dose. Administered after you got back from Lear's place. Who wants your dog subdued? And why?"

50

Peacock chair

♥

Farrell thumped his tail as Emma approached, but he didn't lift his head from the hearthrug. She squatted to stroke his soft ears. "Sleeping it off, baby?" she crooned. "Did a nasty person drug my boy?"

Ray cleared his throat as the morning room door opened. Paul Barker strode through it. A grin split his face as he noticed Emma. "Just the person," he declared. He crooked a finger at her after nodding to his father. "Come with me, please."

Emma glanced up at Ray and considered resisting. Hunger gnawed at her stomach and tiredness created a nagging ache at her nape. She sighed and rose, her legs shaky beneath her. "I'll meet you in my lounge," she stated. Paul waited for a beat, glancing from her to Ray and then leaving. His outdoor shoes squeaked as they moved from oak floorboards to tile.

Emma leaned close enough to Ray so he could hear her whispered instruction. "I just remembered. Gwendoline said Arnand Dubois took a sleeping tablet and stayed in bed until later than usual. We need to find and confiscate whatever is left of his supply."

Ray wrinkled his nose. "He seems so mild-mannered. I can't imagine him drugging animals and whacking women with shovels."

Emma struggled to hide her expression of distaste. "That's because you don't yet know what I've found out. We need to take his, plus any others, out of circulation." She snapped her fingers and moved towards the corridor. "Oh, and don't get caught. Bunny went to the third floor for a nap."

"I'll carry my toolbox this time," Ray suggested. "Nobody notices a tradesman."

"Right." Emma shot him a smile, but her gaze strayed to the sleeping dog. "Do you think he's okay?" she asked.

Ray offered a confident nod, but Emma sensed he faked it for her benefit. He tilted his neck to the left as though tipping water from his ear. "He came good before, but maybe the second dose was bigger."

"Please find the pills," Emma breathed. "We need to protect the dog and the other people in this house."

Her phone buzzed with another Facebook message as she walked along the corridor. It gave her an excuse to drag her feet. Allaine apologised for the slew of weird photographs, courtesy of Nicky and Kayleigh. *'The snow is melting,'* she advised. *'You need to catch the killer fast because these kids are going stir crazy. I can't keep them trapped up here indefinitely.'*

Emma squeezed her eyes closed. No one could keep Nikolai Andreyev hostage for long. It left her with little choice. Detective Inspector Paul Barker unnerved her, but she promised to cooperate.

Emma stepped into her lounge. Her nerves jangled. Paul knelt before the hearth, a knotty pine log in his right hand. He laid it in the flames with consummate care. His ski jacket lay across the arm of Rohan's chair. A thermal shirt covered his brawny arms.

Ray oozed a rugged handsomeness. But his son possessed the fine bone structure seen in photographs of his late mother. She'd retained an elfin beauty and swathes of tumbling brown curls. Those same waves brushed against Paul's lashes as he studied the fire.

Emma slammed the door loud enough to make him jump. His lips twitched as he rose.

She gulped at the unfamiliar fire in his eyes. Paul brushed wood flecks from his palms as he strode towards her, his gait purposeful. A frisson of fear travelled from Emma's heart to her brain. In less than a second, she'd stuffed her phone into her pocket and readied herself for an attack. Her right foot dropped back, and her fingers curled into fists. Her left wrist ached with the action. She couldn't bend her fingers around the rim of the splint. It left her one-handed. And all the while, her brain whirred, identifying Paul as a friend when his body language spelled out latent aggression.

She couldn't take the risk. "Touch me and I'll hurt you!" she spat, her words issuing an inadvisable threat to the serving police officer.

He rushed her, but with overwhelming emotion instead of violence. His arms closed around her. Air rushed from her lungs as her breasts pressed against his chest. She hadn't expected it.

Her palms sweated. Paul smelled of pine and wood smoke. His cloud of need engulfed her. His role gave him natural authority, and he stepped over the decency line with frightening ease.

Rohan's image rose before her. She'd loved him since her sixth year. Her rescuer. The ache of his absence and the uncertainness of his injury overrode her paralysis.

"What are you doing?" It emerged as a shout, carrying the force of her desire for release. She pressed her hands against his chest, uttering a cry of agony as her wrist protested the splint. He freed her, not just because of her violent shove but in surprise at the litany of swearwords she grunted. Emma dipped at the waist and clutched her left arm to her body, the filthy words spewing from between her gritted teeth.

Paul cleared his throat and stepped back. But he didn't apologise. Emma rose, her eyes watering and her expression furious. "What is your problem?" she yelled at him.

"You!" He faced her square on, a red flush spreading up his neck and into his cheeks. He lifted his hands to his forehead and pushed his fingers through his hair. "You're infuriating!"

"I am?" Emma retorted. She skirted the police officer, stalked to Rohan's chair, and tipped the ski jacket off the padded arm. It sank to the floor with a susurration of waterproof fabric. She huffed and balanced her forearm across her thighs. Gathering her courage, she turned her head to glare at him. He hadn't moved from the door, but his gaze flicked to his fallen jacket and the rejection it embodied.

Paul seemed to give himself a mental shake, his body trembling and his teeth clamping over his lower lip. He strode towards the couch, stopping to lift a mobile phone from the coffee table. Changing his mind, he didn't sit, but walked to the mantel and rested a hand on its antique shelf. His knuckles showed white through his tanned skin. Emma watched him unlock his phone screen and scroll using the side of his thumb. Seconds later, she heard her own voice and froze.

"You recorded my conversation with Bunny?" Her chin flattened as her jaw hardened. "That's illegal and inadmissible."

Antagonism flashed in Paul's eyes. He turned to face her. "I don't intend to use it in court, Emma!" He waved the phone in his hand. It shook and threatened to drop it into the hearth. "I've recorded all the interviews so far, and no one has objected. But you requisitioned the room if you recall, and you somehow activated the record button." His lips pulled back in a sneer. "You recorded yourself speaking to a potential murderer!"

"Right!" Emma remembered the uncharacteristic hardness of Rohan's chair. She'd sat on Paul's phone. "Bunny didn't kill Kathleen, but that's why you assaulted me? Because I'm an idiot?"

"I did not assault you!" His jaw dropped open. The anger drained from his face. He ran a trembling hand over his eyes. "I didn't mean to," he breathed, perhaps realising his mistake with the finality of a hammer blow.

"I told you not to touch me seconds before you did it!" Emma growled. "You're lucky my wrist is hurting, otherwise I'd have laid you out flat." She rushed on as his lips parted in protest. "And don't use the assaulting a police officer line because it won't work. Not when I tell Ray and then my husband."

Paul blanched. The embarrassed hue faded to leave a whitewashed complexion. He looked sick. It reminded Emma of Kathleen's colourless cheeks. Acid rose into her throat.

"I'm sorry." The apology came too late. "I like you. Always have." He licked his lips and bowed his head, letting his gaze fall on his sturdy boots. "I wanted to ask you out years ago, but then your husband showed up again." He shrugged. "Guess I regret a missed opportunity."

Emma pursed her lips, resenting the flush of sympathy which pressed against her resolve. Instead, she shook her head in a slow arc. "That's your problem, Paul," she countered. "I've never given you the slightest encouragement." She lifted a finger to silence him as she sensed him preparing to offload. "If you can't control yourself, you need to leave my home." Thoughts of Christopher invaded her mind and strengthened her spine. Her half-hearted rebuffs didn't deter his hope. It led to disaster and an endless pit of sadness and hurt feelings.

Emma swallowed. "Why did you want to speak to me? I've told you everything I know." She jerked her chin towards his hand. "It's irrelevant now, isn't it?" She rose with a sigh, still holding her wrist across her stomach.

"Emma!" He took a step towards her, his features twisted into a mask of agony and despair. "Be careful," he warned. "Stay out of it. Whoever hit that woman across the face meant business." He patted his phone against his sternum for emphasis. "I lifted her into the freezer, Em. She weighed nothing. There are no defensive marks on her fingers and not a single sign of a struggle. They wiped her out with excessive force. And that killer is walking around your house." He swallowed as he finished his emphatic speech.

"Okay." Emma nodded. "I'll be more careful. But who do you think killed Kathleen Dubois?" She inhaled and shook her head as Paul stared at the rug beneath his boots. "Bunny didn't do it. I agree our conversation puts her right in the spotlight. But she wants to leave the whole sorry nightmare in the past. I believe her. Gwendoline is a complete airhead. I think it devastated Bunny how she's turned out."

She recalled the incident in the lobby when Gwendoline arrived, indignant and blaming Bunny for her shoe malfunction. And when Bunny offered Kathleen a hot drink, Gwendoline rebuffed and embarrassed her. Emma quailed inside, the incidents creating a miserable catalogue of mistreatment. She imagined her sparky son behaving towards her with such obvious disdain. Her heart burned.

"I disagree," Paul replied. He'd collected himself, regained a police detective's bearing, and set aside his misplaced affection for Emma. His shoulders appeared squarer, and his jaw set in hard angles. "Kathleen

Dubois ruined Bunny Cathcart's daughter and got her arrested. Revenge is the best motive for an impassioned, unpremeditated murder." He ventured closer, but kept his hands locked by his sides this time. "And that's why I'm concerned for you." He lowered his voice to a gentle cadence, his emotional confusion leaking into his words. "You sequestered yourself in a room with a potential killer, Emma. I forbid you to take any more risks."

Emma choked on the overt command. Even Rohan didn't prohibit her, no matter how foolish her ideas or actions seemed. She bristled and decided not to tell him about the drugged dog, or the shoe sizes of her guests. "Whatever you say, Detective," she replied.

The door clicked behind her, and Emma stared down at her shaking right hand. But she couldn't decide if the anger caused her chest to tighten. Or overwhelming sadness.

51

Drafting chair

♥

"Emma!" A shout issued from upstairs. She turned right and headed towards the back staircase, recognising the urgency in Ray's voice. "Emma! Bring Paul!"

"What's happened?" Monty walked from the lobby towards her.

Emma retraced her steps and found Paul already behind her. "Ray wants you," she stated. "And me."

"Not you!" He administered a rough shove to her shoulder like an overbearing father. "Stay here!"

"Hey!" Monty called. His voice rose in indignation.

A spirit of defiance caused Emma to ignore Paul. She powered up the stairs on his heels, making the familiar turns with more skill and racing him to the top. Ray met them on the second floor, his colour mottled. Sweat beaded on his forehead.

"What's happened?" Paul demanded.

"Is it Bunny?" Emma pressed her right hand into a fist. "Is she okay?"

Ray gripped Emma's right shoulder. "Run downstairs and grab my blue first aid kit." He waggled his eyebrows at her. "From the top cupboard. You'll need a chair to reach it."

"Speak to me!" Paul urged. "What the hell's going on?" He followed his father up the narrow staircase to the servants' floor.

Emma didn't waste time waiting for the explanation. She trusted Ray and followed his direction. Farrell gave a happy woof as he spotted her in the corridor. He picked up speed and met her outside the kitchen. His furrowed brow smoothed as he shook off his enforced slumber. The solidity of his ebony body pressed against Emma's calf. She blew out a ragged breath.

"What's happening?" Monty demanded. He dogged her steps, desperation in his eyes.

"Gwendoline's hurt!" Emma hissed.

Dyfed released a high-pitched scream as Emma blasted through the door. He clutched Ridley's knotted fingers as the men lurked beside the Aga. A bowl smashed against the tiles as Ridley released it in shock. Each held a spoon and shared the remnants of the soup.

"Sorry!" Emma shouted. She pointed to the dog. "Farrell, stay!" White crockery shards had spread outward in a hazardous pattern of destruction for soft toe beans. The dog dropped onto his rump, confused but obedient.

Emma dragged a chair through the mess and used it to access the highest cupboard. "Grab this!" she commanded, dragging a heavy box from the top shelf. Hands took it while she descended. Once on the ground, she saw Dyfed clutching it to his chest. Filled with medical equipment and weighing several pounds, Emma knew she couldn't carry it upstairs one-handed. She glanced around for Monty, but he didn't follow her into the kitchen. She grabbed Dyfed's upper arm, surprised by the twig-like muscle beneath his suit jacket. "Carry this upstairs for me?" she begged. "To the third floor."

Ridley released a whine of discomfort at their potential separation. He set both spoons on the counter and, to Emma's surprise, followed them. They reached the third floor landing as Ray dashed from the first of the single bedrooms. The dog pattered up behind them. Ray snatched the box from Dyfed's hands.

"Is Bunny okay?" Emma demanded. "She came upstairs for a nap. I should have stopped her."

Ray jutted his chin forward and peered at her from over the box. "Blonde hair, short skirt?" He flapped his hand in front of his chest. "Black and red corset thing?"

"Gwendoline?" Emma's jaw dropped open. "What's happened to her? Where's Bunny?" Dread snaked around her heart and squeezed. Was her character judgement so poor? Had Bunny Cathcart killed Kathleen and then attacked her own daughter?

"Drugged," Ray said. He waggled his eyebrows at Emma, and his lips flattened into a line.

"Sleeping tablets?" she whispered. Her gaze slid to the open bedroom door and Paul's bowed head. He'd lifted Gwendoline to a sitting position with her torso slumped against his shoulder. She moaned with each slap of his hand to her already flushed cheek. Emma gulped. "We didn't grab them fast enough, did we?"

Paul's gaze slid to Emma, and he frowned. "We'll talk about this later!" he snapped, as though holding her responsible for Gwendoline's condition.

Emma left Ray unfurling a new plastic cable and examining the date on a bag containing clear fluid. She turned to find Dyfed and Ridley still blocking the landing. "He's setting up a drip," she told them, her tone flat. "He knows how to help her. We can't get an ambulance out here until the snow melts. He'll do his best."

"It's snowing again." Dyfed pointed through an open bedroom doorway. Rumpled sheets and pillows left askew showed where Arnand Dubois had slept alone. The narrow window at the junction between the ceiling and wall usually showed the sky. But the maelstrom of white flakes bouncing against it restricted the visibility to nothing.

Emma groaned. "Can this weekend get any worse?" she whispered.

A high-pitched scream from downstairs made her wish she hadn't asked. "Help!" a female voice wailed. "Somebody help me!"

Emma left Dyfed and Ridley clutching each other on the third floor. Fatigue dogged her steps as she pelted down the servants' stairs, across the landing and down the next set. Her wrist clattered against the banister as she spun around the last turn, arriving in the corridor at a run. Farrell accompanied her, more alert than he'd seemed earlier. Emma's slipper soles squeaked against the tiled floor as she whirled from side to side.

"Here!" Flora rose. She pushed herself away from a bundle of rags just outside the kitchen door and ran towards Emma. "It's Monty! You must help him!" She grasped the front of Emma's jacket in her panic and administered a firm shake.

"What's the matter?" Bunny appeared from the lobby end, her tiny feet speeding up as she assessed the situation.

"Where did you go?" Emma rounded on her, fear and aggression exploding from her chest. "You went upstairs for a nap!"

"I couldn't sleep." Bunny recoiled, taking a cautionary step backwards. "Sir Robert knocked on my door. We found a chess set in the morning room. I'm beating him." Her thumb and forefinger made a pinching action as though selecting a pawn. "I used the bathroom off the lobby and heard screaming. What's happened?"

"Help Monty!" Flora seized a swathe of jacket sleeve in her white-knuckled fingers and dragged Emma to kneel beside her husband. "Do something!" She released her grip as Farrell delivered a warning bark.

Emma stared down at Monty. The retired schoolteacher lay on his back on the tiles. His position appeared less haphazard than Kathleen's undignified end. One arm rested beside him, the smooth palm facing upwards, and the fingers curled. The left arm covered his face as though protecting him from a blow. Streaks of blood stained his white shirt sleeve, masking the injury. Emma didn't want to touch him. She never again wanted to experience the sensation of raw chicken beneath her fingers. But Flora sobbed and bent double as though her stomach might split. "Help him?" she begged. "Someone's attacked him."

"Where's that policeman?" Bunny slipped an arm around Flora's rounded shoulders. Flora seemed like a leviathan beside her. Bunny had to stand on tiptoes to offer comfort.

"Oh, there you are." Sir Robert shuffled along the corridor, his white curls bouncing with every movement. His soft soled slippers made no sound on the tiles. Farrell ran to him, turning his body to escort the man to rendezvous with the women. The old barrister released a groan. "Not another one!" he huffed. "This really is too much!"

Emma stared up at him in mute appeal. For a moment, nobody moved or spoke. Then she cleared her throat. "Sir Robert, please, can you go up to the third floor?" She jabbed her thumb towards the rear staircase. "Go that way. You'll find Ray and Detective Inspector Barker with Gwendoline. Tell them Monty's hurt."

Sir Robert skirted Monty's feet and scuttled away. Overweight and unfit, he huffed up every step until the sound died.

"Help him!" Flora implored.

Emma blew out her ragged breath and seized Monty's limp wrist. Her fingers sensed a faint warmth. She placed the pad of her middle finger over his artery and felt the rhythmic beat of a pulse. "He's alive!" she exclaimed. Relief coursed through her. She leaned across and pulled the bloodied sleeve from his face.

A horizontal gash scored his handsome forehead. The blow had exposed the fatty layers, but Emma saw no exposed bone in the cut. A blue bruise raised the skin on either side of the narrow opening. It had bled with the usual vigour of a head wound, but not to excess.

"Flora?" Monty groaned and called for his wife, his voice weak and croaky.

She dropped to her knees beside him, her tears still drying on her cheeks. "What happened?" she breathed. "You went to fetch a glass of water from the kitchen and didn't return. I came looking for you."

"The kitchen?" Bunny stared at Emma. "Didn't that smiley man rush at us with a meat cleaver?" She clapped her hand over her mouth. "Did he do this to you, Monty?"

"Perhaps. I don't remember." Monty clung to Flora's hand and closed his eyes. "I got to the kitchen door, and the attack came from nowhere." He tried to sit up, his eyes swimming with pain. Flora tucked herself behind him, balancing his crown against her bent knees. She stroked his fringe away from the gash with gentle fingers.

"He's cold," Emma said, releasing Monty's wrist. She stared up at Bunny. "Please, can you fetch a blanket from the lounge? I don't think Paul locked the door behind him."

Bunny nodded and navigated around her. She returned in seconds, carrying a plaid throw from the back of the sofa. Emma draped it over Monty's prone body and tucked the fringes beneath him.

"I feel silly," Monty croaked. "Let me go back to the morning room with Flora."

"No." Emma shook her head and twisted her lips into an expression of regret. "I need Ray to check you over before we let you stand. She doubted Ray would come unless he'd stabilized Gwendoline. But Paul could get details of the attack while they waited.

Farrell sniffed Emma's hair before settling beside her. His hazelnut eyes had regained their sparkle. His jaws parted in a massive yawn. He leaned his weight against her, interwoven solidarity and laziness.

Emma recognised Ray's heavy tread with a groan of relief. She counted his steps from the servants' stairwell to the top of the back stairs. Clump, clump, clump. He'd kept on his boots and jumped down three steps at a time with his long stride. Muted thuds revealed Sir Robert puffing behind him like a musical backing track.

Ray skidded to a halt beside Emma, casting his eyes over Monty's prone body. "For pity's sake!" he sighed. "Who's doing this?"

52

Bentwood chair

♥

The former army medic assessed Monty's condition, while everyone else gathered in a knot. Bunny wrapped a protective arm around Flora's waist. "What is going on here?" she whispered to herself.

Emma remained silent as Ray performed his checks. He knelt on the floor beside Monty, turning to seek Emma in the group. "I need some saline, gauze, and medical tape." He issued the command, and she nodded and stepped towards the kitchen door.

"Don't go in there alone!" Bunny shrieked. "The crazy cleaver waving man is in there."

Emma exhaled and baulked against the unflattering description of Dyfed. "He's upstairs with the detective. Gwendoline collapsed. I was with him and Ridley when Flora screamed."

"Oh." Bunny's brows knitted into a line. "If Gwendoline is sick, someone should tell Arnand." She pursed her lips but showed no inclination to find and inform him. Emma saw conflict flash in the tiny eyes masked by the giant spectacle lenses and pitied her dilemma.

"I'll do it," she offered. "After I fetch the medical supplies for Ray."

Farrell followed her into the empty kitchen. His nose crashed into the backs of her knees as she paused and fixed her gaze on the door frame at eye level. Emma pursed her lips and pushed open the door.

Farrell bounced into his warm bed by the Aga with enthusiasm, but didn't lie down. Emma groaned. "Watch the broken bowl," she urged. He watched her clamber onto the chair she'd left there earlier. She pulled down Ray's everyday medical kit, the one containing sticking plaster and the usual necessities. The dog followed her as she left, carrying the plastic box under her right arm.

"Thanks." Ray took it from her with a smile and opened the lid. His expert fingers dug into the compartments. He'd sat Monty up and leaned him against the wall. His pink slippers poked from beneath the plaid blanket. They looked pathetic and a little drunk.

"How did it happen?" Emma skirted the group and stared down at the pitiful scene.

"They got him from behind." Flora turned to face her, her eyes glittering. "We're not safe here, Emma. Whoever killed Kathleen came for Monty." Her fingers writhed together at her stomach, clenching and releasing in a spasm of fear. Bunny patted her back in a gentle, settling motion, but her slippers pointed towards the stairs. She ached to check on her daughter.

"So, did they hit you with something?" Emma asked. "How did you get the gash on your forehead?"

Monty dabbed his lips with the back of his hairy hand. He hissed in pain as Ray pressed iodine over the open cut. "I walked along the corridor to the kitchen. Heavy footsteps came up behind me. As I turned, I felt a shove to my shoulder blades just before my forehead smashed against the door frame. My teeth rattled in my head, and I went down like a stone." He poked out his tongue and wiped the blood from his lower lip. "I've bitten my cheek."

"I'm sorry this is happening." Emma's fingers sought Farrell's head, and he looked up at her and edged closer.

She sighed. "I'll check on Gwendoline and then find Arnand."

"What happened to Gwendoline?" Alertness entered Monty's slumped frame, and he used his hands to push himself higher. "She's family."

"Sit still," Ray ordered. Monty sunk back against the wall.

Flora covered her face with her hands. "Oh, my goodness!" she breathed. "This is personal. First Kathleen, then Gwendoline, and now Monty. Who's doing this to us?"

"I don't know," Emma admitted. "Detective Inspector Barker will figure it out soon."

She patted her thigh, and the dog flanked her to the second floor. Bunny didn't follow, though her gaze tracked Emma's progress as far as the first sharp turn. Emma dragged her phone from her pocket and sent Ray a one-handed message on social media, asking him to protect the blood stain on the door frame. She copied her words into a text message, but it refused to send. The cell tower was still out of action.

Dyfed and Ridley still occupied the split level landing on the third floor. They'd released their hold on each other and sat on the top stair. Emma offered them a smile and stepped into Gwendoline's bedroom. She lay on the narrow bed with her arms crossed over her stomach. Her closed eyes made Emma think she was still unconscious, but they shot open when her slippers squeaked across the threshold. "Oh," she grumbled. "It's just you."

"Thanks," Emma retorted. "It seems a drug overdose hasn't improved your mood."

"I ache all over!" Gwendoline barked. "And I didn't do this to myself!"

The unpleasant tang of vomit hung in the air. Gwendoline had puked in the antique water jug. Paul leaned against the windowsill, drawing breaths from the icy air seeping around the frame. He rested one foot on a wooden chair. His knee supported the sagging arm holding a bag of clear liquid. A cable ran from its underside into a canula in Gwendoline's hand. "Do you want to take a turn?" he asked. "I've used both arms and they ache now."

Emma pursed her lips and made a stand. "No thanks. You're doing a great job. I came to tell you what happened downstairs."

Paul perked up. His spine straightened, and he set his foot on the floor. But the arm holding the drip bag sank, and he switched sides. "Tell me!" he ordered.

Emma shot a sideways glance at Gwendoline. She sensed the other woman's piercing blue irises fixed on her face. Ignoring her, she relayed the essential details.

"So," she finished. "Ray's taking care of Monty in the downstairs hallway. He'll have a headache for a while and perhaps a concussion."

Paul winced. He changed arms again and patted his jeans pocket. "Can you write all that down in my notebook?" he asked. He flexed his shoulders and peered at the liquid level in the bag. "This is taking ages," he grumbled. "What will happen if I lay it on the chair?"

"The bag will fill with her blood instead," Emma stated. "She's behaved like a total bitch all weekend. I'd just do it."

Gwendoline gasped with indignation and her gaze swivelled to Paul. Her lips pursed, but she said nothing for once.

Emma pushed her fingers into Paul's front pocket. It took her closer to him than she wanted. She gripped the hard upper edge of his book. He leaned back to enable it to slide free, and Emma avoided his gaze. She popped the tiny pen from within the spine after retreating to the tiny writing desk.

Scratches covered the antique wooden surface, too historically precious to obliterate. She recounted Monty's description in slanted handwriting. She also detailed the clues about the dog and the sleeping tablets. After some thought, she glanced up at Paul. "I'll alibi Dyfed and Ridley. They were upstairs with us when Flora screamed. Dyfed carried the medical box. Monty wasn't on the floor three minutes earlier."

Tapping the pad with the nib of the pen, she considered Gwendoline's blank expression. "There's also a blood stain on the kitchen door architrave."

"Thanks." Paul held out his hand for his book.

"I'll leave it here." She poked the pen back into the spine and lined the book up against the front of the desk.

Paul's lips parted. But Emma didn't intend to replace it in his pocket. Hunger filled his eyes, not just at her proximity. He wanted to go downstairs into the thick of the crime. Emma pitied him. Gwendoline was beautiful and alluring until she opened her mouth.

Glancing down, Emma realised the dog hadn't entered the room with her. She turned to leave. "Make her hold the bag herself." She jerked her head towards Gwendoline. The other woman's lips puckered to produce a dimple in the centre of her chin. "She looks recovered enough to me."

Emma stepped into the hallway. Gwendoline squeaked behind her but wasted the energy. Dyfed and Ridley sat on the top step with the dog wedged between them. His tongue lolled with happiness as the men stroked his furry ears and chest. All three jumped as Emma walked onto the landing. Farrell's tail beat against the wooden floorboards like a drum.

"You're fine." Emma smiled. "He'll take as much of that as he can get."

"Is the poorly lady better now?" Dyfed's eyes stared up, wide and filled with concern.

Emma wrinkled her nose. "No. She's still a bitch." She skirted their feet and walked down the first three steps. "Where's Chloe?" she asked, turning. "You usually stick together."

"She's looking for Dad." Dyfed's eyes protruded like boiled eggs. They seemed huge in his pale face, the irises reflecting an unknown terror.

"He's here?" Emma froze, her body tilted at an awkward angle. "Gareth is here?"

Ridley rocked on the step, his shoulder moving Farrell's left ear back and forth like a wiper blade. "No, no, no!" he whispered.

Dyfed stretched an arm around the dog and the distressed man. "She's just making sure," he stated, his tone calm and reasoned. "She checks every ten minutes in case she sees him coming. Then we can all hide under the bed. Like last night." His angular jaw still bore the painful smile, even as he hinted at a coming devastation.

"What will you do when this is over?" Emma waved her right hand around the stairwell to encompass the disastrous weekend, Wingate Hall, and their inevitable journey back to reality.

Dyfed shrugged. His fingers gripped a swathe of Ridley's jacket. It seemed to calm the man, and he ceased rocking. "Hide," he said. "From the people."

"People?" Emma dropped her chin. "What people? Does Gareth have other workers?"

"No, no, no!" Ridley began rocking again.

Emma patted the air between them. "Don't worry for now," she soothed. "It's still snowing. No one can cross the roads or fields today. You're all safe." She paused on the step and offered them a lifeline. "Farrell, stay," she said, her tone commanding. "Guard them."

The dog's maw shut with a snap after licking each man's cheek.

Mission accepted.

53

Panton chair

♥

"Well, that seemed weird." Emma studied Ray's actions as he replaced the blue medical box on its shelf. His height made the chair redundant. He glanced sideways at her and raised an eyebrow in question. Emma swept crockery shards into a pile with a broom. "Dyfed just told me that Chloe checks all the windows every few minutes in case she sees Gareth. Then they're going to hide under the bed. Apparently, that's how they spent last night."

Ray shrugged. He moved to the sink to wash his hands. "Paul doesn't know why the charge sergeant released him last night. He thinks they had enough to keep him until they scheduled a new court date."

Emma clicked the fingers of her right hand. "Yeah, but Dyfed said they'll hide from *the people*. Does that mean Gareth intends to turn up here with some nasty friends?"

"He can try." Ray's jaw set into hard lines. "Oh, and thanks for telling the girl's father about her collapse. He arrived upstairs just as I set the drip up on the hat stand."

"What hat stand?" Emma frowned.

"The old one from the servants' hall in the basement." He winked at her as he dried his hands on a towel. "Paul didn't want to give me the key, so I made him hold the drip. I figured he'd give in eventually, but then you called me downstairs." He grinned at her from across the room. "His arms were like jelly by the time I got back to him. I used the opportunity to grab more wood at the same time."

Emma pursed her lips to contain her wicked snigger. "Where is Paul now?"

"Interviewing the guy with the gash on his forehead." He waggled his eyebrows and released a heavy sigh. "I'm going to run out of medical supplies if this continues."

Emma nodded. "Did Gwendoline say what she'd taken?"

His eyes widened as he shook his head. He folded his arms and leaned against the counter. "She's absolutely certain she took nothing."

"So, what then?" Emma pushed a line of crockery ahead of her. "Has the person who drugged Farrell made themselves busy with putting the guests to sleep?"

Ray blew out a breath through his nose. He pursed his lips and stared at the tiles. "I made her vomit." His nose wrinkled in remembered distaste. "Paul salvaged some of it in an evidence bag. He'll get it tested. She said she felt fine until just after lunch. So, it fits that someone slipped drugs into her food."

"Did you get to search any of the rooms before you found her?"

"Yeah." He nodded. "I went through all the double rooms and the two singles at the far end of the floor." His fingers pushed into his trouser pocket, and he pulled out a blister pack of pills. "I found these in the second from the end. There are seven missing."

"Christos," Emma breathed. "Two for the dog and three for Gwendoline?"

"Maybe." Ray gnawed on his bottom lip. "Or perhaps he brought a half-empty pack and took one last night."

"What are they?" Emma crossed the kitchen and took the packet from Ray's fingers. "Temazepam. Don't you need a prescription for this?"

Ray took the packet from her and shoved it back into his pocket. "Each tablet contains 20mg. A doctor might prescribe up to 40mg per night for someone with real sleep difficulties. But only over a limited period. The dog didn't need that much. 20mg would do it."

"So, two for the dog and five for Gwendoline?" Emma blinked at him in horror. "You think he tried to murder her?"

Ray shrugged. "I'm not sure, Em. Maybe he just wanted her to shut up for a minute. She's hung off his arm the entire day. The woman doesn't know what silence is."

"A drastic way to get some peace." Emma turned and leaned her backside against the Aga. Warmth filtered through her jacket and soothed the tired muscles in her spine. Her sore knees ached beneath her sweatpants. "So, here's what we have. Kathleen died in the downstairs hallway between midnight and two thirty. We think Christos borrowed the boots, used the shower, and left them in my bedroom."

"His feet are three sizes too big, but carry on, anyway."

"Christos brought Temazepam with him and could have drugged Farrell and Gwendoline." She clicked her tongue. "But we also know Arnand Dubois had sleeping pills with him."

"Why would he drug his own daughter?" Ray spread his palms before him. "And the dog?"

Emma blew out a frustrated exhale. "Did you find any other tablets in the rooms? You might still need to check Gwendoline's, Bunny's, Mavis', the major's and Sir Roberts." She twisted her lips. "Don't worry about Sir Robert. He borrowed heart pills from the major. I doubt he brought anything else. No one expected to stay overnight. So, why bring sleeping pills to an evening event?"

"Gwendoline told me her family rented a hotel room for two nights. It's possible her father brought his medication with him rather than leave it there."

Emma nodded. "That's fair." She straightened her spine and loosed her hair from her ponytail. Mahogany curls tumbled over her shoulders. "There's only one thing for it. With Gwendoline out of action, I need to turn my charm on Christos. I'll check his actual shoe size and ask him for drugs."

Ray sighed. "Subtle, Em. Real professional." He turned away before clicking his fingers and facing her. "You should know my son has a crush on you."

Emma flattened her lips into a line. "Yeah. I figured," she responded.

"Be careful." Ray flapped his hand. "With Christos. Not with Paul. One's dangerous and one isn't." He left the room after zipping up his jacket. His heavy tread squeaked along the corridor.

Before Emma left the kitchen, she finished removing the smashed bowl one-handed. Then she photographed the blood smear on the architrave. She sent copies to Paul and Lear using Messenger. Wizardry with cling film and tape protected the area from smudging. She stood back to admire her handiwork and tiptoed to the lounge door. Paul's voice vibrated through the heavy oak, his tone steady and confident. Emma couldn't discern Monty's replies. She ached to sneak into the tunnel and listen, but figured they'd almost finished.

With feet dogged by reluctance, Emma walked towards the lobby.

A chill hit her within seconds of leaving the corridor. Light streamed around the inner door, coupled with a cloud of white steam. It filtered through the gap like a dragon's breath. Emma jogged towards the source and yanked the inner door wide. Christos jumped and released a gasp.

"What the hell?" Emma demanded.

The tall man stood in the vestibule, shrouded in a eucalyptus scented vapour. Emma flapped her hands to push it away from her face. "Sorry!" he gasped. "I'm so sorry." He switched off his vape with an extended fumbling action. "I know you said no vaping indoors, but I can't go outside. Drifts block all the external exits. And the windows don't open on the third floor." His voice held a whine.

Emma leaned against the door frame. She stared at the white carpeted lawn. Snow covered the grass and crept up nearby structures to soften their edges. "It's fine," she replied grudgingly. She glanced down at the black slippers encasing Christos' feet. They poked from the hems of his smart trousers like hooves. Emma frowned. "Aren't those a little small for you?" She feigned concern. Screwing up her features, she flattened her lips into twin lines of angst. "I'm so sorry. The store had nothing above a size twelve for men." She patted her chest. "This event happened at short notice. I dashed to the Pound Shop and bought up everything they had."

Christos shrugged. "These are fine." He relit the vape and hid behind the ecstasy of sucking in his flavoured air.

Emma's head jerked back hard enough to bump her crown on the door frame. She ached to rub the painful spot, but resisted. "Oh, but your dress shoes seemed so much bigger." Her voice wavered with excitement.

Christos smiled back at her. Vapour escaped from both sides of his mouth. "Rented," he said. "I cancelled my original order when Mavis lost the venue. Figured she'd abandon the whole thing."

"But she didn't." Emma spoke through gritted teeth. Mavis never intended to. She'd planned to strong-arm Freda into hosting it.

Christos shrugged. "It's the Christmas season. By the time I called them to reinstate the order, they'd loaned out the last size ten." He grinned as Emma cast her gaze from his feet to his wrinkled shirt collar. She could have kicked herself for falling into the trap. His irises glittered as though she'd undressed him. "A small fat guy took the shoes. But he didn't need a suit for someone over six feet tall."

Emma's phone buzzed in her pocket.

'Sorry, been busy,' Lear had written. 'Cell tower still screwed. Done some online checking. Christos Smaragdis doesn't exist.'

Emma pushed her phone into her pocket. Her heart pounded. A pink flush lit her cheeks.

Christos grinned, misunderstanding her discomfort. Ray's voice screamed in her head, telling her to leave it. The game had changed. She wasn't equipped.

But Rohan Andreyev never backed away from a fight.

Emma's lips twitched with another question for the fake Greek. She decided to channel Rohan.

54

Stacking chair

♥

"When did you meet Gwendoline?"

An unpleasant expression crossed Christos' handsome features. His nose wrinkled as he drew in another puff from his vape. He paused a moment before replying. Emma already knew the answer, but wanted to hear him lie. If Lear couldn't find him, he'd used an assumed name. She hoped to tie him in knots a little before asking for his real identity.

Christos switched off the vape and shoved it into his jacket pocket. He tugged at his shirt collar, turning at the same time to rest his arm on the door frame above her. The lower level of the vestibule put them nose to nose. A eucalyptus haze covered Emma's head as he breathed into her face. "You're exquisite," he mused, his lips curving into an affable smile. A strand of his silky hair slid over his left eye and bounced on his lashes.

"But then there's Gwendoline." Emma pursed her lips and readied her right fist. Despite the pain in her knees, she guessed she could aim one of them between his legs to disable him.

His lids fluttered closed for a beat. "She's nuts!" he exhaled. "I met her on a dating app. Saw her photo and thought we could have some fun." His lips slid into a wicked grin. But it faded fast. "I'm not interested in being catfished, so we organised a video call." He groaned. "Then she opened her mouth!" He dropped his chin and almost head butted Emma. She shifted sideways just in time. Christos pressed his free hand to his chest. "She didn't want fun. The only thing she wants is a husband, a tribe of kids and a fat wallet. I blocked her when she started planning the wedding." He stepped back and turned to view the snow blanket through the narrow side windows. His voice held a faraway edge. "You could have knocked me over with a feather when she climbed on the bus last night. Just my bloody luck!"

"When did you disable the Wi-Fi in my bedroom?" Emma kept her tone casual, throwing out the question and expecting his ready denial.

One eyebrow arched upward as he turned to stare at her. "How did you know?" he demanded.

"I didn't," she replied. A stunned silence surrounded them for a second. Then she said, "But I do now." It explained her inability to summon the Google Assistant on her phone in the night. It required the internet. She sent a silent apology to her innocent son.

Christos blew out a ragged breath. "She tried to load a picture of us to her Facebook page during the awards ceremony. I have former acquaintances I'd like to avoid." He cleared his throat. "But then her phone wouldn't connect to the internet. So that darned old lady gave her the password to your Wi-Fi."

"What old lady?" Emma groaned. "Freda."

Christos nodded. "I wished she hadn't." He shrugged and stared at his slippers. "So, I needed to stop Gwendoline posting the image. But she's persistent. She even tried to get into my bedroom during the night."

"You heard her knocking?" Emma cocked her head.

Christos replaced his arm against the frame above her. He leaned close enough to kiss her. She fought the urge to recoil from his eucalyptus breath and the slimy persona hidden beneath the attractive wrapping. "I swapped rooms." He lifted his chin and whispered into her fringe. "I'm too tall for the single beds." His breath coasted across her cheek. "I'm too big, baby."

Emma clamped her teeth together to avoid laughing. He'd never met her husband. Oblivious, Christos warbled on. "I nipped across the corridor and grabbed the double after everyone went to sleep. The caterers slept in one room together."

"So, who took your room?" Confusion dropped Emma's jaw as she sifted through the possibilities.

Christos shrugged. He engaged the booster on his charm offensive and stroked her jaw with his soft fingers. "Monty," he said. "He ran a bath before anyone else woke up. I nipped in to use the toilet while he grabbed a towel. Maybe Flora snores." He leaned forward, his lips brushing Emma's forehead. "Do you snore, baby?" His soft lips drew into a smile. "I don't mind."

Emma kept her nerve, though his proximity sickened her. It took all her resolve to remain in his orbit. "What time did you disconnect the router?" Her voice wobbled with fear. "How did you know where to find it?"

His lips brushed her cheek. She couldn't lift her head without inviting a kiss. She jammed her chin down and waited for his answer. He'd become distracted, his fingers tugging at the zipper of her jacket. It edged lower by degrees. Emma pressed her fingers over his hand to halt the movement. "Be a good boy. Answer my questions," she whispered.

He inhaled and his kisses ceased. His breath warmed her cheek. Emma wanted to scream. "I slipped in when you went downstairs last night," he replied. The hoarseness of arousal made his voice husky. "Your dog is useless. It didn't even wake up."

"Who told you where the router is?"

"Too easy." He slipped his fingers into the back of her hair. The gentle massaging had the opposite effect than intended. It caused Emma to tighten every muscle in revulsion. "At first, Gwendoline couldn't get a signal. Freda told her to stand towards the back of the room because the router was overhead."

Emma gulped. "You went outside in the night to vape, didn't you?"

"So? I thought you liked a naughty boy." Christos' lips closed over hers, his hot breath filling her mouth. He moaned and his chest rose and fell with the heightened speed of lust.

Emma's knee hit the spot. It crushed his erection with devastating accuracy. His head dropped in agony and her right fist connected with his symmetrical jaw. She pushed with both hands, shoving him backwards with enough force to topple him against the front door. A searing pain shot through her left wrist. Two falls and a shove completed the break.

Christos' head smashed against the heavy wood. The door remained staunch. Centuries of storms, inside and out, hadn't rocked it. Christos' empty head left no mark. But his scalp cracked like an eggshell. Blood trickled across his throat and into his rented shirt collar.

Emma's phone vibrated in her pocket again. She dragged it free with shaking fingers.

'Found him,' Lear had written.

She read the message aloud as Christos inspected his split head. His fingers shook. The broken vape leaked pink liquid on the vestibule tiles.

'Christos Smaragdis the Greek is Chris Smith from Hull,' Lear concluded.

And Emma laughed until her sides ached.

55

Curule chair

♥

"What now?" Paul collected a sobbing Emma from the lobby floor. He crushed her to his chest. Her mouth filled with the rustling fabric of his ski jacket. Dribble darkened the material.

"Emma?" Ray spun her around by her shoulder. Her chin clattered Paul's chest. Ray's eyes flashed at her coursing tears and her wide open mouth. "What happened?" he demanded.

"Chris Smith," Emma wailed. "Chris Smith from Hull!"

Christos pitched onto his knees and crawled to the step. Blood seeped from his crown. "She attacked me," he croaked. "She's raving mad. Arrest her."

Emma snorted. Spit projected onto Paul's coat, and she shrieked again. "Chris Smith!"

Why did no one understand her? Greek Christos Smaragdis was a fake. A conman, like Bunny said.

"Emma, stop!" Ray grabbed her wrist. His fingers closed around the splint. He shook her arm. The broken bones ground together. The lights flicked off.

Emma hit the lobby floor like a brick.

She woke in the morning room. It felt like seconds later. Freda's concerned face hovered over her. Chamomile laced her breath. A hint of cooking sherry undermined the herbal façade. She stepped back as Emma pushed herself upright, using her right arm. "What happened?" she demanded.

"You attacked Christos!" Gwendoline elbowed Freda aside. A tussle ensued as Freda fought for prominence. "He's bleeding!" Gwendoline raged. "You drugged me, hit Monty and..." Her chest hitched. "And you killed my mother."

"Whatever!" Emma snarled. She closed her eyes and assessed her pain levels.

"Hey." Ray's warm fingers stroked her cheek. He'd squatted in front of her, obliterating the elbow fight. "Sorry." He winced. "I panicked. Grabbed the wrong hand. Your wrist is knackered."

Emma groaned. She laid back against the sofa arm. "I figured. It's numb. Thank goodness."

She covered her eyes with her right forearm. "Check my phone."

"It's here." Paul stepped forward. Ray took it from his outstretched hand. He unlocked the screen using the same code as the burglar alarm. His lips curved down in a silent rebuke.

"What is it?" Paul leaned over his shoulder. Ray realised the mistake at the same time as Emma. Her eyes flashed as he speed-read the message and shoved the phone into his jacket pocket.

Ray rose with a sigh. "New information."

"From where?" Paul's brows crinkled in disbelief.

"Doesn't matter." Ray pointed his index finger beyond Gwendoline. Emma's curiosity burgeoned. Christos bled into a white handkerchief. He occupied a nearby armchair. "Someone's playing a game with us," Ray said. "Aren't they, Mr Smith?"

"What?" Gwendoline spun around fast enough that her skirt lifted. Emma blinked at the lithe thighs and perfect buttocks. "Christos?" She blocked Emma's view as she set her hands on her hips.

"Chris Smith from Hull." Ray's voice held respect. The clever alias had stuck admirably close to the truth. It revealed casual arrogance.

"How do you know that?" Paul held his hand out for the phone. "Let me see."

Ray crossed the distance in two strides. He yanked Christos up with one elbow. The man's body leaned sideways. He clutched the handkerchief against his bleeding crown. His coat tails drooped like a ladybird's crushed wings. "Just ask him," Ray stated, his tone flat.

"This is a nightmare!" Gwendoline pressed her hands against her cheeks. "I can't date a man from Hull!"

"Excuse me, I'm from Hull!" Sir Robert's affability disappeared beneath his indignation.

The major laid a settling hand on the lawyer's shoulder. "It's more that he's lied," he soothed.

"For the money." Bunny rose from an armchair on shaking legs. She squared her shoulders as though she'd discovered a hidden well of confidence. "He wanted the treasurer's role. My friend in the Leicestershire Arts Society tipped me off a few weeks ago. He's cleaned out their account, but they can't prove it."

Flora gasped and pressed a hand over her mouth. She rounded on Christos. "Did you empty our account, too?"

He hung from Ray's grip like a limp rag. His head shook without enthusiasm.

"He didn't get the chance," Bunny clarified. "Besides, someone got there before him, didn't they?" She glared at Mavis, who seemed to shrink in place. Her portly body bowed as though her legs couldn't support her weight.

"I'll pay it back," she whispered. "I promise. But I didn't take it all."

Ray jerked his head at Paul. "Guard the door," he growled. He turned to Freda. "Is everyone here?"

Her dress swished as she cast around the room. "Yes," she concluded. "Oh, except the caterers."

"Leave them out of it," Emma said. She placed her feet on the rug and gripped her wrist against her stomach. "They aren't responsible for any of this." She rose, her vision blurring around the edges.

Paul hadn't moved. He stared at his father with narrowed eyes. "What are you planning?" he demanded.

"A body search." Emma twisted her lips. She singled out Sir Robert from the crowd. "Sir, will you position yourself in front of the door?" she asked.

With a nod of his furry head, he strode to the only internal exit and took up sentry duty. His body vibrated with importance.

"You can't do this!" Gwendoline snarled.

"Why?" Emma rounded on her. She pointed to the woman's flimsy skirt. "You carry no handbag. I can't imagine where you'd secrete anything in your outfit. What's the problem here?"

Gwendoline's gaze flicked across the room to her father. Such a tiny movement. But it alerted Emma to some hidden motive for her evasion. "Detective Inspector Barker, do you have the authority to conduct this search?"

Paul nodded. He seemed lost for words.

Undeterred, Emma instructed Ray to search the major first. He acquiesced to Ray's careful frisking without dispute.

"Just heart pills," Ray concluded, stepping back. He handed the blister pack to Major Mallory-Eaves. The older man tucked it back into his wallet. "Thank you, Sir."

"Good." Emma smiled at the military man with the spiky moustache. "That means I'm not such a terrible judge of character." She pointed to the French doors. Snow banked against the glass, but she wanted to take no chances. "Please, could you guard those for us?"

"Certainly." The major strode across the rug with purpose. He took up his position opposite Sir Robert with a curt nod.

Ray searched everyone's pockets and the women's bags. With great reluctance, Paul ran his hands over arms, legs, torsos, and clothing. Ray extricated mobile phones, mints, fluff, and loose coins from various jackets and trousers. Flora's handbag disgorged paracetamol and anti diarrhoea tablets. The other women possessed similar emergency medication.

Monty lay on the sofa nearest the fire. He agreed to a search but remained lying down. Paul found only a phone in his trouser pocket. Gwendoline glared at Paul for the duration of his contact with her smooth skin. She pursed her lips as though this wasn't her first dalliance with a police search. Christos' wallet betrayed him with a driving licence in his real name. Bunny carried no purse or pockets. She kept a battered mobile phone in her bra.

But Ray hit the jackpot with Arnand. His fingers produced a plain cylinder, which rattled when he shook it. A blister pack contained only two sleeping pills. Emma watched in fascination as Ray inspected the tiny writing on the cylinder. Paul handed back the sleeping tablets with a shake of his head. "Herbal," he declared. Narrowing his eyes, he asked Arnand, "Does valerian work?"

Arnand frowned. "Not bad," he admitted. "Not as good as prescription medication, though."

Emma piped up from the fringes of the crowd. "Did your wife use any pills?"

"No." Another dead end.

But Ray's body appeared rigid. His eyes held the glassiness of deep thought. "Why do you have these with you? he demanded." He popped the lid of the cylinder and sniffed.

"Vitamins." Arnand's eyes glittered like river stones. His beige aura became grey.

Ray shook two into his palm. Emma gasped as he bit down on a pink tablet. Paul's eyes widened in horror. "Don't!" he cried.

Ray's nose wrinkled. "Iron tablets. Was your wife anemic?"

Arnand shifted from one foot to the other. "No." He cleared his throat. "These are mine."

"Mum couldn't take iron," Gwendoline observed. Her voice held a high, girlish note. She peeked at Christos beneath her eyelashes before remembering his disgrace. Her expression shuttered. "She had a special condition. From birth."

"What?" Paul joined his father. Their shoulders touched.

Arnand coughed. Awkwardness descended over him as he visibly squirmed. "Hemochromatosis," he murmured.

Ray squinted at the tiny writing on the cylinder. "These are high dose." He stared at Arnand. "You don't look anemic."

Arnand flattened his lips across his teeth. He pushed shaking hands behind his back.

"Bag," Ray demanded. He waited for Paul to pull a freezer bag from his jacket pocket. He dropped the cylinder into it.

"Iron tablets?" Paul's chin jerked back, and he peered at his father. "Why do I want these?"

Ray heaved out a breath. "You just do," he murmured. "Trust me."

56

Prayer chair

♥

"What now?" Paul spread his hands and stared at Emma. His hazel irises flared with anxiety. The tension hiked among the gathered guests. They'd complied with the strange requests but rallied in the ensuing silence. Emma sensed herself about to lose control of them.

She turned to face Gwendoline. "Who wrote *Her Ladyship*?" she demanded.

The other woman scuttled across the rug and sank onto the sofa beside Christos. He peered at her from beneath his fringe. She stared down at her hands, the fingers twisting in her lap.

"Your mother didn't write the poem?" Paul seized the fragile thread and pulled. "You seemed adamant about that. She didn't write it and she didn't read it to the group last night."

"Poem?" Mavis blustered. Her breasts wobbled as she reconfigured her usual effrontery. She set her hands on her hips and waddled towards the detective. "Of course, Kathleen read us a poem. Are you stupid? She won competitions for her work." She waved a flailing hand around her. "Why do you think we came here?" She sucked in a breath and sealed her lips over the ready insult about Wingate Hall and its mistress.

Paul faced Arnand. The older man remained standing, his hands clasped behind his back. "I, er..." He cleared his throat again. "No, she, er...Kathleen didn't write that."

"So, who did?"

Paul nodded to Emma. "Do you remember the words?"

"Yes." How could she ever forget them? She gritted her teeth and recited the spiteful ditty from memory. *'Her Ladyship.*

Her voice, like onions, such a pungent assault,
Harsh and crunchy, our ears to halt.
Her laughter, like the bitterest citrus zest,
Leaves tongues twisted and hearts unimpressed.'"

"Is that about you?" Freda released a gasp and rose from her seat. The action deflated her lungs and left her chest concave. "Is that about Emma?" She spun on her heels and glared at each member of the Society. "Well!" she huffed, uncharacteristically running out of words. "Well!"

"It's not about her!" Gwendoline shouted. Her voice bounced off the rich oil paintings. A row of Ayers' lords and ladies peered down at her. "My mother didn't write it!" She bent double in her seat. The fury in her movement caused Christos to list towards her on the shared cushion. He winced and dabbed at his head. Dried blood flaked onto his white collar. Gwendoline stared at her father. "Tell them!" she demanded. "For once, say something!"

Arnand's voice held a low rumble. He swallowed and fixed his gaze on Paul as though willing the others to vanish. "Kathleen didn't write that," he asserted, his voice firm.

Emma cocked her head, wondering why she didn't see it before. "It's in the same voice as her winning poem," she mused. "The one about food and emotions." She tucked in her elbow and supported her painful wrist. "One person wrote both poems. Someone in this room."

Everyone denied it. No one had written the offensive poem. Including Kathleen.

Paul allowed them to leave the morning room. He took Arnand to the lounge for an interview. Emma's nerves jangled as though electrified. Ray grew frustrated with her. "Keep still!" he exclaimed. He spread his hands in defeat, a roll of crepe bandage unfurling in his fingers. "I can't secure the bones if you jiffle!"

"It's too hard!" Emma wailed. "I'm missing something important."

Ray secured her wrist in the splint and began wrapping. "Christos admitted he borrowed the boots last night to go outside to vape. He's tall enough to notice the key on the mantelpiece. He claims he checked all the jacket pockets in the armoire and stole whatever he found."

Emma's jaw grew slack. "Like what?" she demanded.

Ray shrugged. He bent lower to tape the bandage in place. "Loose change. Cash." He waggled his eyebrows. Colour flushed into his cheeks. "A burner phone I left in my right boot."

Emma grunted as pain shot through her forearm. "Why didn't you find it in his room?"

"He hid it between the middle rung and the mattress under his double bed. We thought that room remained empty."

"We did." Emma pursed her lips when he didn't answer. He saw it as a failure of his duty. The dereliction burned in his chest. She winced as Ray fixed the sling in place. "Don't make me wear this. It hurts my neck."

"Do as you're told," he growled.

"Did Paul ask Christos about Rohan's greatcoat?" She squinted up at him. "Did he see it in the armoire?"

"Yes, he asked, and no." Ray sighed over Emma's next question. "He didn't see it there when he sneaked downstairs at one o'clock. Kathleen already had it."

"Did he ask Monty about the Temazepam?" She chafed against the sling's restriction. "Or Flora. They didn't share a room like we thought."

"Paul's dealing with it." Ray lifted the ski jacket over her shoulders and waited as she pushed her left arm into the sleeve.

"I can't cope like this," she grumbled. "My jacket will keep falling off."

Ray leaned across the table and snagged a giant nappy pin. "I'll fix it in place," he said. His irises danced with mischief.

"Help me into the tunnel?" Emma begged. "I want to listen to Paul questioning Arnand."

Ray blew a raspberry. "I don't think so." He laughed at her irritation. "Behave."

Emma resented having overseers. She chafed against the restrictions. As soon as Ray released her, she headed for the coach house.

Winston slept in the master bedroom. His shoes hung off the end of the mattress. Emma stared at his pale complexion and worried. She tugged the bedspread over his icy form. "Don't die Winston," she whispered. "We don't have room in the freezer."

"I'll try not to," he growled. She jumped back and clattered against the open door with a shriek. No suitable retort came to mind.

"I'm going into the tunnel again," she croaked. He didn't reply.

57

Butterfly chair

♥

The sling restricted her movements in the narrow space. Emma slunk to her original position, finding it harder to remain silent.

"You're sure you don't know who wrote *Her Ladyship*?" Paul's casual tone belied his fox-like inquisitiveness.

"No." Fabric rustled as Arnand squirmed.

"But you acknowledge it sounds a lot like your wife's poem?" Paper sifted under Paul's fingers. "I seized this notebook after I arrived. Pages are loose. It's very fragile. But the writing has a similar style to the winning poem."

"My wife is dead!" Arnand barked. "I will not sully her memory. You're calling her a cheat. It's unacceptable! A slur on Kathleen's work!"

Paul tutted. Frustration filled the sound. "You said you borrowed the grey coat from the armoire?"

"Yes. Everyone disappeared upstairs. We didn't know where they went. Kathleen's fingers were like ice. I saw the wardrobe and trusted the homeowner wouldn't mind. We brought no warm clothing to the evening. A mistake, in hindsight."

"Because of your wife's illness? Can you give me the name of her doctor?"

"She hated hospitals!" Arnand shouted. "Her diagnosis came from childhood. She lost a baby because of her stupid disease. Useless medics failed her. She refused to see one after that."

Paul waited a beat before changing direction. "I'm sorry for your loss. Let's return to last night. You're certain Mrs Dubois didn't remove her shoes after putting them on to leave?"

"No. I offered to help her, but she resisted. She wished to sit by the fire."

"Yes. In the morning room. Why did you leave her there? Alone." A veiled rebuke lurked beneath the enquiry.

Arnand sighed. Sadness and exhaustion mingled. "Monty arrived. He promised to bring her upstairs when they finished chatting."

"He said she didn't want to go. Why didn't you return for her?"

"I took a sleeping tablet."

"So, you did. But you admitted they weren't a knock-out drug."

"People saw me go to bed," Arnand insisted. "I didn't wake until this morning."

Disappointment thudded in Emma's chest as Paul thanked Arnand for his time. The squeak of leather betrayed him standing.

No one returned to the lounge. Emma waited in the tunnel until her legs grew numb. She crept to the coach house and crawled through the half-door. The TV burbled from the sitting room. Winston waved a hand over his shoulder as she reached for his chair. "Still alive," he said.

Emma retreated. She got as far as the lobby before hearing the raised voices. She'd almost blasted into the open but slid into the folds of the curtain in the last second. The musty scent of old fabric assaulted her nostrils.

"How could you do this to me?" Monty took a threatening step towards Gwendoline. She stood on the bottom step of the main staircase. It gave her a height advantage. "I'll never forgive you for this." He balled his fists by his sides. "You'll get nothing else from me. Ever!"

"You could spare it," she replied. "Just the one." Her lower lip wobbled, and she tilted forward. Her arms curled around his neck. "You can't abandon me now, Monty." Her fingers caressed his angry cheek. "Gwenny needs a tummy tuck. You promised."

His profile relaxed, the features melting like warm custard. Emma watched in horror as Gwendoline dragged her sharp nails along his skin. Monty reeled back, but not before she'd drawn blood. "I'll tell," she snarled. She adopted a high, beseeching voice and pressed a hand to her breasts. They bounced like basketballs in her decorative corset. "Daddy, I need to tell you what Uncle Monty did to me."

"You bitch!" he snapped. "You took everything from me!"

Gwendoline shrugged, unafraid of him. She jiggled her breasts in his eyeline. "Did you like my trick with the sleeping tablets? Bought them off the internet last week especially. I hear Flora snored until this morning. The dog ate the first attempt." She slid her fingers into her corset and massaged her supple breast. "Lucky, I removed them from here before the detective frisked me."

"Flora deserves none of this!" Monty's inaudible whisper communicated desperation and disgust. At himself, or at Gwendoline?

"She can't resist a fattening scone. Fat for a fatty. She didn't even taste the powder. Maybe she gobbled it down too fast." Gwendoline sighed. Her breasts rose and fell in Monty's eyeline. "They're vile. I took one after we found Mum's body. But I dropped the second one in the lobby. It disappeared." She giggled. "The detective thinks Christos drugged me. I only needed two more pills to fall into a deep sleep. That big dude put his fingers down my throat." Retching sounds echoed off the walls.

"This all needs to stop!" Monty begged. "I've nothing left for you to take! Stay away from Flora. She's done nothing to you!"

Gwendoline's hand shot out so fast, Emma inhaled. She covered her mouth to muffle her shock. Gwendoline grabbed the back of Monty's neck and tilted him forward, crushing her lips against his. He released a ragged groan filled with anguish. His arms fluttered by his sides as though attempting flight. But he didn't pull away from the kiss.

"I don't like Flora. Too bossy by half. And a little too much awareness. Now, no more bad Monty," Gwendoline whispered. "There's lots I can do to your lovely wife. The wrong word here, or a little overdose there." She bopped the end of his nose with a manicured index finger. "Let me take care of everything from now on. I hid the pills in Christos' room." Monty appeared frozen by her presence. Bewitched. She spoke with her lips against his. "I thought he might make a lovely meal ticket, but I'm losing interest." Her tongue protruded, running a line around Monty's lips. He shivered, his hands still by his sides. His eyelids fluttered closed.

"What do you want?" he moaned.

"Your silence." Gwendoline pressed her body against his. She enfolded him, his face disappearing into her cleavage. He didn't pull away, despite the gash across his forehead. "You know what about?"

Monty's head shook, an indecisive action. "I can't," he whispered. "It's cost me everything."

Gwendoline chuckled. Such an evil sound from between her delectable lips. She'd turned the man to putty in her hands. "Oh, Uncle Monty," she breathed into his ear. "You still have so much more to lose." Her irises sparkled as she toyed with him. His trousers fluttered with the shaking of his knees as she kissed him again. Her fingers brushed across his nipples and his arms snatched at her waist. The air crackled with desperation.

Emma had seen enough.

58

Windsor chair

♥

Christos lurked in the kitchen. He leaned his rump against the Aga and stared through the window. His body jerked as Emma entered the room. The blood-stained handkerchief fluttered to the floor, and he held his hands in front of him. "Truce?"

"Okay." Emma slumped at the kitchen table. "Stay over there then."

Christos retrieved his handkerchief. He swiped it across the back of his head and inspected the faint mark. She didn't apologise.

"Why did you leave the kitchen door open after you returned last night?" Emma faced him, her eyes narrowed. "Why put the key back on the mantel but not close or lock the door?"

Christos licked his lips. He stared at the ceiling. "My hands were too cold. I took the key with me and vaped outside for a while. A blizzard started. It cleared after half an hour, and I waited in a nearby outbuilding." He shuddered as though testing the memory. "My fingers froze. I couldn't feel them. So, I pushed the door closed and threw the key onto the mantel. I got to bed just in time, too. Gwendoline tapped on Monty's door a little later."

Emma considered what she'd overheard. Gwendoline claimed she'd knocked on Christos' door before two o'clock. She didn't realise Monty and Christos switched rooms. And why drug poor Flora? Emma remembered Gwendoline's warning. Because she could. She'd later planted the pills there, aiming to throw suspicion on Christos. She'd hadn't ruined his alibi for Kathleen's death but thrown shade on Monty's instead.

"Why did you put the boots on my hearth?"

Christos shrugged. "I left them there to dry. I had this crazy idea you might walk in, see me naked in the shower, and join me. But the hot water ran out, and I panicked. By the time I remembered them later, someone had locked the door."

It sounded plausible. Emma remained silent, pawing through the evidence.

"No one will speak to me." Christos sounded surprised. "That's why I'm hiding in here."

Emma raised an eyebrow. "Ripping off local groups doesn't help you make friends."

"I didn't steal from them!" His voice rose in protest. "Mavis got there first. Mind you, she's adamant she only took twelve. But because fifteen thousand is missing, they'll pin it on me."

"Yeah," Emma mused. "So, if you didn't steal the other three, who did?"

"I don't know." Christos rubbed his eyes.

"Hey," Emma said. She turned to face him, studying his expression. "Did you see a shovel in here last night?"

"During my wanderings?" A smile lit his lips. "I did. Leaned against the sink. A bit of snow came in with me. I cleared it out and leaned the shovel against the door. I wasn't careful. My hands were too cold. Perhaps it fell afterwards, and the door opened. I'm sorry."

Emma stared at the space. Then back at Christos. "I don't suppose you wiped off your fingerprints?" she asked. It seemed a silly question to ask an invited guest.

His shoulders swallowed his head like a tortoise. He grinned at her, that bad boy smile. "Of course," he replied.

Emma sought Paul. She now knew only the murderer's fingerprints remained on the shovel. Thanks to Christos. But the missing money from the Society's accounts troubled her. Mavis had ceased lying, so why deduct three thousand pounds from her debt?

Ray flew down the rear stairs as Emma exited the kitchen. He almost smashed into her. "Where's Freda?" he demanded.

Emma shrugged, her expression blank. "I don't know. Why?"

Ray growled in his throat. "Paul wants to interview her. He's taken Mavis back to the morning room and sent me upstairs to collect Freda." He dodged around Emma and strode along the corridor towards the lobby. "Send her to the lounge, if you see her," he called over his shoulder.

Emma sighed. Her body ached. Her bruised knees increased their complaint. She wanted to go to bed, not chase around the house after Freda.

She limped towards the coach house with reluctance. It surprised her she'd rather spend time with the obnoxious Winston. A shrill sound reached her as she passed the lounge. She halted, her slippers squeaking on the tiles. "You'll say nothing!" An angry male voice rose in response. "I'm warning you!"

Emma turned the brass knob, and the door creaked. A spooky, guttural groan. The man spun, whipping around Freda's stricken frame like a satellite and settling behind her. His bent arm clasped her around her thin neck. A kitchen knife reflected the speckled glow of the chandelier. The lights danced as his hand shook. A line of blood trickled from Freda's jawline and soaked the delicate collar of her dress.

59

Cross-back chair

♥

"I'm sorry, Emma. This isn't personal."

She snorted, her reply devoid of humour. "Right. I'll remember that." She stepped into the room but left the door open.

"I'm so sorry," Freda gasped. "I'm responsible for this whole mess." Her voice rose to a squeak as Monty pressed the sharp blade to her throat. Emma tensed. Freda's delicate skin covered the livid blue arteries like threadbare nylon.

"Why, Monty?" Emma spread her hands, palm upwards in a truce. "Why this whole charade?"

He blew out a ragged breath. Gwendoline's nails had left dents in his flushed cheek. The red welts jarred with the gash across his forehead. Ray's paper stitches increased the look of a man falling apart at the seams.

Monty's exhale disturbed the fluffy white curls hugging the nape of Freda's neck. His right heel edged backwards until it hit the hearth. "I owe you that, I guess," he conceded. His features relaxed, returning to their handsome proportions. The gentle school teacher emerged from beneath the agonised, twisted sneer. His shoulders lost their tension, and the blade slipped level with Freda's collar. "I've written as Larissa Le Strande for over four decades." He released a dramatic sigh. "She stole my best poem. She entered it into the competition, and it won." The gash across his forehead glistened.

Emma's mind emptied. Monty set the blade against Freda's protruding jugular, though his lips flattened into twin lines of regret.

"Larissa stole your poem? I'm confused."

"No!" Monty's agitation rose. "I'm Larissa. That bitch stole my poem."

"This is about copyright theft?" Emma startled him. Her voice rose to a squeak of disbelief. "You took an old lady hostage over a stolen poem?" She took a step forward and Monty's head reared. His forearm increased its pressure against Freda's throat.

Spittle rattled like a gunshot as he snarled at Emma. "You have everything you ever wanted. Your rags to riches story is local legend!"

Emma held her breath. Her gaze slid to Freda and her thirst for notoriety. How much did she betray her to the local gossips? Her teeth ground together as she surveyed Monty's lithe frame for potential weakness. A swift kick to his left knee would unbalance him, but she risked an accidental slice across Freda's narrow throat. One could tumble into the fire. Or both.

"He killed Kathleen Dubois," Freda whispered. Her eyeballs swelled in her waxy complexion. "I've waited all day to speak to the detective."

Monty cleared his throat. "Shut up!"

"Why?" Emma edged forward a step. "Because Kathleen stole your poem?"

He gulped. "I wanted to write. To commentate on life." His chest swelled with inner pride. "A publisher bought my collection. Larissa Le Strande found recognition with The Bloomsbury Publishing Set. The industry could enjoy forty years of my outpourings. Then she stole my best poem."

Emma exhaled. "The one likening food to emotions?" Another step. "You can challenge the ownership of intellectual property." She affected a soothing tone, drawing out the syllables and slowing her speech. "You can forensically track amendments to file documents. Flora could swear an affidavit." Another step. "Rohan could help you with the computer evidence."

As Emma studied the vein twitching beneath Monty's jaw, she realised her offer lacked any substance. He'd killed a woman. No one would care about his poem.

"I didn't keep it on a computer. Gwendoline stole my notebook!" Monty hissed. "My entire collection. The publisher saw my poem in the University Times. They withdrew their support. I'm blacklisted. Me!" Spittle hazed the surrounding air. He inhaled an agonised breath. "Kathleen writes spiteful limericks. Nothing publishable. She took my place as the Writer in Residence. Mine!"

Emma breathed through her nose. It didn't calm her pounding heart. "Mabel said Gwendoline entered the poem on Kathleen's behalf." Monty's features caved into a ghoulish mask. Emma had stumbled on the reason for his argument with Gwendoline. He wanted his poetry and his reputation restored. But she'd blackmailed him with his own indiscretions. She'd stolen his notebook during one of their seedy assignations. That fact alone had silenced him.

A trickle of blood slid along Freda's protruding tendon. The blade nicked her tissue paper skin again. Emma pointed to it, drawing Monty's attention. "You've hurt her!" she cried. Her voice rose with indignation. "She's bleeding."

Monty's lashes flickered. "I didn't want this."

"Careful!" Emma shouted, as his grip tightened against Freda's chest. More blood turned Freda's collar into a scarlet fringe. "What do you want?" She turned her palms outwards and held them aloft. The sling tugged at her neck.

Desperation cast a greyness over his complexion. "Let me leave. You'll never hear from me again."

Emma swallowed. Monty's short-term release wouldn't end well. The police would pick him up before he reached the nearest town. If he didn't die of hypothermia first. "Fine." She reversed a full step, her hands in front of her. "But first, tell me what happened with Kathleen?"

Monty's eyes narrowed. They became glittering pits in his blanched face. Rapid blinking accompanied his trembling lips. "I spoke to her last night after she sent Arnand away. She treated him like dirt. He left like a scolded cat! I promised I'd walk her upstairs." He gulped, and the blade shook. "I demanded my notebook. She knew the poem didn't belong to her but just scooped up the praise for my work. She laughed at me. Threatened to burn it." A tear trailed down his cheek.

"The detective has it," Emma soothed. "He knows she didn't write the poems."

"But I watched her pull out a page from her coat pocket and toss it into the fire. My life's work."

Emma's knees locked with the effort of remaining still. "Paul noticed some missing pages. Perhaps they fell out during the awards night, and she didn't notice. She picked them up later and put them in the coat pocket. She burned one to upset you, but threw the remnants into the kindling bin. The first few stanzas of *Her Ladyship*. But you didn't kill her then, did you? You walked away."

"But I saw him later." Freda's voice croaked. Monty had arched her spine backwards, so she stared at the chandelier. "I used the bathroom. He snuck upstairs to the third floor at twenty-five past two. Murder leaves a stain on a man. He doesn't want me to tell the detective, but I must."

So, Freda ended up as a reluctant hostage. She knew too much.

"Did you smash Kathleen in the face with the shovel?"

"An accident!" Monty shouted. "That idiot Christos came upstairs like an elephant. He disturbed Flora. She wanted a cup of tea." His chest heaved. "I found the shovel where I left it. I meant to replace it behind the panel while the kettle boiled. Then Kathleen appeared in the corridor."

"So, you hit her?" Emma quailed at the memory. He'd almost sliced off her face.

"Let me leave. Don't come after me. I'll release Freda when I'm clear."

"No." Emma shook her head. Her dark curls tapped her shoulders as though in agreement. "It's too cold for her outside." Her brow furrowed at the blue line spreading around Freda's lips. "She's going into shock. Let her go. Leave through the kitchen door. The key is on the mantel." Emma narrowed her eyes at her former friend. "Get out and stay out."

Monty withdrew the blade from Freda's throat, retracting his arm until she drooped on shaky knees. Emma stepped forward to take the nonagenarian's negligible weight. She collected a trembling Freda into her arms.

A cool blast of air curled around her shins. As Freda sank to a heap of bones on the hearth, Emma heard the kitchen door open. It squeaked inward, and the drift cascaded onto the tiles. Snow crunched in a rhythmic beat.

Emma sat Freda in a nearby armchair. She ran across the corridor. Monty had gone. The imprint of his slippers left scuffs through the drift. A metre from the house, deep shafts showed he'd sunk to the knees with each stride.

Freda sobbed, her crabbed fingers shaking as she swiped them across her eyes. "I'm sorry," she wailed. "I'm so sorry."

Emma's thoughts turned to Kathleen Dubois. The last lines of *Her Ladyship* now applied to her. The poem thief laid in a basement freezer, the epitome of the stolen words. A chill slid down Emma's back.

'Her gaze, like a fish, icy and blind,
Frozen in death, leaving no warmth behind.'

60

Tandem chair

♥

Flora sniffed into a well-used tissue. Flakes littered the table. Her shoulders heaved. "He'll die out there," she breathed between sobs.

"A friend put in a call to the police. And Search and Rescue." Emma stroked Flora's bowed shoulder. She'd messaged Regan, and he'd used the satellite phone to contact Rohan. Her husband raised the alarm from his hospital bed. At least he had a working cell tower nearby.

"How? We still have no phone signal!" Flora folded in half and pressed her face against her knees. "This event was a disaster from the start."

Emma bit her lower lip to stem her agreement. She sensed she wouldn't stop if she let her mouth run about the Lit and His Society's behaviour. The sky cleared through the lounge window. Snatches of an icy blue gleamed above the puffy cumulus clouds. But the temperature didn't budge. The snow remained deep and impassable.

Monty's fleeing footprints had glistened with ice long after he left. Ray refused to chase him through the grid locked countryside. Paul had begged to no avail. His father wouldn't risk his own life for a murderer.

"They'll arrive as soon as they can," Emma promised.

Flora rocked in the hard dining chair. "No!" she wailed. "I need them to search for my husband, not waste their time here."

Farrell whined and leaned his jaw on her knee. His doleful eyes twinkled up at her. She cast an absentminded hand over his soft ears, drawing comfort from his warmth.

"I'm confused about something," Emma said. A few facts had bothered her since listening to Monty. She nudged a mug of sugary tea towards Flora. "Drink this, it'll help."

Flora exhaled and sat up straight. She cupped the mug in her shaking hands. "What?"

"I overheard Gwendoline say she'd used a scone from the buffet to drug you last night. But Monty mentioned you both woke when Christos went to bed."

Flora sniffed. She wiped her nose on her furry sleeve. Strands of rabbit pelt attached to her cheeks and chin. "I didn't eat it," she stated. "That girl hates my guts. Always has. Twisted little thing even years ago when I taught her. I wouldn't trust her to spit on me if I caught fire."

Emma licked her lips. She trod with care through her next sentence. "But Monty didn't bring your tea. He didn't return to your room at all. Why didn't you notice?"

Flora's lips rested against the lip of the mug. Her eyes became glassy as she stared at the scarred pine table. She remained silent for so long, Emma doubted she'd registered her question. Then, as though electrified, Flora inhaled. She set her mug on the table with force. Hot tea slopped over the side and wet her fingers. "I don't want to talk about it."

"Oh." Emma's heart landed in her stomach like a brick. "Because you thought he spent the night with Gwendoline?"

Flora's gentle eyes morphed into fiery dots in her strained face. "I said, leave it!" she snarled.

"How long have you known?" Emma whispered.

The slap took her breath away. It caught her beneath her eye and left a stinging, hand-shaped welt. The chair legs skittered against the tiles as Emma leapt to her feet. Flora screamed, a stomach clenching wail. It took a second for Emma to register the dog's teeth clamped around Flora's offending wrist.

The kitchen door flew open. Ray stood in the gap. Rage filled his expression. Emma backed towards the sink, comforted by the hard edge against her spine. "Farrell, drop!" he commanded. The dog released Flora's arm. He slunk to Emma's side and sat on her foot. No one rebuked him.

Emma kept her cool hand against her painful cheek. "She hit me." Her words wavered in the air before her.

Paul appeared behind Ray. His face bore a quizzical expression. His gaze switched from Flora to Emma. But the fight had left her. She clutched her wrist where the dog's teeth broke the skin. Shock robbed Emma of words to describe the incident. Ray crossed the room, and his burly arms enfolded her. She fought the urge to cry.

A glance at Flora showed a friend she no longer recognised. Nicky's beautiful, spirited teacher had retreated behind a vengeful, bitter façade. There seemed no point sparing her feelings anymore. Emma cleared her throat and wriggled free of Ray's grasp. Paul blocked the doorway, his rapid blinking betraying confusion.

"Monty and Gwendoline are lovers." Emma's voice shook. "That's how Gwendoline stole his poetry book. She entered his best poem into the university's competition under her mother's name. I'm not sure why. Spite, perhaps. But Monty couldn't tell anyone what she'd done. He knew she'd expose their affair. And how else could he explain her access to his personal items?" A gulp intruded on her words. "Flora didn't eat Gwendoline's scone and wasn't drugged last night. Monty came downstairs, and I believe she followed him. He didn't kill Kathleen, did he?" She stared at Flora's blank expression. "The wound seemed deeper at the initial point of impact, just beneath her right eye. Monty's tall, but his height matched Kathleen's. Only a downward stroke could cause the thinner end of the shovel to cut through to the bone so deeply at her cheek. A strike by Monty would distribute an even pressure across the blade." Emma inhaled, surprised when her lungs locked. "Christos leaned the shovel against the back door. But Monty said he retrieved it from where he left it. Against the sink. So, you killed Kathleen. And he's covering for you."

Flora shook her head from side to side, a slow, deliberate rocking motion. "No," she breathed.

Emma's fingers balled against Ray's jacket. "Then why did you send Ray away from the third floor earlier?" she demanded. "Were you searching for Monty's poetry book?" Her gaze slid to Paul. He tapped his inside pocket and the freezer bag containing the notebook rustled.

"I asked Mr Dubois for his wife's belongings as soon as I arrived." A heavy frown bisected his brow. "It's the first thing I did after examining the body."

Flora sank against the chair's spindles. She resembled melting snow. She pursed her lips together as though willing herself to remain silent.

Emma leaned against the sink. Ray released her. His elbow bumped her upper arm as he mirrored her stance. "When did you realise Kathleen used Monty's poem for the competition?" She kept her voice soft.

Flora shook her head. "Last night," she whispered. "Monty sank into a huge depression when his publisher cut him loose. He didn't give me a reason. I recognised his poem when Kathleen read it aloud. And then I saw her pass Monty's book to Arnand."

"So, you searched Mr Dubois' room for it? You couldn't find it and Ray disturbed you."

Flora's shallow nod confirmed Emma's theory.

"Why not keep Monty safe with you the previous night when Christos woke you? Why send him out for tea? Especially when you knew Gwendoline occupied a room just metres away."

"I didn't suggest the tea. He did." Her lips pursed. A tear trickled along her jaw.

"And then you panicked. You suspected he'd found an excuse to meet Gwendoline. Monty used the main staircase, but you cut down the servants' stairs. It meant you reached the kitchen first. You found the open back door and the fallen shovel. It was freezing. You reasoned no one had gone outside. So, you considered the morning room. Perhaps you imagined a tryst by firelight. You snatched up the shovel and left the kitchen in a temper. But you ran into Kathleen in the corridor. Gwendoline's mother and the poem thief."

"And you killed her?" Paul's jaw clenched. Little surprised him as a detective. But he'd never imagined the tall, mild-mannered woman could exact such vengeance on an elderly woman. Disbelief flickered in his eyes.

"An accident," Flora whispered. Her words mirrored Monty's. "I heard footsteps and rage built in my chest." She patted the top button of her coat as though it held a blockage of unshed fury.

"You thought it was Gwendoline?" Emma pitied her for the error. Gwendoline Dubois deserved a shovel to the face. She'd toyed with a man's marriage and his dreams. And he'd become an addicted passenger on her train of destruction.

Paul swore. "We need to find him," he breathed.

Ray shrugged. He cared little for Monty's guilt or innocence. "I'm not going out there again," he growled. And folded his arms across his chest.

61

Pulpit chair

♥

"But someone smashed Monty's forehead into the door frame." Ray pushed a mug of hot chocolate towards Emma. "I figured he'd worked out who murdered the victim. And they went after him."

Freda whimpered in the chair opposite Emma, and he ignored the intimation. He'd patched the knife wounds to her throat and declared her fit for the detective's questioning. After Paul finished with Flora.

Emma considered donating the fortifying drink to Freda's pitiful cause, but a glance at Ray's stern face dissuaded her. She took a sip and closed her eyes in pleasure. "Monty did that to himself." She exhaled a lungful of angst. "The blood stain on the architrave ran vertical. His gash was in line with his eyebrows."

"Horizontal." Ray snapped his fingers. "Right. He wanted the biggest cut possible, so he turned his head sideways and nutted the frame."

"He did." Emma sighed. "Gwendoline faked her drugging episode. Did you know that?"

Ray's lips screwed upwards into an arch. "No one can simulate pupil dilation. She seemed genuine. Shallow breathing, fluttery heart." He shook his head, still not convinced.

"She took enough to make herself sleepy, but not to put her in danger. But she'd planted the sleeping pills in the wrong bedroom. She didn't implicate Christos, but Monty."

"Did he know that?"

"Not when I ran into him outside the kitchen. I just told him Gwendoline was hurt."

Ray's lips slid into a scowl. "So, he injured himself to throw Paul off course. Just in case anything blew back onto him?"

"But I noticed the blood stain didn't match his cut."

"Is he protecting Flora?" Freda's voice warbled into the silence.

Emma shrugged. "Only he knows his own thought processes. But I believe he saw her swing the shovel.

She ran back up the servants' stairs not realising he'd witnessed everything. He checked Kathleen and discovered she'd passed away."

"So, he returned the shovel to the lobby, just like he told us." Freda shuddered. She jabbed a gnarled finger towards the counter. "Could I trouble you for one of those delicious chocolate drinks?"

Ray sucked in a breath. He turned to the kettle, but Emma noticed his grimace. Freda often used him as her personal hired help. Emma dropped her chin. She promised herself she'd deal with the things she'd let slide. As soon as the Lit and His Society departed.

"That's calculating behaviour," Ray remarked. He busied himself with a fresh mug and a spoonful of chocolate powder. "Putting the murder weapon back where it belonged."

"I think that's what woke me." Emma ran her finger around the rim of her mug. "The panel clangs if you don't close it just right. My bedroom is above the lobby. The timing fits." She lifted an ice pack from the table. Wincing, she placed it against her flaming right cheek. "It also explains why Monty hid in the spare bedroom."

Ray snorted. "Yeah, could you climb back into bed with your wife after watching that?" He glanced at

Emma and his fingers stilled. "Let me clean that cut under your eye first. It's still bleeding."

Emma sat up straight and dropped the ice pack. She raised her hand to ask for silence. Her gaze fixed on a point beyond the house. "What's that noise?" she whispered.

Thwack. Thwack. Thwack.

Snow flew past the window like an avalanche. It slammed off the sill and shattered into bouncing fragments.

At the same moment, two phones emitted a vibration. Ray pulled his free, but Emma didn't bother. Farrell barked. Her chair squealed against the tiles as she shoved it backwards with her knees.

"What's happening?" Freda rose, clutching her hands to her throat. "What now? My nerves are shattered." She screamed as the house exploded with noise. It's inhabitant's footsteps pounded from upstairs. Her gnarled fingers swept over her eyes.

Ray stared down at his phone screen and frowned. His work worn fingers sent a reply to Regan.

Emma reached for the door knob. She no longer cared about evidence or murder. The desire to get outside overwhelmed her senses. The kitchen door banged against the pantry as she wrenched it open. Paul appeared in the corridor, his hand pulling the lounge door closed behind him. Flora's sniffs carried in his wake. "What's happening?" he demanded.

The remaining Lit and His Society members poured from the main stairs and the morning room. They surged together like meeting streams. Emma reached the end of the corridor and burst through them. The dog kept pace with her, emitting frantic warning barks. She cannoned Gwendoline into the armoire without regret. Sir Robert helped the other woman upright, but Emma ignored them.

She reached the front door first. Snowflakes pelted the west of the house as though sandblasting its stone façade. The windows creaked with the force of the growing gale. Emma wrenched open the inner door and stepped into the vestibule. Then she pressed her nose and forehead against the glass, her heart pulsing with the thwack of the helicopter's powerful blades.

62

Elizabethan chair

♥

Ray reached Emma's side as the house vibrated with the force of the powerful rotors. The helicopter's dull khaki paint stood out against the pristine snow. Murmuring came from behind them, but Emma tuned out her guests' curiosity.

Ray tilted his phone screen towards her with a grin. His bulk excluded the throng pressing behind him. *'Incoming.'* The approaching helicopter negated Regan's warning.

"We're good, Em." Ray slipped his arm around her shoulders and pressed a kiss to her temple. "He obviously pleased someone enough to send him home in an RAF Puma. Emma grinned up at him. She wanted to improve on his description. Better than good. Her heart skipped with pure euphoria. Farrell watched through the window. A whine slipped from his chest, low and continuous. His ears perked and drooped with excitement.

The helicopter couldn't land on the deep, unstable snow. A blizzard whirled beneath it in ever decreasing circles. A blur of movement indicated the side door sliding open. The wheels grazed the snow, and its black maw disgorged a slew of objects. They plunged earthwards and disappeared into the drift.

A gasp of dismay rippled through the group. The Puma rose into the air, snow swirling around it like desert sands.

"No!" Mavis wailed. "Come back!" Her volume altered as she spun, gathering the combined misery of the crowd. "Why is it leaving us behind?"

Ray barked out a laugh and turned from the front door. He edged Sir Robert and Gwendoline aside with his broad shoulders as he stepped from the vestibule. "Did you think the government sent a helicopter to taxi you home?" He snorted, his chest rock-hard against Mavis' indignation. His arms spread wide, and he herded the crowd away from Emma. "Into the morning room," he commanded, his voice echoing.

"But what did the helicopter want?" Bunny's squeak rose over the others. "Why did it come here?"

Condensation fogged up the antique glass as Emma watched her husband push himself upright. He struggled with the drifts, hindered by a prosthetic leg and a useless arm. Sniper strode beside him, lifting each leg as though concrete encased it. Snow puffed up with every step. When Rohan stumbled, Sniper held out a steadying arm. "Take it," Emma whispered. Her plea coated the glass. "Ignore your pride. Come to me." She smoothed the steam from the glass with her right fist. Sniper had looped his arm around Rohan's waist and supported him on their painful walk across the lawn. Three others followed, one small enough to resemble a child against the landscape. He disappeared almost to the waist with each heaving step.

Voices still complained behind her. Emma heard Sir Robert's soothing tones. A glance saw them collected in the lobby like worried sheep.

"Move, Em!" Ray appeared beside her. He carried the shovel he'd brought with him a lifetime ago. He pointed to the lobby and commanded the dog to wait. They moved onto the threshold and watched him work. A blast of cold air took her breath away as Ray yanked open the heavy oak door. Snow cascaded into the vestibule and covered his boots. Warm air puffed from between his lips as he went to war with the drift. But not the stuff inside. He set about clearing a sliver of the steps nearest the ornate iron banister.

The visitors took an age to cross the lawn. Every step cost them energy and time. Emma dragged Nicky's ski mittens from the armoire and stuffed her right hand into one. It closed around her fingers like a clamp. But she joined Ray's fight, rolling the vestibule snow into a ball. She pushed it around the floor one-handed, gathering up the icy debris. It became almost too fat to pass over the narrow lip of the entrance and onto the steps. Farrell watched her, desperate to join the game but mindful of Ray's command.

Emma gritted her teeth. Grim determination mingled with temper as she pitched the snowball onto the landing and down the stairs. It bounced, shattering with every impact. Ray glanced back at her and smiled. He didn't tell her to go inside with the complaining, dissatisfied crowd. Her effort made little difference, but he let her do it, anyway.

The visitors reached the driveway's edge. A spiralling wind swirled the snow as though Wingate Hall welcomed them. Sweating but still eager, Ray continued digging. Emma stepped onto the wide landing in her slippers. The crunch beneath her soles punctuated the scraping of Ray's shovel. She saw he'd cleared a narrow tunnel almost to the bottom step.

Energy flowered like a sunburst in her chest. She ached to run past him and explode into Rohan's arms. Sharing her sentiment, Farrell took a flying leap from behind her. He disappeared into the drift covering the stairs. Flakes dotted the air above the oval hole. The men's progress increased as they navigated the buried bus to find a clearer section of the driveway. Farrell met them, bouncing as though riding a pogo stick to move through the snow. They waded towards Ray.

He switched his shovel into his left hand before saluting Rohan. Emma heard a murmured greeting beneath the swishing of her pulse in her eardrums. Ray shook hands with the three strangers before Sniper wrapped him in a bear hug. They turned as one towards the stairs. And Emma.

After wasted minutes of slipping and sliding, they reached the front door. Emma shook the gloved hands of the three newcomers. They introduced themselves, but she only remembered the woman's name. Marian Slade. Medical Examiner. Emma had mistaken her for a man as she'd struggled through the snow. She smiled at the two male police officers and waved them into the lobby.

Sniper followed. He waggled his eyebrows at her as he removed his heavy gloves. A sleight of hand mimicked a stopper, plunging into a syringe. He brought out the worst in her and she poked out her tongue. Gaiety lifted her spirits until she experienced a light-headed giddiness. It seemed too long since she'd laughed or joked with anyone.

She didn't watch her husband struggle with the stairs, sparing him the humiliation. Ray walked up behind him, acting as a break if he fell. Farrell bounced up at the rear. Rohan didn't fall.

Emma's lower lip trembled as his breath filled the vestibule. She turned aside, aware of her audience. A tear slipped from her chin and spattered her ski jacket. The cold air burned the cut on her cheek, left there by Flora's nail. She ground her teeth together, her jaw locked in place. She ached, body and soul.

"Dorogaya." Rohan whispered the endearment the moment he stepped over the threshold. His heavy coat hung off one shoulder. It matched hers, although lacked the undignified nappy pin. His good arm wrapped around her and crushed her against him. His Parka hood flopped over them both as though offering privacy.

Ray took charge of the onlookers. He herded them into the morning room and left them with the burlier of the police officers. The door closed and his steady tread echoed along the corridor. With him went the medical examiner and the other officer. Marian Slade's journey would continue to the basement freezer with Paul.

Emma's throat squeaked as she fought for control. Her resolve slipped with the audience gone. Rohan released her and pushed the hood back from his face. His angular features regarded her. The bluest of irises sparkled from eye sockets, bruised by exhaustion. "It's nice to be home," he growled. His voice vibrated through Emma's feet and warmed her chest.

She stared up at him, her smile wavering. Her excuses and apologies melted before the kindness in his handsome face. She said, "You didn't miss much."

Farrell barked. One doggy eyebrow rose as he called out her lie.

63

Koken barber chair

♥

The extra manpower brought considerable relief. Detective Chandler kept the Lit and His Society members corralled in the morning room. Sergeant Pollard handcuffed Flora and kept her sequestered in the kitchen. Paul interviewed the other miscreants after slipping Monty's knife into Emma's very last freezer bag.

Mavis returned from the lounge sobbing. She passed Emma in the lobby and halted. "I'm sorry," she murmured without looking up at her. "Such a terrible strain, always waiting for someone to discover my theft. I'm glad it's over."

Emma knelt in the hearth, the poker in her right hand. "What did Paul say?" she asked.

Mavis bristled. She hadn't lost all her effervescent self-righteousness. "He predicted theft charges in my future." She gulped, the sound audible in the silent lobby. Her hand brushed away the tears on her cheek. "Perhaps not prison," she said, forcing positivity into her voice. Wretchedness descended over her. The soles squeaked as she turned her fluffy slippers towards Emma. "Do you think the Literary and Historical Society will banish me?" she whispered. "It's all I have."

"I don't know." Emma rose. Her world had righted itself with the helicopter's arrival. She'd listened to her children's excited voices with the cell tower restored. Generosity burgeoned in her heart. "Perhaps make peace with Freda," she suggested.

She'd just finished reviving the fire as Christos slunk past. His hair stuck on end as though his interview with Paul had stressed him. He watched her feed the last log to the flames. "Ah, Emma," he purred. "Our life together has so much potential. I'm still game if you are." He poked out his tongue and ran it beneath his top teeth.

"No, thanks," she replied. She rubbed her sooty hand on her sweatpants. "Not interested."

"Problem, dorogaya?" Rohan's voice rumbled from behind Christos. Though his prosthesis caused a limp, it didn't rob him of the eerie ability to creep up on the unsuspecting. Christos turned, his eyes widening. Rohan towered above the tall man, reducing him to something average. Unused to it, Christos blinked. He took a step away from Rohan's defined chest. For a moment, he assessed him, taking in the sling, the muscular build, and the man's powerful energy.

Rohan's invisible forcefield defied competition from a confidence trickster. "Er, hi." Christos shot a nervous glance at Emma. She denied him an introduction.

"Detective Inspector Barker sent you to the morning room." Rohan's low growl held a latent threat. He took a step forward, staring down his angular nose at Christos. A blond eyebrow quirked in question. Rohan never asked twice.

"Bye then." Christos gave a feckless wave to Emma with his right hand. His façade crumbled in the face of genuine masculinity. Proud shoulders rounded, bowing him low. He scurried towards the morning room and closed the door behind him.

Emma stepped out of the hearth. Rohan's right arm pulled her against him. He nuzzled her hair. She breathed in his familiar scent. "I'm filthy," she murmured against his shirt.

"Fighting talk." He bit his lower lip and smiled at her, a suggestive hint behind his flashing blue irises.

"We do need to talk," she replied. Not what he'd meant, but a necessary segue. "I'm sorry we argued before you left. You were right about everything. The truth hurts."

Rohan pressed his index finger beneath her chin. She didn't resist the upward pressure. "I love you," he whispered. His lips closed over hers. Warmth flooded her body.

A throat cleared behind Rohan. "Excuse me." Paul's tone held awkwardness.

Rohan winked at Emma and turned to face the detective. "Da?" he answered.

Emma snuggled beneath his good arm. She pressed her splint against her stomach. The sling hung from her neck like a scarf, already discarded.

"A local farmer located our person of interest on his property." Paul tilted sideways to include Emma in his news. "Monty Jones reached an adjacent estate before collapsing. The snow ploughs reached the main road an hour ago. My colleagues will meet him at the hospital. It'll take a while for the ambulance to make both trips."

Emma inhaled. She struggled to catalogue her emotions. Monty had befriended her through the school. She'd liked the Jones' family. A lot. "How is he?" she managed. "He went outside in his slippers." She pushed away the mental image of the pink fluff and Monty's laughing eyes.

"Not great." Paul wrinkled his nose. "Hypothermia. The farmer panicked. His call suggested Mr Jones is suffering from a mental breakdown." He forced a smile on his lips and nodded to Rohan. "Mr Andreyev," he said.

Rohan studied the detective as he strode towards the morning room. Paul reappeared with Gwendoline. Her eyes bulged as she noticed Emma snuggled against Rohan.

Emma couldn't resist it. The words tumbled free like acid. "Oh, Gwendoline, you haven't met my husband, have you?" She lifted her chin and narrowed her eyes. It amused her that Gwendoline picked a battle over a conman. She and Christos deserved each other. Petty. But delicious.

Rohan didn't glance twice at Gwendoline's swinging hips. He didn't notice the covetous glances she shot in his direction. She followed Paul, delaying at the entrance to the corridor.

"Mrs Andreyeva," he whispered. He brushed soot from Emma's nose. "Victory suits you."

Rohan accompanied Emma into the shower. Someone knocked on the door as he ran his lips across her naked shoulder. The dog barked from his fireside bed. But Emma had locked the bedroom door, and they ignored the intrusion.

Rohan perched on the seat in the shower cubicle. Emma settled across his lap. A healthy flush coloured her skin in the forgiving lights. She ran her index finger over the waterproof plaster covering his wound. A transparent window framed the grizzly bullet hole. Emma bent to place a gentle kiss over the injury, her lips barely grazing the smooth membrane. A smaller exit wound at the back wore a similar covering. He'd been fortunate. A different calibre could have splayed his back like an exploding melon. "How much does it hurt?" she whispered.

The shower's gentle spray soothed her aching shoulders. Warm water washed away the day's stress. Rohan gathered her closer. Her breasts grazed his powerful pectorals. "Not as much as losing a leg," he murmured. "Or my zhena."

"Your wife?" Emma purred. She kissed the end of his nose. "Oh, we won't tell her." Her right hand slipped between them, finding his hardness. She turned to face him with a smile. Rohan's wide hands cupped her buttocks in invitation. And she accepted.

64

Mission chair

♥

The shower took longer than Emma intended. Her hunger for Rohan increased with each slow kiss. After they emerged, she used cleanser and glass spray to banish all the imaginary traces of Christos and his ridiculous designs on her.

She snuggled in a towel on the antique four-poster bed, staring down at her swinging feet. Her gaze flicked to Rohan as he inspected his wounds in the mirror. "Rookie mistake," he breathed. Grabbing the towel, he scrubbed at his blond hair one-handed until it resembled a harvested hay field.

"Yours?" Emma asked.

"Lear's."

Her lips formed an 'o', but no sound emerged. No wonder Regan seemed edgy and distracted. He glanced back at her and smiled. A dimple appeared in his right cheek. "Don't worry. I won't fire him. This time."

"He'll learn." The plea filled Emma's voice. "He needs more training." Her own words betrayed her. Rohan relied on each member of his team to perform their task without error. Mistakes cost lives. Or caused a .45 sized opening in someone's flesh. The thought stymied her. A wave of gratitude coursed through her. The decision didn't rest on her shoulders.

"The bank paid a premium bonus." His lips curved upward. "They offered me a year's contract. I'm to find loopholes in their system and plug any gaps."

Emma's hazel irises twinkled. "Are there any?"

Rohan grinned at her. He straightened the cuff of his prosthetic leg and smugness settled over him like a mantle. "Oh yes," he replied. The smile remained as he considered the data feast before him.

Emma shed her towel and inspected her bruised wrist. Blue and purple lines spread like an infection. She held it up for his opinion. The abandoned splint and crepe bandage spread like a disjointed snake on the hearthrug. "Does this look broken to you?"

Rohan blinked, but his gaze didn't leave her breasts. "Perhaps." He didn't sound sure.

Emma dressed one-handed. She dragged out another tee shirt and sweatpants. A thick pullover replaced the dirty ski jacket. Even with a bullet wound, Rohan managed with less huffing and puffing. He slipped the sling over his head and settled his elbow into it.

Emma traded her disgusting slippers for heavy socks. She jammed her phone into her pocket and waited for Rohan. "Farrell, come," she commanded. The dog exuded a heavy sigh and squeezed his eyes closed.

Rohan frowned. "Can't he stay here?" He cocked his head and studied her pursed lips.

"No." She clicked her fingers and Farrell shoved himself up with exaggerated reluctance. He sat for a moment, hoping he'd misheard. His nose pointed towards the warm, comfy spot he'd made. "Come!" she insisted.

She locked the door behind them. Rohan raised an eyebrow but didn't comment. She carried the splint in her right hand, the bandage trailing as far as her hip. She stopped at the top of the main staircase. "Is The Bloomsbury Publishing Set real?" she asked.

Rohan shrugged. "It sounds familiar. Why?"

"Just a feeling. Virginia Woolf belonged to the original Bloomsbury Set in the early 1900s. And I know of Bloomsbury Publishing, which started forty years ago. I've just never heard the two entities combined in that way."

"I can check." Rohan pulled his phone from his trouser pocket.

"Do it downstairs," Emma urged. She took it from him and added it to the splint and bandage. The chill air caused her to shiver, the fire hardly dispelling its harsh edge.

They reached the kitchen in search of food. Ray greeted their tired entrance with amusement. He smoothed the dog's ears and petted his ruff. "How's our resident junkie?" he murmured. Farrell strolled to the Aga and hurled himself into his bed with a deep sigh.

"What?" Rohan stopped with his hand on a chair-back. He blinked in alarm at Ray.

Emma groaned. "It's a long story." She dumped his phone on the table and waved her bandage. "Please Doctor, can you redo this?"

Her dynamic with Ray changed in Rohan's presence. He relinquished his fatherly role and rebuked her less. "You need an X-ray." Even his voice sounded gentler. "It's definitely broken."

"I fell over the body." Emma winced as she explained her injuries to Rohan. She pointed to her cheek with her free hand. "And Flora clocked me. Hard."

"You'll live." Ray grinned at her. He finished taping the bandage in place. A cursory search of the table revealed no sling, and he shrugged.

"How do you spell Bloomsbury?" Rohan's fringe bounced against his lashes as he peered at his phone screen. Emma sounded out the letters and he shook his head. "I tried that. You're right. The Bloomsbury Publishing Set doesn't exist." His lips twisted, and he assumed his thinking pose. Emma watched his fingers coast across the screen. "Ah." He hissed and sat upright. "Here." He spun the phone. She leaned across the table. A website bloomed to life, a riot of pastels and cursive fonts.

"It's real?" Her heart lightened. "A genuine publisher?" Despite his sins, Emma still wished to restore Monty's poetry to him.

"No. Sorry." Rohan pushed the phone closer to her. "I replaced the letter 'o' with numeric characters. Zeros. It's a scam site." He scrolled for her, his view upside down as Emma sat transfixed. A tab took them to a pricing page and then the terms and conditions.

Emma blinked, mesmerised by the sloughing of information. Her fingers brushed his as her world tilted. He grounded her, just like always. "I don't understand."

"It's a vanity press." Rohan zoomed in to the price list. "Real publishers pay the author. They provide editing, cover design and, often, an advanced royalty. The advance is offset against future earnings. A vanity publisher is a glorified printer. The author pays them for each service. In return, they claim intellectual property rights." He flicked the screen and squinted as the website page scrolled. "There." He jerked his chin in time with his finger tap. "The standard fee for publication is three thousand pounds. Editing, cover design and marketing incur individual extra charges. But good luck getting your rights restored if you sign that contract. Look at the terms and conditions."

Emma threw herself back in her chair. A dark pall settled over her expression.

"What's wrong?" Ray took a step towards her.

Emma exhaled. "I know who stole the extra money from the Lit and His Society's account," she said. Her flat tone betrayed the dull thud spreading from her chest. She pushed Rohan's phone towards him. "It's all for nothing." Hopelessness caused tears to bud in her eyes. "Kathleen died for dashing a man's false hope. This entire weekend was a monumental sham."

65

Spider back chair

♥

Depression shrouded Emma like a cloud. Kathleen Dubois died for nothing. A non-entity blacklisted Monty, making him angry enough to start a family war. But for his affair with Gwendoline, he could have shouted about the poetry theft from the rooftops.

Emma sat at the kitchen table and seethed. "Gwendoline." She murmured the woman's name with enough spite to strike her dead with a thought. "At the root of everything and yet still stinking of roses." The hideous Kathleen had ultimately died in her place.

Ray's eyebrows hiked almost to his hairline. He didn't comment. But Rohan reached across the table, his wide hand closing around Emma. "Settle, dorogaya." His gentle tone soothed her. "Sud'ba will find her." The accented Russian word for destiny. He squeezed her fingers. "The ambulance just left Clive Merton's place with Monty. Merton is using his tractor bucket to clear the lane between us."

Emma glanced at Ray. He nodded and waggled his phone. The text glinted blue on his screen. Her spine straightened with eagerness. "We could get rid of them all today?" Her chest inflated as she dared to hope.

"Our thoughts too." Ray jerked his head towards Rohan. "I could clear a narrow strip to the main gates and create enough space to open them. It'll take a while."

Rohan's nose wrinkled as he considered the proposition. Always the strategist. "It's deep," he mused. "Perhaps use your energy just at the gates. Merton could clear the driveway faster with his machine once it can get through."

"Yes, sir!" Ray tapped his temple in a diluted salute. The plan energised him. "I'll grab my gear and get on with it." He dipped to pat the dog's head. "You coming, Faz?" Farrell yawned wide enough to disconnect his jaws. He grumbled as he rolled onto his other side. "Oh." Ray shrugged, appearing hurt. But he left the kitchen in a rush, eager for action.

Rohan leaned across the table and retook Emma's hand in his. His gorgeous lips parted to speak but halted at her sudden rigidity. The door slid open by a slow degree. She watched, tensing as it swung inward. Rohan spun to assess the threat, his right fist already balled. Dyfed's grinning face poked through the gap. He surveyed the kitchen. His gaze landed on Emma. Then Rohan. He released a high-pitched scream and withdrew his head.

Rohan crossed the distance to the door in three giant strides. He swatted the heavy oak aside like a bug. His long reach netted the fleeing Dyfed in two seconds flat. He hauled him into the kitchen. "Who's this?" he demanded. Dyfed dangled from his collar, his feet almost off the floor. He squirmed in Rohan's powerful grip.

"It's okay," Emma soothed. She rose, her hands outstretched. "It's Dyfed. He's with the caterers."

Rohan's fingers sprang open, and Dyfed dropped onto his heels. His eyes darted around the room and his lips flapped like an oxygen starved fish's. Emma walked towards him, and he winced. "You're fine," she soothed. "What can I get for you?"

"Who screamed?" Urgency filled Paul's voice. He arrived in the kitchen on squeaking soles.

Dyfed closed his eyes as though wishing himself into a vacuum. His body shook. "The man," he whispered through partly opened lips. "The man said we're leaving."

"Ray?" Emma rested a hand on Dyfed's shaking shoulder. "Yes. He's clearing the driveway with our neighbour. You can leave soon. Perhaps not in your van. It's stuck, isn't it?" She spoke as though to a frightened child. Her palm moved in a stroking motion.

Dyfed's eyes filled with tears. His chin rose as Paul edged closer. "Make her stay," he begged. His hands wrung, his knuckles bumping his chest. "We like it here. Make her stay with us."

"Who?" Paul stiffened. He threw his shoulders back but didn't interrupt.

"Mum!" Dyfed's breathing quickened. His terrified irises betrayed the unfortunate, permanent smile. "Don't let her leave."

Paul swore. He exited the kitchen at speed. His boots pounded along the corridor towards the lobby.

"Where's Chloe?" Emma kept her tone soft. Her fingers rubbed raised circles into Dyfed's thin shoulder beneath his worn footman's coat.

"Gone," he murmured.

Shouts echoed around Wingate Hall as Paul and his colleagues pulled the place apart. He raged through every room, yelling at his subordinates. Rohan intervened when he blasted into the kitchen to demand a master key. Dyfed screeched and dived under the table. "Enough!" The walls amplified his voice and echoed it along the corridor.

Paul screeched to a halt in the doorway. He blinked in shock.

"You're scaring him!" Emma crouched beside the table to reassure Dyfed. But he scooted away from her outstretched hand.

Paul bristled with indignation. "This is a police investigation!" His voice rose without matching Rohan's.

"And you lost a suspect." Condemnation oozed through Rohan's glare.

"You said they could stay on the third floor," the constable protested. "I asked you about it. You said they had no connection to the murder."

An embarrassed flush hurried from Paul's neck to his cheeks. "They don't. But they need to stay here." He silenced, lost for words. Losing interest, Rohan sat down again. He rested his right forearm on the table. Dyfed skittered closer to his legs, hiding in his shadow. "I need a master key." Paul snatched back his authority through bluster. "You have locked rooms. I need to check them." He focussed on Rohan, growing frustrated when he didn't reply. "Key!" His voice rose.

Rohan's eyes rolled upward in casual disrespect. He glared at the detective. The conflict caused tingles to run along Emma's spine. Poor Ray shovelled snow from the driveway, unaware of the brewing dispute. She stepped into the fray. "I locked the rooms before the guests arrived. They don't have access."

A low keening emitted from beneath the table. Dyfed curled into the foetal position and moaned. Paul's eyes danced with antagonism. Ray's gentle son had retreated beneath the obstreperous façade. He directed his question to Rohan. "Captain Andreyev, I demand a key." He held out his hand, his palm bouncing with every pulse beat.

Rohan tilted his head back. Emma cringed at the devilment in his grin. "I cannot give you permission," he said, his tone level. "I do not own Wingate Hall or its environs." His smile didn't falter.

Emma exhaled. She faced Paul. "I can waste time showing you through empty rooms for the next hour," she stated. "Or we can ask Dyfed when and where Chloe went." She crouched beside the table. "Dyfed?" She spoke with gentleness. "What made Mum leave?"

"The man." He kept his eyes closed and wrapped his arms around his shins. His bones would crack if he made himself any smaller.

"What man, darling?" Emma asked. A wet nose against her ear conveyed the dog's presence. Farrell slunk beneath the table and sat beside the stricken man. Dyfed relaxed enough to cling to the dog.

"He said we could leave soon. We sat by the lobby fire, keeping warm. Mum heard him. He went outside."

"Yes, Ray." Emma offered a gentle smile. "The big man who helped you bring food in from your van?"

Dyfed nodded.

"What did Mum do then?" Emma supported herself with a hand on Rohan's thigh. Her knees ached with the pressure of crouching.

"She said, 'They'll come for us. I need to get away.' And she ran out the door behind the man."

"What about Ridley? Did he go with her?"

Dyfed's head shook. His spindly neck resembled a crane arm, his skull a loose wrecking ball. "He's hiding," he whispered.

Emma smiled at his bowed head. "You stay there and cuddle Farrell," she soothed. "Like before."

She rose and contemplated Paul. His jaw showed through his cheek as he clenched his teeth. Admiration for her had turned to hatred with Rohan's return. She saw it in his glittering irises. "So," she concluded, her tone firm. "No need for a pointless search. Chloe went out through the front door. I'm guessing she's working her way around to her van right now." She jabbed her thumb at the door behind her. "If you wait out there long enough, I'm sure she'll turn up." Ice dripped from her voice.

"What about the other one?"

Emma exhaled. "I believe you'll find him under a bed on the third floor. You can leave him there for now."

Paul took a calculated step towards Emma and his voice rumbled through his chest. "I know there's another man here too," he hissed. "Two separate people mentioned him." He dropped his chin and stared at her through the tops of his eyes. "Where's the old man you're keeping quiet about?"

Rohan rose. His bulk filled her peripheral vision. He edged himself between Emma and the detective like a wall. "You're referring to my father," he growled. "I

invited him to stay in the coach house for the weekend."
His chin jutted forward. "After his chemotherapy. He's
sleeping right now, but I'm sure he won't mind your
intrusion later."

Emma gulped. Her mind ran through a series of
checks and her panic increased. She didn't remember
closing the tunnel or shutting the airing cupboard door.
Did she leave the vacuum cleaner in the hallway?

"Come on, sir." Detective Chandler shot a nervous
glance at Paul's livid profile. "I'll go through the front
door. You cut her off at the back."

The breath whooshed from Emma's lungs as Rohan
drew all the oxygen from the room. "Good idea," he
snarled at Ray's son.

Detective Inspector Paul Barker had drawn the battle
lines. But Rohan Andreyev had scorched them into his
psyche like a brand.

66

Acapulco chair

♥

Emma and Dyfed coaxed Ridley from beneath the bed. Dust balls coated his elbows as he sobbed and rocked. He edged into the corner nearest the wash stand and clung to Dyfed.

"Can I help?" Marian Slade stepped into the fray with unexpected assistance. Gentle and easy-going, she sat on the bed and told the men some humorous stories about her kitten. They showed no interest, but her lyrical voice brought an instant calm.

Emma plonked beside her on the mattress. A spring dug into her bottom. She experienced momentary sympathy for her unwanted house guests during their long night of the soul.

Marian watched Dyfed stroke Ridley's tight curls. She frowned. "This is all a bit strange, isn't it?" she whispered.

Emma nodded. She sifted her uppermost thoughts into coherent questions. They took her in a different direction. "Please, can I ask you about Kathleen Dubois?"

Marian pushed her lips into a pout. An older woman, she'd aged with dignity. Greying curls trailed from her ponytail. Hazel eyes sparkled with mischief. She loosened the zipper on her heavy jacket and nodded. "You can ask. I may not answer."

"Thanks." Emma exhaled. "Why did Ray insist Paul seized the iron tablets from Kathleen's husband?"

Marian tutted. "I understand everyone overheard the discussion about hemochromatosis?"

"Yes. Arnand Dubois said she got an early diagnosis."

"Let's talk about another patient with this condition," Marian began. "Not our victim, you understand?" She widened her eyes to punctuate her meaning. A beat passed while she waited for Emma's nod. "Someone suffering from hemochromatosis can find relief by donating blood often. It dilutes the iron content. Under no circumstances should they take high-level doses of ferrous sulfate."

"What if they suffered from white coat syndrome and refused medical treatment?" Emma gnawed at her lower lip. "But they'd know not to take iron tablets, wouldn't they?" She picked at a loose thread on her bandage. "So, they'd avoid them."

"Exactly." Marian beamed. "If they knew."

"Oh." Emma considered Arnand's reaction to Ray's discovery of the plain white cylinder's contents. She closed her eyes to better access the memory. "Arnand gave Kathleen a pill at the awards night. I saw him." A frown bisected her forehead. "She demanded it. He didn't want to give it to her."

Marian's brows rose beneath her fringe like twin suns. "Interesting," she mused. "Perhaps it isn't an attempted murder, then."

"What?" Emma jerked so hard she almost tipped off the mattress. Her calves clanged against the metal frame.

Marian shrugged. Her tone became musing. "No one begs for iron tablets. I'd suggest she believed they were painkillers. She must have been in terrible pain most of the time." She clamped her teeth over her lower lip, aware she'd said too much.

Emma's phone vibrated in her pocket. Not a message, but a call. She peered at the screen, and Marian used the opportunity to escape her questions. Rising in a rustle of heavy fabric, she walked from the room with a purposeful gait.

"Hey." Emma answered her phone. Regan's voice held an uncharacteristically high pitch. He didn't give her time to say anything else.

"Why is everyone running around in the courtyard?" he demanded.

Emma rose, aware of the tense set returning to Dyfed's shoulders. "Who is?"

She'd abandoned the police officers earlier, leaving them to hunt Chloe. Emma cared more about Ridley's distress. But Regan couldn't mean the detectives were running around the courtyard. Paul must have caught Chloe within minutes of Emma walking upstairs. "I don't know," she mused. "What can you see?"

"A skating rink. And people rolling around all over it."

Emma clopped down to the second level, then used the servants' staircase to reach the corridor. The kitchen door stood wide open, the rear of Chloe's van still where she left it. Poking her head outside, Emma spotted Paul Barker and his detectives playing an uncomfortable game with a frantic Chloe. They bobbed up and down like falling skittles in the drifts as she evaded them.

Disgusted, Emma slammed the door on the icy temperatures. "The detectives can't catch the caterer." She spoke into her phone, still connected to her conversation with Regan. "I'm tempted to lock them all out there."

Regan chuckled into her ear. "It's entertaining. Is she a suspect in their murder case?"

"Nope." Emma slumped into a kitchen chair. "She seems like a woman just trying to get by whilst her partner beats her and takes all her cash."

"Nice."

Rohan walked into the kitchen. He ducked to clear the lintel and frowned at the ball of tape blocking the catch. "Rohan's here," Emma said to Regan. The connection ended, and she stared at her screen in confusion. "He doesn't want to talk to you." Her hazel irises twinkled with mischief as she gazed at her husband. She jerked her head towards the courtyard. "Didn't you fancy joining in? It looks like fun."

Rohan's arched nose crinkled at the bridge. He used an unfamiliar Russian swearword. Emma didn't need a translation. He delivered it with enough force to provide understanding. "I watched them from the coach house. Winston is still laughing."

"Oh!" Emma's eyes widened. "I forgot to put the vacuum cleaner away or hide the tunnel."

"I did it." He didn't rebuke her error. Just covered it for her.

"Why chase Chloe?" Emma remarked. A shout carried from outside. The game continued, three against one. "Where can she go in this weather? Monty ended up next door and now requires medical treatment." She shrugged. "Perhaps they'll all give up once they're soaked to the skin."

Rohan tugged her to stand and commandeered her chair. Once seated, he pulled her into his lap. "She is a rabotorgovets."

Emma curled her right arm around his neck and peered at him from beneath her lashes. "What?" Her voice rose at the end.

"Rabotorgovets." He pursed his lips after giving the Russian again. His eyes became glassy. "I can't think of the English word. Indentured, perhaps." His fringe bounced against his lashes as he stared up at her. He smoothed his right palm along her spine. "No. There's no agreement for labour. They are slaves. She is a slave master. Is that correct?"

"I understood the word!" Emma gasped. "That's not the problem. I just can't believe it!"

"Da." His fingers coasted over a dent in the table's edge. Stephie cut her front teeth there. The wood bore the two perfect imprints with dignity. "Slaves, da?" he repeated. His lashes fluttered as he gazed up at her. "I received a call from a senior Home Office contact a few minutes ago. Because of our work, Wingate Hall is a protected address." He slid his jaw sideways to create a pensive expression. "Do you wish to explain why Detective Inspector Barker arrested a known slaver and gave our address last night?"

Emma groaned. She used her right hand to shield her face. "I don't believe this," she whispered.

"No matter." He wound his good arm around her and pressed his cheek against her shoulder. "When these crazy people leave, we can get our deti home. Da?"

Emma nodded, the action filled with exhaustion. "Yes," she replied with a sigh. "The second these crazies leave, we'll bring our children home."

67

Aeron chair

♥

Clive's tractor rumbled up the driveway an hour later. A contingent of police SUVs followed it. Flora, Gwendoline, Arnand and Christos left in the first wave. Emma didn't say farewell to them.

With Chloe in handcuffs downstairs, Dyfed and Ridley fell to pieces. They took refuge together beneath the narrow single bed on the third floor. Two police officers, a nurse, and a lovely man from the Red Cross tried to coax them out. But Ridley sobbed for his mother and Dyfed wouldn't leave him.

"Slaves?" Emma whispered the word as though saying it often might negate its effect. "Here, in Market Harborough?"

The man from the Red Cross pushed his auburn hair away from his forehead. His gentle lips turned down. "It's common," he replied. His low voice rumbled through his wiry beard. "These two men don't know they're slaves. Their owners gave them a bed and food, small treats perhaps in return for work. It's possible they believe this life is better than homelessness."

"Better?" Emma pressed her fingers over her lips. "How is it better?" She shook her head at the memory of their hunger. And how they'd spent all night on the cold floor without bedding. Her chest ached with pity. And with guilt. "I knew something felt wrong," she admitted. "But if the blizzard hadn't trapped everyone here, they'd have left last night."

"And you'd have thought no more about them." The man touched her shoulder with his giant paw. His words held no rebuke. "Don't blame yourself," he said. "How could you know? They're afraid of their masters. Threatened away from casual conversation. They wouldn't say anything to alert you to their predicament."

Emma nodded. Her muscles prickled with a million tiny needles. "They wouldn't talk to me," she admitted. But she said the words for her own benefit, not his. "Ridley doesn't know if that's his first or last name."

The man inhaled. "I've seen worse."

"You do this a lot?" Her eyes widened.

"Four or five times a year. I'm a volunteer. We'll take these guys for a shower, clean clothes, and medical care. They'll get a psychological evaluation and ongoing counselling. Cases like these are the saddest. They just don't realise they're slaves. Can you imagine the trauma once they see what they've missed? And then learning to function independently in society instead of someone telling them what to do and think?"

Emma's shoulders slumped. "Will they stay together?" She pictured Ridley without Dyfed and wondered how he'd cope.

"I don't know," he replied.

Emma swallowed. "Could they stay here?" she asked, her voice small.

The man patted her shoulder again. "No. The police will take them miles away from here. Witness protection. They'll need to testify against their masters."

"Are you sure Chloe isn't a slave, too?" Emma turned to him, her features sharp and imploring. "Gareth beat her. I saw the marks. He used her money to gamble."

His head shook from side to side, his irises glittering with emotions she couldn't fathom. "No," he replied. "She isn't a victim, Mrs Andreyeva. Not at all."

When Ridley grew hysterical, Emma fetched the dog. Fresh from a frolic in the snow with the detectives, Farrell padded upstairs with her. Perfect prints tracked behind him on the floorboards. His soaked tail swished with happiness and restored equilibrium. It cast water droplets in a wide arc around him. The icy temperatures had banished his chemical hangover. But his excitement at the newcomers had filled his social bucket to overflowing. He crawled under the bed with the frightened men, subjecting himself to their hugs and murmurings. His tail thudded against the boards. But when he shook himself, both emerged screeching.

Everyone withdrew from the bedroom. They left the nurse and the Red Cross volunteer, still speaking to Dyfed and Ridley. Emma jumped at Dyfed's explosion of grief. She couldn't cope. Abandoning the police officers, she ran downstairs.

As her feet pounded against the wooden treads, her rage built in her chest. She ached to find Chloe, to smash her to a pulp for what she'd done. What she'd sanctioned, explicitly or otherwise. Long strides carried her down the back stairs, her temper boiling with each step. Paul had kept the other offenders in the lounge. With them gone, that's where he'd keep Chloe. Emma spun around the corner, fury directing her steps to the lounge.

And then her feet left the floor.

"Put me down!" she shouted as he spun her. His powerful body dipped, and the ex-paratrooper slung her over his shoulder. The cloying scent of tobacco shrouded her head. With her left arm useless, she beat against his back with her other hand.

The lounge door remained closed, but Detective Chandler appeared from the kitchen. Sergeant Pollard followed on his heels. "What's going on?" the latter demanded. A mug of tea listed in his left hand.

Before Emma could scream for help, Sniper's voice rumbled through her. "We're fine," he stated. "Nothing to see here."

"There is!" Emma growled. She smashed her fist against the corded muscle on one side of his spine. "There is something to see here!"

"The captain wants his wife." Sniper threw the statement over his shoulder.

Emma lifted her chin in time to see the officers walk back into the kitchen and close the door behind them. They'd worn the same nonplussed expression as hers earlier. She'd known something wasn't right about Chloe's group. Yet, she'd mistrusted her own instincts. Officers Chandler and Pollard repeated her error. Perhaps in their world, strange men carried wailing women over their shoulders all the time.

"Release her!" Winston spoke first as Sniper carried Emma into the coach house. Rohan turned towards his team mate with an expression of bemusement.

"You wanted her," Sniper replied. He dumped her upside down in an armchair and stood at ease. "Here she is."

Emma struggled to orient herself. She rose like a leviathan from the cushions, her hair a tangle of curls. Sniper had thwarted her anger at Chloe and so she turned it on him. He cackled with laughter and sidestepped her first launch, but Rohan stemmed her second. His strong fingers closed around her elbow and held on until she ceased wriggling.

"I'll return to the control centre via the tunnel." Sniper turned and left. He shot Emma an inflammatory smirk as he exited the coach house. The basement door echoed as it clicked shut behind him. But his smirk lit a spark in her chest, and she tugged against Rohan's grip.

"Let me go!" she shouted.

His jaw showed through his cheek. His fingers closed harder around the joint. "Why?" he asked. His tone remained level. "Because you want to bash in the brains of the rabotorgovets? And anger the detective some more? Or because you're channelling your fury into a futile action as a salve to your guilt?"

Emma gasped as the tension lost her body. Her lips parted, ready to deliver a hail of indignation. Her right hand moved fast, aimed for Rohan's tanned cheek. "How dare you!" she snarled. But she'd forgotten he still clasped her elbow. He jerked his hand, and her slap went nowhere.

"Stop!" Winston commanded. He sank onto the sofa and released a dramatic sigh. "Save the drama for the bedroom, Alexei!" His skin had lost its awful greyness and the dangerous spark had returned to his blue irises. He focussed his steely gaze on Emma. "Alexei needed to silence you. Fast, Emmaline." A grey eyebrow rose as he peered at her. "You have a far bigger issue than the slaver in your lounge, girl."

Emma gulped, their seriousness washing over her like an icy surf. "What's bigger than two men kept in servitude?" she demanded. But her voice sounded weak against their combined might.

"Dolan!" Rohan snarled.

Emma looked from one to the other. "I don't understand."

"He's free." Winston's lyrical tone held a springy quality, as though he enjoyed the animosity between Christopher and his son. His right hand gave a languid flick.

"He escaped!" Emma closed her eyes and exhaled. "I knew it!" Not Winston roaming the grounds then, but Christopher Dolan. She'd sensed him, felt him tug on their shared connection. Her lips parted in a tut of exasperation. Rohan studied her with accusation oozing from his sharp features. His irises glittered like diamonds. Powerful enough to cut glass.

"I heard someone near the stables last night. I asked Regan to check the grounds, but he found no one." Emma's elbow hung limp from Rohan's fingers. She realised fear and anger had fuelled his horrible comment. She noticed then how his hand shook. Instead of fighting him, she pressed her body against his hip. Offering solidarity. "Nothing will change." She made the promise without looking at him. Her jaw hardened. "I don't want him near this house, or me."

"He didn't escape," Winston informed her. "The government recruited him for their own means. Then, the fools turned him loose. So, I suggest you rid your house of your unwanted guests within the hour." Winston rose. His voice had the strength of an autocrat, but his body complied like an elderly man's. He clung to the sofa arm before trusting his balance. "And then fortify this place like a prison."

68

Lectern chair

♥

The Market Harborough Literary and Historical Society left. They filed through the front door the same way they'd entered. This time, they edged along Ray's narrow tunnel of cleared snow until reaching the driveway. They clung to the hand rail. An assortment of taxis awaited them on the main road. The entitlement had left along with their dignity. Fraudsters, murderers, liars, and cheats had infiltrated their top notch society.

Gwendoline shot Emma a haughty sneer as she clip-clopped over the threshold. She carried her feather boa over her arm. Her breasts bounced in their corset. Emma spared her a moment of pity. She'd arrived in a haze of glamour and arrogance. She left alone, orphaned by murder and its consequences. Her lover sat in a hospital bed with hypothermia, a police officer at his side. Detective Barker hadn't yet decided on Monty's charges. Obstructing a murder enquiry vied with conspiracy to commit murder. Christos' eligibility faded with his embezzlement charges. So, Gwendoline Dubois left alone.

Emma pursed her lips and watched her fingers curve over the banister rail. She still wondered if guilt precipitated Gwendoline's actions with the poem. A final sendoff for a dying woman, perhaps. An unwitting admission of culpability.

Only Sir Robert gripped Emma's hand and pumped it with enthusiasm. In her peripheral vision, Emma noticed Mavis sliding on the icy driveway in her silly shoes. She released a screech of alarm, which everyone ignored. "Thank you for a lovely weekend," the old barrister enthused. "Wonderful. Exciting! Tip-top!"

Emma blinked back at his strange review of a monumental disaster. "You're welcome." She dragged out the words, not sure of their appropriateness. Rohan glowered from behind her. His gaze raked the buried bus and the oak trees lining the driveway. Alert. Watching. For Christopher Dolan.

Major Mallory-Eaves flattened his lips as he stepped into the vestibule. "You'll let me know when I can collect the bus?"

"Yes." Emma nodded. "It's a shame about the open door and the drift inside it. You might need a garage to tow it back to town."

Rohan stiffened. His muscular biceps tensed against her spine. Lockdown meant no access to anyone outside of the family. Not even to rescue a stricken school bus.

"Bye," Bunny said as she passed. "Thanks for everything." She hustled after Gwendoline without waiting for a reply.

To Emma's surprise, Freda dumped a suitcase beside her feet. She turned to beam at Ray. "Take this downstairs for me, dear," she instructed. "I'm leaving too."

"You are?" Emma hadn't prepared for her exodus yet. It knocked her off kilter like a rogue wave. With a muted growl, Ray hefted the suitcase and followed the major.

"Yes, dear." Freda air kissed both cheeks. "Mavis and I have reached an understanding. She'll board with me while she sells her house. Then she'll pay back the Society's account with interest."

"She'll stay in the residential community?" Emma frowned. "Is that allowed?" Images floated past her inner vision of the arch-enemies cohabiting. And the subsequent bloodshed.

Freda's eyes boggled as she considered the question. Her thin chest shook as she shrugged her shoulders. "I've no idea," she mused. "Oh well. Better to apologise than to ask permission."

Sadness enveloped Emma. It wrapped around her and squeezed her chest. She couldn't conjure any wonderful words of love or appreciation for the old lady. Not on the spur of the moment. But one question still plagued her. "Freda, why did the Society's members boycott the event? Is it me or the Hall they object to?"

Freda reared back in shock. Her lower lip flapped as though she'd lost control. "Noooo!" she cried after a moment's recovery. "Goodness, no! Not you, Emma! Kathleen. Nobody liked her when she lived here. She wrote spiteful limericks about most of the people in town." She tapped her temple. "Old people have long memories, despite what others might think. The woman was an absolute bitch. Nobody wanted to see her lording it around." Her features smoothed into gentle hills and valleys. She clapped her hands together.

"I bet they're all sick with envy now. We've had the best murder mystery weekend in the Society's history." Leaning forward to whisper to Emma, spittle landed on her chin. "Same time next year, dear."

"Oh, I'm not sure about that," Emma began.

But Freda jabbed a black marker pen into her hand. "Please return this to Nicky. It's come to my notice it's not as described." Her brows waggled as Emma shoved it into her pocket. "It's not an eyebrow pencil. That child charged me a pound."

Rohan loosened behind her. He laughed for the first time since learning of Christopher's release. Emma's usual smirk didn't surface. She grabbed Freda's thin hands and gripped them. "I'll visit soon," she promised. "We can walk to the Baptist Coffee Shop and catch up on gossip."

"Righto." Freda turned towards the stairs. She still wore her slippers as she stepped onto the landing. "Wait!" she bellowed into the white landscape. Ray's slow pivot revealed the hunching of his shoulders. Freda clapped her hands. "I'm seventy-two," she lied. Shaving two decades from her age, she held out her arms to Ray. "Carry me down the stairs. There's a splendid chap."

To Emma's amazement, he obeyed.

Ray dumped the case on the driveway and stomped back up the stairs. The suitcase wobbled before falling over backwards. A haze of flakes wafted upwards from its impromptu sojourn in the nearest drift. Emma's lips parted as he hefted Freda into his burly arms. His heavy boots took each tread with care as though he carried a precious artifact.

Freda grinned like a teenager. She wafted her left hand in a royal wave over his shoulder. "Bye bitches!" she cried. Emma covered her mouth to prevent her shriek of laughter from escaping.

The reigning Lady Ayers relinquished her choke hold on Wingate Hall.

Freda had left the building.

If you liked the Market Harborough location, you might be interested in **_Artifact_**, also based in the town.

Visit my website at ktbowes.com and if you use the Buy Direct button, you can get 50% off the purchase price by using the code VIG0XFGCW9 at the checkout.

Please review *Murder in The Actuary's House* for me? It enables other readers to find and enjoy my novels. They rely on your opinion as much as I do.

You can leave a review on your favourite platform. I'm really grateful to you.

I have a Patreon channel which is where I release my novels first.

For as little as $3 a month, you can read my work, chapter by chapter, just minutes after I've written it. Members of the $10 tier get 5 brand new chapters per week, and to share in a monthly Zoom call with me.

Patreon also runs a free trial for readers who want to see if they like it before committing.

Take a look around, or just binge read my backlist at https://www.patreon.com/KTBowes

I also have a mailing list which I'd love for you to join.

It's easier to be more candid in a monthly newsletter and to talk about my life and my writing process.

If you'd like to join me there, visit my website and click the link. In return, you can pick up four free novels delivered straight to your inbox.

Copyright Notice

♥